W9-CAW-503

THE

FAIREST

AMONG

WOMEN

Also by

Shifra Horn

Four Mothers

Shifra Horn

THE FAIREST AMONG WOMEN

TRANSLATED FROM
THE HEBREW BY *H. Sacks*

ST. MARTIN'S PRESS NEW YORK

www.stmartins.com
For information on a reading group guide for *The Fairest Among Women*, visit the Web site listed above.

Designed by Lorelle Graffeo

Library of Congress Cataloging-in-Publication Data

Horn, Shifra.
[Yafah ba-nashim. English]
The fairest among women / Shifra Horn ; translation from the Hebrew by H. Sacks.—1st U.S. ed.
p. cm.
ISBN 0-312-26590-5
I. Title.

PJ5055.23.O75 Y3413 2001
892.4'36—dc21

2001019263

First published in Israel by Keshet, 1998

First U.S. Edition: July 2001

10 9 8 7 6 5 4 3 2 1

AUTHOR'S NOTE

In April 1948 a bloody battle for control of West Jerusalem took place between Arab and Israeli armies. The wealthy inhabitants of the Arab neighborhood of Katamon, with its beautiful stone villas, suffered as a result of the fighting. Caught between the two armies, the neighborhood was subjected to a barrage of bullets and shells, and the lives of the residents became intolerable. As the fighting continued to rage, they fled, leaving behind them uneaten meals, unmade beds, and all their possessions, for unknown destinations, with the clothes on their backs and the keys to their houses around their necks, hoping and believing that the war would soon be over and they would be able to return to their homes. The neighborhood was conquered by the Israeli army, and the original residents were never allowed to return to their homes.

When the battle was over the magnificent empty homes were taken over by Jewish refugees from the Jewish Quarter of the Old City, which had been conquered by Jordanian Legionnaires. They were joined by those fleeing from the borderline neighborhood of Mamilla, at the foot of the Old City walls, which was subjected to heavy bombardment and bullets from Jordanian snipers. Broken in body and spirit, Holocaust survivors, who had left behind them in Europe the ashes of their murdered families and their memories, homes, and property, crowded together with Jewish exiles from the Arab countries, who left everything behind them and emigrated to the Promised Land.

In the rooms of the abandoned villas of Katamon these refugee families set about trying to rebuild their ruined lives and to forget the sights of death and war.

This book is dedicated to refugees all over the world, violently uprooted from their lives in the shadow of war.

THE

FAIREST

AMONG

WOMEN

one

ALI HAMOUDA'S HOUSE OF NOTES

The earliest event etched on Rosa's memory was a noise. A strange, muffled, swishing sound, unlike anything else she had ever heard, filled her with dread on the night they moved into the new apartment and became the first memory of her life. This muffled noise, which easily prevailed over the routine, familiar crackling of the guns and thunder of the shells, made her hair stand on end and disturbed her sleep.

In years to come, when she tried to recapture it for her children, she said that the noise sounded like the dragging of bodies, many bodies, of people no longer alive.

All that night, while Angela, her mother, hastily packed their few possessions in British ammunition boxes that smelled of grease and gun oil, taking care to put her slain husband's things in a separate box on which she wrote, in black ink, AMATZIA, the crackling of gunfire went on echoing in the town, interrupted by the muffled dragging noises and people's hushed voices. What exactly they were dragging there she didn't know, since she was still only a little girl. And when she tried to approach the window, to penetrate the darkness and see what was causing the noise, her mother screamed at her to get back into the room and closed the shutters.

Even the Jewish soldiers of the Palmach, who had won the bloody battle of the Saint Simon Monastery and invaded the affluent neighborhood of Katamon, which emptied overnight of its Arab residents, were unable to stop the noise. It turned out to be caused by carpets, legions of brightly colored carpets rolled up into thick, heavy sausages and dragged, like prisoners bound hand and foot, through the streets of the town on the night after the battle. The magnificent carpets, which had never left their homes, were peeled from the cool stone tiles where they had been slumbering peacefully for years in the rooms of the affluent villas of Katamon and hauled against their will away on the looters heels'. Humbly they were dragged through the dust, leaving furrows in the ground as they passed, their brilliant colors blackened with the filth of the streets, the threads woven and tied by the strong, nimble fingers of the young women weavers coming loose. Where the carpets went, who dragged them away, what floor tiles they were covering today, and whose feet were cushioned by their softness—nobody knew the answers to Rosa's questions when she grew up and tried to solve the mystery of the walking carpets.

In years to come, whenever she came across a magnificent carpet in the homes of friends or relations, she would look closely and search for signs of dragging, in case it turned out to be one of the looted carpets that had terrified her with their muffled noise on the night after the Battle of Saint Simon.

The next morning they moved from their narrow room in Mamilla to the new house they had been allocated in Katamon. Its Arab owners had fled in panic and made their way in a sad convoy of cars and loaded wagons that crept along the Hebron Road to an unknown destination. All the way from Mamilla to the abandoned neighborhood of Katamon, little Rosa walked with one hand held tight in her mother's and the other imprisoned in that of her uncle Joseph. The household goods, the mattresses, the quilts, and their clothes and those of the dead Amatzia preceded them on a ramshackle baby carriage made of wood. Rosa remembered the bare back of the porter pushing the baby carriage heaped with the greasy ammunition boxes. The back was broad and glistening with sweat, and the dark hairs growing on the round shoulders stuck to the wet flesh. When they arrived Angela argued over his fee, and he went away cursing and spitting in disappointment.

Splendid villas greeted them in their new neighborhood, and the tense stillness in the air underlined the chirping of the birds hiding between the boughs of the mulberry trees, palm fronds, and pine needles as if they were afraid of being hit by a stray bullet. The house that had been assigned to them and that, together with its inhabitants, was to decide Rosa's fate and set her life on its predetermined course, was built of chiseled pink stones veined with red. Tall, narrow windows, framed in jutting stones, looked at them curiously under arched eyebrows and half-lowered blue blinds. Rosa raised her eyes and saw the rusty remains of the rain dripping from an iron gutter projecting from the corner and gaping at her like the beak of an ancient bird. The downspout climbed up the wall of the house to an ungainly roof covered with orange tiles, which reminded her of a fez. The iron gate, shaped like a potbellied treble clef, opened wide with Oriental hospitality and greeted them with a merry squeak that broke the tense silence. A vast hall, stripped of carpets and furniture, welcomed them in; and a fresh smell of lavender mixed with the sweet scent of the jasmine twining round the window bars, designed by the music-loving owner of the house to look like musical notes, assailed Rosa's nostrils. Like a trespasser on somebody else's property, afraid that the rightful owners would emerge to chase them away in disgrace, Angela took Rosa's hand, pressed it tightly to her bosom, leaving white pressure marks on her palm, and set out with her to explore the deserted rooms on either side of the hall.

In the kitchen they found a cold meal set on a spotless damask cloth, covering a magnificent mahogany table that appeared to be crouching in the corner on legs carved to resemble lions' paws. Rosa felt the pitas and marveled at their unexpected hardness, gazed at the black olives gleaming seductively in their bath of green oil, examined the soft white goats' cheese called *labneh*, whose sour smell pervaded the house, and tried to breathe in the aroma of the black kebabs threaded on little skewers, around which a swarm of glittering flies was buzzing. She longed to break off a piece of pita and dip it in the *labneh*, but Angela's bony hand shot out and slapped Rosa's dimpled little one. The insulted child withdrew her hand from the tempting food and burst into the frustrated screams of a hungry little girl whose food has been snatched from her mouth.

"It's not ours," Angela explained. "It's not our food."

"So whose food is it?" she asked when she calmed down. Although her mother usually took care to answer all her questions, this time she did not bother to reply.

Like someone rudely shaken out of her sleep in the middle of the night, Angela walked around the house in the wake of the man in uniform who had been waiting to meet them. She pointed to the room she wanted and asked for it in a weak voice. Rosa was surprised at her choice. The room was full of excrement, and there was a strong smell of urine in the air. After scrubbing the floor and scattering Amatzia's possessions about the room, Angela tried to put Rosa to sleep in a new-looking wooden bed she had dragged in from the adjacent room. Rosa looked suspiciously at the bed, on which plump little angels were painted in soft pastel colors, and sat down on it hesitantly. With a weary movement of her hand Angela motioned her to lie down, and she curled up obediently and sank into the soft mattress. But just as she was falling asleep she suddenly sprang up as if she had done something wrong.

"Whose bed is this?" she asked.

"It's yours now," Angela answered in a confidential whisper.

"But someone slept in it before. Another little girl slept in it; where is she now?"

"The little girl went away, and now it's yours," said Angela.

"Then the bed isn't mine, and I'm not allowed to sleep in it," said Rosa firmly, remembering the pita and *labneh*.

"If you don't want to sleep on it you can sleep on the floor," her mother answered crossly.

Worn out, Rosa sprawled out on the new bed, thinking of the sounds she had heard the night before, of the little princess on whose bed she was sleeping, and of the painted cherubs playing her to sleep on their harps. With sweet sounds in her ears and images of golden-haired princesses dancing in front of her, Rosa closed her eyes and fell asleep. The mattress, which still held the warmth and the smell of that other little girl, who had gone, never to return, who had wet its kapok with her tears when she was sad and dreamed sweet dreams in its depths, quietly and submissively embraced the heavy body of the new little girl who had found a refuge in it.

That night Rosa met her. She was a little girl of her own age wearing a ruffled white dress, with airy lace gloves as white as snow on her hands and spotless white socks and patent leather shoes on her feet. Around her neck hung a big, heavy iron key, tied to a white silk ribbon and dangling against her chest like a precious locket. If she hadn't been so short, Rosa would have taken her for a bride. She looked at the girl in alarm and realized that she was looking at her own image, as if she were looking at herself in a mirror. The two little girls stared wide-eyed at each other.

Rosa dared to break the heavy silence. "Who are you?"

"Who are you?" the little girl answered like an echo.

"I asked first. Who are you?"

"You're sleeping in my bed," the strange little girl said in a quiet voice, her face as expressionless as if the angel bed had not been stolen from her.

"It's mine now. My mother said so," Rosa retorted, holding on to the wooden railing firmly, as if the mattress were about to slip out from under her body.

"But before it was mine," said the stranger quietly, afraid to wake Angela and Joseph, sleeping soundly on their bedding on the floor.

Rosa knew that the little girl was right, and she held her tongue because she didn't know what to say. Then she gathered the courage to ask, "What's your name? Mine's Rosa."

With inexplicable obstinacy the stranger refused to reveal her name, and Rosa decided for her: "If you don't want to tell me your name, I'll call you Rina," she announced, happy to give her a name of which she was particularly fond at the time.

The strange little girl rolled the name round in her mouth like a ball: "Ri, Rin, Rina," and with lackluster eyes accepted her new name.

"What's that key?" Rosa asked, and weighed the key in her hand.

"It's the key to my house," she replied, hesitating.

"And where is your house?" asked Rosa, even though she knew the answer.

The little girl didn't answer, as if she hadn't heard the question.

"So where are you sleeping now?" asked Rosa. "My mother told me today that you're sleeping in the bed of another little girl who went away."

Rina was silent. With her snow white hand she signaled to Rosa to make room for her. Rosa turned down the blanket, and to her astonishment the little girl got into bed with her clothes, her gloves, and her shoes on. Rina laid her head with its halo of curls on the plump pillow next to Rosa's, and in a tone of command said to her: "Now we have to go to sleep." Rosa snuggled up to her obediently and fell asleep.

When she woke up in the morning the little girl was gone. In her place she found a huge doll with a hard china face and a soft body, cheeks painted pink, blue glass eyes, and a magnificent tower of yellow curls tied with a red silk ribbon. The doll wore a white ruffled dress, and on its feet were soft kidskin sandals. Rosa looked in horror at the doll's dead eyes, which looked back at her with an accusing expression, and pushed it away with a cry. The doll fell onto the tiles, which were decorated with pictures of leaves and fruit, and its hollow skull hit the floor with a dull thud. By some miracle, the doll's head remained intact.

"What's wrong?" Angela rushed up to her, picked the unwanted doll up from the floor, and examined its head for cracks. "Look what a beautiful new doll you've got," she said, trying to infect Rosa with her enthusiasm.

"It's not my doll," the little girl answered accusingly.

"It's yours now," said Angela and put the doll back on the bed. Rosa shrank into herself, trying not to touch the lifeless body lying beside her and staring at her with cold glass eyes. She tried to tell Angela about Rina, but her mother, who was busy arranging the room and unpacking the boxes, only pretended to be listening, nodding in agreement, and Rosa knew that she hadn't heard a word. Later on she overheard her mother saying to Joseph: "If we hadn't moved into this house they would probably have slaughtered us, like they did my poor husband, Amatzia, and it's lucky for us the army arrived to save the town, and in any case they're living in our houses now and sleeping in our beds and wearing our clothes and eating our food, and we're doing to them exactly what they're doing to us." Rosa, who didn't understand what she meant, asked her uncle Joseph, but he refused to elaborate on his sister's words, and afterward she heard him scolding Angela for planting unnecessary fears in the child's heart.

The next night, before she got into bed, Rosa put the rejected doll into an ammunition box she had found in the yard and padded it with an old towel. She placed the box with the doll inside it next to her bed. "This is your bed," she said to the doll. "You're not allowed to get into my bed." That night Rina visited her again. She was glad to see the doll and told Rosa that her name was Belle, because she was the most beautiful doll of all. She picked the doll up carefully—"because her face is made of china and it can break"—and showed Rosa how to turn it over so that it said in a high, piping voice: "Mama, mama, mama." Then she asked her to take good care of the doll and keep her dresses clean and showed her how to look after Belle's hair.

After that Rina appeared every night and lay down beside her, and she became her best friend—until the day that Rachelle, Ruhama, and Ruth, her new friends, arrived in the house. Rina, her night friend, couldn't take part in their daytime games—jump rope, catch, and hide-and-seek—and their friendship cooled off a little. She would reappear mainly on lonely nights when the icy winter wind played whistling tunes on the musical notes of the window bars. Then she would stand pale faced next to the bed, ask about the doll, Belle, and Rosa would invite her into their bed, calm her fears of the thunderbolts and lightning flashes, and explain to her that they were not gunfire or shells, because the war was over long ago. And when Rina calmed down, Rosa would tell her in a whisper that the whole world was full of little girls sleeping in the beds of other little girls who were sleeping in the beds of other little girls, and that there was no end to it, because this was the way things had to be.

A few days after they had moved into the splendid villa, which boasted the name "Ali Hamouda's House of Notes" and was registered in the government offices as "Abandoned property, block 142, house number 5," they were joined by refugee families who had escaped from the Jewish Quarter of the Old City, whose eyes still reflected the terrifying sight of the Jordanian Legionnaires surrounding them on all sides and whose ears echoed with the thunder of the shells. Tattered clothes, diapers gray with washing, and sheets stained with blood and excrement were hung out in front of the house, over the lavender bushes, hiding the splendid entrance from the eyes of passersby. The air grew dense with cigarette smoke, and the odor of sweat mingled with the sweetness of cheap perfume, the reek of menstruating women, babies' shit, salted herring, garlic, cabbage soup. All these plus the bad breath of rotting teeth and smells of mold and rust suddenly filled the house, rudely thrusting aside the delicate scents of lavender and jasmine that had greeted Angela, Rosa, and Joseph when they first arrived.

It was then that Rosa began to notice the patches of lighter color on the walls, hinting at pictures that had been torn from their place by an anonymous hand; the marks left by the scraping of heavy furniture on the tiles, furniture that had disappeared together with the rolled-up carpets; and the piles of books in fine covers that had been pushed into a corner and served the refugee families as fuel or as toilet paper. At night she would hear the screams of Mischa, whose arm was tattooed with a row of five blue numbers; the shrill cries of the many babies crowded into the rooms; and the groans coming from the writhing bodies of Mr. and Mrs. Cohen, whose little cubbyhole was separated from Angela's room by a gray army blanket.

There were five families living in the house. The Cohens had received the dressing room, a little cubbyhole leading off Angela's room, which was the best bedroom in the house.

In days to come, when strife and contention increased in the house, Rosa would hear her mother explaining to the other residents that she was entitled to the best room because her husband had been killed by an Arab murderer and she had a fatherless child to look after, as well as a brother who was also an orphan.

Mischa occupied the kitchen, and whenever anybody needed a drink of water in the middle of the night he would wake from his troubled sleep, sit up in his rumpled bed clad in striped pajamas sour with sweat, and rub his eyes with his ruined hands. At the sight of a ghostly figure wandering round the kitchen he would break into a series of screams in Polish. Until they took pity on him and requested all the residents to keep a supply of drinking water in their rooms in order not to disturb his rest, because his penetrating screams in the dead of night woke not only the inhabitants of their own house but also the people living in the villas next door to it.

The entrance hall, previously the grand salon of the house, was occupied by the Warshavsky family from the conquered Jewish Quarter. A black-clad and long-bearded father, a mother so brittle and angular that it seemed her body would snap in half at a touch, and six small children crowded into the room, sleeping on mattresses on the floor. At night the mattresses covered the floor, and by day they were stacked in the corner in a colorful heap the children liked to clamber up and dive off, straight onto the hard floor. The oldest child was Ruhama, who was Rosa's age, as skinny as her mother, pale and fair-haired. Ruhama, whom everyone called "the shrew," would secretly pinch the bottoms of her one-year-old twin brothers whenever her mother asked her to change their diapers, and she would tell Rosa forbidden things about husbands and wives and what they did to each other at night. The spacious, windowless room smelled permanently of wet diapers.

The Zilka family, consisting of five people, lived in the room opposite Angela's. The father of the family, who in Iraq had been a man of means, an accountant who always dressed in suits, now had a job as a construction worker. Every evening he would sit in the entrance to the house next to the lavender bushes, rolling amber worry beads between his fingers, drowning his misery in arak, and cursing the day he had decided to emigrate to Israel with his family. After that he would try to approach his wife, and she would yell at him that his breath stank and that she would only allow him to touch her when he got rid of the disgusting smell.

Their daughter, Rachelle, boasted long, thick black hair that looked as smooth and shiny as if she ironed it every morning with a coal iron. Her flat nose and pitted skin, humped and cratered by the ravages of smallpox, detracted only slightly from the glory of her hair. Her brown, almond-shaped eyes turned purple when she was angry, and she was never short of reasons for anger. Rachelle was known for her hard character, her forthright common sense, and her need always to be right. Nobody in the house would ever forget her endless arguments with the sharp-tongued Ruhama, with one saying, "That isn't so," and the other saying, "It is so," and continuing ad infinitum with, "No, it isn't," and, "Yes, it is." This bickering would only stop when the irate residents screamed at them both to shut up.

The Sharabis—father, mother, grandmother, and the little girl, Ruthie—were the last family to move into the villa, and they received the little room at the end of the hall. Ruthie, whose complexion was café au lait and whose glittering emerald eyes shone at night like a cat's, joined Rosa, Ruhama, and Rachelle in their games. When they jumped rope the serious, responsible Ruthie would keep watch on her tiny grandmother, who sat on a low stool at the entrance to the house, a pointed black hood tied over her head and her fragile legs wrapped in shiny trousers trimmed at the edges with a strip of embroidery. People said that she was a hundred years old, and attributed her longevity to her diet, which consisted morning, noon, and evening of fenugreek and *ghat*. With the obstinacy of the old she would use her gums to chew the intoxicating leaves she crammed into her toothless mouth. When she had drained the gum-darkening juice to the last drop, she would spit out the blood-colored dregs in an energetic sideways spit that would have put a far younger person to shame.

And when the children were bored, Joseph, the oldest child, would gather them around him and keep them occupied. Once they stole, at his command, a ladder made of rough whitewash-spattered planks, and with its help invaded the wide storage space over the kitchen ceiling, which was high enough to walk upright in. Quietly, so as not to wake the snoring Mischa napping in his fortified kitchen, they took out china plates and dishes with lacy edges, of whose existence nobody was aware but them, and ran with their booty to the open field. There they formed a line and, one after another, in exemplary order, at Joseph's command, they hurled the china at the gray rocks, gold-rimmed plates, soup bowls, heavy crystal glasses, coffee cups decorated with flowers, gravy boats, and delicate vases made of colored glass. And when they went away they left behind them a pile of broken china mixed with shards of glass and crystal sparkling like diamonds in the sunshine.

When the stock of china and glass ran out, Joseph discovered the movie theaters in the town. He took advantage of his sister Angela's preoccupation with her daily worries, played hooky from school, and made the rounds of the movie theaters. He would go in in the middle of the movie and pay the price of half a ticket. At the end of the movie, before the lights went on in the hall, he would run to the toilet and hide there, standing on the seat so that his feet wouldn't give him away. And when the lights went out he would sneak back in and see the first half of the movie he had missed.

Later on he found himself jobs. At the Edison Cinema he sold waffles, at the Ron he pasted up posters, at the Zion he acted as an usher, and at the Orion he swept the hall. In this way he was able to see a number of movies a day and all the movies showing in town. And when he came home to change his clothes and eat, Rosa would sit beside him, and he would tell her the plots of the movies he'd seen and hum the tunes to her. Angela would pretend to be busy with the housework and listen in secret; and her memories would ferment in her body, her longings for Amatzia would make her heart contract, and her eyes would fill with tears.

After about a year, Angela began repeating to anyone willing to listen that the house was falling apart. The creeping disintegration started in the garden, lapping with its dry tongue at the green plants. When it had finished with the plants it climbed up the downspout and ravaged the roof, after which it slid straight through the windows, invaded the rooms, and finally seeped into the walls themselves, crumbling them and destroying the water pipes and electric wiring. The first one to notice the changes in the garden was Rosa. The lavender bushes and jasmine that had previously surrounded the villa disappeared into thin air, taking with them in silent protest the scent of their flowers. Soon the garden was taken over by hostile nettles, stubborn couch grass, and thorns. Tall prickly brambles provided shelter for snakes and black scorpions that emerged on the hot summer nights and invaded the rooms in quest of the coolness provided by the thick walls of the house.

Responsibility for the drainpipe, which had come loose from the wall, was taken by Mousa Zilka, Rachelle's brother, who liked climbing up it to the roof. In the summer its dry beak gaped with the helplessness of a dying man, and the painful gurgles it made in winter, when whistling winds banged it cruelly against the wall, made the residents' flesh creep. The iron shutters, attached to the walls by little metal soldiers wearing fezzes on their heads, got stuck, and the stones around them grew rusty. When the shutters were removed, the windows were shattered one after another by the wild ball games of the Warshavsky and Zilka children. After that the tiles began falling from the roof; the water came out of the taps muddy and rusty, making loud, spluttering noises as it did so; the toilet overflowed, wetting their shoes and overpowering the medley of smells in the house with its pungent odor; and at exactly the same time the musical gate at the front of the house was torn from its hinges, leaving a mute, gaping hole behind it, like an open wound exposed to the ravages of the wind. The high ceilings of the house began to sprout black rosebeds of mold, and mossy green growths spread their spores through the air and gave Mischa asthma attacks that sounded like the barking of hungry dogs and kept the other residents awake at night.

At the same time the invasions from outside increased. Long columns of black ants with menacing pincers carried away the herring tails left over by the Warshavsky family and the pita crumbs the Zilka children dropped on the floor. Due to the large amounts of food consumed in the crowded house, gangs of famished gray field mice appeared and built their nests of gnawed rags deep in the recesses of the closets. In their wake came mangy, flea-bitten cats, who stalked the rooms in search of the rodents as if the house belonged to them. Quite independently bands of little pink geckos joined the pilgrimage to this Mecca of houses, the rapid beating of their hearts exposed to view behind the transparent skin of their bellies. Making shrill little chirping noises, the geckos would set out on nocturnal hunts for the glittering green flies swarming round the ceilings and leaving tiny black droppings behind them. Skinny spiders with long, trembling legs arrived on the heels of the flies and began diligently weaving their beautiful, sinister webs in the corners of the rooms, waiting patiently to trap the flies and methodically covering the ceilings and walls with the artistry of their delicate, closely woven nets.

Rosa would often hear her mother lamenting her bitter fate and complaining of the crowded living conditions that made her life so difficult. One day she heard from Mousa Zilka, with whom she cuddled and kissed in hidden corners of the house until Joseph caught them at it and beat them soundly, about a family who lived in a building not far away and who had had a great stroke of luck. The father of the family had simply wanted to hammer a nail into the wall, and to his astonishment he had discovered a treasure trove of gold coins and jewels. They had sold the lot and bought a new apartment in the nice Jewish neighborhood of Rehavia, where they now lived all by themselves.

While everyone was discussing the treasure trove with glittering eyes, Rosa equipped herself with a long, rusty nail, and late at night, after her mother's sighs turned to light snores, she called Rina and consulted her. Rina joined her in their bed in her ruffled dress and her patent leather shoes, which she never took off and which never wore out. She listened gravely to the story and admitted that there was a treasure trove in the house, but she refused to reveal where it was hidden. "I don't need your favors," said Rosa, and began gently tapping on the wall next to the bed and listening intently to the sounds it made. After choosing a place that sounded particularly dull and hollow and was well hidden behind the pink frame of the angel bed, she began digging into it with the nail. When she had done for the night she stuck the nail deep into the kapok mattress, until only its flat head showed. The next night she groped for the cold tip of the nail, pulled it out, tapped it on the wall, listened to the dull noises it made, and continued her digging. She did this every night, searching for the treasure hidden by the previous occupants of the house before they fled. Angela, who cleaned the room every day, was at a loss to understand where the little heaps of plaster and whitewash under Rosa's bed came from.

"This house is falling apart," Rosa heard her complaining to Mrs. Zilka. "Wherever I go I find sand and whitewash and bits of plaster."

"I have the same problem. The house is full of sand, and I can't understand where it comes from."

"However much you clean it keeps on coming back." The

women concluded their conversation with a sigh and went on energetically hanging up their washing.

At the end of their first year in the house the hole Rosa had dug in the wall broke through into the Warshavskys' room. Through it she could see what was happening in the room and hear the noises made by the family at night, and at last she was able to understand what Ruhama had meant when she told her what her father did to her mother at night.

When the icy winter winds whistled through the rags with which they tried to seal the broken windowpanes, and the dozens of holes and tunnels drilled in the walls by the children in search of the treasure were discovered by their parents—the tension in the house reached a breaking point. Angela argued that the crisis was precipitated by the walls, which were as riddled with holes as Swiss cheese and which conducted the sights and sounds from room to room and family to family. It was enough to open your ears next to the wall in order to hear what the Zilkas thought and what the Warshavskys got up to in the secrecy of their room—and the mystery of the Zilkas' disappearing pitas too was finally solved when an accidental look through the hole in the kitchen wall revealed Mischa, his bony hands trembling with greed, breaking off a piece of the hot pita baked by Mrs. Zilka in the clay *taboun*, beneath which merrily burned two thick volumes of the *Encyclopaedia Britannica*.

The signal for the outbreak of hostilities was given when Angela asked the Cohens to try to get through the night without their usual moans and groans, since she had two children in her room and it wasn't nice for them to hear the kind of sounds that should only be uttered in private. The next day Shoshana Zilka told Angela that Mrs. Cohen had spread a rumor through the neighborhood that she was harassing her because she was jealous of her conjugal life with her husband.

That evening Angela lay in wait to catch the Cohens at it, and when in the silence of the night they began to make their nauseatingly familiar noises, she flung aside the gray woolen blanket dividing their rooms and screamed at the top of her voice.

"Quiet! I'm sick of the pair of you! And if I wanted a man like you, I could get a million for a *mille*," she yelled at Mr. Cohen, who sat up in bed, naked and confused. His face went red, and he tried desperately to cover his damp, drooping member, which had gone limp in shame. It burrowed under his body like the head of an ancient tortoise, trying to disappear into the depths of his groin, which was covered with frizzy black hair. The corner of the sheet he had enlisted to cover his shame was torn violently from his hands by his wife in order to cover her own nakedness.

A terrible commotion broke out in the house, with everyone hurling insults at everyone else. The first target was the Warshavsky family. Everybody complained of the dirt they left behind them, of the stinking diapers, of the leftover herring that made the whole house reek, and of their sleepless nights because of the incessant crying of the Warshavskys' new baby.

Shlomo Zilka was called a drunk and his children, gangsters. Rosa was accused of bringing all the ants and mice with the slices of bread she hid under her mattress. Even the quiet Sharabi family was not exempt; they were rudely informed that their bodies stank of fenugreek and that people were fed up with their spitting on the floor and the stains it left all over the house. The height of the uproar was reached when in sudden solidarity they all turned on Mischa and told him that he frightened the children with his shrunken skull, his bloodshot eyes, the number tattooed on his arm, and the horror tales he told them of starvation and human beings turned into soap. And when everyone was yelling at Mischa, Angela added that it was because of these stories that her Rosa had started stealing bread at night and hiding it under her mattress.

The first to break was Mischa, whose nerves were shot anyway. Stiff as a sentry at his post he stood in the middle of his accusers, stopped his ears with his skeletal hands, their swollen veins pulsing with anger, and in a terrible voice he cried like a wounded animal: "Quiet!" Then he went to town, bought a big lock, fixed it onto the kitchen door, and prevented the other residents from entering his territory and using the sink and the stove. And they all had to buy primuses and oil rings and wash their dishes and their vegetables under the garden tap.

It was then, as Angela told her friends, that Rosa's ravenous hunger, which was never to leave her, took hold. As if a hole had opened in her stomach, she would eat everything she could lay her hands on without any discrimination. Angela blamed the poor wretch. "It's all because of Mischa." After he barricaded himself in the kitchen, Rosa was the only one who found a way to his aching heart and assuaged his loneliness. She would speak to him sweetly from the other side of the locked kitchen door and ask him to tell her about the camps. She was the prettiest little girl in the neighborhood, and he would open the door a crack. Her golden curls, her slanting sapphire eyes set in a round face with a translucent skin, and the organdy frocks in which her mother dressed her with the help of the parcels from distant relatives in America made her look like a doll, and she was Mischa's favorite. As if afraid of being caught red-handed, Rosa would glance quickly to the right and the left, slip through the half-open door, and sit down on Mischa's bed, always rumpled and soaked with the sweat of his night terrors. Then she would take off her black patent leather shoes, fold her feet in their spotless cotton socks beneath her, and place herself at the disposal of Mischa and his stories.

Having received the green light to go ahead, Mischa would begin with the unchanging ritual she found so enjoyable. With a skinny hand trembling with suppressed desire, he would fish out from under the mattress a few of the soft, flat cookies spotted with green mold that he kept especially for her, offer them to her, take one for himself, and begin telling her his stories. From him she heard of his wife and child, who never returned, and of the hunger in the camps, which was so terrible that the inmates ate potato peels and the bark of the single tree growing in the concrete yard. And of the people with bloated bellies who gave up the ghost under the cold iron sky of the camp. With shivers running down her spine, she would take another of his sweat-soaked cookies, sniff it with relish, scrape off the green mold with her fingernail, bite into it, and ask him to tell her about the people who were turned into soap and about his first meal after the liberation, and how in spite of the explicit orders of the doctors he had eaten and eaten until he almost died. Toward the end of the visit she would ask him to show her his arm. And he would roll up his sleeve, as shy and blushing as if she had asked him to undress completely in front of her. When the blue tattoo was exposed in all its shame she would touch his dry skin with her finger, gravely stroking each numeral in turn. And with his flesh coming out in goose bumps he would read the numbers out loud to her, teaching her addition and subtraction, multiplication and division with their aid, and she would learn it all by heart, with the result that she knew how to read and write numbers and do arithmetic long before her three little friends.

Full of stories and hungry for food she would kiss him good-bye on the gray stubble of his sunken cheek and slip back to her room. If neither Angela nor Joseph was watching, she would raid the icebox and polish off its contents, and in case she felt hungry during the night, she would take the loaf Angela was saving for breakfast and Joseph's school sandwiches to bed with her, where she would fall asleep with her mouth full of half-chewed bread. In the morning she would wake to her mother's furious shouts as she searched for the missing loaf and blamed everyone, but especially Mischa, for its mysterious disappearance. After she discovered the column of ants leading to Rosa's hoarded food, where they had entrenched themselves in a nest of breadcrumbs, she bought a lock for the icebox and opened it only as required.

"I'm not about to stand for hours in line to buy food for the family, and beg for extra coupons, and risk getting caught on the black market, just so you can gobble everything up in a single evening," said Angela, who nevertheless took food from her own mouth to give to her daughter, and grew thinner as Rosa grew fatter.

Thus deprived of her natural sources of nourishment, Rosa made the rounds of the residents, putting on her saddest expression, the expression of a poor fatherless child that melted the hardest hearts, and sat as a welcome guest at the meals of the other families. She would open her supper with herring, sour cream, and baked potatoes at the Warshavskys and continue at the Zilkas with highly seasoned eggplants, soup full of weeds pulled up from the garden, and a thin, steaming Iraqi pita baked in the clay *taboun*. At the table of the Sharabis she ate sponge bread dipped in fatty marrow soup and finished off with a sharp salad and a phosphorescent green sauce made of fenugreek. When she returned to her room she would ask Angela to make her an omelet from egg powder with a spinach patty, polish off a jar of yogurt, gulp milk straight from the saucepan where it had been put to boil, break bread with her hands, take half the loaf to bed with her and hide it under her mattress, where she shared her hoard with the new kingdom of ants that had come into being immediately after the previous one had been liquidated by her mother. The cookies she loved best of all she kept for Mischa.

With Mischa she celebrated the biggest and longest feasts of all on the Day of Atonement. When the other occupants of the house wandered round their rooms like ghostly shadows, their dry mouths giving off the bitter smells of empty stomachs, their faces pale, and their tongues coated white, Rosa would escape the punishment of the fast and slip away to knock on Mischa's door. He would open the door a crack, check to see who it was, stretch out a skinny hand and pull her into a kitchen full of the smell of cooking. On the table she would see delicacies that never made their appearance there on ordinary days of the year: black bread thickly spread with butter, a pink ham for which he had paid a fortune to the administration officer of the nearby Greek Embassy, potatoes boiled in their skins, sweet carrots cooked in wine and raisins, a finely chopped salad, onion rings bathed in oil, black olives, and fresh cookies for dessert. After they had eaten their fill they settled down on the bed, and Mischa would play with her curls, kiss her dimples, stroke her skin, and tell her stories about the camps. Then she would ask him why he never fasted on Yom Kippur. Mischa would fix his dull eyes on her transparent sapphire ones, stroke her arms and legs, weigh his words gravely, and answer her in the same words year after year: "There, in the camps, every day was Yom Kippur. There we fasted enough to last us all our lives, and even if I live another thousand years I still won't use up all the days I fasted there. For this Yom Kippur I've already fasted," and he would raise a glass of wine to the sooty kitchen ceiling, winking at Rosa and declaring: "Let's have a happy holiday!"

Some say that Rosa's aversion to bathing stemmed from Mischa's stories. Every Friday afternoon, when all the residents were freshly bathed, their hair soft and shining from the laundry soap with the picture of a menorah stamped on it, the house would fill with Rosa's screams as she battled Joseph and her mother in the bathroom. These battles would leave blue bruises on her plump flesh and half-moons of bleeding little holes on their hands, a painful reminder of her pointed teeth. After a lengthy, stubborn struggle in their room, they would finally succeed in imprisoning her hands in theirs, and Joseph would carry her, kicking and screaming, to the bathroom, where he would throw her onto the floor and with Angela's help strip off her clothes, push her into the tub, and peel the dirt off her with a rough loofah that left fine red scratches all over her skin. When her body was scoured and her hair clean, they would lead her back to the room wrapped in a stiff towel and dress her in her Sabbath clothes.

Many years later, when Rosa already had children of her own, Angela reminded her of these forced baths.

"Why didn't you want to wash?" she asked her.

Rosa reflected a little before she replied, shook her head, and said with a serious expression: "It was because of the camps."

"What camps?" asked Angela in surprise.

"The extermination camps," said Rosa quietly.

"What have the extermination camps got to do with washing?" asked Angela incredulously.

"They led them into the showers on the pretext that they had to wash," said Rosa, "and there they gassed them, and afterward they made them into soap."

"Mischa told you that, didn't he?" asked Angela.

"I don't remember," she lied. "I don't remember where I heard those stories," Rosa replied with lowered eyes, the terrible scenes described by Mischa coming back to haunt her.

Rosa grew fast and soon outstripped her friends—Ruthie Sharabi, Rachelle Zilka, and Ruhama Warshavsky. When they walked through the neighborhood streets together Rosa looked like their big sister, with her hefty body and swelling breasts that kept getting heavier underneath the broad bands of cloth her mother wound tightly round her chest to flatten them. Sometimes, when they tired of jumping rope and playing hopscotch, the girls would hide from the boys in the yard, behind the Warshavskys' tattered sheets hanging out to dry, and discuss grave and weighty matters. Their favorite subject was what their lives would be like when they grew up. Rosa, who was an only child and longed for brothers and sisters, would jump in first and declare with shining eyes that above all she wanted a husband and a lot of children, even seven or eight, the more the better.

Ruhama, who suffered because of her little brothers and detested the patter of their little feet, would shake her head in disagreement and announce that she, of course, would have a husband, but she didn't want any children, because children meant trouble, diapers, noise, dirt, and aggravation, like her mother always said, and besides, it was a shame to waste money on them. Whatever money she had she was going to spend on herself and on a beautiful house full of flowers.

Rachelle naturally wanted a husband and children, but not too many: "One or two is enough, because three's already too many." And, unlike Rosa and Ruhama, she knew that she wanted a profession. She wanted to be a bank clerk and to count lots of money every day. "And anyone who touches money all day long will have money, because money sticks to your fingers, my father says so," she would whisper to her friends with gleaming eyes.

And when the three of them looked at Ruthie, waiting to hear her plans for the future, the little girl would lower her emerald eyes to the ground, pluck a stalk of wood sorrel with her slender fingers, put it to her lips, and chew on it without thinking, until the delicate, sour taste filled her mouth and brought a grimace to her face.

"Well?" they would press her.

"I don't know," she would say in embarrassment. "I don't know what to want."

"If you don't want anything, you won't have anything," Ruhama warned her. "No husband, no children, nothing. You have to want."

And Ruthie would become confused under the pressure of her friends, look with lowered eyes at the stalk of wood sorrel, which had lost its crispness and turned into a limp, masticated lump, sigh, and say that there was no need to ask for anything.

"Then you won't have anything," Ruhama would sum up. And as always when she wanted to annoy Ruthie, she would sing:

Once upon a time I went to Yemen,
I saw a little black boy eating a lemon,
And he'll be Ruthie's husband, a match made in heaven.

Since none of the girls had ever seen a black boy, and the way Ruhama said the word made it seem like a curse, the idea of their friend marrying someone like that seemed shocking and threatening to them. Ignoring the insulted tears beginning to drip from Ruthie's emerald eyes, Ruhama would announce that it was time to return to their jumping and hopscotch.

In her spare time Angela began to tell fortunes by reading coffee grounds. She had learned this skill from her aunt Lise, who knew how to read coffee cups like an open book. First she told the fortunes of the neighbors, and when they came true the neighbors brought their friends, who brought more friends, all fearful and curious to know what lay in store for them. A lot of banknotes accumulated in Angela's hands, joining the money brought home by Joseph, who had graduated from high school and was working in the movie theaters of the town while waiting for his military service to start. When she had a tidy sum, she applied to the Housing Ministry. As a widow she received a grant, and they were moved from the villa into a small apartment on the third floor of a new building in 10 Shabazi Street, one of the jerry-built housing projects in Katamon G, whose outer walls were covered with a jigsaw of orange stones amateurishly stuck in the plaster by builders new at the trade.

In the new building they were greeted by three small rooms, a kitchen, a gleaming bathroom, and a private toilet. Without any urging, Rosa shut herself up in the bathroom and spent the whole day soaking in the warm water, scrubbing her skin and stripping off old memories. She emerged in the evening, the tips of her fingers swollen and wrinkled as a washerwoman's; her flesh pink, fragrant, and shining; her long hair shampooed, and her eyes radiant. Suddenly Angela realized how she had grown and how beautiful she was, and Joseph, who was angry with her at first for keeping him out of the bathroom, gazed into her calm eyes, drowned in their blue lakes, and forgot all his grievances.

Although Rosa had asked Rina to move into the new house with them, Rina refused with incomprehensible obstinacy. And when Rosa pressed her, she said that the villa was her home, she had the key to the front door hanging round her neck, and she would never move. Rosa was tired of her oppressive silences, the lacy dress that never got dirty, and the games she made her play with the doll, Belle, and she didn't miss her at all. They left the angel bed, which Rosa had outgrown, behind in the villa, and took only the doll as a souvenir, even though Rosa refused to play with it. And when Angela found the doll thrown under Rosa's new bed, she dusted its dirty dress and set it on top of the wardrobe as an ornament. From its perch the doll would stare at Rosa with its cold eyes in mute reproach and remind her against her will of the old house, of Rina, and of the nights they had spent together. Soon Belle's hair was full of dust, glittering spiderwebs reached from her elaborate curls to the ceiling, and her lace dress turned gray with grime. One day, during the spring cleaning in honor of Passover, Angela picked the doll up and turned it over. But Belle was silent, and no cry of "Mama, mama, mama" escaped her lips. With a heavy heart Angela shook out her curls and gave her a new hairstyle to match Rosa's. Then she wiped away the dust powdering her china face, took off her lace dress, and washed it carefully. Together with a handful of sharp-smelling mothballs, she wrapped the naked doll and the laundered dress in an old sheet, and after some hesitation she buried them deep in the closet next to the dead Amatzia's winter clothes.

"When you get married and have a daughter, you can give her the doll," she said to Rosa, or perhaps to herself, and continued her spring cleaning.

A few weeks later they were joined in the new neighborhood by the Warshavsky and Zilka families, and at the end of the year the Sharabis too received an apartment of their own and moved in with Ruthie but without the grandmother. "She died in the middle of chewing *ghat*, and when they took her body to bury it, it was as dry and light as if there was nothing left of her but skin and bones," said Ruthie. And when Rosa started school, the girls from Ali Hamouda's House of Notes were all together again in the same class.

Many years later, when Rosa had children of her own, she would grow sick of the sight of the neglected houses and the yards full of thorns and junk surrounding her and suffocating her soul in Katamon G.

Then she would take her children for walks at twilight in the neighborhood of Old Katamon, among the magnificent villas of the Arab effendis who had abandoned their homes and property in their panic-stricken flight. The streets that had once borne Arab names were now named in honor of Jewish acts of heroism and historic dates. As they went from street to street Rosa read the names out loud and explained their significance. From Portzim Street they climbed up to Palmach Street, down Tel Hai to the Twenty-ninth of November Street, and from there to the streets of the Thirty-five and Conquerors of Katamon, and to Relief Convoys and Water Distributors Streets, commemorating the siege of Jerusalem.

When she wandered round the streets of Old Katamon she remembered the night of the looted carpets, and she wondered what had happened to them and where they were now. The well-tended villas made of chiseled Jerusalem stone looked to her like palaces. Here and there the flags of foreign states flew from imposing houses, with limousines bearing diplomatic license plates parked outside them. Rosa would point to the flags and explain to the children: "That's the Greek flag, that's the Italian, that's Sweden, and that one's Chile." She would pick fragrant honeysuckle flowers from the fences as she walked and show the children how to suck out the sweet drops of nectar. When they passed jasmine bushes she would decorate their heads with the sweet-smelling blossoms, and from the passionflowers she would pull off the long, slender petals to reveal the shy little man hiding inside them to the children. She would peep with them through the slats of the wooden fences and devour with her eyes the flourishing gardens and the people serenely sitting and walking in them.

And when she approached Ali Hamouda's House of Notes, she would slow down and stop. Surrounded by her children, she would stroke the gleaming wrought-iron gate adorned with the treble clef, and widen her nostrils to take in the scent of the jasmine mingled with that of the lavender bushes, which had grown back, covered with fragrant purple flowers. Then she would point a trembling finger to the half-open green shutter and whisper to the children as if she were telling them a secret: "That was our room." And they would stare wide-eyed with disbelief at the magnificent villa standing opposite them surrounded by trees and lavender bushes. Rosa would try to explain to them that in those days it wasn't like it was today, when only one family lived in the house—that then a number of families were obliged to crowd in together. And they would listen to her politely and ask to go back to their own familiar neighborhood.

When Rosa realized that they didn't believe her stories, she began visiting the house on her own. On the days when longings pierced her body, she would hide behind the fence, and her eyes would invade the window of her room and grope their way blindly among the familiar furniture. In her mind's eye she would see the icebox, the doll, Belle, the angel bed, and Rina. And when in her imagination she lay next to her on the mattress, she would be assailed by the old smells of the air heavy with cigarette smoke and sweat mixed with cheap perfume, the stink of soiled diapers, the smells of mold and rust. And when she encountered Mischa's face she would hurry home with a great hunger gnawing at her stomach, and she would not be appeased until she had opened the fridge and devoured its contents. With her stomach full she would sit on her armchair and swear that she would never visit the house again, until a force stronger than she was carried her back there again.

two

THREAD OF SAFFRON

*On winter nights, when a cold wind raged out*side and blew through the cracks in the windows of the third-floor apartment on 10 Shabazi Street, Angela and Rosa would snuggle up under the thick kapok quilt and play the memory game. In spite of their urging, Joseph refused to join them, burying his head in a book and ignoring their invitations. Rosa was always the first to begin, but her memories ran out too quickly. After all, she was only a little girl, and little girls don't have many memories, Angela would console her, and at her request she would tell her the memories she loved best of all, the memories of her uncle Joseph when he was a baby. And while Angela spoke, Rosa would giggle and steal sly looks at the hefty, broad-chested Joseph, whom she could on no account imagine as a baby.

"When Grandma Fortuna gave birth to Uncle Joseph at home and we all crowded curiously round his cradle, we saw a perfectly ordinary baby: purple, wrinkled, and angry, like any other baby. Nothing about him warned us of the troubles to come." This, more or less, was the standard formula with which Angela opened the story of Joseph when he was a baby. And Rosa, who had heard the story dozens of times and could quote passages from it by heart, was never satisfied, and would ask to hear it again and again in spite of her uncle's vociferous protests.

Angela's stories on those winter nights began with the childhood she never had in the little village of Za'afrana, next to the Libyan capital of Tripoli, and the story of her own birth, which she had heard from her mother in one of their rare moments of intimacy. The story would pass before her eyes like tear-jerking scenes from a movie, and the deep insult it had planted in her would come back to swell her heart and choke her throat.

When Angela was born her father, Jacob Janah, whose friends in the synagogue Hebraicized his name and jokingly called him "Señor Wings," was very disappointed. Janah demanded of his wife, Fortuna, that she give him a son, and Fortuna, who knew that she was carrying a girl because her sister, Lise, had seen it in her coffee cup, refused to let her daughter out and kept her imprisoned in her body until the end of the tenth month. And every day the baby kicked desperately at the walls of her mother's stomach and begged to be let out, until one day she butted violently against the sac enclosing her and tore a long slit in it with the long nails of her little fingers, and the waters broke in a strong jet. And when the water flooded the floor, they forced Fortuna onto the bed and sent for Victoria the midwife. Ignoring Fortuna's despairing screams, Victoria pushed her hand into the gaping hole revealed between her forcibly parted legs, and extracted the baby's head with ease. With practiced movements she freed the shoulders, and with one little pull the baby's body slid out. At first the midwife was appalled at the sight of the scowling little face, which was furrowed by deep lines, as if the baby had grown old due to its prolonged stay in the womb. Then she looked at the hands waving in the air, which were swollen with water, rough and lined as those of an old washerwoman, and when she finally lowered her eyes to the bottom of the little body she saw that the male member she had expected to see was missing. And without that member, Janah had warned her, her life wouldn't be worth living.

In her alarm the midwife dropped the big copper basin full of hot water, which hit the stone floor with a terrible clattering noise, splashing its contents and scalding her thighs as it did so. At that moment Janah burst into the room, so large and frightening in his appearance that the midwife began trembling all over, as if she were to blame for the sex of the child. Under the angry and disappointed eyes of the humiliated father she quickly cut the umbilical cord, pressed down on the mother's abdomen to eject the afterbirth, and ran away as fast as her legs would carry her.

On the day that Angela was born, a son was born to their neighbors, David and Malka Bokobasa, whose small and meager saffron fields bordered the splendid Janah fields. Jacob Janah suffered terribly at the lavish party thrown by his neighbors for little Solomon's circumcision. Crushed and humiliated, he sat in the "Jacob's Ladder" synagogue, to whose building fund he had made a handsome donation, and watched enviously as the worshipers went up to Bokobasa, slapped him on the shoulder, congratulated him on the birth of his son, and respectfully called him "Abou Solomon." Only a few came up to Jacob, and with pitying looks tried to console him with remarks along the lines of, *Don't take it to heart, A daughter is a sign of sons to come,* and *Next time you'll do better.* His enemies looked at him with malicious, gloating expressions, and in mocking, insincere voices wished him the same good fortune as his neighbor. Janah fled the synagogue in shame, called David Bokobasa to him, and made a pact with him.

"Since both our children, yours and mine, were born on the same day, it's a sign from heaven that they were meant for each other, and that they should marry when they come of age," he said, without looking Bokobasa in the eye.

"And what if they don't want to?" Bokobasa made bold to ask in a hesitant voice.

"What if they don't want to?" Jacob scornfully mimicked his neighbor's trembling voice. "So what if they don't want to?" he repeated with a shout. "They won't have any choice in the matter. We'll betroth them right now, in the cradle. Let's see them not agreeing. This is a vow we're making here, and you don't break a vow, and if anyone does break it he'll bring trouble on his head."

And David Bokobasa, slighter and weaker and poorer than Janah, couldn't oppose him. He shook hands with him and vowed that his son and Janah's daughter would marry, and woe betide anyone who broke the vow. Janah went home satisfied, shook his wife Fortuna's shoulders, woke her up, and told her to prepare for the engagement ceremony.

"But the child's just been born," she implored.

"Do as I tell you," he snapped. "You didn't give me a son, so Bokobasa's son will be mine," he added and got into bed. And Fortuna didn't sleep a wink all night.

After giving birth to Angela, Fortuna's womb closed. Some say that it was the fear of producing another girl and bringing fresh misfortune to its mother that caused it to close up. For eight years the womb persisted in its rebellion. Every thirty days, with the precision of the appearance of the new moon, it spat out the unfertilized eggs and the bed of mucous membrane it had grown for them, and obstructed the passage of the spermatozoa quivering with their desire to mate. Cunningly it beckoned them and invited them in, only to kill them in the trap it had dug for them in its black depths. But when Angela was eight years old, one determined spermatozoon, with a long, strong tail and a pointed, thrusting head, succeeded in crossing the deathtrap and reaching its goal. Nine months later Joseph was born.

At this point in the story Angela's face would grow grave, and her eyes would cloud over. Familiar with the phenomenon, Rosa would keep quiet and with uncharacteristic patience allow her mother to commune with her memories. After a few moments of silence, she knew, Angela would take up her story again with renewed vigor.

Her ears still ringing with the yells audible throughout the village, the yells of triumph with which her father greeted the news of the birth of his son, she remembered that at first everybody feared the opposite: that Jacob Janah was reacting with screams of disappointment to the news that his wife had given birth to a daughter. But when they heard the truth from the midwife, who emerged from the house with her head held high, as proud as if she were personally responsible for the birth of a male child, and a big bundle of money together with a few bags of saffron in her apron, all of them, Jews and Muslims, closed their shops in his honor and went to congratulate him. So overjoyed was the father that, together with his guests, he polished off the entire contents of the wine cellar, adding threads of saffron to the bottles to improve the flavor.

Never before had the village seen such celebrations; even the memory made Angela feel weak. For seven days and seven nights, until the day of the *brith*, the house swarmed with visitors eating delicacies yellow with saffron, drinking, singing, and telling jokes. Women whose hands were painted with saffron instead of the usual cheap and commonplace henna circulated among the guests bearing trays laden with food, while the father, proud as a peacock, led them in convoys to the baby's room. Ignoring Fortuna, who was still exhausted from the difficult birth, as if she had had nothing to do with bringing his son into the world, he would whip the blanket off baby Joseph and reveal the miracle that had been vouchsafed him and for which he took all the credit. Then he would wait for the flattering and obsequious cries of admiration that were music to his ears, and when the guests murmured words of praise for the baby's erect penis, he would modestly lower his eyes and with his chest puffed out in pride he would whisper: "Just like his father."

For seven days and seven nights Janah forbade Joseph to be diapered, and ordered the nurses to lay him in his cradle with the lower half of his body exposed, broadcasting the tidings of his maleness to the world. And in order to avert the evil eye from his first born son, Victoria the midwife was summoned to cover the walls of the room with the yellow prints of her splay-fingered, saffron-painted hand. On the day of the *brith* female relatives and neighbors arrived and with open mouths and rolling tongues uttered joyful ululations that mingled with the wails of the baby as the mohel snipped off his foreskin, while Janah stood by, watching like a hawk to see he didn't cut off too much.

"And what was Joseph like?" Rosa would ask. And Angela would recover and say: "Joseph was a baby like all other babies, a perfectly ordinary baby, not too big and not too small, not too fat and not too thin, not too beautiful and not too ugly, just an average baby.

"It happened right after the *brith*. The baby began to eat. He ate voraciously. At first he ate for two babies, and then he began to eat for three, and then for four, and when he began to eat for five babies he finished all Granny's milk." Angela remembered how her father yelled at her mother then that because of her little breasts, which he had always mocked, the baby didn't have enough to eat. He tore the hungry, screaming Joseph from his mother's arms, wrapped him in one of the white cotton sacks in which he packed the bundles of saffron, and carried him round the village in search of a wet nurse. The moment he was taken from her arms Fortuna knew that her son was lost to her forever. From that day on she was allowed to see him only at night, through the window of the nursery where he slept in the light of the oil lamp, while a strange wet nurse counted his breaths.

His lips pursed with anger against his wife, whose milk had dried up, Janah strode through the village with the hungry, wailing baby bundled in a sack on his back. On the outskirts of the village he found Allegra. They say he found her by following the terrible sound of her weeping, the weeping of a mother who had lost her baby. He found her sobbing on the grave of her baby son who had died suddenly in his sleep. Her black garments were ripped and covered with ashes, her face and chest ravaged by the deep scratches she had inflicted on herself in her grief, the hair she had torn from her head lay around her on the ground, and her naked breasts dripped milk onto the fresh mound of earth. As if she weighed nothing at all, Janah pried her clinging fingers from the little grave, picked her up in his strong arms, and carried both his burdens home, one wailing from hunger and the other with grief for her dead baby. From that moment until the day her milk dried up and she was sent away, she never stopped crying.

"When Joseph finished Allegra's milk," Angela continued with her story, "and her tears dried up together with her milk, they gave her a bundle of small change and sent her home." Angela remembered the scene vividly: Allegra clinging to Joseph, her dry eyes wide open, her gaping mouth screaming as she refused to part from him and wept tearlessly.

"After they dragged her off Joseph by force, they brought him a new wet nurse. When her milk dried up, and they couldn't find another wet nurse in the village, Janah went to the nearby town and hired three wet nurses for a large sum of money—Georgette, Juliet, and Nazima—and they all lived with us in our house. In order to ensure a steady supply of milk, it was decided that Georgette would feed him in the morning, Juliet in the afternoon, and Nazima in the evening. And each in turn would enter the nursery with laughing faces and bursting breasts and leave it with sad expressions and dry, depleted bosoms. Before Joseph turned one, he had dried up the milk of all the wet nurses in the area, and Janah decided that he had to be weaned.

"During the course of his last breast-feed, the screaming Joseph stuck his milk teeth ferociously into the dry nipple of the evening wet nurse, Nazima. And the sudden silence that fell on the house when he closed his mouth was broken by the agonized shrieks of Nazima, who screamed as if a band of devils had fallen on her and were eating her alive. But Joseph was undeterred by her shrieks, and he clung to her like a leech and refused to let go. For three days and three nights he remained with his mouth clamped around the dry nipple, while Nazima screamed in pain and silent tears of hunger and sorrow poured down his cheeks. Why was he silent? Because his mouth was gagged by Nazima's milkless nipple. And how was poor Nazima's nipple finally freed? Grandma Fortuna went to consult the wise women of the village and tried everything they advised. One of them told her to rub pepper mixed with tobacco on his gums, another advised her to pinch his mouth and squeeze it till he choked, and a third recommended massaging and tickling the soles of his feet until he laughed and the nipple slipped out of his mouth. But nothing helped. So Granny sent them all away and boiled goat's milk on the stove. When the milk boiled over, the smell penetrated the baby's nostrils, and he opened his mouth, dropped the nipple, and burst out crying so loudly that all the neighbors came running to see what had happened. In the meantime they flooded his open mouth with the goat's milk, and he swallowed and swallowed and swallowed until he fell asleep."

At this point in the story the pungent smell of goat's milk filled Angela's nostrils, and she saw her little brother tottering on his fat legs into the kitchen, sniffing the milk Fortuna was boiling on the stove, and drinking it in bucketfuls. Before her eyes she saw her father coming into the yard with a herd of black goats following him obediently, little copper bells tinkling on their necks. With glazed eyes she remembered how her mother would milk them into tin buckets and boil the milk, still warm and bubbling from their teats, until it brimmed over in white, airy foam and put out the fire with a whispering sound.

And when she felt Rosa tugging at her sleeve, Angela would rouse herself and continue her story. At the age of two Joseph would no longer wait for the milk to boil. He would steal into the pen, evading the watery eyes of the goats surrounding him, choose the ones that were suckling their young, and while the kids were still clinging to their mothers and butting their stomachs in order to quicken the flow of milk, he would feel their teats to find the fullest. With a hefty kick he would chase away the suckling kid and clamp his lips around the wet, quivering teat freed for his use. The kid robbed of his food would stand next to its mother, looking on helplessly as the milk flowed into Joseph's stomach, stamping its hooves, bleating, and butting its hornless head into Joseph's broad back.

In the light of this new development, Janah decided to wean the kids as soon as they were born, and he instituted a new order in the pen. No sooner had a newborn kid fallen onto the straw behind its mother and hurried to attach itself to her teats than Janah would detach the tiny mouth and, ignoring the protests of the mother, bear away the fruit of her womb, its hair still wet with amniotic fluid. He would teach the newborn kid to suck from a rubber nipple attached to the plug of a wooden barrel, which he filled with milk diluted with water. And while the mothers lamented their stolen babies with heartbreaking cries that caused the kitchen maids to stop up their ears, the kids learned to feed themselves from the rubber nipples, butting the wooden barrels with their soft heads as if to quicken the flow of milk. Thus Joseph was at liberty to attach himself to the teats of the mother goats and drink to his heart's content without any interference from their offspring, and he spent so much time among the goats that sometimes it was difficult to tell them apart.

"So Joseph was really the son of a nanny goat," Rosa would whisper into her mother's ear, so that her uncle wouldn't hear.

"That's what the children in the neighborhood and at school thought, they called him 'son of a nanny goat.' And when he came near they would hold their noses and complain about his smell. They claimed that even though Joseph had been weaned from the goats at the age of five, their smell still clung to him. They said that his blue eyes were as watery as a goat's, and when he grew up they blamed the goats for the hairy pelt that covered his body and said that he would never find a bride.

"Joseph grew and grew and grew," Angela went on, and at this point in the story Rosa chimed in and echoed the refrain: "And he grew and grew and grew."

"Until the next-door neighbors complained that they could hear him growing in the night," continued Angela. And she remembered the loud, strong sounds of Joseph growing, mingling with all the other noises that disturbed the neighbors in their sleep—the croaking of the frogs, the whimpering of babies in their dreams, the bleating of the hungry kids and their pining mothers.

"How do you hear a child growing?" Rosa would ask again, even though she had heard the story dozens of times before.

"A child's body makes a special sound when it grows."

"And what sound does growing make?"

"There's a special sound for grass growing, a special sound for trees growing, and a special sound for children growing." Angela would repeat the categories of sounds that Rosa, in spite of all her efforts, had never succeeded in hearing.

"But what does it sound like?" she persisted.

"It's impossible to explain, you have to hear it."

"But when will I hear it?"

"When you have children of your own, if you stay awake all night you'll be able to hear them growing."

"Did you hear me growing?"

"You grew quickly, just like Joseph, and we all heard it, Joseph and I and all the people in the house," Angela replied, and added that at the age of one year Joseph had worn clothes to fit a two-year-old, and when he was five he looked like a boy of ten, and Grandpa Janah, who suddenly began to age rapidly, was afraid that Joseph's accelerated growth would be the death of him.

"But why did the way Joseph grew worry Grandpa?"

"Because the bigger and stronger a child grows, the weaker his parents grow, because the growth of the child brings old age to his parents.

"And then," Angela continued her story, "a wise woman in the village told them that children only grow in their sleep. Not in the daytime when they're running around and playing. And in order to slow down the tempo of Joseph's growth, they decided to wake him up at night every hour on the hour."

To help him achieve this end, Janah bought a wooden clock with a red, pointed roof and a porthole closed with a green shutter set in its center. When they opened the shutter they found cogs and wheels and a little painted wooden bird. "A cuckoo bird," explained Angela, and added that after they had all peered inside the clock, listened to the sound of the pendulum and the ticking noises made by the innards of the clock, Janah hung it over Joseph's bed, where the cuckoo faithfully performed its function. Every hour on the hour, day and night, it would pop out and stick its beak right into Joseph's ear. In the beginning Joseph would wake with a start at the bird's shrill cries, sit up in bed in a panic, and refuse to go to sleep again for fear of the bird's cruel beak and ear-piercing cries. But after a month he grew used to it and slept soundly through the hourly racket. And so Joseph went on growing, and the neighbors went on complaining, protesting at the cuckoo cries too, and Janah discovered new white hairs in his beard. Then he went and bought a bigger clock and hung it up next to the first one. Two birds now popped out at once, and like a pair of old friends who hadn't seen each other for years, they would stand on the little balconies of their houses and call out the time to each other every hour on the hour. And since by their combined efforts they failed to wake Joseph, Janah decided that if two were better than one, three would certainly be better than two, and he bought a third cuckoo clock. But Joseph was so used to their calls by now that even this reinforcement failed to disturb him, and the sound of his growing, accompanied by the cries of the cuckoos, went on waking the neighbors from their sleep. That year, when he turned six and began to go to school, he was as big as a bar mitzvah boy.

At this point in the story Angela's voice would break, and she would fill up with an ancient bitterness, the poisoned fruit of an anger that had never been resolved.

The same bitterness welling from Angela's throat would return many years later to prove to Rosa that her mother had never recovered from the incident that had upset her nights, wrought havoc with her sleep, emaciated her body, and ruined her youth.

"In their wisdom," she would resume, in a voice hoarse with resentment, "they decided that I had passed the age of growth. And since I was nearly a woman, I didn't need to grow anymore, and I didn't need to sleep. And so they made me responsible for stopping Joseph's growth and hung the cuckoo clocks over my bed, right next to my ears. Every night for two years I would wake up in alarm on the hour, since I had never grown used to the noise of the cuckoo calls. Then I would have to go to Joseph's bed and shake him violently until he woke up, so that he would stop growing for an hour. Since I was an obedient child who always did what her mother and father told her, I never got a decent night's sleep. I went to school with black circles round my eyes, and if you asked me what they studied there I wouldn't know what to tell you, because I was fast asleep."

"And Joseph? Did he stop growing?"

"Because of my shaking Joseph would wake up for a few seconds every hour, complain that I was disturbing his rest, sometimes hit me in his sleep, turn his face to the wall, and go straight back to sleep. In the morning he would get up taller and as fresh as if he hadn't been woken up at least ten times during the night. Until I couldn't take it anymore and asked my father's permission to emigrate to Israel. And he, of course, refused. And when I tried to rebel against him, he locked me up and hid my shoes and clothes. My mother found the key, let me out, gave me her shoes, and helped me to escape. And when I reached Kibbutz Givat-Rimonim, where I met your father, I put my head down on the pillow, and they told me afterward that I slept for a week."

"And who woke Joseph when you left?"

"Janah brought Moustafa. Moustafa was an orphan who was glad of the warm bed and good meals they gave him, and in exchange he did your grandmother's shopping for her in the market and woke Joseph up at night. Joseph went on growing during Moustafa's time too, because, or so I heard, he wasn't too strict about his work and sometimes slept the whole night through."

"And who woke Joseph when he arrived in Israel?"

Angela smiled at the question: "When Joseph arrived in the country and came to live with me, you'd just been born, and you woke him up with your screaming. It was then that I bought him his first cuckoo clock, because he'd grown so accustomed to the ticking of the clock and the cries of the cuckoo every hour that he couldn't fall asleep without them."

With a complaint that sounded as bitter as if the whole thing had happened yesterday, Angela would conclude her story by saying that while Joseph grew up to be a tall, broad-shouldered man, she herself had remained small and shriveled, as if her brother had grown at her expense. Then Rosa would ask to see the family portrait, and Angela would take the picture, covered by a strip of white sheet, out of the drawer next to her bed. Four people stared out at her from the photograph, two of whom she knew very well. Rosa would move her index finger over the picture, traveling from one to the other, and even though she knew the answer, she liked asking in a babyish voice: "And who's this?"

"That's Grandpa Janah with Grandma Fortuna next to him." And Rosa would gaze for the umpteenth time at the tall, strong man with the hard, cruel face. His wiry hair stuck up on his head like the black bristles of a brush, and a thin waxed mustache shaded his upper lip. Her grandmother stood next to him, apologetic and self-effacing, looking the picture of misery. Her lips turned down at the corners, with deep lines on either side of her mouth; her downcast eyes evaded the camera and stared at the floor of the photographer's studio.

"And here's Joseph." Rosa gently stroked the hulking boy, a head taller than his sister, stretching his lips in a pathetic attempt at a smile in order to please the photographer.

"And here you are," she pointed to Angela, who looked like a little girl even though she was already a young woman about to set sail for Palestine. She was sloppily dressed in a loose garment that blurred the womanly contours of her body and made her look even thinner and more wretched than she was. Her coarse washerwoman's hands, too clumsy to pick the saffron flowers, hung lifelessly at her sides.

And when Angela again covered the photograph with the strip of sheet, she remembered the first time Rosa had seen it. She had gazed intently at them all and suddenly burst into peals of bell-like laughter.

"Joseph was the son of a nanny goat, but you've got horns," she said and pointed to the pair of fleshy horns her brother's upraised fingers had caused to sprout from her head. And Angela, who had seen the picture hundreds of times, couldn't understand how she had failed to notice the horns before. And after that, whenever she showed the picture to Rosa, she would look for the horns and wonder how he had made them grow without her sensing it, and how she had failed to notice them after the photograph was developed and sent to her in Palestine.

In time to come, when Joseph perpetrated the terrible deed that devastated their lives, Angela would think about what he had done to her right under her nose and the horns he had given her behind her back, and wonder why she had ignored the ill omen immortalized in the photograph and engraved on her fate many years later. For if she had known what Joseph was going to do to her, she would have taken steps to stop him, and no doubt everything would have been different.

And before she went to sleep Rosa would make her regular request to her mother, that if she heard her growing during the night she would wake her up, several times if necessary. Pouting and defiant, she would repeat that she didn't want to grow. If she grew up Angela would grow old, and old people always died in the end, and she didn't want to lose her mother ever. Angela, whose heart contracted every evening anew, would kiss Rosa's heavy eyelids as they drooped and closed of their own accord, and promise to wake her up.

And when Rosa was sound asleep and Joseph went out as usual to the movies, more memories would be patiently waiting their turn to surface. Then the memories would hover before Angela's eyes, flickering in orange and yellow, blinding her with a sudden flash that made her stomach turn over, and covering her head, her arms, and her legs and clothes with foul-smelling yellow scales. Together with the scales her first memory of her father would rise to the surface. The memory was of his gigantic hands, whose palms were yellow, as if he were permanently ill with jaundice, and the bittersweet smell coming from his clothes, his hair, and his breath. And when she remembered her father a bad taste would rise to her mouth, reminding her of the taste of the food she had eaten throughout her childhood and girlhood, and a slight sensation of nausea would overcome her, filling her mouth and making her stomach contract.

Almost all the dishes served at her father's table were liberally flavored with the king of spices, threads of saffron, even though they were worth their weight in gold. Her father owned the biggest saffron fields in the area, and only he could afford a diet of exclusively orange dishes. He would always say that they were good for a man's virility and a woman's fertility. Janah, who liked to impress people, refused to call the flowers he grew in his fields saffron. His flowers, of all the saffron flowers grown in the purple fields of the village of Za'afrana were called by their Latin name, which sounded more important to him, as befit the king of spices. And when he spoke of his flowers to his friends in the synagogue or his drinking companions, he would begin with the words, "My *Crocus sativus,*" knowing that he was making a mighty impression on his audience. He used this Latin name so often that the villagers who called him, to his face, "Señor Janah," and in the synagogue by his Hebrew name, "Señor Wings," began calling him "Señor Crocus" behind his back. After his son was born he would proudly pepper his speech with the words "my son, Joseph," and so the honorary title "Abou Joseph" was added to his name.

A few months before the picking season began Fortuna would grow nervous and restless. She would pinch Angela for no reason, raise her voice to her, secretly shake Joseph, Janah's pet, and make the servants' lives a misery. "She acts as if her periods last for months instead of days," the kitchen maids would whisper behind her back. And while Fortuna turned into a nervous wreck, Janah grew relaxed and happy.

And in the autumn months, when the stigmas were picked in the early hours of the morning, after the dew had dried on the petals of the flowers and before they opened to soak up the sun, the fields would be invaded by young girls whose hands were white and transparent, whose fingers were long and supple, and who moved as gracefully as dancers. Like delicate butterflies the maidens danced among the lilac-colored flowers, and plucked the corollas gently from the calyxes. After the purple flowers had been removed from the green stems, the saffron pickers would carefully break off the stigmas with their fingertips, taking care to count three stigmas for every flower. Then Janah would take one of the threads in his fingers and crush it, checking to see if it left the sweet-smelling crimson stain that did not come off easily even when scrubbed with soap and water. And the deeper the color of the stain and the longer it lingered on his hands, the more satisfied he was and the higher his prices soared. When the hands of all the pickers turned orange, Janah would collect the stigmas and dry them on soft sieves made of horsehair set over smoldering coals, until the right smell wafted into his nostrils. Then he packed the orange gold in little cotton bags, which together with the threads of saffron inside them each weighed no more than a gram.

And as Angela remembered, the smell of saffron would rise in her nostrils and she would be filled with nausea. The orange color that danced before her eyes throughout her childhood became hateful to her, and when she grew up she refused to eat anything in shades of orange. Carrots, pumpkins, oranges, and tangerines were never to be seen on her table during her marriage to Amatzia, and she never used mustard to flavor meat. And when Rosa asked her to cook pumpkin for her, to peel her a carrot, or to squeeze the juice of an orange for her, she would do as her daughter asked with revulsion, as if she had asked her to take a life, and she would try to avert her eyes from the sight of the loathsome color. Then she would hurry to wash her hands and scrub them with soap and disinfectant as if they had been branded with an indelible stain.

three

THE GREATEST LOVE IN THE WORLD

Although she was still a young woman when she was widowed, Angela made up her mind never to get married again. When people brought up the subject she would purse her lips and refuse to answer. Spiteful tongues said that for lack of a man in her bed she concentrated all her energies on Rosa and her ringlets, and she would end up with a spoiled, ungrateful little monster on her hands. And behind her back the neighbors claimed that it was for the very same reason that she had it in for the Cohens, who had shared her room in Ali Hamouda's villa and noisily celebrated their conjugal bliss behind their curtain every night. The sanctimonious lectured her that it was unhealthy to bring up a child without a father figure, and those well-versed in the Talmud quoted: "The sages ordained that a woman should not be without a man."

Shoshana Zilka and Mrs. Warshavsky would ask her in confidence how she could stand being without a man for such a long time, and try to introduce her to widowers and divorced men. When she turned their offers down in disgust, they patiently explained that she had no call to be so choosy, since she herself was far from being the fairest among women: She was short and skinny, her breasts were shriveled, her hair was thin and mousy, her eyes were as dull as if she hadn't had a good night's sleep in her life, her hands were coarse as a washerwoman's, and her teeth were loose. For the matchmakers who came knocking at the door and the many others who tried their luck she had one answer: "In spite of my appearance I had one great love, a love so great that even if you put all the romantic movies in the world together you wouldn't find anything like it. I'll never have a love like I had with Amatzia again, and I'm not prepared to settle for less."

In years to come, when Rosa grew up and asked her why she

never remarried, Angela would explain to her that a widow, especially if she had lost her husband in tragic circumstances, should never betray the memory of her beloved husband by marrying again. After Rosa got married Angela would confess that she remained single for fear of upsetting Amatzia in his grave. "A new man in my life," she said, "would have made him jealous, and he had already suffered enough. And this jealousy would have endangered my new husband's life, and very likely your life and my life too, because a jealous, wounded man will always seek revenge, even if he has to climb out of the dungeons of hell or interrupt his feasting on the Leviathan with the righteous in heaven to do so." Only when Rosa had children of her own would Angela tell her of Amatzia's great love for her: "There is no greater love in the whole world, not even in those movies Joseph screens in his movie theaters that make everyone cry."

In his passion Amatzia would tell her that he loved all of her, and even though she knew the answer she would ask him to explain in detail what he meant. Then he would tell her patiently, for the umpteenth time, that he loved not only her external, visible organs, but also her internal, invisible ones. If he could, he would have kissed her heart, stroked her slippery liver, listened to the whispering of her lungs, peeped into her intestines, and worshiped the darkness of her womb from within. "And there isn't a man in the world who loves your outside and inside equally, and it was my luck to find the only one of his generation capable of it. And since his love was so concentrated and intense that it would have been enough for a thousand women, they took him away from me quickly, because what he gave me in his short life others could never have given me if they lived to be a hundred. And what he gave me then was so much that I'm still using it today, drawing on that great bank of love day by day, hour by hour, minute by minute." At the same time Angela knew, and she told Rosa so, that she had to be thrifty in her use of the great fund of love he had showered upon her, for if she was too extravagant she would use up everything in the reserves he had left behind him. When this happened she would know that it was time for her to join him and take up her life with him at the point where it had been cut off.

Nobody could understand the story of the love between Angela and Amatzia, a sturdy, good-looking kibbutznik who excelled at folk dancing and playing the harmonica. Years after he was murdered, the members of Kibbutz Givat-Rimonim were still bringing the matter up at their meetings and blaming themselves for not preventing his marriage to the girl who had brought catastrophe down on his head. They would discuss it for hours, trying to understand once and for all what Amatzia had seen in Angela to make him want to marry her, and how they had failed to see the writing on the wall. They had all seen him helping her to carry the baskets of oranges she had picked to the collection point, but none of them had realized that he was motivated by love. The romantics among them thought that the big, strong Amatzia had fallen in love with her because she looked so fragile that she had aroused his protective instincts. The more sophisticated argued that perhaps it was precisely because Angela, who was well aware of her limited attractions, was the only girl on the kibbutz who didn't try to ingratiate herself with him that he was drawn to her and fell under her spell. Some claimed that Amatzia's marriage to Angela was a rebellion against his parents and the kibbutz members, who had expected great things of him, the fine, firstborn son of the kibbutz. The compassionate and soft-hearted were of the opinion that he had decided to marry her because he felt sorry for her. Her parents, on their way to rescue her from his clutches, had both died on the same day, and since he was a youth with principles and a highly developed conscience, he had taken the responsibility for their deaths on himself.

Only a small minority dared to admit that it was love, a very great love. For even though they had lectured him day and night, insisting that he deserved a better-looking, better-connected, and healthier woman, Amatzia had rebelled against his parents and comrades, abandoned everything, married her with a ring and a rabbi, because that was what she wanted, moved into the Mamilla quarter of Jerusalem with her, and lived with her there in poverty.

It seemed that the dire prophecies of the elders of the kibbutz and their unremitting efforts to separate the couple only strengthened his love for her. And she, grateful to him for choosing her over all the other girls, tried to requite his great love. The old folks in Mamilla well remembered the couple living parsimoniously in their cramped little room. At night they would hear Angela's shouts of joy and Amatzia's deep groans in response. Night after night the pair of them kept their neighbors awake, until they decided to send a deputation of pious women to Angela, to put the fear of God into her and tell her that it was sinful for a woman to go to bed with her husband night after night all month long without skipping a single day for the uncleanliness of her menstruation and without going to the *mikvah* to purify herself of her blood. And when the women of the neighborhood met to consult over the watermelon seeds laid out on colorful blankets to dry, they came to the conclusion that she was probably pregnant, since only a pregnant woman could sleep with her husband every night without skipping a single day, and they decided to leave her alone.

In spite of the austerity that left Angela's body even skinnier than before, except for the rounded little belly sticking out of her skirt, and although there were days when they did without a hot meal, Amatzia and Angela did not give up their other love, the love of the cinema. Once a month, Angela told Rosa, when they had succeeded in saving a little money, they would take turns buying a single ticket and going to see a movie. The other one would wait outside the movie theater and for days on end would feed on the details and listen in suspense to the story of the plot. Together they would hum the tunes and reenact the most important scenes, the scenes of love and kisses.

Their love, which was greater than all the love stories they saw in the movies, came to an abrupt end. The warning sign came a week before Rosa was born, an event they were anticipating with all the eagerness of a couple in love. That night, after they had satiated each other's bodies, and Angela cuddled up blissfully in Amatzia's arms and waited for sleep, she sensed the baby crying inside her. For a long time she lay on her back with her eyes open and listened to the stifled weeping rising from her body. And when the crying grew louder and the beating against the walls of her stomach grew harder, she could stand it no longer and she woke Amatzia with a gentle shake and told him what was happening to her.

"Amatzia, the baby's crying inside me."

Amatzia sat up in bed.

"Are you sure your labor isn't beginning?" he asked anxiously, afraid they wouldn't find transportation to get them to the hospital in time because of the curfew.

"No. She's just crying. The baby's crying. I don't know what's wrong with her," she repeated.

All that night Amatzia lay by her side, stroking her face, kissing the baby in her stomach whose crying he couldn't hear, and trying to calm them both, until the sky turned pink and the exhausted Angela fell asleep in his arms.

A few hours later, when he went out to look for work as a porter, he was murdered by an impassioned Arab coming out of the Temple Mount on the Muslim holiday of Id-al-Fitr. His ears ringing with the Mufti's call to kill the Jews, he plunged his dagger straight into Amatzia's stomach and sliced his liver in two. For hours he lay bleeding in the sewage canal next to the main street leading to Mamilla, until the river of blood flowed down the hill and collected in a puddle at the entrance to the Valley of Hinnom, alerting passersby to his plight. When they followed the trail of blood they found him lying on his back, his body dry and drained.

Angela said that he had left the house quietly in the morning so as not to wake her. When she woke up in a panic, the hollow of his body next to her in the bed was already cold. After drinking her morning coffee she overturned the empty cup on the saucer and did the same with the muddy dregs of Amatzia's cup waiting for her in the sink. She did this every morning without his knowledge. After washing her face and combing her hair she examined the results. The dry coffee had congealed on the sides of her cup in a strange configuration of spidery black trickles she was unable to decipher. Alarmed, she examined Amatzia's cup and saw the figure of a big-bodied man lying at the bottom of the cup with a huge hole gaping in his stomach. She knew immediately that a calamity was about to befall him. In an act of desperation she did something unthinkable in coffee-reading circles and poured the remains of the cold coffee standing in the pot into her cup. She quickly drank the sinister black liquid, and with the bitterness choking her throat she poured the dregs straight into Amatzia's cup, covering the evidence with a new layer of grounds. With a pounding heart she examined the results. The figure of the slain man looked back at her mockingly, in a new configuration of coffee grounds swollen with water. She burst out of the house like a madwoman and ran through the streets in her dressing gown, her huge nine-month-old belly sticking out in front of her. With prayers and vows she tried to turn away the evil fate swooping down on him, and with tears bathing her face she stopped the passersby and asked them if they had seen her husband, but nobody could tell her where he was.

In the afternoon rumors reached the quarter of an unknown young man that had been murdered. Immediately afterward her brother, Joseph, who was living on a kibbutz arrived on a surprise visit. In the evening, when the policemen knocked on her door accompanied by two neighbors and a nurse from the hospital, Angela was waiting for them, with Joseph holding her hand and her face as white as a sheet. The room was sparkling with cleanliness and she was wearing her one and only maternity dress, whose collar she had already torn as a sign of mourning.

They buried Amatzia on the Mount of Olives under the cover of darkness. Preceded by an armored car and surrounded by armed British policemen to prevent violence and bloodshed, the bier made its way up the bare, rocky hill covered with tombstones, and there they laid him quickly to rest in the hastily dug pit. That night Angela's mind took pity on her and effaced the fragmentary images, the words and gestures, which if she had taken them in would no doubt have driven her to throw herself into the pit after her husband.

Angela did not remember the sight of the bloody towel pushed deep into the gaping wound in the body of the man who had loved her as no other man was capable of loving.

She didn't remember the hateful words and the accusation—"Murderess!"—hurled at her by her mother-in-law.

She didn't remember how the kibbutz members who accompanied him to his last resting place stood around the grave like a hostile wall, and shooed her away like a chicken when she tried to approach.

She didn't remember how she had pushed her way through them, supporting her vast belly with her hands.

She didn't remember how the fatherless baby had struggled inside her, crying and beating its little fists against the walls of her womb.

She didn't remember how she had chased them all away and fallen on the grave, digging her nails into the mound of freshly dug earth and refusing to move even when a policeman's baton came down lightly on her shoulders, and how in the end the British policemen had been forced to pick her up in their strong arms and carry her away, kicking and screaming.

A few hours later, when she was sitting shiva for him with two neighbor women at her side, feeding her sugar water and mopping up her tears with a big handkerchief, she noticed her black fingernails and she couldn't remember how the dirt had gotten there. And when she wanted to know if Amatzia had suffered when he was stabbed, the mourners explained to her that Amatzia hadn't felt any pain, that the stab of the knife is felt by the victim like a hard blow and afterward, when the blood begins to flow and the life drains out, a sense of lightness spreads through the body, until the soul escapes and flies up to heaven. And Angela listened to the explanations, and she couldn't understand how healthy people, who had never been stabbed in their lives, could know with such certainty how a stabbed man felt at the moment of the stabbing and after it, until the moment when the soul departed from the body.

And when the city of Jerusalem was divided, and the grave remained on the other side, she could no longer go and visit it—until the Six-Day War rejoined the two halves. Then she went up to the Mount of Olives and, with the crackle of gunshots still reverberating in the blackened mountains, she looked for the grave. For months she searched the hillside every day, until she knew every rock and tombstone, identified the people buried there by name, remembered the dates of their births and deaths, and knew who lay next to whom. But she never found Amatzia's grave. During those dark days of searching, when Angela thought painfully of the husband who had disappeared from her life without leaving a grave behind him, her thoughts turned willy-nilly to her parents, who had vanished without a trace.

The tragedy that had taken place a month before her marriage came back now to haunt her, and she saw her parents swallowed up by the sea on their way to Palestine, together with another forty-five people on board the ship hit by a British naval mine meant for another vessel. And when she wept on Amatzia's vanished grave, she wept too for the memory of the parents she had never had a chance to mourn. For immediately after the news of their death she had married Amatzia, and she had been unwilling to mar their happiness together with her grief.

Angela did not yet know that one of the passengers on the ship plying its way though the dangerous sea, teeming with German submarines and mines below and hostile fighter planes above, was Solomon Bokobasa, the boy born on the same day as she was and promised her in marriage with a handshake. As a child she had blocked her ears with her thumbs when her mother told her how her father had forced David Bokobasa to make a pact with him. And when she saw her intended, whom everyone called "Solomon the Praying Mantis" because of his swaying gait and the way he prayed in the synagogue, she would run away, refusing to believe that when she grew up she would have to marry him. But her mother told her that once the fathers had sworn an oath to each other, she had no choice in the matter, because whoever broke his oath would be cursed. And during the sleepless nights imposed on her by her father, Angela would think about Solomon the Praying Mantis and the oath their fathers had sworn, and she knew that she would rather die than marry him and give birth to little praying mantises just like him.

As soon as her letter with the news that she had fallen in love with a kibbutznik from Givat-Rimonim reached her parents, they began making hasty preparations to sail for Palestine, terrified in case she married him and brought the curse down on their heads. They ignored the warnings broadcast every day on the radio that anyone setting sail while war was raging on the seas was taking his life in his hands, packed their possessions, and boarded the ship, laden with presents and accompanied by Solomon Bokobasa, dressed in his best Sabbath suit. In big traveling trunks they crammed wedding outfits for the bride and groom, copper trays, tin kettles, carpets, amulets, solid gold bracelets, rings studded with rubies, goat's hair blankets, and a ton of preserved food flavored with saffron. Janah took all his property with him to Palestine, as well as four sacks of saffron, two years' harvest, which he hoped to sell in the land of Israel and the surrounding countries and make a fortune. For three days the ship sailed, until it hit the mine, which blasted a huge hole in its hold. At the very same moment a storm broke out at sea and the ship was engulfed in water. Soaked to the skin, Janah held on to his son, Joseph, trying to protect him from the waves raging all around and lashing the deck with long tongues of foam, sweeping away everything they encountered in their path. But when he found himself standing up to his waist in water tinged a bright yellow color, he went out of his mind, forgot his son and his son-in-law-to-be, and rushed off to rescue the soaked sacks of saffron. He clung to them with all his might and main until a great wave came and washed him off the sinking deck into the sea, and as he plummeted into the black depths he caught a final glimpse of his precious sacks bobbing gently on the waves above, turning the foam yellow as they floated slowly away.

Three days later a passing merchant ship found the sole survivor of the wreck, Angela's hulking brother, Joseph, floating on top of the sacks and beating the yellow waves with his big hands. For months afterward ships sailing in the vicinity of the wreck reported sighting yellow, bitter-smelling waves and thousands of dead fish with orange scales floating on their backs with their white bellies turned up to the sky.

Since, with his big body and serious face, Joseph looked far older than his years, the sailors who had saved him were astonished to see him squatting day and night on the deck with his thumb in his mouth and tears pouring endlessly from his eyes. He didn't stop crying until he reached Palestine and was reunited with his sister as she stood under the marriage canopy with Amatzia. On the kibbutz, people made fun of his big body and serious face and put him to work at the hardest and most physically demanding jobs, justifying their actions on the grounds that his sister had robbed them of the finest of their sons, and however hard they worked him he could never make up for their loss of the unique and irreplaceable Amatzia.

When Amatzia and Angela left the kibbutz, fed up with the hostile attitude of the members, and moved to Jerusalem, and Joseph remained of his own free will, the kibbutz treasurer claimed that he did so as a conscious act of atonement for the departure of his renegade brother-in-law, while Angela believed that he stayed on the kibbutz because he did not want to burden them.

But the real reason Joseph stayed was rooted in his love of the movies. Every Friday night the kibbutz members would gather on the lawn in front of the dining hall and wait for the movie of the week to be screened. Joseph would sit by himself, apart from the rest, and as the pictures flickered on the screen the tears would drip from his eyes. At the end of the movie he would steal into his bed in the corner of the tent and, his eyes swollen with weeping, he would turn his face to the canvas wall and pretend to be asleep.

On the day that Amatzia was murdered Joseph went up to Jerusalem, and when the policemen came with the terrible news he was already there, waiting for them at his sister's side. For years Angela tried to get him to explain to her how he knew what had been revealed to her in the coffee grounds, but he only shrugged his shoulders and said: "I just felt that you needed me."

And at the end of the week of mourning, as soon as they returned from Amatzia's grave, her labor began. Without being asked, Joseph packed a little bag with a nightgown, underwear, a toothbrush, and soap, accompanied her to the bus station, and in the bus he sat beside her on the hard wooden bench, supporting her huge belly in his strong arms so that she would not be jolted by the turns in the road and hurt the baby inside her. And when they reached the hospital and Angela collapsed onto the bench bent double with pain, he gave her particulars to the reception clerk. And on Angela's registration form, in the place reserved for the name of the father, it said "Joseph Janah" and in brackets "Kanafi," the Hebrew name given him by the officials of the Jewish Agency when he arrived in the country.

Supported by her brother, Angela walked to the delivery room, lay down on the bed, and parted her legs. And when the baby tried to cleave through the darkness of her womb and tore her body apart in its efforts to reach the light, Angela's screams pierced the ceiling and burst through the roof and rose high into the sky to announce the birth of his daughter to her husband in heaven.

Rosa, whose birth was natural but difficult, was a big baby. She weighed six and a half kilos, and all the doctors and nurses came to see the gigantic baby who never cried, not when she was born, or when they slapped her on the buttocks, or even when she was hungry. When all the other babies in the room were screaming to high heaven over such trifles as hunger, noise, or wet diapers, Rosa lay on her back with the spasm of a smile fixed on her face, infecting anyone who looked at her and her smile with a strange, tingling happiness. She was the most famous baby in Palestine, and got her picture in the newspaper when she was only two days old.

"A reporter and a photographer came to the hospital to ask about me," Angela told her daughter, basking in the memory, "and they took a picture of you smiling in your crib." Charitably Rosa would look for the umpteenth time at the yellowing picture, which Angela had covered with hard plastic to protect it from the ravages of time, and listen to her mother telling the story she had heard a thousand times before: how in order to emphasize her remarkable size they had photographed her with the other babies born on the same day lined up on either side of her, looking like underdeveloped embryos in comparison to the blooming, fully formed Rosa. Then she would read out loud what was written under the picture on the front page of the newspaper: "The biggest baby in Israel born in Hadassah Hospital in Jerusalem." The main item described the baby and gave her weight, and the last line referred the reader to the middle of the paper and the sad story spread over two pages there. Under the screaming headlines: BORN FATHERLESS, the article told the sad tale of Angela, who had lost her husband a few days before giving birth to her daughter, and showed a picture of her, small and emaciated, clasping a huge baby wrapped up like a mummy to her undernourished bosom.

From the minute she set eyes on the big, kicking red bundle in the nurse's arms, Angela was conscious of Rosa's beauty, which was in striking contrast to her own faded looks. Even then, as she looked at the baby placed in her arms, she knew that her daughter would be the fairest among women. On her bald head she saw a mop of golden ringlets, and when she looked into her dark, bleary eyes she saw the bright blue hiding in them, and knew that they would be so deep and clear that you would be able to see right through them. Angela examined the delicate ears and saw that they were perfectly formed and set close to the baby's head like a pair of seashells, and on her bare gums she saw the teeth that would grow strong, straight, and even, gleaming with a whiteness that would never dull. When she removed the diaper wrapped tightly round her body, she saw the many dimples that would pucker her flesh in a benediction of beauty, and her long, full legs. Then she opened the baby's clenched fists and examined her fingers. She counted five fingers on each hand, and immediately noticed the index finger on the right hand, which was particularly long, and she knew that her daughter, blessed with those long, slender, supple fingers, would be a lucky woman, able to pierce the cigar-shaped buckwheat *koubeh* dumplings from end to end and stuff them with ease, and that her reputation as a cook would spread far and wide. And when the baby murmured, she heard her laughter, which would be clear and strong and echo in the chambers of the heart, turn the heads of men, and drive them crazy. But none of that could blur the effect of the thing that loomed up in front of her eyes, impudent and defiant, and turned her knees to water: the magnificent bosom that Rosa had grown during the nine months of her stay in the womb. For baby Rosa had been born with breasts.

*   *   *

And when Angela came home she put the baby to bed in the wicker basket she had bought from the Arab woman who took figs to the market in it. Surrounded by the smell of figs, her magnificent bosom bound up and flattened by a diaper, the baby gazed with her clear blue eyes at the people poking their heads into her cradle and smiled her most enchanting smiles at them.

She soon grew into the prettiest little girl in the kindergarten and the prettiest little girl in the school. She was always a head taller than her friends. Her body was rounded and padded; she had dimples in her knees, her arms, and her buttocks, and dimples in her cheeks when she smiled. Her breasts were round, heavy, and firm; and her pink nipples were always erect. Her slanting eyes laughed at everyone she met, and her fair hair was combed into elaborate curls.

Every morning Angela would wake her up two hours before school began. Like a doll on a spring Rosa would sit up in bed with her eyes closed, dreaming her interrupted dreams and entrusting her head to the hands of her mother, who patiently rolled her hair, curl by curl, into a magnificent mop of ringlets. Rosa's head soon became a commodity in its own right, and the neighborhood hairdressers added it to their repertoire. Under dying, setting, permanent waving, and straightening, to this very day you can still find advertised in the hairdressing salons of Katamon G "Ringlets à la Rosa." Once this style entered their list of treatments, the hairdressers watched Rosa like hawks. With sweet words they would invite her into their establishments, part the ringlets, weigh them in their hands, feel each ringlet admiringly with their fingers, consult one another as to the lotion used to set it, secretly sniff the fragrance wafting from her head, and try to get her to tell them what her mother put on her hair. Despite all their efforts to solve the mystery, none of the neighborhood hairdressers succeeded in emulating Rosa's ringlets. Dozens of little girls in Katamon G boasted hairstyles similar to Rosa's then, but they all lacked Angela's "finishing touch," as she put it, resolutely refusing to reveal her secret formula to anyone.

Rosa would parade proudly through the neighborhood, and her crown of ringlets would draw flies, gnats, bees, butterflies, and other winged insects as into a sweet and deadly trap. In the evening her mother would remove the insects that had found their death deep in the ringlets' honeyed trap, shampoo her hair with laundry soap, and the next morning she would set to work, parting and curling and applying her secret formula all over again. If not for her heavy body, Rosa might have been invited to take part in the beauty contest for little girls, but Angela did not encourage her daughter to lose even a single kilo, explaining to her repeatedly: "That's what men like. Fat, juicy women, with something to take hold of. The more there is of a woman the better they like it."

Armed with her mother's theories, Rosa feasted on Angela's cooking, and while her school friends tortured themselves with diets, she put on more and more weight. Her cheeks filled out, her dimples deepened, and her skin tightened over her limbs. In order to underline her daughter's beauty Angela saw to it that she wore only the finest clothes. Huge parcels of magnificent second-hand dresses, their fabric stiff and rustling, which had clad the bodies of pink-cheeked distant cousins on Sabbaths and holidays, arrived in the mail from America. These dresses, swelling like bells over their petticoats, Rosa wore to school and to play with her friends in the afternoons, and since she had a lot of dresses, she wasn't afraid to get them dirty or torn. She stood out in the playground among her friends in their white cotton blouses and short blue gym pants, whose elastic constricted their young thighs. As they gathered around and fingered the rustling, transparent material of Rosa's new dress, admiring sighs and whispers would rise from every side. "Another new dress," they marveled. "How beautiful," and, "I wish I had a dress like that."

Only Ruhama, watching with an envious glint in her eyes, did not come up to feel the stiff, gauzy stuff of the diaphanous dress. Rosa heard from Ruthie that Ruhama talked about her and her fancy dresses and said: "Even if people sent me a hundred dresses like that I wouldn't wear them, not even on Sabbath, because they're ugly and they make Rosa look even fatter than she is." Rosa tried to ignore these comments, which pierced her as painfully as long, sharp pins.

And the more beautiful Rosa grew, the more Angela declined. But in spite of her skinny body, her dreary looks, and her teeth, which began falling out one after the other, dozens of suitors came calling at the house. She would meet these men in the park, the street, or the grocery store. Before they looked at her they looked at Rosa. And they longed to stroke her golden ringlets, to kiss her dimples, caress her smooth clear skin, and bounce her on their knees. When they raised their eyes from Rosa and encountered Angela's suspicious stare, they would quickly put on expressions full of benevolence and declare that they would be happy to adopt the pretty child and give her a father. Afterward they would come calling with gifts: food, toys for Rosa, fabric for dresses, books, and movie tickets to ingratiate themselves with Joseph—who, after Amatzia was murdered, came to live with them and took on the role of the man of the family. The rich men, the ones with cars, would take mother and daughter for drives in the Jerusalem hills. The others would take them both for walks around the town, for Angela never went out for a walk with one of her suitors without taking Rosa along. When Rosa grew older and no longer joined her mother on her outings, the stream of suitors dried up and turned to a meager trickle, until in the end they all disappeared, as if there were no more eligible men left in the country.

When Rosa strained her memory she remembered almost everything. Big Morduch had a fruit and vegetable store in the city center, and he would bring her the freshest fruits, and while she ate them he would pinch her cheeks and claim that her blush was due to the healthy vitamins contained in the fruits. Rosa was the only child in the kindergarten whose lunch box included red apples in winter and orange loquats in summer. Next in line was Yakov the Butcher, who kept the freshest, juiciest chicken parts for them, and who secretly pressed her thighs like a slaughterer examining an animal before he killed it, and whispered in her ear that she was getting fat because of the meat he brought her. Yonah the Tailor volunteered to sew their dresses for free, and as he took her measurements, he would feel Rosa's breasts as if by accident, slide his hands over her butt, and look deep into her eyes with an innocent expression, as if his hands were moving of their own accord. Affectionately Rosa remembered Simcha, the chestnut vendor, and how she would warm her hands in winter over the big basin full of scored chestnuts crackling appetizingly on the smoldering coals. Rosa liked feeling Simcha's hot hands as they dropped the chestnuts he had pulled out of the fire for her into her pockets, from where they spread a warm glow through her body. In the summer Simcha would exchange the basin for a big, steaming cauldron in which he boiled bearded, yellow corn on the cob over a little bonfire. In exchange for kisses on his sunken cheeks, he would present Rosa with as many soft ears of corn wrapped in dripping green leaves as her heart desired.

Rosa remembered a long list of men who all wanted Angela, but she knew that Angela didn't want them. With the airs and graces of an impoverished queen her mother received them in the thorny yard of the house, accepted their offerings, and refused to give them her hand. Not one of her suitors, she boasted, had ever been allowed to set foot in her room in Ali Hamouda's House of Notes. And even when they moved to the new apartment in Katamon G and Rosa had a bedroom of her own, none of them was allowed into this room, which Angela called "Amatzia's room," and where she kept all his things as if he were still with her. The bristles of his old shaving brush were still stiff with the residue of the soap he had never rinsed off. His broken comb was full of the curly, straw-colored hairs uprooted from his scalp on the morning of his death. His swollen shoes with the cracked soles were still waiting for his feet underneath the bed. His clothes were hanging in the closet, the dirty underwear he had thrown into the laundry hamper on the eve of his death had never been washed and been preserved as they were at the bottom of the hamper, and his smell still lingered in the air of the room as if he had just left and would soon return. Only his framed pictures hanging everywhere, preserving his life on the kibbutz and his work in the cowshed for posterity, and the wedding picture of them on top of a haystack had been added to the room after he died. Angela told Rosa that all through the ceremony she had sneezed into the rabbi's face, and she had only discovered years later that she was allergic to hay. Every day she lit a candle in honor of Amatzia's memory, until the day she died, a few months before the birth of Angel, her last granddaughter.

Every Thursday afternoon, Angela's market day, Rosa would steal into Amatzia's room. With a serious expression on her face, resolved that this time she would cry, she would sit on the bed and try to commune with her father's memory. But at exactly these moments, as if to spite her, happy thoughts would come into her head and distract her from the sorrow and grief she was determined to feel. In her mind's eye she would see cream cakes, mountains of ice cream, and stuffed roast chickens, and the smell of freshly baked bread would fill her nostrils. With a strenuous effort she would try to banish the delightful sights and delicious smells invading her on every side and threatening to ruin her grief. Resolutely she would force herself to concentrate on the image of the father she had never known and on the feeling of loss that should obviously have accompanied this bitter fact. But in spite of her efforts to concentrate on her pathetic state, happy sights and thoughts kept stealing back into her head.

As a last, desperate measure she would take her father's picture down from the chest of drawers, contemplate it at length, and try to concentrate on the handsome stranger looking at her through the glass. As she gazed intently at the friendly face his light eyes would come together and unite into one, sticking out of the middle of his forehead like the single eye of the Cyclops, as if on purpose to make her laugh. At the sight of the new aspect she had given her father Rosa would burst into laughter, replace the photograph on the chest, pick up the shaving brush and deliberately prick her fingers with the stiff, unrinsed bristles in order to hurt herself and make herself sad. But even the contact with her father's personal possessions did not make her feel close to him. Then she would close her eyes and whisper his name over and over until her jaws grew tired: "Amatzia, Amatzia, Amatzia, Amatzia." And when in the end the chant came out in the garbled form of "Matza, Matza, Matza," she would burst into peals of laughter, as if she had just heard the funniest joke in the world. When she finished performing the "ritual of Amatzia," as Angela, who sometimes came home from the market early and peeped through the door in secret, called it, Rosa would slide off the bed and firmly slam the door behind her, as if to prevent the visions of her father from interfering with her life. Then she would carry on with her games with a light heart until her next encounter with him, when Thursday came round again.

And when Angela would tell Rosa about Amatzia and show her the pictures of their wedding, Rosa would meet the faces of her grandmother and grandfather standing next to their son under the canopy like a hostile wall. She would often ask her mother to take her to visit her father's kibbutz and meet her only grandparents. And Angela would explain again with pursed lips that her grandmother and grandfather lived abroad, and that it was impossible for her to visit them. The subject came up on her every birthday and every Rosh Hashanah, when she would receive a greeting card from them, without an envelope or stamp. When she grew up she realized that her grandparents, who had been living on the kibbutz all those years, refused to have anything to do with Angela, whom they blamed for murdering their son, and ignored the existence of their only granddaughter. The greeting cards were written by Angela herself, twice a year.

Angela's nights were dedicated to Amatzia's memory. Every night Rosa would hear her holding long conversations with her dead husband, telling him about her life, trying to keep him from worrying, and describing Rosa to him in glowing terms—her beauty, her outstanding performance at school, her friends, and her activities in general. Then she would ask him again, as she had asked him every night when he was alive and his warm body was clasped in her arms, why he had chosen her when he could have had any girl on the kibbutz, all of whom set their caps at him, the strongest and best-looking young man in the whole of the Emek. After discussing the subject with him at length and explaining the lack of logic in his choice, she would thank him for choosing her above all the other girls and for the love he had given her, which would be enough to last her for the rest of her life. Then she would take her leave of him and say good-night.

A few minutes after this Rosa would hear her mother's restless body rubbing itself against the starched sheets. With strange, tingling sensations tickling her groin, she would listen to the creaking of the springs and the clattering of the bed as it thudded slowly and rhythmically against the wall behind it, and finally to the hoarse moans that indicated that quiet was about to settle on the house as her mother sank into a deep sleep. Only after she heard the soft whistling of the air as it escaped from her mother's lips would Rosa allow herself to go to sleep. As long as she lived in her mother's house she would listen to the sounds she made at night, and when she sometimes went to sleep over at her friend Rachelle's house, she would have difficulty in falling asleep without them.

And when she couldn't fall asleep she would talk to Rachelle about the future, about the husbands they would marry and the children they would give birth to. Then Rosa would return in her imagination to a field of flowers on a false spring day and find herself standing in the middle of that field, trampling the soft grass with her feet as the smell of the sap rose in her nostrils and the first rays of the sun warmed her body and a bright rain of butterflies descended on her head. And she would fall asleep at last.

four

FOUR BUTTERFLIES, FOUR HUSBANDS

Rosa would have four husbands. Ever since she had been a child, everyone in Katamon G was of this opinion. If anyone had asked them why they thought so, they would have been unable to explain how and when this idea had sprung up and become a rumor that crystallized into a firmly held belief and turned into a self-fulfilling prophecy. But all the inhabitants of Katamon G would repeat the number like a mantra and whisper it in the secret of their homes and yards.

And when Rosa walked down the street, the neighborhood urchins would line up on either side of her like a guard of honor and call out in time to her steps: "Four, four, four." Angela didn't like this silly joke, and she would rush at the teasing boys and shoo them away with yells and threats and the heartfelt wish that they wouldn't have a single wife between them. And since she looked like a witch out of a fairy tale and was known for her ability to see into the future, they would take fright and scatter in all directions with embarrassed giggles. Still, all the way to school Rosa would hear the number "four" bouncing at her like a rubber ball from between the bushes, from behind the telegraph poles, from the stairwells, and from the shuttered windows of the dark houses. When her uncle, Joseph, who was already a soldier, came home on leave he would demand that she show him exactly which of the neighborhood boys had teased her, but she refused to tell him. Well aware of the bone-cracking strength of his hands, she preferred to swallow the insult rather than seek redress from the uncle who was as jealous of her as a loving husband.

No wonder, therefore, that she hated the number four, hated it so much that she avoided counting it among the other numbers, refused to say it aloud, and in the end invented a new name to replace it, "flor." And when her friends wanted to tease her, they would invite her to jump rope with them and count her jumps out loud. And Rosa, who in spite of her weight had no rivals in jumping rope, would wear them out, reaching "florty" and then "flor hundred," until their wrists hurt and they begged her to stop and turn the rope and give them a turn to jump. In arithmetic lessons Rosa would do her best to avoid the teacher's eye, and whenever she was asked to solve a problem whose solution included the hated number, she would deliberately give the wrong answer. And Angela couldn't understand why her daughter, who was such a good pupil, had begun to fail in arithmetic, a subject in which she had formerly excelled.

When Angela pressed her, Rosa explained that it had all started on that sunny, false spring day, three weeks after Hanukkah, the day the pupae turned into butterflies. On that day spring burst out in all its strength and banished with its radiant face the gloomy days of winter. Warm breezes drove away the clouds, caressed people's faces, penetrated their bones, and warmed their hearts with the false promise of spring. The mild weather confused the plants, making the grass sprout and the flowers embedded in the earth bloom. They raised their colorful heads, stretching their crumpled petals and spreading false sweet scents afar. Thus they waited, decked out in their finery and perfumed like brides, for the go-betweens to come and help them carry out the commandment of be fruitful and multiply. With their petals quivering in the warm breeze they dazzled the eyes of the insects flying around them, and in the heat of the moment they made no distinction between flies and bees, grasshoppers, beetles, butterflies, and flying ants. For in the work of reproduction all are welcome. Dazzled by their beauty, the creatures circled around them, seduced by the glorious sight, dived deep into their open, greedy mouths, picked up their pollen, sipped the nectar from the wide goblets offered them, and bore away with them the tiny yellow bits of eternity sticking to their legs and wings and covering their bodies.

That week Rosa's ears buzzed with the hoarse, broken mating cries of the neighborhood cats, the barking of dogs driven mad by the distant smell of a bitch in heat, and the clattering of copulating tortoises. Only just emerged from the bowels of the earth at the end of their winter hibernation, and before they had a chance to warm their cold houses, the tortoises advanced on the humped mates waiting for them in suspenseful silence. Slowly they approached them, their black eyes oozing a transparent mucus, and when they found what they were looking for they began knocking loudly on their shells, calling them to come out. And when their calls went unanswered, they embarked on armored warfare, ramming the females with their hard bodies until their heads and tails poked out of their shells. And when the female saw the insistent suitor facing her, she would stretch out her tail and wait with infinite patience for her armored knight laboriously to mount her humped house. When he reached the top, the climber would close his beady eyes and attach the opening of his tail to the still female. Rosa, who felt sorry for the female tortoises, would chase the desperate suitors away, and they would return and climb onto the females' backs again and cling to them as stubbornly and resolutely as if their lives depended on it.

That same week, which was particularly hot and full of the sounds of copulation, all the butterflies broke out of their cocoons at once, as if they had received a sign from heaven. Then too a rain of butterflies came down and covered the earth, the trees, and the stones in a thick layer of bright butterfly dust. All the inhabitants of Jerusalem came out of their houses and went into the fields to see the shower of butterflies and collect them in heaps in brown paper bags. That year in the Mahaneh Yehuda market they sold pictures of sunsets made of red butterfly wings and pictures of pirouetting dancers in tutus sewn from the torn-off wings of pink and white butterflies. And next to the mountains of summer fruits, on display for sale, were giant butterflies trapped in heavy wooden frames and protected by glass, their soft bodies fixed to cardboard by long pins and their bright wings outspread.

Among the people wandering like dreamers in the fields where the butterflies and sunbeams danced a demented dance of beauty were Rosa, Rachelle, Ruhama, and Ruthie, the "four R's from Ali Hamouda's House of Notes," as everybody called them even after they had moved to the new neighborhood.

It was Ruhama who dreamed up the idea that stuck Rosa with the number four and determined her fate in the preordained future:

"If we stand still, the butterflies will think that we're flowers and come to us. Afterward we'll count how many butterflies each of us managed to attract. And we'll know how many husbands we'll marry."

"But you can only marry one husband," grumbled Rachelle, who was always in a bad mood and always wanted to be right.

"The butterflies will tell us how many husbands each of us will marry," Ruhama repeated, and told them all to stand in a row, close their eyes, and think that they were flowers.

Shaking with suppressed laughter the girls stood with their eyes closed, while the desperate butterflies whirled around them like confetti, taking advantage of the single day allotted them and showering them with colored rain.

Spectators said that the heaviest shower of butterflies rained down on Rosa. With the flutter of their silky wings tickling her cheeks she stood between her friends, her heart pounding, her fists clenched, praying for one and one only. Afterward Ruhama told all forty pupils in the class, who told their parents, who told their neighbors, who told their relations, who took the news outside the city, how Rosa stood there, surrounded by a soft, bright, fluttering cloud, and when they opened their eyes they counted four gorgeous big butterflies caught in her curly hair.

"You'll marry four men," pronounced Ruhama, and went up to her friend with one miserable gray butterfly caught in her own hair, trying to free itself with weary flaps of its wings. On Rachelle's head they found one brightly colored butterfly, while Ruthie's head had none.

"And you won't have even one husband," Ruhama said to her in a scornful tone, and to add salt to the wound she hummed the tune that always brought boiling tears to Ruthie's eyes, bringing it up to date in order to adapt it to the new circumstances:

Once upon a time I went to Yemen,
I saw a little black boy eating a lemon,
And he won't be Ruthie's husband in a match made in heaven.

Then she hurried off to spread the tale of Rosa's four butterflies and accused her of trapping them on purpose. For when she told the story to every passerby, she added that it was all because Rosa smeared her hair with sugar water, and she herself had seen how the butterflies clustered round her, trying to suck the nectar from her hair.

As a result of the story the whole neighborhood knew that Rosa's glorious curls weren't natural. Angela, so they said, fixed her daughter's hair in those elaborate ringlets after first rinsing it in sugar water. When Rosa found out about the stories spread by Ruhama, they had a terrible fight, as a result of which the camp of the "four R's from Ali Hamouda's House of Notes" was split down the middle. Rachelle took Ruhama's side, and Ruthie took Rosa's. Later on Rachelle rejoined Rosa's camp, and announced that she had finished with that wicked Ruhama forever. One month later she changed her mind and maneuvered successfully between the two camps.

And so it would be in the future too, even after they were married women with children. Rosa would make friends with Ruhama again only many years later, after the death of her first husband, when she would knock on her door and hold out the face of her husband spread over a big poster, rolled up and fastened with a rubber band.

five

THE LOVE OF UNCLES

Of the "four R's from Ali Hamouda's House of Notes," Rosa was the first to marry. She was the first girl in her class to marry, and perhaps she was also the youngest girl to marry in the whole of Jerusalem.

If the choice had been up to Rosa, she would probably have married Shraga Matzliah, the best-dressed boy in the class and the most outstanding at sports. In spite of the ban imposed on boys by the girls in those days, and vice versa, Rosa loved Shraga. Faithfully she dragged her love with her from class to class of elementary school, for eight whole years.

When she sat next to him on the bench in class and he stroked her leg under the desk, she was sure that he was meant for her. With the insight of a girl who would one day be a woman, she sensed that Shraga was a part of her, a part of her body, a part of her soul, and that very soon, as she confided in Ruthie, after making her swear that she would "die in Hitler's black grave" if she told her secret, she and Shraga would be married. And when Ruthie said that she was a head taller than he was and a husband should always be taller than his wife, Rosa replied confidently that her mother had told her that at their age the boys were always shorter than the girls, and afterward they shot up while the girls stopped growing. And even if Shraga stayed short and she went on growing, she didn't care, because she loved him with a true love that nothing could spoil, not even differences in height.

Rosa knew for certain that she would marry him after he kissed her in the gym when they were in the eighth grade. This kiss opened a door to a new world of feelings, strong sensations, and desires. And when the door opened, they stood on its threshold and felt the sensations and delighted in the magic of the place where they found themselves. Trembling all over, they sniffed the smells of lust surrounding them, saw the provocative sights on every side; new tastes that had never visited their palates touched their tongues, and their ears rang with the sweet sounds of moans and tender words of love. And in those moments they were swept up body and soul in a tempest that bore them to a destination from which there was no return. And as she embraced his slender body and pressed him to her heavy breasts, he slid his tongue between her teeth and promised to marry her.

The taste of that kiss, with its fresh scent of plucked oranges, stayed with her for a long time, even after Shraga himself disappeared from her life, leaving a faint scent of rotten oranges on her hands and clothes. The smell, which took a long time to evaporate, was a constant and painful reminder of her first love. And it would come back in full force at the beginning of winter, when the first consignment of oranges reached the market and their sharp smell would spread through the air, invading the houses and announcing the arrival of the cold days to come. Then the pain would shoot through her body, cleaving its way through the tangle of her memories, pouncing on her suddenly and without any advance warning.

People said that the reason for the Matzliah family's panic flight from the neighborhood had to do with Joseph, who had heard about the famous kiss from Angela, who heard about it from Shoshana Zilka, who heard it from her daughter, Rachelle, who heard it from Ruthie, who made her swear that she would "die in Hitler's black grave" if she told. That same day Joseph marched to the school, alarming both pupils and teachers with the grim expression on his face, which was more frightening than usual. Without any preamble he marched straight into the principal's office and overturned his desk. Many days afterward Levana, the principal's secretary, was still excitedly telling anyone who would listen that as he turned the desk over, which he did with one casual push of his hand, Joseph muttered that if any of the boys in her class dared come close to his niece, he would crack his head like a coconut. In the neighborhood nobody knew exactly what a coconut was. The children knew the sweet called "Cocos," a soft, pink, nauseatingly sweet roll with a white center, manufactured by Havilio, while their parents knew the poor substitute for margarine marketed during the years of austerity, called "Cocozine," which tasted horribly like soap, and was manufactured, so it was said, from coconut oil. But neither the children nor the adults had ever seen a coconut in their lives, and the threat to crack someone's head like a coconut sounded particularly serious and frightening coming from Joseph, who had probably read about the coconut and even seen its picture in one of the encyclopedias he sold from door to door.

That same day the principal summoned the Matzliah family and asked them to control their son. The next day Shraga didn't show up at school, and the same week the family packed their belongings and moved to another town. The neighbors claimed that Joseph and the upturned desk weren't the direct cause of their precipitate departure, since they had been planning to leave for some time. Others claimed that they might have been planning to leave, but Joseph had forced them to put their plans into practice and execute them on the spot.

For days after the parting Rosa stayed home from school, and uncharacteristically refused to take a bite to eat. Her whole body ached, and she was sure that she was going to die. When she was asked where it hurt by the doctor they took her to see after she had refused to eat for three days, she said that her stomach hurt, her head hurt, and her heart hurt. When the doctor's blushing hands moved over her body, listening to her heart, palpating her stomach, and tapping her back, she told him in a whisper, so that Angela wouldn't hear, that she felt as if her arms and legs had all been amputated together. And when she heard him talking to her mother in a language she didn't understand, she knew for sure that he was telling her that she was going to die. Defeated and helpless, she felt his hands climbing to her golden curls, and she wanted to tell him that her hair hurt too, but she was afraid he wouldn't believe her. And when they left the room Angela told her that the doctor had decided not to give her any medicine, because "time would do the trick."

All the way home she groaned in pain at every step, and she couldn't understand what the doctor meant and what trick he was talking about. When she stole a glance at her mother and saw her calm expression, her anger welled up. She was going to die, and her mother didn't even care.

Years later, when she was a wife and mother, she would sometimes feel the same dull pain striking without any warning, piercing her body and creasing her face into an expression of suffering. Then she would whisper to Angela, who saw her suffering, that she was having another attack of the "Shraga pain." And Angela would shake her head and repeat the sentence she had been repeating to her all these years: "A long time has passed since then, and anyway you were children." Then she would remember her own love for Amatzia, which had not dimmed with time, and the pain of her loss, which had only increased with the years, and she would hold her tongue and embrace Rosa compassionately.

If she could only have known what would happen to her beloved daughter after Shraga left town, it is doubtful that she would have allowed things to take the course they did take. And when she thought about what had happened, she would blame herself for her blindness, and wonder how she could have let it happen right under her nose and failed to see what was so obvious. And the more she pondered the painful affair, the less she understood how she could have been so cheated and deceived by the fate that lay before her plain and clear to see, how it had changed its spots, mocked her and tormented her, shamed her in public, and spoiled all her plans.

In those days of remorse Angela suffered severe headaches that affected her entire body, bored into the roots of her teeth, made her sick to her stomach, and produced flashes of hateful orange light that danced in front of her eyes and blurred her sight. And when she emerged from her room at the end of an attack, she looked confused, pale, and exhausted. On the days of her headaches, when she talked to Rosa and her grandchildren, she would pass easily and unconsciously from one language to another: from Hebrew to French and from French to Italian and from Italian to Arabic, and nobody could comprehend her words or her meaning.

The people in the neighborhood said mockingly that "Angela slipped up on the job." She told everyone's fortune and knew in detail what was going on in every house, who would marry whom, who was cheating on her husband, how many children this one would have, and why that one would remain a virgin to the end of her life. "But what can you do? The shoemaker always goes barefoot," they would add with a sigh. People who had never believed in her powers and who despised astrology, tarot cards, and coffee cup readings, said that it was all because of Rosa's beauty, which was the dangerous type that drove men mad and made even the most rational of them not responsible for their actions. Angela had brought this trouble on her head because she herself had cultivated her daughter's beauty and femininity as if they were the most important things in the world.

* * *

And when Angela heard these remarks she remembered Rosa's early years, the war she had waged against her burgeoning breasts, and her attempts to suppress the signs of her daughter's femininity, until she had given up in despair. When she first saw the breasts that had grown on her daughter's body when she was still in the womb, Angela had screamed in alarm, and Rosa had screamed right back. The doctor had reassured her and said that it was a common phenomenon, especially in female babies, and that the swelling on her chest would go down in time. Angela believed him, rocked the baby in her arms to calm her, and after a week and a month went by without any reduction in the size of the breasts, which grew bigger and heavier with the growth of the baby, and the doctors she consulted were at a loss, she knew that she had to do something. At first she put the baby down on her stomach so that the weight of her body would flatten the prematurely ripened breasts. When this failed to have any effect, she bound the magnificent bosom tightly in a diaper every day to reduce its size. For years she waged a daily battle against the breasts until her strength failed her, and when Rosa turned seven she gave up and loosened the bonds forever. As soon as they were freed from the confines of the tightly bound diaper, Rosa's liberated breasts sprang up, growing and flourishing until her premature development brought catastrophe down on her head.

But her Uncle Joseph encouraged her burgeoning femininity. He chose clothes for her that showed off her figure to advantage, rehearsed her in feminine gestures and seductive smiles, and taught her the facts of life. Angela would tell her friends that from the moment Rosa was born he had helped her enthusiastically and shared the burden of bringing the child up with her. He had looked after her when she went out to do the chores, he would change her diapers, kiss her dimples, rock her on his knees, and tell her stories.

And when she started school he sat with her patiently and painstakingly arranged the eraser, the pencil sharpener, the compass, the indelible pencil, and the colored pencils in the heavy wooden pencil box with its two layers and sliding lid. Then he covered her reading book in cloth, which he sewed with a red seam, and her notebooks in brown wrapping paper. In the morning, while Angela fixed her ringlets, he made her a sandwich from thick slices of white bread spread with margarine generously sprinkled with white sugar. To the sandwich he added a ripe banana, crammed it all into the embroidered cloth bag with her initials on it, and pulled the red cord to close it.

And when Rosa bit into the sandwich and felt the sweetness of the sugar on her tongue, her heart filled with love for her uncle Joseph. At night she lay in her bed next to his and listened to the heartbreaking sighs he heaved in his sleep. And when she was woken by frightening dreams, she always found him by her side, stroking her cheeks and hair. Angela told everybody that Joseph would be a wonderful father because he knew how to take care of babies, and in spite of the serious expression on his face he knew how to make them laugh. She also said that Joseph knew exactly when his niece was going to wake up, taking up his position by her bed a moment before she opened her eyes, which was why she never woke up screaming for attention, knowing that her uncle would always be there for her.

When she grew older, he would take her out to the sunny fields surrounding the neighborhood and teach her all the reproductive secrets of the flowers and the butterflies. He would open the petals and show her the pistils and the stigma and reveal the secrets of creation to her. And Rosa would compare Joseph's explanations with those of Ruhama, who told her in secret about husbands and wives and what they did with each other at night. At those moments she remembered the struggling bodies she had seen when she peeped through the hole she had drilled in the wall in Ali Hamoudi's villa: Ruhama's mother and father rolling round on the bed, writhing and twining and groaning.

When Joseph went into the army it was ten-year-old Rosa who sewed the insignia onto his uniform, pricking her finger with the needle and leaving traces of her blood on the stiff cloth. Every Friday she would wait in suspense for the clump of his army boots on the stairs. The moments of his homecoming were the happiest moments of her life. Then he would pick her up and swing her in the air, kiss her blushing dimples, compliment her on her curls, and tell her that she was growing so fast that soon she would be a proper lady. Then he would open his rucksack and spill its contents onto her bed, chocolate, crisp cookies, cans of preserves, and food he had gone without for the sake of the women he loved. And Angela, tired of standing in line in the half-empty shops during the austerity regime after the war, with all her ration coupons swallowed up in the bottomless pit of Rosa's stomach, would accept the gifts gladly and bury them deep in the pantry to keep them from vanishing at once. After they had partaken of the food he had brought, Rosa would stroll through the neighborhood hand in hand with him, so that everyone would see her soldier uncle, and all her tormentors who flung the hated number in her face would never dare to raise their heads when Joseph was by her side.

Nobody in the neighborhood could understand how Angela, who read the omens in the dregs of her household's coffee cups every morning, had been unable to predict the future. And furthermore, how it was possible that she, so sensitive to the feelings of others, had been blind to what was happening in her own house, right under her nose.

It happened when Rosa was fourteen, although she already looked far older than she was. Her height, her elaborate hairstyle, her ripe body, and her heavy breasts drove men wild, and they would stop her in the street and make suggestions to her. Rosa would blush beneath the eyes undressing her, run home, and consult Joseph. And Joseph would pacify her, gently stroke her cheeks, kiss her dimples, and ask her to describe her harassers so that he could beat them up.

In those days, after being discharged from the army, he found a job selling encyclopedias from door to door. The apartment was stacked with volumes of the *Hebrew Encyclopedia* and the *Young People's Encyclopedia, One Hundred Personalities, The Wonders of the World, Fun with Science, Countries and Nations,* and *Famous Composers.* All the knowledge in the world, Joseph told her, was written there on the finest paper and abundantly illustrated. In the neighborhood they said that at night Joseph read the books he sold, and by day he bedded the women who opened their doors to him. They would stand in front of him, their bodies still warm with sleep, wrapped in flimsy robes, their hair in pins and rollers, and their skin smelling of male sweat and morning coffee. With amused expressions they would look into his sad, liquid eyes, appraise his muscles, let their eyes travel to his fly, and open their purses. Then they would open their hearts to him, unbutton his trousers, and finally part their legs.

And Joseph, with his growing knowledge of the world and the bedroom, would tell Rosa about distant lands, world explorers, famous sailors, and exotic animals whose names she had never heard before. And, whispering into her reddening ears, he would reveal all the secrets of love and reproduction to her.

When he had saved a bit of money, he bought an old motorcycle with a sidecar, and with Angela behind him and Rosa in the sidecar, he would drive to the Tel Aviv beach. When they reached the sea, after the terrors of the hairpin bends of the road, they would get off the motorcycle with trembling legs, blocked ears, and eyes squinting from the effort of catching the sights flying past them on the way. And once their feet were standing on firm ground, they would begin to fix their hair rumpled by the wind, and wipe the traces of the black fumes emitted by the motorcycle from their faces with their spotless handkerchiefs. Joseph would lead them straight to the wide steps leading down to the beach, where they would lie on towels and expose their white bodies to the sun. When their skin turned red Joseph would take the two women of his life to eat ice cream and chocolate cake in Café Roval in Dizengoff Street. He would wait for them patiently while they window-shopped, inspecting the new summer dresses and imagining themselves in the spike-heeled shoes. On the way back he would stop in Ramleh, buy two ice-cream cones, and present them to the women with a theatrical flourish.

On the day it happened, Angela, Joseph, and Rosa came home, exhausted and red-skinned from the late summer sun, straight to the news of the war being broadcast nonstop by the radio, its lights twinkling in time to the marching songs played by bellicose military bands. In spite of her weariness Angela started tearing old sheets into strips and pasting them, with Joseph's help, onto the windowpanes. Worn out and worried, her bones aching, she went to bed earlier than usual. After telling Amatzia about the events of the day and expressing her fears of this new war, because even though it was far away in the Sinai Desert, "you never could tell," she fell asleep after the usual sounds of rubbing, thudding, and moaning.

Rosa and Joseph remained awake in the silent house. Rosa looked anxiously at her uncle pacing the room like a lion in a cage. Nervously he turned the knobs of the radio and listened to the news streaming from the instrument in a number of languages and reverberating tensely in the air. The excited voice of the *Voice of Israel* announcer dominated the rest, overshadowing the quiet British tones of the BBC and the loud, belligerent voice, solemn and threatening, coming from

Radio Cairo. "The IDF invades Suez," "All leave canceled in the Egyptian army," "Nasser summons army chiefs," "Arab armies advance toward the borders"—the radio played these announcements in Hebrew, English, and Arabic. Frightened to death, Rosa got into bed, secretly feeling the loaf of bread she had hidden under her mattress in honor of the new war in the Sinai Desert. Her sleep was disturbed by the shouts of "War, war, war!" echoing throughout the neighborhood. It was the old woman in the opposite building with the blue numbers tattooed on her arm. The next day people said that she had run down the street naked as the day she was born until people in white coats caught her and took her away to the hospital.

Terrified out of her wits, Rosa jumped into bed with Joseph, dressed in the brief baby doll pajamas her mother had given her for her fourteenth birthday. As she had done when she was a child frightened by a nightmare, she snuggled up next to him under the blanket and told him falteringly about the things she had never shared with her mother or her friends. She told him about Hitler, about people disappearing from their homes in the middle of the night, about the death camps, about the women with shaved heads, about the people turned into soap, and about the fear that all these things would happen again, to them here in Jerusalem, at the hands of the murderous *fedayeen.* Joseph kissed her forehead, stroked her cheeks, played with her curls, and whispered deep in her ear that here in his arms she was safe, and he would never let anyone harm the little girl he loved.

His whispering in her ear sent unfamiliar shivers down her body, spreading and expanding like cellophane paper crumpled into a tight ball inside a clenched fist and suddenly opening up when the fingers relaxed. From the soles of her feet to the top of her head she felt the new sensation, making her nipples tingle and the hairs on her body bristle, until she could barely breathe. Rosa giggled in delight, uttered little cries of excitement, and asked him to whisper in her ear again, because it made her feel good. Hastening to comply, Joseph stuck his tongue right into the delicate concha and nuzzled the fleshy lobe with his lips. And with her soft squeals of delight making his head spin, he ran his tongue down her throat until he encountered her nipple, and without paying attention to what he was doing he found himself sucking on the crinkly little mound and felt Rosa's body stiffening in his arms. With hesitant, groping movements he slid his hand between her legs, where a welcoming wetness awaited him. And when he heard her moan he pressed his loins to her body, and soothed her in a practiced, up-and-down rocking motion until a stifled cry pierced his ears.

Afterward she sobbed tearlessly in his arms. Joseph stroked her face, smoothed her hair, and tried to kiss her on the lips. Rosa pushed his head away, avoiding the touch of his lips on hers, loosened the grip of his arms around her body, slid out of his bed, and crept silently into her own bed. Alarmed, he asked her not to tell anyone, not even Rachelle. And with tiredness spreading through her body and making her limbs heavy she fell asleep, the place between her legs stinging like a burn.

The next morning Rosa's hair rebelled and refused to coil into ringlets under her mother's practiced hands. With a mop of unruly curls crowning her head she left for school, feeling her mother's worried eyes on her back, probing and searching, piercing her flesh and penetrating deep into her body, which had grown old overnight. Rosa didn't remember what she was taught that morning, and the self-defense instructions relayed by the old men in uniform did not reach her ears. When she came home early because of the war, Angela told her tearfully that they had come to take Joseph into the army and sent him to the south. With a feeling of relief at not having to meet his eyes, she shut herself up in her room, and concentrated on the strange feeling that was still pulsing between her legs. She felt lonely and wished that he was there, so that she could confide in him about the events of the night, but then she remembered that he himself was responsible for what had happened to her. Confused, she sat on her bed and tried to feel longings and concern for her uncle fighting in the desert and defending them here. But instead she felt a new anger welling up in her, swelling her throat and pressing on her chest until she thought that she would choke. Swaying on her feet, she left the house, whispering that she was going to visit Rachelle, and slamming the door behind her.

A few weeks after Joseph had returned from the war, his hair red with desert dust and his clothes stiff with dried sweat, Rosa's breasts started to swell. When she began throwing up in the morning, Angela's suspicions were aroused and she dragged her to the doctor in a panic. That night, sitting with Rosa in the kitchen under the bare bulb on the ceiling that was reflected in her eyes and turned them red, Angela stared into her daughter's eyes and demanded that she tell her who the father was. Then Joseph came into the kitchen, asked Rosa to go to her room, and conferred with his sister at length in a low voice.

Through the closed door Rosa could hear her mother's sobs and her uncle's soothing words. "She's only fourteen. They'll put you in prison. What have you done?" Angela wept, torn between her love for her brother and her love for her daughter. Later on, lying in bed and telling Amatzia the events of the day, Angela peppered her words with sobs and sighs that went on echoing for hours through the house.

Rosa curled up in her blanket, and for the first time in her life, in perfect coordination with her mother's sobs, she felt the warm tears flowing down her cheeks. Full of shame she turned her back to Joseph, and, with her wet cheek on the pillow and her hands between her legs, she tried to recapture the painful-pleasurable new sensations she had experienced with her uncle. In the morning he came up to her bed, stroked her curls, gently shook her shoulder, and before she was fully awake he asked her to be his wife. Confused and sleepy, she sat up in bed, covered her bust with the sheet, and since she had always obeyed his commands and never refused him anything in her life, she answered him this time too with a weak Yes.

All day long she lay in bed whimpering like a baby that had just discovered how to cry. She wept for the past, the present, and the future, for all the years she had never cried. The reservoir of her unused tears burst, overflowed, and flooded her. Rosa didn't know why she was crying. At first she thought the weeping had started because of the father she had never seen and continued because of Rina, the little girl from Katamon who had been expelled from her home. On the way she remembered Mischa the refugee; and when she thought of Shraga, the love who had disappeared from her life, her sobs increased. When she had finished crying for Shraga she cried for her uncle Joseph, who was about to become her husband, whom she loved in a completely different way from the way she had loved Shraga, with a love whose meaning she was unable to comprehend. When she finished crying for Joseph, she began to cry in fear of the baby she was going to have without knowing what she was going to do with it, and in the end she cried for herself, for her ruined childhood and her dreams, which would never be realized. When she had nothing left to cry for she stopped crying.

The dam of tears remained dry throughout her marriage to Joseph. The unused tears collected again and flooded her, so they said in the neighborhood, when her last daughter, Angel, was born.

Five rabbis sat on the bench and debated the question of how to permit the marriage of a minor. In the end they decided that if she brought them two hairs "from the nether regions of the body, the place where hair is known to grow, she is a girl and may be considered henceforth to be mature." After this they discussed the situation of the widowed mother; her brother, Joseph, who had been orphaned at an early age; and Rosa's delicate situation, and they permitted the marriage to take place.

One month later Rosa stood beneath the wedding canopy, surrounded by her friends, her little stomach peeping out, while Joseph's erect member threatened to rip his trousers in anticipation of the night he would spend with his wife under the protection of the law. Rabbi Elbaz, pale as death, looked from the low neckline of the bride's dress to the swelling in the trousers of the groom.

Rosa's marriage made her famous. A week before the wedding, without any advance warning, a reporter who introduced herself as Galya turned up at their house, praised her beauty, told her that she looked far older than her years, and asked her a lot of questions. Then she asked to look at the photograph albums. Pleased by the attention, Rosa sat by her side and explained to her in detail who the people in the photographs were, and also showed her willingly the studio portrait taken of her in the nude by Rahamim when she was one year old, a big baby with a diaper wound around her chest, her body padded with layers of fat, her bottom sticking up, her head crowned with yellow curls, her eyes wide open, and her lips parted in a smile to reveal two glittering teeth. The next day Galya arrived at the school accompanied by a photographer, and Rosa saw all the children, especially the girls, crowing round her in the playground at break.

The article, spread over the two center pages, was published on her wedding day, and the guests sitting at the tables passed the paper from hand to hand. The story was accompanied by pictures and described the beautiful little girl from Jerusalem who was getting married in the fourth month of her pregnancy. In the long and detailed article her closest friends, Ruthie and Rachelle, were also interviewed, telling the story of the butterfly game, describing their secret dreams, and boasting that Rosa was their best friend. The rival newspaper too carried an article about the wedding, containing interviews with a psychologist who dwelled on the catastrophic consequences of marriage at such a young age; and with a doctor, who spoke of the dangers of marriage between relatives and the harmful effects of giving birth at such a young age. Rosa's homeroom teacher also contributed to the article, expressing her hope that Rosa, an outstanding student, would continue her education—not at her school, of course—and recommending that she go to evening classes. And she added that she hoped very much that Rosa, the queen of the class and a social leader, would not set her friends a bad example.

During the service Rosa couldn't rid her eyes of the sight of Ruhama, who had turned up at the wedding even though she hadn't received an invitation. With her sharp elbows she pushed her way straight to the canopy, stationed herself there between Ruthie and Rachelle, and raised her index finger high in the air, as a sign that this was husband number one.

Rosa glanced at Joseph's strained face, and at that moment she felt that she loved him and she would never have another husband. She knew that her love for him was not like her love for Shraga. It was a different kind of love. But when she tried to clarify the difference to herself, she was unable to do so. In time to come she would understand that she loved him out of habit, and love that grows from habit isn't like real love.

With the marriage contract in his hands and Rosa and Angela hurrying behind him laden with gifts, Joseph made for their bedroom, pushed their two iron beds noisily together, and tied them to each other with stout wire that he bent easily in his strong hands. Then he asked Angela to give him her thickest sewing needle, laboriously threaded the eye with string, and while Rosa and Angela were busy unwrapping the presents, he sewed their mattresses together, enveloped by the pungent smell of seaweed bursting from the holes in the cloth. "So that no one will find himself sinking into the gap between them in the middle of the night," he explained when his wife asked him to come and help them open the wedding presents.

When his work was done, he came into the living room, said good-night to his sister, and extracted his niece from the wrapping paper, the saucepans, the kettles, the trays, the bowls, the plates and the glasses that covered the sofa and chairs and floor. Ceremoniously he carried the bride over the threshold of the room in his arms and put her down gently on the joined mattresses, which enveloped her in the smell of the sea.

From that night on the sound of bouncing springs and the thud of the bed against the wall of the next room ceased, as if Angela had renounced her private life for the good of the new couple. And when her longings for Amatzia pierced her body, she would bury her head deep in her pillow and call out his name in muffled cries of pain that reached Joseph and Rosa's room and froze their bodies for a few seconds in the position of their lovemaking. Then Angela would sink into her bed and tell Amatzia in a whisper of the events of the day. And Rosa and her husband would detach themselves from each other and lie calm and satisfied, listening to the movement of Angela's lips until they fell asleep and woke up to the smell of strong coffee and almond cookies she had baked for them in the early hours of the morning, when they were still fast asleep, clinging together like a pair of abandoned kittens.

In the morning, about two hours before the school janitor rang the big bronze bell, Angela strode resolutely into the married couple's room and shook Rosa awake as she always did. While she went on sleeping sitting up, her mother curled her ringlets, gave her a cup of strong coffee to drink, and sent her off with a sandwich to another day of schooling, of which she remembered nothing, sunk as she was in dreamy reveries about the enjoyable events of the night before. It was only after weeks of battling Rosa and the school administration, which had no desire to see among its pupils a girl whose swelling stomach was a sign of her disgraceful behavior, that Angela gave up and sent the girl to evening classes. There she stood out among the day laborers and artisans intent on getting an education in their blue overalls stained with grease and whitewash. The sharp smell of sweat exuded by their bodies after their day's work would assail her nostrils when she entered the classroom and make her sick to her sensitive stomach.

At night she would come home, her hand supporting her belly and announce that she was never going back to school again. If Angela hadn't insisted on continuing to treat her like a schoolgirl, it is doubtful that Rosa would have graduated from high school, since she had plenty of excuses for shirking her lessons: She was a married woman now, and it was her duty to look after her husband, and now she was pregnant, and now she was breast-feeding the baby, and now she was pregnant again, and how could anyone expect her to concentrate on her studies. But every morning Angela would wake her up two hours before school began, fix her ringlets as if she were still a regular schoolgirl, and force her to sit at the table and do her homework. And in the afternoon she would drag her, almost by force, to the classroom. Uncomplainingly she cooked for Rosa and her husband, washed the baby's diapers, and at the graduation ceremony, four years after her marriage, Rosa stepped up to the platform with her belly about to burst and a three-year-old bowlegged toddler clinging to her skirt, and received a certificate to say that she had graduated from high school with distinction.

When Angela looked at her pregnant daughter, memories of her own pregnancy came back to her. When she lay in bed at night, discussing the events of the day with Amatzia, she would feel the heaviness of her belly and Rosa kicking inside it. The more Rosa's belly grew, the more Angela felt the heaviness in her own body, and the pains she had once felt came back to torment her emaciated body and weary soul. That was when she began to go downhill, the irreversible cycle of life leading to its inevitable end. As Rosa's breasts filled out and stood up, Angela's breasts emptied and shriveled and surrendered to the force of gravity. As Rosa's hair thickened and curled in snakelike waves down her back, Angela's hair grew thin and gray. And when Rosa's eyes began to shine and flash, Angela's tired eyes, embedded in a network of fine wrinkles, sank deep into their sockets. Above all Angela suffered from wobbly teeth, which began to fall out one by one. Nothing helped, not even the eggshells she ground up with her few remaining teeth, or the sardines she swallowed whole, or the chicken bones she chewed or the marrow she sucked out of the hollows of soup bones. The doctors said she suffered from a lack of calcium, and that if she had taken proper care of herself in time, the condition might have been prevented. On the day her last tooth fell out and she found her gums naked and riddled with holes where her teeth had once been, she took action and ordered a magnificent set of shiny white porcelain dentures, and from then on she dazzled the clients who came to her to have their fortunes told with an artificial, borrowed smile.

In the morning, when Rosa did her homework and Joseph went out to sell encyclopedias, Angela would sit down to drink her coffee, overturn the empty cup on its saucer, and examine the configurations foretelling the events of her day. Then she would collect Rosa's and Joseph's cups and ponder what fate held in store for them, until a soft knock at the door announced the first customer of the morning. Then Angela would shake off her thoughts, open the door, and greet the customer like a welcome guest, usher her into the kitchen, seat her at the scarred wooden table, hurry to the stove, put the kettle on to boil, and open a new packet of aromatic coffee. And by the time the couple came home at the end of the day, the sink in Angela's kitchen was full of dozens of cups and glasses, the muddy dregs of a black fate covering their bottoms and climbing up their sides. Late in the evening they would sit down in the kitchen, steeped in the smell of cooking and the dark aroma of fresh coffee, and while the young couple was busy eating their meal, Angela would tell them about her day.

The poor woman who had no idea that her husband was cheating on her, the one who was carrying a dead baby in her womb, the one who would never get married and many others—their troubles haunted the kitchen like autonomous beings, banishing with their sour breath and the sweaty smell of their fear the subtle aromas of Angela's cooking and filling Rosa's heart with dread. And when Rosa told her mother of her fear that the troubles of others would stick to them, Angela would dismiss it with a contemptuous wave of her hand and explain that what was written in heaven was final, and that no power on earth that could change the sentence. All you could do was predict it, expect it, and prepare for it in order to soften the blow. When she saw the expression of disbelief on Rosa's face, she would explain that she had no choice in the matter, that her destiny as a reader of coffee grounds had been determined even before she had been born, that her uncle had owned a coffee shop in the town, and that she and her aunt Lise had been put to work washing the hundreds and thousands of coffee cups left behind them by the men. Then she and Lise had peered into the cups, examined the configurations of the dregs, and followed their path across the china. She had always felt strange sensations that she couldn't explain and known in advance about the catastrophes about to befall, and joyful events about to overtake, the people who left her the muddy dregs of their coffee as souvenirs. "As if the spirits were talking to me from the cups and telling me stories about the person before me. And I was always right," she told Rosa for the umpteenth time. "If I saw that somebody was going to have an accident, he slipped and broke both his legs in the Turkish bath; and if I saw that somebody was going to win a lot of money, he really did; and when I saw that somebody's husband was cheating on her, he was." And then she would tell Rosa again that for her looking into the dark bottom of the cup was like watching a tearjerking movie: "I see the life of the person opposite me passing before my eyes just like a movie." But when Rosa tried to see what her mother saw and stared intently at the muddy black dregs, all she saw was wet coffee grounds lying in a meaningless shape in the bottom of the cup.

She would often argue with her mother and ask her to stop poking her nose into other people's troubles. It was beneath her dignity, Rosa lectured her, to earn her living from catastrophes, and it was high time she retired and stopped fishing in the troubled waters of these poor unfortunates' lives. And Angela, whose bank balance was swelling like yeast dough and who had bought them a large apartment with its help, right opposite her own, would tell her resentfully to mind her own business and stop interfering in her life. Then Rosa would shrug her shoulders and resign herself to listening, for the umpteenth time, to the horror stories about her unfortunate customers with which her mother regularly regaled them at supper.

Six months after the wedding, when Rosa's stomach was swollen to bursting and everybody said it would happen any day, Rachelle told her tearfully how the class had suddenly been assembled in the school hall and the principal had come and told them sadly that their beloved classmate Ruth had died in the night, and nobody knew how it had come about, since she had been a picture of health and never visited a doctor in her life. Rachelle told her that as soon as all the girls began to sob in terror and dismay in each other's arms, she had heard a loud whisper from Ruhama behind her, overshadowing everything in a black cloud of doom-laden prophecy: "I knew it would happen. Not even one butterfly landed on Ruthie."

Because of her pregnancy, her mother and Joseph forbade her to go to the funeral, but Rosa stole out of the house and followed close behind the stretcher bearing the little body. With her eyes flooded by Ruthie's glittering emerald eyes and her ears ringing with Ruhama's spiteful song, "Once upon a time I went to Yemen," she leaned heavily on Rachelle and felt her stomach pulling her down to the earth.

Screaming Ruthie's name, she pushed her way to the very verge of the grave. The moment the little body, still innocent of any marks of womanhood, was cast into the dark pit, she felt the kicking of her baby, desperate to get out. When she stumbled home she decided that if the baby was a girl she would call her Ruthie, in spite of the objections of her mother, who had always held that it was bad luck to name the living after the dead.

six

CINEMA ROSA

A few weeks after Ruthie, a placid, bonny baby, was born, Joseph's great dream was realized and he opened the Cinema Rosa, his own private movie theater, where he could screen the movies he loved, sad movies about lost people. Even though he was happy in his marriage and loved his newborn baby, he would tell Rosa that there was something missing in his life. When she asked him to tell her what it was, he couldn't explain—for fear of hurting her—that he felt a need to cry until his breath ran out and his eyes were sore.

This need for a good cry, which was so strong and incomprehensible, could not be satisfied by his new family, which brought him many moments of bubbling joy as sweet as honey. And so, when he saw the advertisement that would change his life in the newspaper, he immediately abandoned his job as a door-to-door encyclopedia salesman and the women who opened their purses and their hearts to him and persuaded Angela to lend him the money he needed. The person from whom he acquired the means to make his dream come true was a certain Alfredo, a new immigrant from Italy who had brought with him a large wooden crate containing a shiny black projector carefully wrapped in straw on which was engraved the number 6325 and the imposing name "Parvoset Milano." And when Joseph repeated the words "Parvoset Milano, Parvoset Milano" to himself in a whisper, as if to engrave them on his memory, he would feel a new taste in his mouth, the taste of men and women dressed in elegant clothes talking a language that sounded like music.

It took five stalwart Kurdish porters, gritting their teeth, to carry the machine carefully from the truck to the second story of the building he had rented in Katamon G, which had once been used as a youth club. And when they got their breath back, they took the container apart, plank by plank, pulled out the nails with rusty pliers, and at Joseph's behest made them into long, narrow benches that endangered the backsides of the boys and girls sitting on them, in short pants or thin cotton dresses, with the sharp, nasty splinters that penetrated their tender flesh and refused to come out.

And when the machine was finally fixed to the second-story floor, it squatted there like a monster with two round heads and filled the room with its still, black, oppressive presence until Joseph learned to bring it to life, throwing beams of light onto the screen below and projecting the pictures from the celluloid tape rolled around the little wheels that shone opposite him like gleaming teeth fixed in an eternal smile. He sat for days with Alfredo listening to him patiently explain how to wind the film around the many little wheels revolving one beneath another without order or method. Lovingly he showed Joseph which wheel came first and which last; how to raise the heavy rolls of film without losing his balance and without, God forbid, breaking his back; how to cool the film with the aid of the water circulating in the belly of the machine; what to do with the carbons that focused the pictures; what to do if, God forbid, the film burned in the middle of a screening; and how to mend it with acetone and clear nail polish. Joseph asked him to teach him Italian so that he could read the instructions and acquire a better understanding of the workings of the machine so that he could fix it if it broke down. He learned the language quickly—the language of his first wet nurse, who had disappeared from his life and been forgotten over the course of the years. And the language came back to him like an abandoned lover, reminding him of her presence in the sounds of the sentences that were like music to his ears and the words that tasted as sweet as honey in his mouth.

When the language came back to him he understood that he was ready, and he hired the first movie. Posters went up all over the neighborhood inviting one and all to a free screening of the famous Italian movie *Bicycle Thieves*. Joseph handed out the tickets, sold the refreshments, and projected the film. His knees trembling with excitement, he succeeded in throwing a beam of flickering light onto the silver screen and projecting the moving pictures that wrung the first sobs from the spectators. And when the audience filed out of the hall with tears streaming from their eyes, he knew he had succeeded.

In those days Joseph said that people came to his Cinema Rosa in order to cry, and he explained that there were a lot of people in Jerusalem who wanted to cry but were unable to get the tears out. Some of them were afraid of crying alone in the secret of their houses; others were ashamed of their weakness, preferring to swallow their tears rather than allowing them to roll down their cheeks in public. And when they were at the end of their tether and the tears welled up in their throats, making their hearts heavy and choking their breath, they would come to Cinema Rosa to save their lives. News of the movie theater and the wonders it worked and the relief it afforded to its patrons spread throughout the neighborhood. Satisfied customers told their friends about it on Friday nights around a bowl of salted watermelon seeds, and friends followed them, wiped their eyes on their shirtsleeves, and brought their friends, and soon there was a long line of people who wanted to cry waiting to buy tickets. The place grew so famous that the name "Cinema Rosa" became a synonym for crying. And to this day, years after the place closed down, when the old people of Katamon feel ill treated by life and mutter the words "Cinema Rosa" under their breath, everybody knows that they want to cry.

In Cinema Rosa you never saw lovers who came to hold hands or feel each other's bodies under the cover of darkness. And if any couples did come to the cinema, it was clear as daylight that they were in the middle of breaking up, and that they had come together only to weep for their dashed hopes, for their unrealized dreams, and for the children who would never be born to them. Nobody came to Cinema Rosa to see comedies, musicals, or westerns. Gangster movies were of no interest to its patrons, and war movies, action movies, and thrillers were acceptable only if the protagonists shared their tears with the audience.

Some people tried to explain the source of Joseph's unique talent for finding the films that made the entire audience break into a chorus of tears. The ones who were well acquainted with the family history, as recounted by Angela, said that it was nothing to wonder at, since the milk he drank as a baby had been flavored by the tears of his wet nurse grieving for her dead infant. This fact also went far to explain the glum face of the cinema owner, whom nobody had ever seen smile or laugh. Others added that his gloomy countenance was nothing to be surprised about, since both his parents had died on the same day, when their ship sank at sea, and only he survived, swimming in the saffron yellow waves until a merchant ship rescued him, and ever since then his face had been fixed in a grave, sad expression.

In any event the movies opened the sluice gates and released a flood of tears in everyone who watched them. Those who were ashamed to cry received encouragement and reinforcement from the actors sobbing loudly on the screen in Greek, Hindi, Arabic, Italian, French, and English. And the audience imitated them in Hebrew. But the Turkish movies were the ones in which the actors and the spectators wept the most. Then the lines in front of the ticket booth stretched as far as Tzadok's grocery store. The speculators soon heard about the long lines at Cinema Rosa and the difficulty of obtaining tickets, and they would arrive long before anybody else, buy up large supplies of tickets, and when the window of the ticket booth closed and the sign saying SOLD OUT was hung up in front of the disappointed crowds, they would call the unfortunates left without tickets aside and sell them seats on the rough plank benches for three and sometimes four times as much as they were worth.

And not only the denizens of Katamon came to see the movies. When the rumor that you could have a good cry at Cinema Rosa spread, people came streaming from all over town—refugees who had survived the hell of the war in Europe with tattoos on their arms, battered wives, abandoned husbands, broken hearts that refused to heal, breadwinners who had been fired from their jobs, people with malignant diseases, women suffering from premenstrual nerves, and lost, lonely souls who had exhausted all their reasons for crying and were looking for new pretexts. They all came to Joseph's movie theater, sat on the hard wooden benches, and with the splinters sticking in their flesh, got ready for the ritual weeping. The sticklers would begin to cry even before the lights went out and the curtain went up. Others would begin to sniff when darkness descended on the hall. The more restrained would only start to let go when the slides advertising Bavly's kiosk and Fruma's brassiere and corset salon were shown. When Joseph screened the cartoons before the main feature, the entire audience pulled out their handkerchiefs as if in obedience to a silent command. During the Carmel newsreels the first sobs were heard, and when the subtitles announcing TRANSLATION BY JERUSALEM SEGAL TEL AVIV came on, loud bellows of lamentation rose from the hall of the accompaniment of trumpeting from noses stopped up by the overflow of tears draining into them. And by the time the film began, their eyes were so bleared and blinded by tears, that many of the spectators only heard the voices without seeing the pictures. When the lights went on in the hall as a sign that the movie was over, the red-eyed audience would slip out with bowed heads, dripping noses, and a weight off their hearts.

From the aperture in the wall of the projection room Joseph would watch until the last people left, wiping his eyes with a vast white handkerchief and blowing the vestiges of the liquid from his nose with a loud, trumpeting noise, tuck his unruly shirt back into his pants, and go down to the ticket booth to count the day's takings. There he would pile the tattered notes and worn coins in neat stacks, make complicated calculations on the back of an old poster, and when he was finished he would set aside, with a gloomy expression on his face, a number of notes for the entertainment tax, the recreation levy, the security stamp, the immigrant absorption loan, and the sales tax.

With the money for Rosa in his right pocket and the tax money in his left pocket, he would go back up to the projection room, repair the film, which had torn in several places, evoking angry whistles from the audience, with acetone and clear nail polish, and prepare it for the screening the next day. Then he would thread the new movie for the following week into the projector, watch it tearfully, rewind it, and finally he would cool the machine and lock the door behind him.

In the early hours of the morning, when the sky was pale pink, he would come home to the new apartment Angela had bought for them. Before joining Rosa he would go into baby Ruthie's room, look at her admiringly, and behave like a loving father in one of the movies he screened. Carefully, so as not to wake her, he would kiss her on the forehead, return a pillow to its place or tuck the blanket around her even if she was already firmly tucked in. During the course of time, as more children were born, he continued to perform this ritual every night. With a clear conscience he would tiptoe into their bedroom, breathe in the air scented by Rosa's breath, switch on the bedside lamp, and gaze lengthily at his wife's face in its soft light. Rosa would lie relaxed on her back, her legs parted, her arms outspread, her bosom rising and falling with her heavy breaths, and her belly, sometimes with a new baby ripening inside it, looming up in front of her.

Then he would feel his member stiffening in her honor, and he would hurriedly take off his clothes, hanging his trousers, their pockets swollen with money, over the back of a chair, and throwing the rest—shirt, underwear, socks, and shoes—in all directions. Carefully he would lie down beside her in the narrow space remaining, put his arms around her, and whisper in her ear the Hebrew translation of the loving words whispered to their lovers by the protagonists of the last movie he had screened. When he was done whispering he would feel her nipples, insert his finger deep inside her, and Rosa would moan in her sleep. When he felt the wetness on the tips of his fingers he would penetrate her from behind, his backside moving to and fro in the rhythm so familiar to them, and she would receive him deep in her body and continue weaving her interrupted dreams.

In the morning she would wake up before him, delve into his right trouser pocket, and fish out the notes and coins she needed for the day. After sending Ruthie to day care, she would rejoin the still-sleeping Joseph and make up for what she had missed in the hour before daybreak. Joseph would mumble the new words of love in his sleep and let her guide him into her body.

And when people told him that in the end he would ruin his marriage by working day and night, with his poor wife going to bed alone night after night, he would twist his mouth into his grimace of a smile and say nothing. During all those years, when he screened thousands of movies at Cinema Rosa, Joseph would scrupulously repeat his nightly ritual with Rosa and the children, until the day when the movie theater was closed, rituals and habits disappeared, and a new life began.

Of all the family Angela alone liked going to see the movies at Cinema Rosa, returning with a bright face, soft eyes, and a light heart. She told Rosa that there in the hall, under cover of darkness, she could let herself go and weep at the top of her voice for the dead Amatzia. Once Rosa allowed herself to be persuaded by Joseph to stay with him and watch the new Turkish movie, *The Virgin from Istanbul*, which had been acclaimed by the critics. With ostentatious boredom she watched the young bride being thrown into the street on her wedding night by her jealous husband, who accused her of having had other men before him, and being reunited with him in the end after keeping faith with him for many years of banishment. And when she left with her dry eyes lowered against the accusing looks of the moist-eyed audience, she declared that once was enough to last her the rest of her life, and since she had no reason to cry she would never watch one of those tearjerking movies again.

Many years later, after Cinema Rosa had closed down and Joseph passed away and the troubles began to pile up, she searched the town for just such a movie theater, so that she could release all her pent-up tears, but she never found one.

seven

A LIFE OF HABIT

During the years when Joseph was busy with his cinema, screening the movies and crying with the audience, Rosa lived a "life of habit," as she described it in her conversations with Rachelle. One after the other the pregnancies she had initiated arrived, with the easy births in their wake. When she came home from the hospital with a new baby in her arms, its brothers and sisters would line up to inspect it curiously and then to perform the ritual of kissing the new arrival on the cheek and solemnly repeating the name given it by Joseph. The house filled with children and the smell of babies.

In those days Rosa was busy kissing plump stomachs, nuzzling firm buttocks, and nibbling tiny hands. She loved seeing the first heart-shaking smile, hearing the gurgling chuckles, and smelling the special scent of milk mingled with fine soap and laundry powder given off by their bodies. And when the baby was weaned she would quickly get pregnant again and give birth to a new baby, until all seven were born within fifteen years, leaving their mark on her body in the form of double chins, dimpled flesh, and enticingly rounded curves. After the seventh baby was born, she knew that the wish she had expressed in the wishing game she had played with Rachelle, Ruthie, and Ruhama had come true.

Rosa's life in those days was good, quiet, and predictable, and whenever she needed help she could rely on Angela and Rachelle to come to her assistance. When the firstborn, Ruthie, grew up, she enjoyed taking her mother's place and looking after her little brothers and sisters as if she were their mother and not their big sister. And when Rosa heard the neighborhood women complaining of the hard work involved in bringing up children, she didn't understand what they were talking about, since in her house, with all her seven children, everything ran smoothly and peacefully, and every new addition to the family added to her happiness. The women said that it was easy for her to talk, since "in your house one brings up the other, your mother and Rachelle help out, and all you do is conduct the orchestra and give the orders."

The period of pregnancies and births was marred only by Joseph's insistence on naming his children for movie stars and the protagonists of the movies he showed, preferably the most miserable of them. In the days after giving birth, when she lay and thought about the name Joseph had given the new baby, her anger would well up and she would brood about how different her life would be if only she could stop obeying her husband blindly and doing everything he asked her. But even though she put forward her own suggestions for fresh, original, attractive names, like the names of the flowers and trees she loved, he took no notice and imposed his will on her.

In a regular ritual Joseph would arrive at the hospital at every birth, his face hidden behind a huge bouquet of the flowers of the season, and with a melancholy expression on his face, as if the new baby brought no joy to his heart, he would sit down beside her, stroke her hand, look deep into her eyes, and ask to see the newborn child, so that he could choose the "special name" that would be uniquely suited to it. After deciding on the name he would sit with her for hours, coaxing and cajoling her, until she could withstand his pleas no longer and she would give in to his caprices and accept the weird name he had chosen for her new baby.

Many years later, when the names had taken root in her mouth and become an integral part of their owners, she admitted to herself that perhaps Joseph had been right after all, and her children with their exotic names were indeed special and set apart from the rest of the neighborhood children.

Ruthie, the firstborn, who looked like her grandmother Angela, was the only one who had a normal name, having been born right after the death of Ruthie Sharabi. Ruthie was hardworking and serious, and being the oldest, she was entrusted with a lot of the chores around the house, so that everybody always said that she was a second mother to her little brothers and sisters.

On the day that the wicked Eichmann was sentenced to death, a long, dark baby was born, with an expression as gloomy as his father's. Joseph decided to call him Leslie, after Leslie Howard in *Gone With the Wind,* his favorite movie, which had been shown at Cinema Rosa dozens of times. "And it's a kosher name," he said to Rosa when he saw the expression on her face. "Leslie was a Jew born and bred." And since it was unthinkable to register a Jewish child with a foreign, gentile name alone, he paid lip service to the prevailing mores and added the name "Shimon" to his birth certificate. Leslie-Shimon was an introspective, serious child, he liked playing with toy cars and dreamed of being a truck driver.

Jackie was born, named after Jackie Coogan, who played with Charlie Chaplin in *The Kid*, and in spite of Angela's opposition he was given the second name of Jacob, after the father-grandfather who had been drowned at sea. Jackie grew into a tall, mischievous lad with golden hands.

Scarlett was born, and named after the heroine of *Gone With the Wind*. Since this name jarred on Rosa's teeth like gravel, she added the name Mazel too, the Hebrew version of her grandmother Fortuna's name. Scarlett-Mazel was a fair, pretty girl, quiet and shy, who spent a lot of time playing by herself in front of the mirror and was always busy trying on hats, scarves, old dresses, and Rosa's huge high-heeled shoes, because more than anything she wanted to be an actress.

In the year of the Six-Day War, Lana Turner was born, and her name was Hebraicized into Ilana. Lana-Ilana grew up to be a nervous, sensitive girl who cried easily, and Rosa attributed this to her first days in the world. When the baby was a few weeks old the war broke out, and Rosa huddled with her in the shelter of the dark house, listening to the shells exploding outside. Ever since Lana-Ilana had been an anxious child, afraid of closed places, loud noises, and rude people.

During the war of attrition James Dean was born, with the Hebrew name of Gad, a huge, placid, smiling baby who grew up to be a clever boy, outstanding in mathematics and the heartthrob of all the neighborhood girls.

And in a year during which no event of historical significance took place, the last girl was born, Laura, who owed her name to the movie of this name that was shown in Cinema Rosa, and given the Hebrew name of Liora. Laura-Liora, the youngest and most pampered of the children, tried to comply with her mother's wishes and remain a little girl. When she grew up she went on talking baby talk, lisping, and wearing dresses with ruffles like a little girl's. And even after she married she refused to part with her childhood and wore her hair in braids.

Even though Rosa loved the smell of a newborn baby's skin better than anything else in the world, and was grieved by the speed with which her children grew, after giving birth for the seventh time she decided to stop. And when people asked her why she wasn't prepared to get pregnant again in spite of her love of babies, she gave her identity card as an excuse, citing the fact that it had "seven places to register seven children, and there was no room for an eighth." And when she was told that you could always add another page, she explained that then she would have to fill the new page to the bottom, which meant that she would have to have another seven children, and who had ever heard of a woman with fourteen children? And anyway—she would add the flimsy excuse—the number seven was a lucky number and it would be a shame to spoil it.

Rosa's life was good and tranquil. But while life in her house ran its quiet course, day following day and week following week and pregnancy following pregnancy, things were happening far away that changed the world: The Six-Day War expanded the borders of the state; the peace accords reduced the borders of the state; famines and plagues devastated populations and changed the colors on the demographic maps. Revolutions that took place, regimes that rose and fell, leaders that were assassinated dictated new history books; natural disasters and earthquakes destroyed cities, flattened mountains, changed the courses of rivers, and brought distant continents millimeters closer. All these events stopped at Rosa's door and never penetrated her realm. For her nothing changed; she imposed order and regulation on her life and it went by in a blessed routine, following a course determined in advance.

Only the seven births, the festivals and holidays and the changing of the seasons, and especially the different menus she set for every day of the week, distinguished between one day and the next and accumulated in her memory cells, layer on layer in the gray matter of her brain. New memories would force their way in, assailing the old ones and forming a new stratum of memory compressing the previous one and flattening it with its weight. And one memory followed on the heels of the other until all the memory cells in Rosa's brain were full of the sounds of babies' crying and laughter, sweet smells of bathed bodies and repellent ones of urine and bowel movements. Bottles of milk, wet diapers, emerging teeth, childhood diseases, first days in kindergarten and elementary school, school parties, fancy-dress costumes, PTA meetings, report cards, hairdos, drawings and paintings, graduation parties, entrance exams, stiff army uniforms with stripes on the khaki sleeves, weddings, births, *briths,* and the touch of a new baby's skin. Sometimes, when she tried to dig out of her memory cells an old sight, a familiar sound, or a beloved smell, a newer memory would pop up in her head and usurp the older one, until she no longer knew which of her seven children or ten grandchildren it belonged to and when it had happened. And when she fished facts and figures out of the muddle of memories spinning giddily in her head, she would find herself calling a boy by his brother's name, a girl by her sister's, her grandchildren by the names of her children. And when she tried to tidy up the drawers of her memories, she understood that it was all the same, and rearing one child resembled rearing another, and what was would be, and what had been done would be done, and there was nothing new under the sun, and nothing in her daily life with Joseph would ever change.

Rosa didn't like changes or surprises. "No news is good news," she would say to anyone who asked her how she was and what was new, sure that if she was happy with her life the way it was, any change could only be for the worse. For if something good changed, what could it bring but evil?

"What do I lack?" she would say to her friend Rachelle, who had divorced in the meantime and was supporting her only son with difficulty by her job as a bank teller. "What do I lack?" she would repeat, spitting sideways and making the five-fingered sign against the evil eye. "I have a husband, children, a mother, a roof over my head, and enough to live on, thank God. Any change could only be for the worse."

And so she believed that if in the predictable course of her life she shifted a piece of furniture unnecessarily from its place, did the wash on a day not intended for it, bought the groceries somewhere else, combed her hair in a new style, put her children to bed half an hour later than usual—the change she had made in her routine would lead to another change, which would lead to another change, and so on. Until her whole life would be upset, nothing would be the same, her fate would change for the worse, and calamities would come down on her head. Therefore she took pains to see that nothing changed, as if her life depended on one day being the same as the next.

You could set your clock by Rosa's daily schedule, the neighbors said. Everyone who saw Rosa at Tzadok's grocery store knew that it was exactly half past nine in the morning, and when she went home with her shopping she would do the cooking and the chores allocated to that day of the week: On Sunday she cleaned and straightened up the house; on Monday, Nehama came to remove the hair from her legs and armpits with wax; on Tuesday she laundered, dried, and folded the wash; on Wednesday she did the ironing; on Thursday she did the cooking and cleaning for the Sabbath, and in the evening Aliza the Hairdresser came to shampoo her hair and set it in elaborate curls.

At half past twelve every weekday she had lunch for Joseph and the children ready on the table. After the meal she allowed them to play for two hours, during which time she went to visit Angela, who lived opposite them, and Rachelle, who lived in the apartment below. When the two hours were up, she seated all the children around the big dining table, saw to it that the big ones did their homework and helped those who had problems with their arithmetic or their Bible lessons. Then she would go out for her daily walk and invite them to accompany her.

Sometimes they would go to old Katamon, and she would show them Ali Hamouda's House of Notes and the foreign consulates again and point out the new buildings to them. Sometimes she would take them on the bus to town and buy them American ice cream at Café Allenby in King George Street. When she came home she would prepare supper, consisting of salad, omelets, and yogurt. Before they went to bed she would tell them to put out their clothes for the next day, help anyone who needed help choosing and coordinating color schemes, sew on a loose button, mend an unraveled hem, and darn a hole in a sock with the help of a darning egg. While she worked she would listen to radio programs with the older children. Best of all they liked the Paul Templar detective series, and they would huddle together and shiver with fright at the sound of the wind knocking on the shutters. At the end of the day she would put them to bed, each at the hour appropriate to his or her age, tuck them in, kiss them on the forehead, and wish them good-night and sweet dreams.

When their breathing became calm and steady she would stand next to their beds, smell the childish fragrance of their bodies, and listen to the sounds of the night, trying to distinguish the growing noises made by children in their sleep. And when she heard these noises, she would ask each of them in her heart not to grow too fast, to stay just as they were, small and sweet.

In the morning, after the children had dispersed to their schools and kindergartens, Joseph would go out to attend to his affairs, but not before taking her back to bed as he did every day, taking advantage of the quiet, empty house and enjoying his morning erection to the full, and Rosa would start preparing the midday meal according to the menu of the day. For every day of the week she cooked a different meal for the family, seven different menus that repeated themselves week after week in a never-changing cycle.

At midday, when Joseph hurried home to join his family for dinner, he knew exactly which dishes Rosa would put on the table. He was particularly fond of Sundays, when she made Andalusian almond soup, which was milky white even though it didn't contain a drop of milk, and possessed a smooth texture and a taste like Paradise, flavored with garlic and olive oil.

As a child she had tasted this soup at Shoshana Zilka's parents' table in the villa in Katamon, and when she grew up she ate it at the Jerusalem restaurant where she and Joseph celebrated, on the same date and at the same hour, year after year, their wedding anniversary. When she tasted the soup on their first wedding anniversary, all her senses were awakened and she was flooded by memories, and she ordered another plate, and then another one, and when Joseph paid the bill she pestered Moshe Basson, the restaurant owner, for the recipe and announced that she wasn't leaving without it. With his finger on his lips to indicate that he was betraying a closely guarded culinary secret, he told her that it was an Andalusian soup, and reluctantly dictated the ingredients and method of preparation to her. Afraid that he might change his mind, Rosa hastily scribbled the instructions down on the paper napkin.

When she returned home in triumph she decided that this soup was worthy of opening the week, and thus it came about that the Andalusian almond soup appeared without fail on Rosa's table on Sundays. She could hardly wait for Sunday morning, and at nine o'clock on the dot she would hurry to Tzadok's grocery store, where she chose two hundred grams of perfect almonds one by one, in a long and tedious process that tried Tzadok's patience until it snapped, and every Sunday he would make the same remark: "It's a good thing that Mrs. Rosa didn't decide to cook rice today, or we'd be here till tomorrow morning waiting for her to finish sorting it."

She would put the almonds in a big bowl and pour boiling water onto them. Their thick skins would soften and swell in the boiling water, until long cracks appeared and they split apart. Taking care not to burn her fingers, Rosa would peel off the skin, and when a little mound of naked almonds rose on the marble counter, their white flesh gleaming like ivory, she would soak two slices of dry challah bread left over from the Sabbath in water. As soon as the bread had absorbed the liquid she squeezed it like a sponge and added it to the pile of almonds. Trying to breathe through her mouth she peeled two cloves of garlic and poured five glasses of ice water into a jar. Then she put it all into the mincing machine and turned the handle until she obtained the smooth texture she desired.

After that she tasted her creation, smacked her lips, added three spoons of wine vinegar and a teaspoon of salt, and carefully poured into the bubbling mixture three spoons of green cold-pressed olive oil that she bought from Mohammed, the olive picker from Beit Tzafafa. When a thin layer of white froth had formed on top of the mixture, she poured the fragrant foretaste of Paradise into soup plates and set them on the table. Everything accompanying the soup wasn't really important, but it was always accompanied by rissoles, pastries filled with meat and potatoes, boiled vegetables, and Arab salad chopped fine and flavored with plenty of parsley, coriander, and lemon.

The only changes that took place around her that were impossible to prevent, apart from the obvious ones in growing children, fashions, and her own body, were the changes in the building where she had lived ever since leaving the villa in Old Katamon. Within the space of a few years the square, four-storied building in 10 Shabazi Street had lost its original contours. Sometimes, when she gave it a long look, apart from the casual glances of someone going in and out of the building where he lives, she thought that if she went away for a few years she wouldn't recognize it when she returned.

Porches were closed in, additions were built, new windows opened up, shutters torn out, planters set on windowsills, solar heaters and TV antennas sprouted from the roof, and new families came and went. Every day she wondered anew at the sight of the changes introduced by busy hands. One day all the mailboxes were ripped from the wall, and the ones that weren't ripped out had their doors removed. Only her own mailbox survived, hanging in the air thanks to the big nail that Joseph had hammered into the wall, with the autumn winds that invaded the stairwell rocking it from side to side with a jarring, metallic creak. The flaking whitewash on the entrance wall too was something Rosa watched with interest. At first the whitewash would erupt in a rash of swollen boils that would burst of their own accord, leaving a frame of new flakes that would drop to the floor in a layer of fine yellowish powder. Sometimes she would notice the round gray marks made one on top of another by the blows of a football aimed hundreds of times at the same spot. They were joined by the striped prints of the soles of the sports shoes of particularly angry boys who let off steam by kicking the wall. Rosa was sure that it was these same boys who had smashed the lamp over the door and stolen the lightbulbs from the stairwell and the landings, causing the residents to grope their way blindly in the dark. She knew that they were also responsible for the huge slogan sprayed all the way across the rough orange stones of the outer wall of the building, proclaiming sadly: LIFE IS LIKE THE HAIRS ON MY ASS—SHORT, HARD, BLACK, AND STINKING. To this motto other philosophical statements had been added during the course of the years, expressions of distress and noble ideas, huge hearts pierced by arrows, declarations of loves and hates and giant drawings of intimate body parts, all of them sprayed in red and black paint the residents were unable to erase.

When the sweet baby scent of her last child turned into the prickly smell of ordinary sweat, Rosa sensed that her life was about to change. She would quickly complete the chores of shopping, cooking, and washing, and until the children returned from kindergarten and school she would pace the rooms of the house, looking for something to do and complaining to herself about the way the days were dragging out now that there was no new baby for her to look after.

The new occupation came to her accidentally-on-purpose when Joseph asked her to grow a scented plant, "never mind what," for the habdalah ceremony he strictly observed every Saturday evening to distinguish between the holy Sabbath and the ordinary days of the week. Rosa, who knew his weakness for the smell of lavender, whose fragrance had been etched on the scent cells in his brain on their first day in the House of Notes, took a bus to Farhi and Sons plant nursery in Talpioth, and asked for a lavender bush. They led her into a big hothouse covered with torn sacks, and gave her a tiny pot containing a pathetic looking gray shoot, mentioned its Hebrew name, and told her that its scented flowers could be used not only for the habdalah but also for flavoring roasts and for brewing tea with medicinal properties for treating coughs, colds, pneumonia, and insomnia. Before Rosa could transfer the little cutting to a permanent pot it grew into a many-branched bush sprouting hairy purple heads that spread a delicate scent in the air. And no sooner had she picked a twig for Joseph's blessing than it was immediately replaced by two new branches covered with purple flowers.

When the bush grew big and strong, in spite of the constant use she made of it for the habdalah, in cooking, and in brewing tea, she decided to prepare a dried herb from its blooms. She would gather the flowers when they opened in the evening, after the sun had beaten down on their heads all day and dried up the night dew. Then she would spread them on a net and protect them from the sun and the dew. Sometimes she would tie the twigs in bunches and dry them upside down in the kitchen. And when Joseph came home late at night from Cinema Rosa, he would breathe the beloved scent deep into his lungs, recover from the sad sights he had seen on the screen, and gratefully kiss the nape of the sleeping Rosa's neck as she waited for him in bed.

After her success with the lavender, Rosa returned to the plant nursery and asked for additional aromatic plants that could be used to flavor food. And the new herbs succeeded too, for Rosa had "green fingers," as the neighbors said. "Everything she touches grows and flourishes, even if she planted a broomstick in the asphalt, stroked it now and then, watered it and talked to it, that broomstick would respond to her coaxing, put out leaves, grow flowers, and even spread a sweet scent for her."

She grew her plants on the little kitchen porch, in any receptacle she could lay her hands on. And when the plants multiplied, Joseph built wooden shelves on all three walls of the porch to make more room for her herb garden. She planted the wild thyme in a big can that had once contained pickled cucumbers, and from its dried leaves she prepared elixirs to sharpen the memory and expel worms from the intestines. The sage she grew in a herring barrel, so that people said of Rosa's sage that it had a heavenly flavor of pickled herrings. The basil took root in an antique kettle. And there was parsley, too, whose roots were used to flavor soup and its ground seeds to flavor fish; medicinal lemon balm, with its delicate taste, which she used to brew tea and flavor salads; yellow chamomile to cure stomachaches and bleach hair; and all kinds of mint for flavoring salads and preparing fresh green drinks on steamy summer days.

And not only common plants grew on Rosa's porch. Many strange and unfamiliar plants took root in her pots and grew like weeds, dotting the green with multicolored leaves and rare exotic flowers. Every morning Rosa would go out into her hanging garden and find some new intruder she had not planted and whose name she did not know, because whenever she left a pot out on the porch, full of loose earth waiting to be planted, the next day she would find it occupied by a new plant the likes of which had never been seen in the Farhi and Sons plant nursery.

And when the well-known botanist Dr. Yavshem paid her a visit, curious about the garden whose fame had spread, he inspected the plants at length, felt the strange leaves with his fingers, frowned, and wondered aloud how this rare foreign plant had reached Rosa's porch if no one had deliberately planted it there. Rosa listened to his speech peppered with Latin names, laughed, and assured him that she had not planted this plant whose name she did not know, whose likes she had never seen in the city of Jerusalem, and which had no doubt been borne there on the wings of the Holy Spirit. For Rosa could not have known that migrating birds that had eaten their last meal in a hot, steaming tropical land had carried a secret treasure of rare, exotic seeds in their fermenting intestines especially for her. And when they flew over her porch in a ceremonial salute they had shed their droppings, studded with the seeds that had ripened and sprouted in the heat of their bellies. And the sprouting seeds had taken root in fertile soil of the pots waiting for them there and grown into plants never seen in the city before.

Over one such plant Rosa found Angela stooping one day, absorbed in feverish activity and muttering to herself. The fingers of one hand were digging in the soil while two fingers of her other hand were savagely and furiously tearing off a modest purple flower with crimson stamens.

"What are you doing?" shrieked Rosa at her mother's bent and violent back. "Why are you picking my flowers?"

"They have to be destroyed."

"But why uproot them? What harm have they done you?"

"They grow those flowers," Angela replied, an expression of revulsion on her face, as if she felt suddenly nauseous.

"What flowers?" whispered Rosa, taking her mother's hands in hers.

"Those saffron flowers," she replied and went into the house.

After things had calmed down and Rosa washed her hands with the hose attached to the tap on the porch, she noticed that her palms were yellow and that they gave off a bittersweet smell. Only after many days of vigorous scrubbing with bleach and disinfectants did she succeed in ridding her hands of their yellow hue. Rosa didn't dare talk about the incident to her mother, but she began to keep a close watch on her. And a few weeks later she saw Angela slipping onto the porch again, making her way through the luxuriant growth, parting the leaves of the bushes and, with a stooped back and an expressionless face, snooping after the purple flowers. When she failed to find what she was looking for she calmed down and returned to the kitchen with a gratified look.

"What are you looking for there?" Rosa asked her.

"The seeds of destruction," replied Angela and said no more.

In those days the porch was full of aromatic plants that looked from a distance like a dark green patch on the expanse of orange flagstones. People would raise their heads to enjoy the sight and say that if Rosa plucked one leaf, the bush would quickly grow two instead, if she pruned a branch a new one would grow in its place, and if she pulled up the entire bush, the seeds it had shed would sprout in a jiffy, grow roots, and produce a new bush bigger, stronger, and more beautiful than the first.

The reputation of the herb garden spread, and the women of the neighborhood would come to Rosa with requests for a branch of sage to dry up the milk in a mother's breasts, or a bunch of basil to get rid of worms, or rosemary to flavor a roast.

Joseph, ever practical, took pity on Rosa, who was wasting her strength on planting, cutting, and distributing herbs for free, and one day he came home with a box of little transparent cellophane bags. That evening he returned early from the cinema, and after reassuring her that the innovation was not a dangerous threat to the routine of her life, the two of them invaded the hanging garden, trimmed branches, picked flowers, and pulled up shoots. Then they sorted out the fragrant bundle and packed it up in rustling bags, and all night long, with green spots dancing in front of their eyes, they discussed the new profession Rosa was about to enter.

The next morning Joseph went around to all the neighborhood greengrocers and sold them the fresh produce. When all the bags were sold, they asked him for a new supply, for Rosa's herbs never wilted or went moldy, but remained as fresh and crisp as the day they were picked. Soon Rosa found herself busy from morning to night with her new occupation: planting and cultivating, pruning and packing the herbs into the little cellophane bags, with delivery boys from the shops coming every day with new orders and the cash to pay for them. At night, when Joseph came home with his pockets full of money from the ticket sales, he would find Rosa's private hoard on the kitchen table, add her daily takings to his, and settle down to the pleasurable task of adding it all up. When he joined her in bed, his fingertips smelling of worn banknotes and coins, he would whisper in her ear the new words of love he had learned from the latest movie, stroke her body, and leave the scent of money on her skin. In those days he would say proudly to the men crowded on the wooden benches in Mousa's hut, drinking red wine and medicinal brandy: "One day Rosa will earn more than I do from those silly plants of hers."

eight

ANGEL WINGS

Rosa became pregnant for the eighth and last time because of a mishap in the Cinema Rosa. On the night of the conception the film got burned during the screening, and Joseph came home early. On that night she had a premonition and she knew beyond a doubt that she was pregnant and that the child she was carrying was different. Of the vision that was revealed to her it was said in the neighborhood that it was a warning from mysterious higher powers guarding her and trying to prevent her from going all the way. But even though she saw the future and knew that the child she would give birth to would turn her life upside down, she did nothing to prevent it. And when she absentmindedly stroked her swelling belly, she felt a strange sensation at her fingertips, unlike anything she had known in her previous seven pregnancies.

Seven children she had borne her husband during fifteen years, and when she turned thirty she decided that enough was enough and she began to take precautions. And when the children grew up too quickly and left home, looking for mates of their own, she looked forward to having grandchildren. And when they appeared, one after the other, ten in number, they brought her new and unfamiliar joys, and she spoiled them as she had never spoiled her own children. She fed them candies, told them stories, took them to the movies, played cards and board games with them, and together with Angela, who had aged a lot by then, she was happy to baby-sit for them when their parents went out at night.

This pregnancy in the fifth decade of her life took her completely by surprise. For from the day the last of her children left home to live their lives and she began to enjoy the grandchildren cradled in her lap, she had stopped menstruating. And from then on she could give herself to her husband night after night without fear of an additional pregnancy that would first stretch her sagging stomach and then slacken it, blacken her teeth, eat away at the calcium in her bones and leave them hollow, make her hair fall out, and cause brown spots to appear on her face.

On the night the event took place that would change the anticipated course of her life and bring disaster down on her head, the cooling apparatus in Joseph's projector broke down in the middle of a particularly sad movie. The film was burned in a number of places, and it was impossible to mend it. The glum-faced Joseph was obliged to return the ticket money to the audience, whistling and catcalling below, and go home earlier than usual.

Rosa received him lying in bed, bathed, perfumed, and wide awake. Her daily takings from the sale of her herbs waited in vain on the kitchen table for the takings from the ticket sales that evening, which had all been returned to the audience. After he told her sadly of the mishap, she comforted him in her arms until he felt the stiffening in his groin, and at the precise moment when all the cuckoo clocks in the house struck midnight, he penetrated her. As soon as he ejaculated and silence fell, she felt the spermatozoa swimming inside her, beating their tiny tails, groping their way through the dark tunnel of her body, sailing straight into her womb, which had been barren for nearly twenty years, and aiming their pointed heads at the target, the egg that had gotten away and survived. As soon as she felt the victorious spermatozoon hitting the egg, she shared her fears with her husband. Joseph, about to bury his head in the pillow and turn his broad back to her, sat up in amazement, bared his teeth stained yellow with nicotine in the grimace that passed for his smile, and waved his hand in dismissal: "You know that's impossible. The door is sealed; there aren't any more children."

The next morning, on her daily visit to her mother, after drinking the ritual cup of coffee Angela would examine behind her daughter's back in order not to annoy her, Angela saw a new expression of pain on Rosa's wan face. After that Angela began dancing attendance on her daughter, fussing unnecessarily, constantly inquiring after her health, asking her if she had eaten, and pressing freshly baked pastries still warm from the oven on her.

After two months had passed, when her breasts began to weigh heavily on her and the nausea rose in her throat every morning, she underwent a series of tests to discover what was wrong, and asked the doctor hesitantly to do a pregnancy test as well. The doctor, who had attended at the birth of Laura-Liora, looked at her with a hint of mockery and said kindly, as if he were explaining the facts of life to a retarded child: "It says here in your file that you stopped menstruating two years ago. You're a rational woman, Rosa. It's not possible." He added that he would recommend she cut down her calorie intake, since she was a big woman, and if she didn't lose weight the menopause might endanger her health.

At the end of the third month she felt the fetus stirring, and after it was seen by the doctors who clustered round her and clicked their tongues as they watched its beating heart and fishlike movements on the screen opposite them, her case was published in a local medical journal and soon reached the daily papers. And when the story reached professional journals abroad she became famous. On a television interview the young host, Danny Barakat, pressed his curly head to the belly of the "pregnant granny" and said that if it was a girl, she would surely be as beautiful as her mother. And with a theatrical flourish, he presented her with his visiting card, with the request that the girl get in touch with him on her sixteenth birthday. And Rosa, blushing furiously at his words under the thick layer of television makeup, nodded wordlessly. But when the taxi they had ordered for her brought her home she threw the visiting card out of the window, stroked her stomach, and made up her mind that when this child emerged from her tired loins she wouldn't let them touch her.

When the tests revealed that the child Rosa was carrying was indeed a girl, she knew that it would be different, because this pregnancy was different from all the others. First her skin tightened on her body and then on her face. Her breasts filled out, and when she inspected the changes taking place in her body in the mirror her nipples pricked up and stared at themselves. Her hair grew thick, her face grew smooth, as if she had been visiting a beauty parlor, her eyes shone in joyful anticipation, and her nails grew so strong that she could paint them red without fear of breaking them. All this the baby growing inside her did for her, as if to compensate her mother for her stubborn insistence on being born.

When Rosa waited her turn to see the gynecologist, the other women in the waiting room didn't give her inquisitive sidelong looks, they didn't whisper behind her back or raise their eyebrows in mute rebuke as if to say that the task of reproduction should be left to younger women. Since she looked like one of them, she had no need to hide her face behind one of the women's magazines and to pretend that the event was taking place in someone else's body and the swollen belly didn't belong to her.

During her pregnancy Joseph began to neglect the cinema and to concentrate on his wife. He stopped bringing the latest tearjerkers to Cinema Rosa, and instead of attending the nightly shows he stayed at home, stroking her protruding belly, cupping her heavy breasts in his hands, and lusting after her even more than usual. He wanted her every day, and the heavier her body grew the more it aroused him, until in the last months of her pregnancy he wanted her all day long, and kept her from doing the housework and tending her plants. After the pleasures of the night, he would take advantage of the erection that woke him from his sleep in the morning, embrace her as she lay with her back to him, and penetrate her gently from behind, to avoid the belly swelling like yeast dough in front of her. And thus he would rock in bed with her all morning, letting go only when she insisted that she had to go and pee, on condition that she came straight back to bed, where he went on delighting in her mountainous belly and heavy breasts till noon. When they were hungry, he would accompany her to the kitchen, stand behind her at the sink and put his arms around her thick waist, rub himself between her buttocks, dig his teeth into the nape of her neck, breathe lewd words into her blushing ears, and when she giggled in embarrassment like a young girl, he would shut her mouth with his lips and suck her tongue. And when she moved about the house he would press his loins to the slit in her backside and rock with her as he clumsily brought up the rear on the journey from the sink to the stove and the fridge, from the washing machine to the laundry line, and from the bedroom to the living room, reluctantly detaching himself only during mealtimes. Then he would sit opposite her, look into her shining eyes, stroke her fresh, taut skin, and sing the praises of her renascent beauty with his mouth full of food.

And Rosa, while enjoying his attention and her rejuvenation, would think of the new baby and the changes it would bring to her life. And when she went at nine o'clock on the dot to Tzadok's grocery, the men in the street would invade her neckline with their eyes and bare her bursting breasts, probe her vibrant body with their stares, and penetrate it in their imaginations with their stiffening members. Then their flaring nostrils would quiver with suppressed lust and with heartbreaking sighs they would breathe in the passionate smells of her secret places, mingled with the scent of Joseph's lavender soap. And they would tail her in twos and threes, following open-mouthed the movements of the maternity dress full of goodies rising and falling on her firm buttocks behind and stretched tight over her burgeoning belly before, until she reached the entrance to her building. When she disappeared into the dark stairwell they would spend hours wallowing in the memory of the smell, and privately discussing among themselves what they would do to her if she fell into their hands. When the rumor reached Joseph he let it be known that if any of the men who dared to dream about his wife fell into his hands he would "smash their heads like coconuts." Since he was a big, strong man and everyone in the neighborhood was afraid of the gloomy expression on his face that boded no good, Rosa was able to go out to do her shopping and walk without fear among the men of the neighborhood, whose slack-jawed stares, heavy breathing, and swelling flies bore mute testimony to everything they were doing to her in the darkness of their thoughts.

But not only men pestered her in those days. The neighborhood dogs too would station themselves at the entrance to the building, throw back their heads, and howl yearningly, with as much tenderness as their stretched throats were capable of producing. And when she walked down the street she was followed by a canine caravan whose rough paws clattered on the asphalt in unison, with a sound like glass marbles rolling along the road. Mangy, battle-scarred alley cats too would approach her, and in spite of their suspicious nature take food from her hands and even allow her to stroke their patchy fur and tickle their tattered ears. Even the crows joined the party, announcing her emergence from the building in a chorus of sharp, metallic caws and accompanying her with a royal escort of beating black wings to Tzadok's grocery and back. And Rosa, who couldn't understand what they wanted of her, would scatter crumbs and bits of food on the kitchen windowsill for them. With uncharacteristic shyness the crows would approach and nibble politely at the leftovers she offered them. And when she came home Joseph would be waiting for her there, full of longing, and do things to her that the neighborhood men didn't dream of in their wildest dreams.

When she consulted Rachelle, her richly experienced friend, about Joseph's insatiable desire for her, and described the guard of honor of neighborhood men who greeted her whenever she left the house, Rachelle giggled and said that she wasn't surprised. Because Rosa had grown so beautiful in her pregnancy that no man with a self-respecting, functioning member in his pants could remain indifferent to her appearance. And she added in a whisper, right into Rosa's blushing ear, that it was a well known fact that if a woman had a husband who desired her every day and went to bed with her every day, some men, exactly like dogs, could smell the smells, see the sights, and hear the sounds. So it was no wonder that they gathered around her, she added, with a hint of envy in her voice.

Even after the tests showed that the fetus wasn't developing properly and the doctors said that she should consider terminating the pregnancy, Rosa continued to stimulate the imaginations of the neighborhood men, and Joseph continued to realize their fantasies with as much pleasure as ever.

Rosa said nothing to Joseph about the results of the tests, and went straight to Peretz the Cabalist in Katamon H. She had first heard his name from Rachelle, who had gone to him immediately after her divorce so that he would tell her her fortune, chase away the evil eye, and make up amulets specially suited to her. They said that he was a great expert at checking mezuzas. He would take the mezuza, look at it through a magnifying glass, and discover all the problems of its owner. His powers were attributed to his genealogy. Peretz was descended from a famous family of cabalists from Baghdad and the great-grandson of a very great cabalist who could bring the dead back to life and speak to souls. Despite his powers, however, Peretz had been unable to overcome his wife's illness, an illness that sucked the marrow out of her bones, shriveled her body, and led to her premature death. When they buried what was left of her, a bag of bones covered with skin, he was inconsolable, and the neighbors would hear him weeping for her in the middle of the night, a terrible, heartrending weeping that frightened children, dogs, and cats and disturbed the rest of the neighborhood.

Everyone in Katamon H knew Peretz, and the children showed

her the path beaten to his door by the feet of all those seeking salvation, lined on either side by brambles and tall, dry thistles sharpening their claws. The thorn-protected path led the seekers from the bus stop through an abandoned junk field to a narrow dirt track winding between low houses, and stopped opposite a house that would have looked no different from the others, but for the dozens of women with hard faces and dull eyes who crowded outside the gate. Their hushed voices mingled in the air with the shrill mating cries of the emaciated cats clustering fearlessly round the battered trash can lying upside down at the entrance to the house.

Rosa shooed the cats away and opened the low iron gate hanging crookedly from a single hinge that creaked rustily at her touch. A sign written in wavering, big black letters announced: PERETZ THE CABALIST LIVES HERE, and a second line announced in red: BANISHES THE EVIL EYE EXORCISES SPELLS AND DYBBUKS RETURNS LOST LOVES AND SOLVES DREAMS. The door with its peeling paint was half open, and Rosa found herself standing shyly in the parlor. Dozens of holy sages, most of whom were unfamiliar to her, gazed at her benevolently from the portraits hanging in a crooked line on the walls, and silently promised her a happy life. Parchment scrolls containing a variety of blessings, closely written in black ink, hung in gilt frames next to the saints and calmed her fears.

Standing nervously at the door was a man dressed in a blue striped suit. In his hand he was holding a fine leather case, gripping it so tightly that his knuckles were white with effort. To an outside observer he looked as if he were about to take off and run for his life at any moment. Rosa looked at him curiously; she knew that he was famous, but she couldn't remember where she recognized his face from. Next to him stood an elegantly dressed woman holding in her arms a thin, pale child, its body twitching spasmodically, and its mouth drooling with transparent threads of spittle that were absorbed by the large bib tied round its chin. From the shabby armchairs and sofa standing round the room eyes stared at her. A low murmur like the buzzing of bees rose in the air. When the women recognized her and greeted her respectfully, she felt their eyes besieging her on all sides, probing into her stomach as if to inspect its contents.

Rosa, who was a sociable creature, shared her problem with the other women, and they told her their troubles. Young girls said that they had come to make sure of a good marriage, and barren women to ask the cabalist to banish the evil eye and open their wombs. The big fat woman sitting next to her told her in a whisper that she had come to ask Peretz to bring the husband who had deserted her back home. Rosa looked at the woman's shabby clothes, the deep lines on her face, her chapped, callused hands, and her dry, henna-dyed hair with its white roots, and suggested tactfully that it might be a good idea to buy new clothes and get her face and hair seen to before she asked for the cabalist's blessing, because if her husband came home now and saw her in her present condition, he would probably go right back to his mistress. Later on Rosa couldn't understand why she had gone on to tell the unfortunate creature that her own husband had never cheated on her, and that he desired her all day and every day, and it was all because she took care of herself, kept her clothes and body scrupulously clean, and never neglected her appearance. When she heard this, the big woman shrank, averted her face, and pursed her lips in pain, and when she came out of Peretz's room her eyes were dripping with tears.

When it was Rosa's turn she stepped into the room separated from the waiting room by a curtain of greasy wooden beads, which did nothing to prevent the waiting women from listening in on their sisters' troubles. In the darkness illuminated only by the memorial candles covering the floor her eyes widened. The white-robed cabalist greeted her warmly, as if they were old friends separated in childhood meeting again many years later. He examined her with a searching look that brought her flesh out in goose bumps, and in a high, reedy voice, incongruous in such a heavy man, he asked her what the problem was. Then he asked her to tell him her name, and the names of her mother, her husband, and all her children, and made complicated calculations on a piece of yellowing cardboard. With a sigh that split her heart he told her to drop molten lead into cold water. With the help of a slotted spoon he removed the pieces of lead from the water and looked at them intently as they stared back at him, like malevolent gray eyes with dilated pupils. When his inspection was over, he asked her for her wedding ring and tied a piece of string round it. Then he took the end of the string carefully between his fingers, and the ring began to swing over her stomach, at first in expanding circles and then strongly to and fro like a pendulum, from right to left and left to right.

In conclusion he looked into her expectant eyes, weighed her breasts in his imagination, and gave her grasses to burn and a liquid with which to bathe her private parts, wrote the names of angels on a parchment scroll in purple ink, and told her to soak it in a dish of water until the letters faded, and drink the water just before going to sleep. In parting he presented her with a blue glass eye. When he saw the confused expression on her face he sat with her for a long time and explained that every child, including the one she was bearing, had a mission on earth, and that she was on no account to consider an abortion. For if she aborted the fetus she would prevent its soul from incarnating in this world, and the soul, prevented from fulfilling its destiny, would return to her in nightmarish dreams, never let her rest, and ruin her life and the lives of all the family, "for every aborted fetus is like a lost soul straying in the world to come." And he added that every woman who had an abortion was obliged to perform a purification ceremony, a *Tikkun Nefashot* for the aborted fetus on the seventeenth of Tammuz, the fast day in memory of the destruction of the Temple, for all the bloodshed in the world today was because of the thousands of abortions performed every year.

As he spoke he gazed wide-eyed at her beauty, passed his hand over her breasts and her stomach, hesitated for a moment, and then said that he saw a girl child who would be like an angel. And when she paid him, despite his protests that no payment was necessary, he instructed her to return after she gave birth, so that he could banish the evil eye from the child, who would be more beautiful in this incarnation than any other, in the past or the future.

Since she had not been given clear answers by the cabalist, Rosa found herself for the first time in her life seeking advice from her mother's spirits. Angela, whose flesh and bones had been ravaged by the years and who was now a shadow of her former self, pretended not to hear the imploring note in her daughter's voice. When Rosa repeated her pleas, Angela explained that it was not in her power to intervene. Every day Rosa visited her mother in the opposite apartment, demanded more and more coffee, and casually left the empty cups with their muddy dregs on the table behind her. And when Angela heard her heavy footsteps on the landing and her door opening and shutting, she would hurry to turn the cup over on its saucer with her skeletal, brown-spotted hands, and for a long time afterward she would sit with her bowed head swaying on its stalklike neck, sighing and communing with the fingerprints of fate.

And when Rosa returned the next day and demanded to know

what she had discovered, Angela would say innocently: "But you don't believe in it. You yourself asked me to stop reading the coffee grounds, so what do you want of me now?"

And when Rosa pressed her, she would explain again: "What's written in heaven is sealed and closed, and no one can change his fate."

"But I still want to know what's written there for me?" Rosa would implore her. "What am I going to give birth to? At least I'll be prepared if I know."

And Angela would purse her lips and refuse to tell her daughter what she had seen in her future and of the change about to cast her into the hard, tangled knot of a new era in her life.

In spite of all her fears, Rosa decided to keep the baby. If this was God's wish, since she had become pregnant against all the odds, there must be some special significance to the event, which was not to be taken lightly. And as if she had forgotten that she had already done it seven times before, she delighted in this pregnancy and worried about it as if it were her first. In the months when the embryo was developing inside her Rosa concentrated on its movements. These movements were not like those to which she had become accustomed in the sixty-three months, or the five and a quarter years, of pregnancy she had lived through in her life. She felt no kicks, somersaults, or hiccups. The movements in her belly were pleasant and gentle, and their touch as soft as the down on the breast of a songbird. To anyone who asked she would say that she felt as if the child were floating on air inside her, and only to Joseph and the children did she confide the sensation of wings, the flutter of feathers, and the chirping sounds breaking out of her belly. They all agreed that the new baby was sorry for her mother who had become pregnant by accident late in life, and she was consoling her from within by the gentle, fluttering touch of a gosling flapping its wings in its nest.

These strange sensations received confirmation from her first beloved grandson, Ruth's son, eight-year-old Dror, who would fix his eyes searchingly on her stomach as if its rounded sides were made of glass and he could look right through them to the fetus swimming in the darkness of her womb. Then he would pass his hands through the air, knit his brow, and announce with the certainty of a seer: "You have an angel in your stomach; she's a gift for me, and I'm going to marry her." And when he said these things Rosa would feel a flapping in her womb, as if the tiny creature inside her were fluttering her wings in agitation. Dror would pass the palms of his hands over the tight-drawn fabric of her dress, caressing his wife-to-be, and uttering soft cooing sounds of love. Then the baby would calm down, and the beating at the sides of Rosa's womb would stop.

"Now she's sleeping," Dror would announce in a gratified tone, put his finger to his lips, and tiptoe out of the room. And in order not to disturb the baby's sleep he would lower the volume of the television in the next room. And Rosa would think about her eldest grandson's promise to marry his still unborn aunt and the strange, ironic twist of fate it represented. For she herself had married her uncle, and in spite of all the gloomy predictions of the doctors about the retarded and deformed offspring that this union between relatives would produce, all her children, knock wood, were sound and healthy and successful without a blemish on their bodies, and this last one too would be as perfect as an angel.

Two months before she was due to give birth, all her seven children arrived in the middle of the day, while she and Joseph were hard at it in bed, and told her that Angela was dead. She had slipped in the bathroom and smashed her hollow pelvic bones, which were eaten away and fragile as glass, to smithereens.

Preoccupied with the life inside her, Rosa accompanied her mother on her last journey, and in spite of the loud wailing of the women around her who had come to Angela to have their fortunes told, she was unable to shed a single tear. And when they went back to the house, she looked dry eyed at Joseph, shedding copious tears outside his cinema for the first time in his life, and bawling at the top of his voice as if deriving immense enjoyment from the act of crying itself. All the seven days of mourning she explained calmly to the condolence callers that she wasn't going to call the child after her late mother since Angela herself had forbidden it on the grounds that it was bad luck to name children for the dead. She told them, too, that her mother had given up the ghost because the supply of Amatzia's love for her had run out, after she had used it up so extravagantly, and now she had gone to join him in heaven in order to obtain fresh rations of love. And Joseph looked at her with damp eyes, listened to her words, hugged her body stirring with new life, and rocked with her, mourning for his sister as if he had been orphaned all over again.

After the week of mourning was over, she went to Angela's apartment and took her father's photograph albums and possessions, preserved as he had left them on the morning he died. When she opened the closet doors in order to sort out Angela's clothes, she found the doll, Belle, wrapped in a shroud and forgotten. A soft white cloud of moths flew out of the doll, leaving little bald patches in her abundant hair and sprinkling her with a silky white powder in their flight. Rosa dressed Belle in the moth-eaten clothes she found at her side, stroked her depleted curls, and rocked her up and down, but the doll failed to produce the expected cry of "Mama, mama, mama." She looked closely at the pretty painted china face, the pink cheeks, the blue glass eyes fringed with dark lashes, the straight nose, and the swollen lips parted in a generous smile to reveal tiny white teeth, and she wished for a daughter as beautiful as a doll.

With a heavy heart she took the doll, her father's belongings, and the glass jar in which Angela kept her false teeth stuck in pink plastic gums. She put the jar on the basin next to the glass with her and Joseph's toothbrushes. And every morning from then on, before she washed her face, she would turn to the teeth sunk in water and greeting her with a friendly smile, and tell them about the events of the previous day. Then she would fish them out of their jar and brush them thoroughly, just as Angela had done in anticipation of each new day. The teeth would rattle and clatter in her hands in a response only she could understand. Joseph would look at her in concern and whisper to the children, who came to visit more frequently than usual, that in view of their mother's delicate condition, they had to be considerate of her, show her understanding, never contradict her, and never ask her to explain the meaning of her behavior, however odd it might seem.

Two months later, on a morning when her stomach felt very big and low, she conversed at length with Angela's teeth, as usual. When she had finished her ablutions she went back to bed, where Joseph bade her good morning and penetrated her as he did every day. At the moment of penetration she heard a snapping sound, and they were both bathed in a stream of clear, warm water. The water seeped into the thick spring mattress and went right through it to the floor, washing away the fluff and gray dust caught in Rosa's long hairs scattered under the bed. Joseph jumped out of bed in alarm, wiped his loins and Rosa's, helped her up, dressed her in her best, and summoned Leslie-Shimon to come at once with his car.

Leaving a trail of little puddles behind her, Rosa was taken straight to the delivery room, and when she lay down on the narrow iron bed she knew that this time it would be a difficult birth. And while all the women in the cold, stainless-steel hall were screaming at the tops of their voices and cursing their husbands for their plight, Rosa gritted her teeth and called on Angela to help her.

Afterward there was a great commotion around her. Rosa remembered only the needle in the bottom of her back and the black pit into which she fell with an enjoyable drifting sensation.

When she woke up she saw Joseph's tearful face opposite her. He told her that they had put her to sleep and in his presence cut open her belly, parted the huge womb that was swollen as tight as a crimson balloon, and removed the baby, who refused to come out of her own accord. Only when she was discharged from the hospital did he dare to tell her that the umbilical cord had been coiled around the baby's neck, as if she had tried to take her own life even before she saw the light of day.

"Your child will stay small," the doctors told her a few hours after she gave birth. And Rosa, exhausted by the operation, fell into a deep sleep from which she woke only at the sound of the orange curtain sliding on its rail and presaging the crowding of the doctors round her bed. The obstetrician, her private gynecologist, the pediatrician, and the midwife were all there.

She looked into their eyes and realized that her premonition had been right and her baby was different. And they looked back at her with a strange combination of sorrow and pity, mingled with professional satisfaction at the rare genetic accident that had come their way like a heaven-sent gift. For a long time they spoke to her about the mutations of DNA caused by marriage between close family relations, and about her good fortune in having given birth to seven healthy children. With gleaming eyes, imagining the many papers they would publish and the lectures they would deliver at medical conferences, they told her that the baby was a hunchback, that her growth would be arrested at about the age of two, and that she might be mentally retarded as well and spend the rest of her life lying on her humped back and opening her mouth only in order to be fed.

Dry eyed, Rosa looked at the deputation of evil angels—so she called them when she described the occasion in days to come—and she told them to fold their white wings, to leave her in peace, and to bring her baby to her immediately. And they glided away, their starched white coats rustling stiffly as they sped down the corridors on their next mission.

After they left the curtain opened again with a loud, tearing sound. Rachelle stood in front of her with a bunch of tired-looking roses in her hands, looking at her with the look she kept for special occasions when she wanted to express sorrow or pity.

"I heard them say that your baby is a hunchback and that she isn't going to grow," were the first words she said. In the cold neon light of the recovery room Rosa could clearly see the scars on her friend's acne-pitted face and the gleeful glitter in her eyes. Even though Rachelle was her best friend, Rosa knew that she was enjoying being the bearer of bad news, and she waited impatiently for her to go.

After a long time, when her breasts were so swollen they were about to burst and the sound of her screams rang through the corridors, they laid the baby in her lap. The baby's dark eyes set in a huge skull gazed at her curiously and unblinkingly, and her head swayed slightly on her neck. As soon as she received the baby in her arms she began to undress her, as she had done with all seven of her newborn babies so many years ago. Gently, as if afraid of damaging the fragile body, she undid the soft flannel garments. The faint smell of laundry powder and the fragrance of baby's skin, mingled with the stench of the black bowel movements passed by newborn babies before they begin to suckle, spread through the room. As if to help her mother undress her, the baby kicked at the white swaddling clothes. With practiced hands that had not forgotten their skill, Rosa loosened the wrappings covering her daughter's entire body as if she were the mummy of an ancient Egyptian baby who had died in infancy.

The baby lay naked on the bed, her shame exposed to her mother's weeping eyes, and with her insides contracting in dread, Rosa saw the humps, or what the doctors referred to as a "genetic mistake." She took a deep breath and looked to see if all the other limbs were in the right place. With a sigh of relief she saw that the navel protruding from her belly like an end of pink rope was exactly in the middle of her body. Her ears were set close to her head, her nose was in the proper place, and she had the right number of arms and legs. Forgetting the dread in the pit of her stomach for a moment,

Rosa delighted, just as she had seven times before, in the tiny nails covering the tips of her baby's fingers. When she recovered from the miracle of the fingernails she lifted the baby up and, as if she were shortsighted, held her right in front of her eyes. With quivering nostrils she smelled the achingly familiar scent of a newborn baby and welcomed her into the world. As if performing a secret rite known only to mothers she kissed her in a fixed sequence on her cheeks, her forehead, on her half-closed eyes, and on each of her tiny fingers. And before she wrapped her up, she examined her again all over, seeking signs of family resemblance.

Afterward, when she told Rachelle about it, she admitted that she was looking for signs of her dead mother. When she failed to find any evidence of reincarnation, she cradled the naked baby in her arms and laid her at her breast. The baby's body was warm and her skin silky smooth, holding out a promise of future beauty. The baby trembled between her breasts, groping like a blind mole for the source of nourishment, and when she found the nipple she gripped it triumphantly between her strong gums. A sharp pain pierced Rosa's body. She looked at the little face pressed to her breast and felt a frisson of pleasurable pain. The pleasure began at the nipple, shooting thin jets of sweet liquid into the baby's mouth, and descended in circles of pain and pleasure to her stomach, squeezing and contracting her empty womb. At that moment a powerful love for this baby awoke in her, greater than the love she felt for her healthy children.

When she tried to explain later how it had happened, she would say that it was as if the humps split her heart apart and left it bleeding.

The next day Joseph came to visit, and this time he didn't bring flowers, as he had done with all seven other births. His face, which was always smoothly shaved, was full of hard gray stubble, and a look of pity such as she had never seen before had settled in his eyes. After him the doctors trooped in, shuffling their feet and looking grave, as if they were the bearers of very bad news. Joseph refused to see his newborn baby and sat next to his wife's bed, holding her hand in his big one and looking into her eyes as the pain deepened in his. Since this time he made no attempt to persuade her to name the new baby after one of his favorite movie stars, and left the choice to her, Rosa knew that this damaged last child would be hers alone. Joseph would have no part of her.

After he had left without giving her a name, all seven children arrived, with a few of the grandchildren in tow, and demanded vociferously to see their sister. With a sour expression the nurse in charge of the neonates complied with their request. She removed the baby sternly from the transparent plastic box, held her in strong hands, and hoisted her high in the air, averting her eyes as if she had nothing to do with her. And when Ruthie insisted on holding her, she thrust her into her arms as if to say, "There it is, that's the situation, and there's nothing anyone can do about it." Then she turned her back on them, wiped the sour expression from her face, and turned her attention smilingly to the other babies, lying side by side like mummified cocoons of pale butterflies.

Late that evening, when Rosa lay waiting for a visit from her mother, she suddenly remembered that Angela had died two months before the birth of her last grandchild. All of a sudden she became conscious of the bereavement that had passed her by, sat up in bed, and burst into loud wails that brought all the nurses on the night shift running to her bed. They plumped up her pillows, massaged her temples, gave her herbal tea, and when they saw that they had no alternative, they put the deformed baby in her arms, in the hope that she would succeed in calming her mother.

Rosa held her baby and rocked her in her arms, and the dammed-up tears burst out. She wept as she had never wept before, for all the years when her eyes had been dry. She wept for her orphaned state, for Rina the little refugee, for Mischa the Holocaust survivor, for her unfulfilled love for Shraga, for the death of her friend Ruthie, for the youth that had passed her by, for her mother who had left this world, for the different child to whom she had given birth, for Joseph who was keeping himself apart from her, and for the terrible change about to take place in her life. And when the tears splashed onto the baby's bald head and wet her clothes, the nurses took her away and gave her mother a sedative.

"It's because she gave birth to a retarded child," the empty-bellied women in the adjacent beds whispered. The whispers seeped through the flimsy walls, swept down the corridors, invaded the rooms, and cast terror into the hearts of the women lying on the narrow beds in the cold, sterilized delivery rooms, with their bellies looming in front of them and their legs in stainless steel stirrups raised high in the air for the convenience of their obstetricians. Afterward the nurses on the night shift told the day shift nurses that in spite of the sedative Rosa had wept inconsolably all night long. Early in the morning her tears dried up, and she held out her arms to her baby with a welcoming smile, bared her breast, suckled her, and cooed at her as if nothing had happened. After feeding the baby she held her in her arms and kissed her tenderly all over her body. The baby belched, looked back at her sleepily, and Rosa felt her breath stopping and her tiny limbs stiffening as her body braced itself to receive the pure pleasure of her mother's kisses and soak up every sign of her love.

And when she came home with the baby in her arms, she was welcomed by a salute from all the cuckoo clocks in the house, repeated ten times, while the gray neighborhood crows flew around the house and cawed excitedly in their cold, metallic voices. That evening when she bathed the baby, Joseph refused to help her as usual, and little Dror volunteered to do it instead.

"I told you," he exulted when she removed the baby's clothes. "My wife is an angel!"

"How do you know that she's an angel?" asked Rosa hoarsely.

"Look, here," the little boy pointed at the tiny projecting shoulder blades of his bride-to-be, stroking them in the air. "This is where her wings are folded." Rosa looked at the two little lumps of flesh projecting from the fragile back, and her hot tears flowed into the bath and salted the water where the mite was splashing.

"Why does she need wings?" she asked.

Dror looked at his grandmother pityingly. "To fly with," he said confidently.

"And when will she fly?" asked Rosa, the tears choking her.

"When the time comes and she wants to, she'll spread her wings and fly," said Dror, and added hesitantly: "And when she flies, I'll fly with her."

After a long silence, he asked: "What are you going to call her?"

"I haven't thought of a name yet," she said, looking down at the bathwater with her eyes full of tears. "Do you have any ideas?"

"I want you to call her Angel," he said in a pampered voice.

Rosa whispered the name absentmindedly, like a soothing mantra: "Angel, angel of God, ministering angel, angel from heaven, my little Angel," forgetting the angel of Death, the evil angel, and the fiendish angels of destruction who torture the dead in hell. When she became accustomed to the name, she realized with a shock that it was the

Hebrew version of her mother's name, Angela, and it was bad luck to call the living after the dead. But when she thought about it, she found reasons in favor of the idea. Since this child was different, since she had given birth to her against all the odds, and since her mother had died so soon before the birth, it was a sign that she was permitted to ignore the instructions her mother had given when she was still alive. To these well-considered reasons, she added the fact that the name had been requested by Dror, her first grandchild, and she couldn't refuse him.

And the name "Angel" in Hebrew, together with the non-Hebrew name "Angela," the date of birth, and identity number were written down by the clerk in the Interior Ministry on a clean new page with seven compartments bearing the title "Children," and added to Rosa's ID booklet. And Rosa stapled the new page onto the old, shabby one bearing the names of her seven previous children, written in different handwritings and tightly filling all seven compartments.

In days to come, when the troubles arrived one on top of the other, her friend Rachelle would say that it was all the fault of the name she had chosen. "If you wanted to call her an angel's name, you could have called her Ariela, Gabriela, Rafaela, Michaela, but Angel? Why Angel? You wanted an angel and came up with something satanic instead."

From the moment Rosa came home from the hospital with the baby in her arms, the change she had so feared happened. Afraid of what lay in store, she ignored the ominous signs hovering in the air and tried as hard as she could to maintain the routine of her life.

Some people said that the crows had been sent to announce the change, because the first time Rosa stepped out of the house pushing the baby's carriage in front of her, they all stopped what they were doing. Every single crow in the neighborhood crowded onto the telegraph wires over her head, perching there like a celestial honor guard of angels of destruction, balancing themselves by flapping their wings and following the baby with their beady eyes. Rosa looked at Angel and thought she saw her raising her eyes to look at the birds and waving her arms as if she wanted to fly with them.

Proof of the honor guard, so the neighbors said in years to come, when people didn't believe their story, were the droppings shed by the crows in their excitement, striping the pavement in straight lines parallel to the telegraph wires they were sitting on. These lines remained there for a long time, in defiance of all the efforts of the street sweepers to get rid of them. And it was also said that the paint on the roofs and the hoods of the cars, which got in the way of the excrement falling from above as they drove past, bubbled and seethed as if they had been splashed by drops of corrosive acid, and a couple of days later it peeled away, leaving an ugly rash of bald spots, as if the cars had been afflicted with smallpox.

And Joseph changed too. The father who had always loved babies and children so much avoided his new daughter and ignored her existence, as if she had never been born. When he came home from his nights in the cinema, he never went into her room to tuck her in. He never shook her gently awake in the mornings or lifted her up in front of his eyes as he had done with his other children; he never held her in his arms or breathed in her fresh smell. And when he came across her by chance, bundled up in Rosa's arms, he would avert his eyes from her and pretend that she didn't exist. And at the same time he avoided contact with Rosa, in case she should abuse his sperm and bring another crooked creature into the world.

The day the doctors informed her that she was permitted to sleep with her husband again, she bathed and asked Aliza the Hairdresser to come by. Aliza set her hair in elaborate curls and fixed them in place with spray. Then she prepared Joseph's favorite dish, the Sunday almond soup, and sat opposite him beaming with happiness, watching every spoonful he emptied into his mouth. Unwillingly Joseph dunked a piece of bread in the white soup, soaked up the liquid, and swallowed reluctantly, refusing to look his wife in the eye. And when Rosa removed the bedspread and signaled that the time had come, he put her off with vain excuses, roamed around the house, and rewound all the cuckoo clocks covering the walls of the living room, the kitchen, the passage, and the bedroom. And when all the cuckoos announced at once that the hour nine had struck, he walked out of the apartment, slamming the door behind him, and went to see what was happening in Cinema Rosa, and from there he went to drink arak at Mousa Zilka's hut. When he came home with a sharp smell of anise issuing from his mouth, he made the rounds of the children's rooms, where seven empty beds awaited their owners who had flown the nest, huddled up in Ruthie's bed, and fell asleep under a ragged poster of two kittens playing with a ball of wool.

When Rosa met him in the kitchen the next morning, he told her that he hadn't joined her in bed because he didn't want to wake her. And he did the same thing the next night too, and every night that week. In those days it seemed to Rosa that her husband had grown old overnight. Her body burgeoning before his eyes and her full breasts failed to stiffen his member as in days gone by. Stubbornly he refused to get into their conjugal bed and avoided all physical contact with her. Like a zombie he wandered round the house in his faded flannel pajamas, fraying in the front and tied around his thick waist with an old silk curtain cord. In the evenings, after Rosa put Angel to sleep in her crib, on her back in order to flatten her humps, she would call Joseph in her most seductive voice, and he would pretend to be deaf, wander into the children's room, and fall asleep curled up like a fetus in one of the seven empty beds.

This soon became a habit, and every night, after winding the cuckoo clocks, he would go to sleep in one of the children's beds. Since he was an orderly, methodical man, he decided that on Sundays he would sleep in Ruthie's bed, on Mondays in Leslie-Shimon's bed, on Tuesdays in Jackie-Ya'akov's bed, on Wednesdays in Scarlett-Mazel's bed, on Thursdays in Lana-Ilana's bed, on Fridays in James-Gad's bed, and on Saturdays he would round off the week in Laura-Liora's bed. On the weekends when the seven children with their wives and husbands and offspring filled the rooms of the house, Joseph would make up his bed on the floor in what had once been his and Rosa's room, curl up like an abandoned kitten, and fall asleep. Then his whistling snores would penetrate Rosa's ears and keep her from falling asleep. And as she lay awake she would think of the distant days when he would stampede inside her every night and then go to sleep with his arms around her, his nose pressed against her head trumpeting into her left ear, keeping her worst nightmares at bay.

nine

A DEAD MAN'S SMILE

Cinema Rosa closed down immediately after Angel was born. Not that Joseph wanted to close it—on the contrary, he wanted to cry then more than at any other time of his life—but the customers simply stopped coming. Joseph claimed that it was all because his ancient projector was growing weak, the light was faint, and the pictures on the screen were losing their focus and sometimes disappearing altogether. He also said that the sound was coming out cracked and dull and it was impossible to hear the heroes clearly as they bemoaned their bitter fate on the screen. The loyal customers of Cinema Rosa, who started avoiding the place, said that Joseph was choosing bad movies, and the latest films he showed failed to make them cry.

In fairness to the deserters it must be said that the rival cinemas had a lot to offer the denizens of the neighborhood, who understandably preferred to sit on soft seats upholstered in velvet, to see sharp-edged pictures on the wide screen, and listen to clear voices coming over up-to-date stereo systems. The big crisis that began that year may also have been due to the hard winter in Jerusalem, which led many loyal customers to abandon the icy hall of Cinema Rosa for the heated auditoriums of the new movie theaters.

Only Rosa knew the truth. When she visited him one day in the freezing, half-empty cinema with Angel bundled up in her arms, she realized that Joseph had begun to muddle up the reels, showing the first last and the last first, and sometimes skipping the middle reel entirely, so that nobody could understand what was going on. At first nobody blamed him, thinking that the films were experimental and avant-garde. But as the plots grew increasingly incoherent, the spectators became increasingly frustrated, especially the movie buffs and self-appointed experts among them, who were embarrassed at their inability to explain the films to the uninitiated. And the audiences began to disappear, taking their tears to new places. The day Rosa found the weeping Joseph alone in the cinema watching a movie without a beginning, middle, or end, she decided on her own initiative to close the place down, and hung up a big sign saying: FOR SALE.

After the cinema closed down, Joseph would vanish right after supper, grunting that he was going to Mousa Zilka's hut, and come home late at night, a smell of cigarettes rising from his hair, lowering his alcohol-bloated body onto one of the children's beds. He spent every evening there, drinking, smoking, and lamenting his sufferings to the men crowding the rough wooden benches, staring dully in front of them in a miasma of smoke and sorrow. Their slack lips, clinging obstinately to wet cigarettes sticking to their teeth, exchanged sad stories of unrequited loves and wasted lives. Shoulder to shoulder, night after night, the men crowded into the little wooden hut covered with a gray, corrugated asbestos roof, out of which burst the mighty boughs of a gnarled fig tree.

How the tree got there nobody knew. One day, Mousa explained to the curious, a sharp little shoot broke through the thick concrete floor. Boldly and impudently the tree pushed aside the concrete weighing down on it and began to thrust its way upward, nourished by the drops of strong red wine sprayed on it by the drunks. As it grew and flourished and put out branches, it began to look down on the people moaning and groaning below. Then it gathered up its courage and, swaying like a drunk, it burst through the asbestos ceiling barring its way to the sun. In those days Mousa would swear to his customers suffering from the raindrops showering down on their heads and the winter winds whistling through their clothes that he had not planted the tree, and perhaps it had been seeded from the leftovers of the dried figs spat out by the workers when they laid the concrete floor. But the old men of the neighborhood told one another on those cold nights, as they warmed their bony hands over olive-oil cans filled with smoldering charcoal, that it was Rosa who had brought the sapling to Mousa, "because Rosa and Mousa had grown up together in the same house in Old Katamon, and when they were children they used to hide away from the grown-ups and fondle each other's bodies, until Joseph caught them at it and beat them soundly. And the beating they had suffered in common bound them together forever." And in proof of their words they pointed to the perfect circle cutting through the concrete and surrounding the trunk of the fig tree, which showed that the tree had been planted deliberately, and not by accident. Others liked adding interpretations to the facts, explaining that "if Rosa had brought Mousa a sapling of a fig tree, it proves that they were in love, but they didn't dare give this love any expression because of Joseph's fanatical jealousy of his beautiful wife." In any event, everyone agreed that Mousa, who received the tree from his childhood love, began to develop strong feelings of affection for it. They said that at night he would water it in secret with the leftover wine in his customers' glasses. And when the spirit took him he would hug the tree and kiss it, and on frosty nights he would wrap a thick woolen blanket around it, whisper his deepest secrets into the knots in the wood that opened up to him like eyes, and share with it his secret love for Rosa.

And when the first fruits of the tree ripened in the summer, the people of the neighborhood would form a long line outside the hut with the hole in the roof, and ask to buy the soft, juicy figs that tasted of wine. The best figs Mousa would put into a brown paper bag and give Joseph for Rosa. And when she received the gift she refused to share the figs with her children. "Because they're full of alcohol and smell as if they're been soaked in wine, and they're not good for children," she would justify herself, and then she would take them with her to bed. Since she knew that they were free of worms, for worms could not survive in wine, she would never split them open and peer inside them suspiciously, but greedily stick her white teeth straight into the soft pink flesh. Then the sweetness would spread through her body, making her limbs heavy and her head spin giddily.

For six months after Angel's birth Joseph spoke neither good nor ill to Rosa, and when she tried to engage him in conversation he turned a deaf ear. And one night, when he came back from Mousa's hut, his mouth reeking of cheap arak and his coat and hair saturated with cigarette smoke, Rosa opened the door and received him with arms outstretched, ready to embrace him, but the embrace never took place, because Joseph bowed his head and evaded her arms. Sadly she followed him to the children's room, where he tried to settle down in Jackie-Ya'akov's bed, and announced firmly that they had to talk. Joseph stared at her, and she felt as if he was looking right through her to the wall behind her. And when she tried to force him to talk to her, and spoke about their lives together, about Angel, and about everything that was happening in the house, he didn't react and behaved as if he hadn't heard a word. When he took off his coat and remained in the filthy pajamas that he refused to remove, not even to be washed, a sharp pain pierced her body at the sight of what he had been hiding from her so successfully. The tall, sturdy body of her children's father was stooped and shrunken. With a serious expression on his face he got up and began wandering round the house, looking for a bed on which to pass his delirious night. Tucked into the bed they had once shared, Rosa listened to the shuffling of his slippers as he trailed through the rooms. She wanted to get up and tell him that today was Sunday, and therefore he should sleep on Ruthie's bed, but she fell asleep before she could do so. And when she found him the next morning in Leslie-Shimon's bed, sucking his thumb while his other hand was busy squeezing his penis, she realized that something had happened and Joseph had begun to mix up the days of the week.

When he finally got out of bed she saw that it was wet and sticky with semen. She put clean sheets on the bed and tried to persuade him to take off his pajamas so she could wash them. But Joseph clung to the frayed pajamas as obstinately as an infant, his thumb stuck in his mouth, mumbling unintelligibly, and she knew that the battle was lost. "We'll wait until Saturday, and when everybody comes for lunch we'll force him to undress and wash the pajamas," she said on the phone to Leslie-Shimon, who from the day his father had begun to decline had inherited his position and taken charge of family affairs.

On Monday night the same thing happened again. Joseph shuffled round the house, holding the top of his pajama pants and looking for a bed on which to lay his stinking, sweaty body. "Today's Monday, and tonight it's Leslie-Shimon's turn," she reminded him. Joseph took no notice of her, upset the sacrosanct order, and curled up in Jackie-Ya'akov's bed, with the reek of his long-unwashed body rising in her nostrils.

And in the coming weeks, as his confusion increased, Rosa knew that there was no more hope. On the nights of the last year of his life he would wander round the house like a man lost in the wilderness, searching for a place to lay down his head. Since he had always been a methodical and order-loving man, Rosa tried to discover a method behind his new sleeping arrangements, but was unable to find any logic or order in it. Joseph had lost count of the days, and even Friday nights, when the whole clan gathered in the house, failed to penetrate the fog in his mind and bring him to his sixth child's bed.

In those days, when her husband shuffled through the rooms seeking refuge in one of his children's beds, she would think painfully of that other Joseph, who would wake the children up on Saturday mornings, fish them out of bed, hold them in a viselike grip, and, as they wriggled in his arms like fish out of water, would rub his bristly chin on their soft cheeks. The children's faces would turn red with the rubbing, and with shrieks of pain and glee they would beg him for mercy. And she would remember how on Saturday afternoons he would put on his thick winter hat with its furry earflaps, lurch around on all fours, swaying like a drunk, and squat in a threatening position in the middle of the living room rug. And when the children gathered around with timid giggles, he would shake his head and swing the earflaps to and fro, and then he would make a very fierce face, growl angrily, and lie down on his back waving his hands and feet in the air. According to the well-known rules of the game, the children would tease him, raise his hat to reveal his always-sad face, and shriek delightedly as he bared his teeth in predatory growls. With shrill cries they would scatter and hide all over the house, and Joseph would lumber after them on all fours. Grinding his teeth menacingly, he would find them one by one, huddling in the corners or hiding under the beds, gather them all in his arms, and throw them in a squirming heap of heads, arms, and legs onto the double bed where Rosa was trying to take a nap. With a leap that shook the bedsprings he would join the pile of wriggling bodies, stealthily fondling his wife as he did so.

And when the children slid off the bed and ran out of the room with screams of pretended fear, he would whisper into her ear with a melancholy face and tearful eyes that he loved her, and that he didn't know what to do with all this happiness, which was too much for him and enough for four men like him. And Rosa would shut his mouth with her hand and tell him not to tempt the devil and bring troubles on their heads.

In days to come, when she thought of his tears and what he had said about happiness, she couldn't understand what had made him so happy, and why a happy man should cry.

In spite of his confusion and the havoc it wrought in his life,

Joseph continued scrupulously to wind the cuckoo clocks. Every evening, when the cuckoos announced the hour of seven with one voice, he would pass from one to another, confiding his sorrows to them, stroking their wooden wings, winding their springs, and preparing them for another day. When he was done he would search for a bed, and the next morning Rosa would find him with his left thumb stuck in his mouth and his right hand firmly gripping his member and squeezing it until his knuckles turned white. In those days Rosa's washing machine worked without stopping, boiling Angel's diapers and the sheets stained with Joseph's urine and semen.

And when they found him shuffling through the narrow neighborhood streets on an icy winter day, naked as the day he was born, with a gang of shouting children chasing him and throwing handfuls of gravel at him, the neighbors were unable to recognize the naked, incoherent creature as Rosa's husband—the tall, proud Joseph. Kind people took him to a shelter for the homeless, and since he went berserk and hit his benefactors, they strapped him to the iron bed with leather straps. In the file they opened for him there they described the circumstances in which he had been found and filed him under the heading "Anonymous."

In the few days he spent at the shelter, the cuckoos stayed inside their houses and the hours went by unmarked by their calls. For three days Rosa made the rounds of the police stations, the shelters, and the hospitals with a photograph of Joseph in better days, until Leslie-Shimon saw a current photograph of his father on the back page of the newspaper, with the caption: "Vagrant old man found. His family is requested to present themselves at the nearest police station." Joseph's eyes stared out of the photograph with a confused expression, and his mouth, with his thumb in it, drooped at the corners. Accompanied by her children and carrying Angel in her arms, Rosa found him in a vast hall full of iron beds, where the reek of unwashed bodies overcame the strong smell of disinfectant. His clothes were saturated with undistinguishable bodily fluids and his body was covered with bleeding insect bites. On every side she saw creatures resembling him, shapeless and lost: homeless new immigrants and foreign workers whose livers were eaten away and whose minds were blank and who had forgotten their names and whose breath stank of cheap industrial alcohol and rotting teeth. And next to them muddled old men with bewildered eyes in whom nobody took any interest and whose children ignored the weekly reminders sent them on the back pages of the newspapers.

Rosa took him home in Leslie-Shimon's car, lovingly bathed his body, dressed the wounds and cracks opening up in his fragile yellow skin, and put him to sleep in their big double bed. When she covered him with the blanket a glint of comprehension flashed in his eyes, and an expression of deathly terror appeared on his face. Like a young man he leaped out of bed and began to wander through the house with the familiar shuffling sound, winding the clocks and stroking the outstretched necks of the wooden cuckoos with his vein-knotted hands.

Already bowed beneath the burden of caring for Angel, Rosa now had to cope with another helpless creature who disturbed her rest and demanded her attention. When she fed Angel mashed vegetables, Joseph would appear in the kitchen and try to snatch the food from his baby daughter's mouth. Because of his teeth, which were falling out one by one, he was unable to eat solid food, and Rosa began to prepare exactly the same food for her daughter and her husband. For hours she would stand in front of the stove, stirring huge pots of boneless chicken, carrots, potatoes, baby zucchinis, and celery leaves. When everything was soft, she would empty the contents of the pot into the blender and purée it into a nourishing broth. After feeding the baby she would sit patiently with Joseph, spooning the purée into his mouth and wiping his chin with the kitchen towel tied around his neck until he notified her with a belch that he had had enough. Then he would look at her with a baffled expression, trying to identify his benefactor. Sometimes he would call her by her name, but more often he would call her by the name of their daughter Ruthie. And as his mind grew more and more muddled, he would also address her as Ruhama, her childhood friend, now a good-looking widow who lived in the building next door. In the days when Joseph was still a virile man, Rachelle had told her with a sour expression of commiseration that the neighbors said that he was having an affair with Ruhama. Rosa refused to listen, and to herself she said that it was all spiteful, jealous gossip, because her husband desired her every day and he couldn't possibly have the strength for another woman as well. Now, when she heard him pronounce her name, she remembered Ruhama's shifty looks and how she would turn on her heel and go into her house whenever she saw Rosa in the street. Suddenly there rose in her nostrils the cheap smell of jasmine perfume that would invade the house and brazenly usurp the delicate scent of his favorite lavender soap when Joseph opened the door. Again she saw the black, red, and blue marks on his shirt collars, and she understood that they came from makeup that didn't belong to her.

She began to suspect that those malicious rumors were true, and the anger seething venomously inside her constricted her throat in sudden hatred for her husband. And when he continued to call her by the name of her rival, she would slap his face and deprive him of his food until the whole house echoed with his despairing cries as he searched the rooms for his bowl. When he began to call for Ruhama one Friday in the presence of the children, Rosa asked them what he meant by it. As if in obedience to a plan agreed on in advance, they all held their tongues and ignored her question, and when she asked again, they made fun of her and said that she had always been suspicious, and asked her what she wanted of their poor old father now, when he wasn't capable of harming a fly. And when she remained alone in the kitchen, Dror, the most faithful and closest to her of them all, came up and whispered in her ear that he had heard his parents at home talking about Grandpa Joseph's love for a woman called Ruhama. Rosa clasped Dror to her ample bosom and rocked him as she wept tears of anger and jealousy for the minutes, hours, days, weeks, and months of love Joseph had stolen from her and given to another. And more than the betrayal itself, she was angry with him for not telling her, for he had always told her everything, because she was his best friend.

And when all her children went home the dam of her tears burst out again. In those moments of weeping, which added up to hours, she forgot all the good things they had shared and remembered only the bad: how he had seduced her that night and gone to bed with her when she was a frightened child of fourteen, how he had taken advantage of his influence over her and persuaded her to marry him. In her anger she blamed him for the fact that she had barely graduated from high school, and because of the children coming one after the other she had never acquired a profession. The tears turned to screams when she remembered all those nights when he told her he was at the cinema or Mousa's hut, but which he must have spent in bed with Ruhama.

At those moments Rosa was sure that he hadn't been satisfied with Ruhama and that he had had other women too. While she was left alone at night to look after the children, he had been out enjoying himself. But most of all Rosa cried for her present situation. Just when she needed him more than ever, her husband had vanished from her life, shirking his duties with the help of a senile disease he had succumbed to on purpose, and leaving her alone with a defective child. Full of self-pity, she thought of her wasted life and of the different life she could have had if only he hadn't seduced her that night when the war broke out. She wept until she had no tears left, and when Angel began to cry with hunger she wiped her eyes and dragged herself to the baby's crib, attentive to her every need.

And while she fixed her eyes on her husband with hard, accusing stares, his condition deteriorated. As dazed as if he had received a terrible blow to the head, he wandered round the house in his outsize diapers and refused to let her wash his body, which reeked of excrement and urine. He spat out the food she pushed into his mouth and looked at her in bewilderment, as if seeing her for the first time in his life, shouting in Italian, which had suddenly come back to him, and calling for Ruhama. And when she summoned the geriatric doctor to the house, he told her that there was nothing to be done, that Joseph's brain now resembled nothing so much as a piece of Swiss cheese, and that he had to be hospitalized before he harmed her or the baby. But Rosa refused and insisted that Joseph would leave her house only to be buried. And every night, before she put him to bed, she would change his soiled diapers, wipe his wrinkled skin with cotton soaked in olive oil, powder his slack behind bristling with the hairs that were once black and were now white, and look pityingly at his penis with its useless erections. After she tucked the diaper firmly round him she would say good-night and take her leave of him, thinking that this night might be his last with her. Then she would go and take care of Angel in exactly the same way.

On the last night of his life, when Rosa said good-night and took her leave of him as she did every night, he refused to go to sleep. He loosened the diaper round his loins and began to hobble round the house, dragging his emaciated legs from room to room with the diaper flapping between his legs like a dirty tail. Remembering what had happened before, Rosa locked and barred the door to prevent him from slipping out and wandering the streets of the town, and tried to guide him back to bed. But he eluded her grasp, and when she despaired of getting him back to his own bed, she put a mattress on the floor in her bedroom, coaxed him to lie down on it, and covered him with a blanket. He curled up and fell asleep immediately.

Rosa didn't get a wink of sleep all night, kept awake by the constant rubbing of his fingers, the snores escaping from his blocked nose, and the noisy sucking of his toothless mouth on his thumb. In the morning, when she saw that he was sleeping peacefully, she took pity on him and didn't wake him up for coffee.

It was only later, at midday, that she heard the silence. When she concentrated on the strange silence she realized that the cogwheels of the clocks had stopped turning, the pendulums had ceased their eternal swinging, and the cuckoos had forgotten to announce the hour. Alarmed, she hurried into the bedroom. With the blanket pulled up to his nose Joseph lay on his back while a swarm of buzzing, glittering, green flies hovered over his head like predatory birds. Rosa moved the blanket and saw his mouth. Around the thumb thrust between his lips, Joseph's mouth was open in a broad, frozen smile of bliss, as if he had been waiting for this moment all his life. She shook his shoulders and his body responded in cold, stiff obedience. She pulled down the blanket and found the fingers of his right hand firmly grasping the rigid member sticking out of his pajama pants like an autonomous being. His whole body was soaked in a pool of fresh semen, the biggest Rosa had ever seen, as if he had ejaculated for the last time in his life all the sperm that he might have produced if he had lived for many years to come.

"And in his death he permitted himself to laugh for all those years when he never laughed," she told her children when she informed them tearfully of his death.

After the undertakers took his body away, the women who worked in the purification chamber told her that at first they couldn't get his thumb out of his mouth, but when they succeeded in doing so the mouth stayed fixed in a broad smile, as if the dead man had been given wonderful news just before he gave up the ghost. And when they tried to pry his hand from his nether parts they were unable to do so, even when one of them gripped the hand and the other gripped the member and they pulled in opposite directions, until they were afraid of ripping his maleness off his body. Even the doctor they summoned to the purification chamber to free the hand from its grip said it was beyond his powers, for the hand and member were welded together into one inseparable flesh.

The women told her too that Joseph's smiling mouth and joviality had infected all those engaged in the sacred task of preparing the body for burial. Thanks to him the purification chamber had been pervaded by such a jolly atmosphere that they had even gone so far as to switch on the radio and listen to the famous cantor Melawski and his children's choir. And to the rhythm of the cantorial songs the undertakers scrubbed the dead man's body from top to toe and shot water into its orifices to clean it from the inside too, kicking up such a racket as they did so that the rabbis came in to scold them for their disrespect to the dead. But when they saw the blissful smile on Joseph's face and gazed appreciatively at the upright member gripped in his hand, they left the room with smiles as broad as his plastered on their faces. And when the water gushed out of his orifices and it was pure and clean and faintly scented with lavender soap, they plugged his rectum with cotton, stood him on his feet, poured nine cubits of water over him, and declared: "He is pure, he is pure, he is pure."

They laid him out on a stretcher in the funeral parlor with his scented body wrapped in winding clothes that had no pockets, for the dead take no property with them to the grave, and his private parts rose shamelessly in the air, lifting the sheet like a proud, defiant mast and causing astonishment and confusion in the mourners coming to pay him their last respects. Stifled giggles broke from the half-covered mouths of the young women as they pointed with trembling fingers at the object of their secret lusts. The young men joined in with admiring and appreciative exclamations, while the old men sighed in self-pity, recalling more virile days.

Struggling to overcome the noise of the crowd pressing up to the body to see the miracle of the erection, the rabbi read the prayers in a nasal voice, rushing through them with untoward haste and doing his best to avert his eyes from the miracle. After he was finished he sat down and asked in a weak voice for a glass of water to be brought to him before he fainted.

Although she was sunk in her grief, out of the corner of her eye Rosa saw her rival, Ruhama, with a scarf tied around her hair and dark glasses covering her eyes, only her eyebrows peeping over the frames in a black-penciled arch of perpetual surprise. Ruhama stood sobbing next to the stretcher, her thin fingers caressing the air above the erect member. Rosa wanted to pounce on her and beat her up in revenge for all those minutes, hours, and days of the great love that had been denied her and bestowed on her rival, but the strong hands of her sons held her down and prevented her from disgracing the family. Her eldest daughter, Ruthie, who couldn't bear to see Rosa's suffering, went up to Ruhama and whispered something in her ear, and she lowered her eyes and beat a hasty retreat, leaving behind her a cloying cloud of the cheap jasmine scent that was painfully familiar to Rosa.

The undertakers rushed him to his grave, trying to elude the crowds of demons that had materialized from the seed spilled in vain, been gathered into the womb of Lilith, and ejected from it in their present form. And when they cast him into the pit the erection towered up from the ground like an impudent plant wrapped in a winding sheet, mocking the gravediggers' attempts to cover it with earth. When all their attempts failed, they addressed the dead man, begged his pardon, turned him over with their strong hands, and buried him with his bottom up and his smiling face to the earth, and his penis digging into the ground as if he wanted to fertilize it.

With trembling knees, supported by her children, Rosa emerged from the cemetery gates, where a tall thin man dressed in a black suit waited for her, holding a glass of cold water on a purple plastic tray. Wordlessly he handed her the glass, watching her with expressionless fish eyes, as the Adam's apple sticking out of his skinny, pitted neck bobbed excitedly up and down in time to her sips. When she thanked him weakly he introduced himself as Yochai the Undertaker or, to be more precise, the director of the cemetery, offered her his condolences in his quiet voice, and blushingly added that if she ever required his assistance he would be happy to be of service to her. Rosa breathed in the smell of the fresh clods of earth mingled with that of crushed roots that rose from his clothes, and looked at the two deep furrows running down his cheeks on either side of his drooping mouth, giving him an expression appropriate to his calling. She nodded faintly to convey her thanks, promised to remember his offer, and got into Leslie-Shimon's car. Yochai hurried after her, tucked her black dress around her legs, and gently slammed the door behind her.

When she got home she asked her children to leave her to her grief, and with nobody to see, she changed the last sheet bearing the traces of her husband's semen. After a moment's hesitation, she folded the sheet into a little bundle, tied it up with a white silk ribbon, and buried it deep in the linen closet.

When she heard the baby's reedy cries, she went into Angel's room and told Ruthie that she would look after her. With a heavy heart she looked at the baby who was responsible for everything. Angel's birth, unintended and unexpected as it was, had upset her life and interfered with its smooth and blessed routine. Because of her one change had led to another and another until it had all ended in Joseph's death. With dry eyes and hard hands she fished the baby out of her crib, quickly and silently changed her diaper, fed her the food Ruthie had prepared for her in advance, and put her down to sleep. She did not make cooing noises as usual or stroke her body or kiss her hair. And as she handled her with fixed, practiced movements, the doll, Belle, who was sitting on the chest with her back to the wall, fixed her with her glassy blue eyes in a cold, hard stare that missed nothing. With an ominous shiver running down her spine Rosa decided to get rid of the doll, which was never really hers and which reminded her of the past. But when she was about to throw her into the trash can in the kitchen, Ruthie snatched her from her hands and scolded her: "Are you crazy? You want to throw such a beautiful doll into the trash? Wait till the baby grows up, and she can play with it." And without asking Rosa she put her on top of the wardrobe.

During the seven days of mourning Rosa saw him winding the cuckoo clocks at exactly seven o'clock every evening. But nevertheless the cuckoos failed to utter their cries, and during the whole of the mourning period they stayed shut up in their little houses. When she noticed that the pendulums too were still, she told Peretz the Cabalist, who had heard of Joseph's death and hurried by to offer his condolences, taking the opportunity to inspect the delights of her body at the same time. Weighing her heavy breasts pressing against the bodice of her mourning dress with caressing eyes, and peeking through the mourner's tear at the neckline, he was happy to explain that for seven days the soul of the dead man hovered in the air of the house of mourning. He would see his family and the condolence callers and try to perform necessary chores in the house. Only after the mourning period was over did the soul leave the house and turn to its affairs in the next world. Once she had heard this explanation from the lips of the cabalist, Rosa was able to tell him how after he wound the clocks Joseph would sit next to her and mock the mourners, curse his children, especially Angel, and stick his hands into the tear in her dress.

Peretz's face grew grave, and he stared into her eyes. "You shouldn't let him occupy your thoughts all the time," he said. "It's only natural for you think about him now, but you should stop it as soon as possible. Constant brooding about the dead harms the living in the end." And he added that in order to get rid of her thoughts about the dead man she had to write Joseph's name on a piece of paper and bury it in the ground close to the threshold of the house. Then she had to take a little rainwater, sprinkle it outside the house, and say: "Just as this water is poured out, so all thoughts of Joseph will depart from me."

Although she knew that she would never do it, she promised Peretz to obey his instructions after Joseph had been dead for a month. During the week of mourning, when his spirit was wandering round the house, before she went to sleep, Rosa would murmur that she forgave him and invite him to join her in bed. In order not to waste precious time Joseph would jump in next to her at once, making the bed bounce merrily, and clasp her from behind in the familiar embrace. As soon as she felt his hands wandering over her body, his tongue poking into her ear, and his member thrusting inside her, she would forgive him for Ruhama, and wake up with him to a morning of love. And when she was asked the meaning of the black rings round her eyes, she would tell her children with a sigh that she hadn't slept a wink all night, she missed their father so much. The marks of the love bites on her neck she covered with a scarf, only allowing herself to delight in the sight of these souvenirs of his passion in the privacy of the bathroom when she bathed.

A month after he left the house she woke from a light sleep early in the morning to the sound of clear and unfamiliar laughter echoing in the room like the delicate chiming of glass bells. She sat up in bed and looked for the source of the sound. She groped her way to Angels crib, and found the baby who had never smiled once since the day she was born, lying on her back looking at a gray crow that was tapping on the windowpane with its beak, as if begging for food, and laughing shrilly. With tears in her eyes Rosa embraced the laughing baby. That morning, long before the alarm clocks went off in her children's houses, all seven of them woke up to the ringing of their telephones and the sound of their little sister laughing on the other end of the line.

"Angel's laughing." Rosa spread the good news through the neighborhood. "She's laughing. She's going to be all right."

"We'll still show those doctors," she said to Dror when he came that evening to help her give his aunt a bath.

"I never doubted it for a minute," he replied. "She's laughing, and she'll talk too, and apart from that she'll be the prettiest girl in the country."

ten

PORTRAIT OF A HUSBAND

From the day she buried her husband, Rosa abandoned her daily routine and began to neglect her appearance, the house, and Angel. She did only what was strictly necessary. She fed the baby and changed her, watered the plants, bought the groceries, met Rachelle for afternoon chats, and all the time she felt a constriction in her throat that made it difficult for her to breathe. She spent hours doing nothing, her dress stained, her hair greasy, the white roots exposed, and her nail polish chipped. Every evening she passed through the rooms, rummaging in the children's beds and searching for traces of Joseph, for his smell and the prints of his body. And when the longings grew unbearable, she would go to the linen cupboard, carefully remove the stained sheet, rub the fabric between her fingers, and with quivering nostrils breathe in her husband's smell.

She especially missed the calls of the wooden cuckoos popping out of their little houses and punctually announcing the hour, and one day in a fit of longing she tried to get them back on course by winding the steel springs with the tiny iron keys. But, loyal to their original master, the birds stubbornly refused to cooperate, and as if on purpose to confuse her, they began popping out unexpectedly at all hours of the night and day, filling the house with a deafening chorus of rising and falling cries that startled Angel from her sleep and made her burst into nervous tears. In despair Rosa decided to leave them alone, but once in a while, when she couldn't bear the silence, she would open the little portholes and peek with one eye at the lifeless birds. And they would stretch their drooping necks and greet her with a single weak, hoarse cuckoo cry.

One long, lonely night she began to hear a nibbling, gnawing sound, and she had no idea what it could be, until a few days later she found a little pile of sawdust at the foot of the oldest clock in the house. One week later she found a similar pile under the clock next to it, and before long her once spotless house was full of yellow sawdust floating through the air, covering the furniture in a layer of pollenlike powder, seeping into the mattresses, and parching her throat. Suspecting the cuckoos, she opened their little portholes and discovered hollow, half-eaten wooden birds too desiccated to greet her with even the weakest of cries. Soon the birds and wooden clocks containing them were completely eaten away by the strong jaws of invisible creatures that Rosa never succeeded in seeing eye to eye, leaving behind them complicated mechanisms of wheels and cogs, pendulums, springs, and clock faces hanging on the walls, to the astonishment of all her visitors.

Together with the disappearance of the cuckoo clocks, the tradition of family dinners on Friday nights vanished too, and one day she found herself betraying Tzadok in the old corner grocery store and doing her shopping in the neighborhood minimart. Ready-made junk food, frozen pizzas, industrial kebabs, veggieburgers, and baby food packed in little glass jars with huge smiles plastered over plump babies' faces on their labels began to fill her kitchen. And canned food, dry crackers, and all kinds of sweets that had never made their appearance in her home before began to fill her pantry shelves.

On the desolate evenings, after the seven daily telephone calls to her seven children, she would sit with Angel, open the family photograph album, show her her father, and stroke the pictures of Joseph looking out at her from his photographs as he bathed in the hot springs of Ein Gedi, stood in front of David's Citadel, sipped beer in Jaffa port, and played with his grandchildren. Angel would gaze at the strange face looking out at her and try to make her presence unfelt, as if she sensed that he had left them because of her. At those moments Rosa did not spare her daughter, and in a voice mingling love, reproach, and righteousness she would say: "Until you arrived everything ran like clockwork. From the day you came you turned my life upside down."

Dror came to visit often, bringing them a few moments of happiness. He would read Angel stories, and she would respond with her merry chiming laugh, he would play horsie with her like Grandpa Joseph used to play with him, try to teach her to clap her hands, bathe her, and put her to bed. When he left and silence descended on the house again, Rosa would go to bed and try to banish harsh thoughts of Angel and how her life had changed from the moment she was born.

In the first year after Joseph died Rosa went regularly to visit his grave. Once a month, at twilight, in an impressive ceremony she would go up to the cemetery with Leslie-Shimon and drive along the paths winding between the silent, crowded tombstones. And when they arrived Leslie-Shimon would place a little stone on the tomb, and Rosa would ask him to leave her alone to commune with his father and come back for her in an hour's time. Ignoring Yochai the Undertaker, who followed her with his expressionless eyes, she would look around to make sure that there was nobody else there. Then she would pour the bottle of water she had brought with her over her husband's tombstone, sweep away the pine needles that had fallen on it, and clean the black lead letters with a toothbrush. After she had finished tending the grave she would prune the lavender bushes planted around it, and arrange the little stones placed on top of it in an order of her own, in a long straight line like a column of soldiers on parade. After inspecting her work she would look around again, and quickly pull down her panties, lift up her dress, sit down with her bare buttocks on the damp tombstone and inform her husband that she had finished cleaning and he could come out now to smell her secret places.

Trembling with excitement Yochai the Undertaker would be waiting for her at the cemetery exit, fawningly offer her a glass of cold water, and watch her full lips as they swallowed the water, his Adam's apple bobbing up and down in time to her sips. Without a word of thanks Rosa would return the empty glass, and he would grip it with his spidery fingers, and with a vigorous sweep of his arm, as if they were in the middle of a bustling city or deep jungle, he would make way for her, conduct her to Leslie-Shimon's car, and open the door for her. After the car had disappeared from view, he would hurry to Joseph's grave. He would stand there for a long time stroking the washed stone saturated with her smell and then raise his transparent fingers to his nose to sniff them, his eyes darting around suspiciously for fear that the dead man would lift the gravestone with his skeletal hands, pounce on him, and wring his vein-roped neck. And when the excitement overcame his skinny body and his legs gave way beneath him, he would sit down heavily on Joseph's tombstone as if to share the charms of his wife's body with him.

Month after month she would go up to the cemetery and perform her rites, until her backside froze in the cold wind of the autumn evenings in Jerusalem. In the long hours she spent there she never succeeded in feeling Joseph's presence. Sometimes she would try to explain this failure by saying to herself that the worms had already eaten his flesh, that his bones had turned to dust, and that he had vanished as if he had never existed. And a body that had vanished, that no longer had any wishes or desires of its own, could not touch her, not even intangibly. Disconsolately she would return home, get into bed earlier than usual, and ignore Angel's existence, as if she were to blame for ruining her life.

A year had passed since Joseph's death, and with the blurring of his presence in the house and the weakening of his smell on the sheet, Rosa decided that she had to do something to preserve his memory. After putting Angel to bed, she emptied all the drawers and shoeboxes in which she kept the family photographs and paged through all the albums until she found the best picture of her husband, the wedding photo taken in Nissim's studio attached to Fruma's brassiere and corset salon, where her many-layered wedding gown had been made. The photograph, taken against a backdrop of red autumn foliage, showed his melancholy countenance split by a gaping mouth, as if he were trying without success to smile. With a sharp scissors she cut him out of the photo and the next day she went round to the modern photography studio in the new mall next to her house, and asked them to enlarge Joseph's face to poster size.

When the enlargement was ready her husband's face looked at her in faded colors with his mouth wide open as if threatening to swallow her up. Under Rosa's scrutiny the young assistant rolled the picture up and slipped it into a thick cardboard tube. From there she went to Tzarfati's picture framers, which was considered the best in town. She looked round at the empty frames hanging on the walls and staring at her with hollow looks, and asked Tzarfati to show her his most expensive frames. A pile of wooden and plastic frames in all shapes and colors rose before her. With a disdainful glance she rejected them all. "My Joseph," she was heard to say, "deserves the best, the finest, and most expensive frame there is."

As she left the shop, cradling the picture in its cardboard tube in her arms, she heard Tzarfati panting behind her. "There's one more frame," he said, "a frame that once held an oil painting from the Renaissance. It was stolen from a museum in Florence," he explained apologetically, as if he had committed the crime himself. "I bought the frame for a lot of money, and I've been looking for a suitable picture ever since." Since Rosa was looking for the most expensive frame on the market, he added, he could offer it to her at the price he had paid for it. Rosa retraced her footsteps, curious to see this prize, and Tzarfati led her into the depths of the shop. With a ceremonious flourish he pulled out the frame, which illuminated the darkness of the shop and dazzled her eyes with its lustrous gold. The frame was made of heavy wood covered with plaster carved in the shapes of flowers and musical instruments and painted shining gold. On the spot she told him that this was the frame she had dreamed of, and in order to reduce the price she pointed out places where the gilt was peeling off, exposing the white plaster underneath it. Eager to close the deal, the framer promised her that he would restore it with all the artistry at his command, cover the white spots, and make it look like new. When she asked him how much it would cost he mentioned the sum in a timid stammer, as if afraid that she would change her mind. But she didn't blink an eye, even though the sum came close to her entire widow's pension for a year. "I have seven working children," she calculated, "and they'll all join forces to preserve their father's memory." She handed over the picture, gave him a deposit in advance, and asked him to let her know when to come and pick it up.

In the following weeks she visited the framer regularly to inquire how the work was going, and when he called to say that it was ready, she asked Leslie-Shimon to go and pick it up in his car. For a week Rosa worshiped at the shrine of the picture as it leaned against the wall in the living room covered with a white sheet, and then she decided to hold a ceremony in honor of its hanging. She postponed the ceremony for another week, so that it would coincide with Angel's second birthday.

In honor of the occasion she worked all day in the kitchen, making a birthday cake, almond cookies, and marzipan balls, and in the evening all the children and grandchildren gathered at the house. After they had raised Angel three times on a chair and wished her health, happiness, and growth, they all turned to the huge picture leaning against the wall. A sigh of admiration broke from their lips as the sheet was removed. Feeling the carved gilt flowers and musical instruments with their fingers and stroking their father's face behind the protective glass they told Rosa that they had never seen such a beautiful frame in their lives. In a joint effort Leslie-Shimon and Jackie-Ya'akov held the heavy picture up on the bedroom wall, moving it up and down, to the right and left, according to Rosa's instructions. After lengthy consultations with the rest of the family, she finally decided on a spot directly opposite her bed, enabling her to see her dead husband every night before she fell asleep, wish him good-night, and wake up with him in the morning.

That night, when she curled up in bed, Rosa looked at Joseph. His teeth bared in a grimace of a smile, his eyes looked back at her lovingly, reflecting the golden light spilling onto him from the frame. "Good-night," she whispered, blew him a kiss, and switched off the light.

In the morning she woke up with a feeling that she wasn't alone. Apprehensively she opened her eyes and encountered Joseph hanging opposite her and looking at her with the warm, familiar expression in his eyes glittering through the glass. It was the same look into which the waking Rosa had been sucked every morning of her married life, when he leaned over her and examined her face framed in her golden hair lying loose on the pillow, until he abandoned their conjugal bed with Angel's birth.

That morning was Angel's first day at the nursery school for children with special needs. Filled with emotion, Rosa waited with Angel in her arms for the van to take her to the day care center. When the door of the minibus slid open, she climbed in and her eyes fell on the handicapped children crowded on the seats and sitting in their wheelchairs. Some of them were as short as Angel, but unlike her beautiful blond child, some of them had flattened faces, gray skins, round eyes protruding from their sockets, dark tongues lolling from their mouths, and spittle dribbling onto the bibs tied round their necks. Children with thin straight hair stared at her with slanting eyes and greeted the new little girl with broken words jumbled together in incoherent sentences. Some of the children were strapped into their wheelchairs, their eyes staring blankly and their arms and legs twitching uncontrollably.

Rosa looked pityingly at the range of disabilities surrounding her and parted tearfully from Angel, who sat among them like a budding flower whose petals had not yet opened. When she got home she went into the bathroom and in order to calm herself and fill the empty hours stretching ahead of her, she ran a hot bath, poured in oil of rosemary, took the lavender soap, and lay there for a long time with the oily water lapping her body and smoothing her skin. She paid special attention to her private parts, viciously uprooting the white hairs growing in her bush with a tweezer, scrubbing herself thoroughly down there with the lavender soap, and washing inside too. She inspected the scar of the operation running down her stomach, puckering the flesh and cutting deeply into it. She rubbed body lotion into the scar, selected her best dress, put it on, and went down to visit her friend Rachelle.

eleven

THE DANCING SCHOOL

"Blessed be he who revives the dead." Rachelle greeted Rosa warmly, made her coffee, offered her almond cookies, and tried to talk to her about the future. "And in order to get ready for life, you're coming with me now to a course in sixties' dancing," she said, and told her about the fantastic teacher whose fame had spread throughout the city and with whom all the women were in love, who had opened a studio in the shelter of a building nearby, where he taught women of their age to dance, bringing the color back to their cheeks and giving them a new appetite for life. "The time has come for you to enjoy yourself," she said. "While the whole country was having fun, dancing, eating, and drinking, you were bearing babies, washing diapers, cooking, and waiting for your husband to come home."

"But I've never danced in my life." With the stab of an old insult, Rosa remembered all the times she had stood leaning against the walls of the school gymnasium watching the folk dances, while all her slender classmates twirled with enviable lightness in the arms of the boys. But nobody volunteered to lift her up and spin her round. Once there was a boy who loved her, who was brave and determined and wanted to prove his strength in front of everyone and impress her, and he invited her to dance with him. But when all the boys swung their partners lightly in the air, his legs buckled beneath her weight and she found herself lying on top of him on the floor, to shrieks of laughter from all those present in the hall.

"The situation has changed," snapped Rachelle, as if she had read her thoughts. "We don't dance folk dances, and nobody has to lift you up in the air." And so saying she dragged her off to the studio in the air raid shelter.

With sounds of joy the teacher welcomed them at the door, but as soon as his eyes fell on Rosa he opened them wide and fell silent.

"You?" he whispered when he recovered his breath.

"You?" she asked, with a blush rising to her cheeks and the intoxicating, tangy smell of freshly picked oranges rising in her nose.

"Me," he went on whispering, as if the two of them were alone in the room.

Rosa recovered first, and looked down at him. He was very short, as if he had stopped growing since she had seen him last, his body was slender, and his thin hair was dyed black and carefully combed and plastered to his head with liberally applied gel, exposing strips of pink scalp and tied back in a pony tail. He couldn't take his beady black eyes off her, and he stretched his lips in a broad smile that raised his narrow black mustache above his even white teeth. As he came closer his body, clad in a purple velvet suit and a red bow tie, gave off a strong smell of sweet orange-blossom scent. In her embarrassment Rosa lowered her eyes to the concrete floor, where they were greeted by the sight of little patent leather shoes that would have fit her ten-year-old grandson Dror.

At that moment Rosa felt a weight on her chest and a weakness in her legs, and a wave of heat engulfed her body and broke out in beads of sweat on her face. She was sure that everyone could see how she longed to free herself of her clothes, rip off his velvet suit, and roll naked with him on the shabby carpet adorning the concrete floor. She closed her eyes and leaned against the wall, praying that nobody would sense what was happening inside her.

"And where have you been hiding your beautiful friend all this time?" he said to Rachelle when he recovered, and slapped her lightly on her butt in pretended rebuke.

"This month she concluded the year of mourning for her husband," replied Rachelle, giving her friend a questioning, reproachful look out of the corner of her eye. "She loved him very much—" she lowered her voice— "and refused to be comforted, and that's why I brought her here."

"Wonderful, you did the right thing!" he crowed, and immediately restrained himself and said to Rosa: "I'm sorry for your loss." But he couldn't keep the happiness out of his voice as he repeated his condolences and went on to promise that he was going to bring some joy into her life.

Wet with perspiration Rosa stepped beside Shraga with a train of women following her every movement through narrowed eyes, inspecting the damp stains spreading under her armpits, and whispering spitefully, loud enough for them both to hear: "Poor thing, she's having a hot flush." Proudly Shraga showed her his kingdom, decorated with vases full of plastic roses in glaring shades of red and yellow, and posters of cool green hills with red-roofed wooden cabins clinging to their sides. He laughed a lot and demonstrated for her benefit his most graceful steps, the ones he kept for special occasions such as competitions and performances under the patronage of the mayor.

Rachelle stuck close to her side, watching her eyes as they looked at Shraga, and counting her smiles in response to his. And when she could no longer bear her suffering she hissed in her ear: "All the women here are crazy about him; try not to monopolize his attention or you'll have them all up in arms against you and nobody in the neighborhood will talk to you." And Rosa replied with a forced smile: "Don't be silly. Look how small he is next to me." And she hoped with all her heart that he would choose her as his partner when they danced.

The worn-out women with their sagging breasts and heavy thighs, dressed in their best and brightest clothes, their swollen feet crammed into their narrowest and pointiest shoes, arranged themselves in pairs. Rosa found herself looking shyly at the tips of her gigantic shoes as Shraga approached her with light, dancing steps and invited her to partner him. "But I've just started," she stammered as the blush spread over her face, climbed to the roots of her hair, and made her ears blaze. "I don't know how to dance," she whispered. "Don't you remember?"

"With Shraga you'll know," he promised her. Resolutely he clasped her around her thick waist, and under the languishing looks of the women he demonstrated with her the stylish steps on Slow to the strains of Frank Sinatra's crooning voice pouring in soft, sweet waves into the air raid shelter. Rosa's feet, unpracticed in the art of dance, stumbled and tripped, but he held her with a strength surprising in someone of his size, and guided her through the steps with his eyes staring straight into the cleavage of her bosom.

When she felt the heat spreading through her body again and the familiar throbbing in her nether parts, Rosa knew that she was betraying Joseph. She hurried to banish the vain thought from her mind and tried to dwell on all her old resentments against him. She thought of the way he had chased Shraga out of town and of how, but for him, she might have married the love of her youth and changed her destiny. And when she had exhausted her anger against Joseph she felt calmer. Surrendering herself to Shraga's arms and the warmth of his body penetrating her dress, she flared her nostrils and basked without guilt in the scent of orange blossom wafting from him.

On the way home Rachelle didn't say a word. With a stony face she said good-bye, went into her apartment, and slammed the door behind her. Rosa climbed to the next floor and as she mounted the stairs she sniffed her fingertips and luxuriated again in the intoxicating scent of her childhood love.

The next day Hannah, Rachelle's former sister-in-law, dropped in to visit Rosa as if by chance, and told her that all the women of the dancing class were furious with her for robbing them of their heartthrob after all the loving attentions they had showered on him from the day he opened his studio in the neighborhood.

Bracha, Baruch the Barber's wife, Hannah told her, was in charge of polishing his shoes. Drora, the greengrocer's wife, ironed his shirts and every evening made him a salad of the freshest vegetables she could spirit away from the shop, chopped into the tiniest pieces. Rachelle, she told her with a sneer, washed his underclothes for him, and before she washed them she sniffed his underpants and socks and almost fainted with the pleasure of it. Yardena, the thirty-year-old spinster, would wake him up in the morning with coffee, *bourekas*, and *haminos*, and strip the blanket off the bed to air, no doubt because he slept in the nude. Nehama would go straight to the bathroom to scrub his back for him, so that it wouldn't be blemished with pimples, and droves of women would call him up dozens of times a day to whisper lewd words of seduction in his ear.

"Do you wonder that they all hate you now?" she asked after concluding the graphic descriptions that brought a deep blush to Rosa's face.

Later that day Rosa knocked on Rachelle's door with a plate of the stuffed cookies she had learned to bake from the late Shoshana Zilka. Her friend took the conciliatory offering from her with a frozen face.

"What did he want of you? Why was he all over you like that?"

she asked, her strong teeth chewing the filling of peanuts and pistachio nuts inside the cookies.

"Don't you remember Shraga?" Rosa replied with a question.

"Where am I supposed to remember him from?"

"He was in our class at school. I can't believe that you don't remember him. You heard the story about me and him from Ruthie, and you told your mother, and she told my mother, until in the end it got to Joseph," said Rosa, trying to refresh the memory of her friend who had caused their separation so many years ago. And when her friend insisted that she didn't remember, Rosa repeated that he had been he had been in their class throughout primary school, and said that ever since first grade they had loved each other and asked to sit on the same bench, and if the teacher refused Shraga would organize the whole class to go on strike. "Because even though he was so small"— she demonstrated his size between her forefinger and thumb— "he had a lot of power over the teachers and the pupils." Then she told her about the love letters he wrote her on the backs of his exercise books, and how he would wait every night under her window until she closed the shutter and switched off the light. And when she saw Rachelle's eyes widening, she added quickly, before she could regret it, that once he had kissed her on the lips, pushed his tongue between her teeth, and vowed that he would marry her and only her. With the taste of oranges on her lips, she told Rachelle that although she had kissed Joseph thousands of times, she had never forgotten that first kiss and the sweetness of its taste.

Rosa was sure that Rachelle remembered the story, but was pretending to have forgotten it because she was indirectly responsible for their separation. So she added that ever since they had been so cruelly torn apart she had thought of him every night with an aching body, until she married Joseph. And even after her marriage, the pain would sometimes return to remind her of Shraga, especially at the beginning of winter, when the first fresh oranges arrived at the greengrocers', and their scent overpowered every other smell.

Rachelle listened to her with glassy eyes, poured her another cup of coffee, and as if the story had made no impression on her, said in a rebuking tone: "You should know that Shraga has never danced with one partner for the whole lesson before. He always changes partners so that we all have a turn to dance with him. We didn't like the way he tried to come on to you, especially in view of the fact that you were recently widowed. We didn't understand why he picked you, of all people, and perhaps it would be better if you didn't come back to the class, because it isn't fair to the other women who want to dance with him too."

But Rosa did go back to the dancing lessons. After a few imploring telephone calls from Shraga, she shampooed her hair and set it in elaborate curls, put on the green dress with the purple sequins she had worn to Scarlett-Mazel's wedding, and the patent leather shoes she had bought for the Passover before Joseph's death, and set out for Shraga's studio. But this time, as he had promised, she was the only student there.

"Couple dancing is something you have to learn, because you're not dancing alone, you're dependent on your partner and you need to be in perfect coordination with him," he explained.

Then he taught her how to take the floor with her partner in as stately a manner as if she were a bride dancing with her groom, alone on the floor under the critical eyes of all the wedding guests. As the lessons progressed, he told her that since she looked like a princess, he recommended the waltz. And then he explained to her that for dramatic dancers he recommended the tango, which had been born in flames more than a hundred years ago in Argentina. To the sensuous he taught the rumba; to the romantic, whose natural rhythm was quick, the salsa; and with the naughty ones he danced rock and roll and the cha-cha.

She soon learned to spin and twirl with him in all the different dances. She was a princess in the waltz, dramatic in the tango, naughty in the cha-cha, romantic in the salsa, and sensuous in the rumba. And when she attained the status of an advanced student, he told her that the way you danced with your partner reflected your relationship with him: "When I see a couple dancing I know who rules the roost at home." Therefore he advised her always to allow the man to lead, because it was up to the man to determine the rhythm and the tone. And when the lesson was over and he accompanied her home, he would tell her about his life on the way, how he had gone to France, studied dancing, and returned to Israel with a teacher's diploma. And he told her too about the women who came to the studio in the shelter, and how the classes with him served them as a refuge from their hard lives and their boring daily chores, and how he paid each of them special, personal attention, and treated her like a fairy-tale princess and the one and only woman in his life. "I give them a romantic illusion and an hour's escape from their husbands and their boring lives, and it's no wonder that they're all in love with me and willing to do anything for me." Rosa listened and she knew in her heart that she was the princess; she was his one and only.

After a month he asked her to go out for coffee with him. Rosa would never forget that first date with Shraga. For a long time he debated which café they should go to, Café Nava or Café Atara in the city center, or perhaps they should choose one of the new, modern cafés that had opened in Emek-Refaim Street in the German Colony. In her ignorance and wish to please him she made the mistake of saying generously that it made no difference to her where they went, and that he should decide. Shraga's face fell, his already short stature shrank, and he looked like a man forced at gunpoint to dance an unfamiliar dance in front of a rowdy, hostile audience. At that moment she realized that it was only in his basement studio that Shraga took the lead, and only there that he determined the rhythm and the tone. When he emerged into the outside world, she had to take charge.

With feelings of pity that grew so intense they almost choked her, she saved him from his sufferings and announced decisively that they would go to the new café in the German Colony. Shraga's face lit up immediately, as if her decision had removed a heavy weight from his heart. In order to avoid any further embarrassments that might ruin the evening she had been looking forward to so much, she informed him that they would walk to the café. As soon as he emerged from his safe shelter, Shraga, so eloquent and entertaining in his studio, seemed to lose his powers of speech. They walked to the café in silence.

When she told Rachelle about it later, she said that although they were both looking forward to sitting in the café, they advanced toward it at a tired snail's pace.

"I'm not surprised," Rachelle said stiffly. "You walked slowly because you wanted to make it last longer." Then she explained to her that couples in love try to make their moments together last as long as possible, so that they can chew them over and savor them afterward.

And when she pressed Rosa to tell her more, Rosa hesitated for a moment before saying: "You won't believe what he talked about when he finally opened his mouth, next to the Greek Colony."

"What?"

"Politics and the state of the economy. And when we reached the café at last, he stayed on the same subject and talked about inflation, unemployment, interest rates, and the foreign exchange rate."

"Are you joking?" exclaimed Rachelle and burst out laughing.

"Believe me, politics and economics."

After hours of solitary brooding about the topic of conversation between Rosa and Shraga on their first date, Rachelle came to a conclusion and ran triumphantly upstairs to Rosa.

"I understand!" she cried with the enthusiasm of discovery. "Shraga wanted to talk to you about some significant and serious subject. And politics and economics was all he could come up with. Otherwise he would probably have sat opposite you eating cake and not saying a word."

"But I wanted him to talk to me about other things," said Rosa in a spoiled voice. "About life, love, about the future," she added and blushed, as if wishing she could take the words back. "And what did he talk to me about? Politics and economics. The things that should have been said went unsaid."

"Be patient," said Rachelle. "Shraga will still say the things you want to hear."

And as if Rachelle had been granted the gift of prophecy, Shraga proved her words and made her prediction come true. A week later he took Rosa to a restaurant, and even though she didn't enjoy the food, finding the stuffed vegetables tasteless and the lamb dry, she liked the idea that somebody else would wash the dishes and loved talking to Shraga, whose tongue had been loosened by an excess of red wine. He wanted to hear about her life. He asked about each of her children, wept when she told him about Angel, and expressed sympathy and amusement when he heard the manner of Joseph's death. When she fell silent, he looked deep into her eyes, caressed her face with his eyes, and said: "I have nothing to tell. I never got married, and I never had children. I sat and waited for you to come back to me."

After three months of flowers, gifts, cafés, and slow dancing in the basement studio, as they sat down to rest on a wooden bench in the gardens of Elisheva House, he asked her to marry him.

"And you should know," he added after the proposal that made Rosa's knees turn to water, "that you owe me. First because we promised each other, and second, because of you I never learned a thing in all those years that I sat next to you in school."

Rosa opened her eyes wide in astonishment.

"Why not?" she asked.

"I couldn't concentrate," he said with lowered eyes. "Don't you remember? I couldn't stop stroking your legs under the desk. Four hours a day, six days a week, twenty-six days a month, ten months a year, for eight whole years."

"I don't remember," she replied, wondering how such an important memory had escaped her.

"How's that possible? For eight years I stroked your legs under your skirt and you don't remember? When I took a rest because my hand was tired, you would kick me under the desk. In the first grade you kicked me with those boots you had, the red ones with the laces, and in the end, in the eighth grade, with the patent leather pumps with the pointed toes. My legs were black and blue from all those kicks. And apart from that, a minute ago I proposed marriage to you and you haven't answered me yet."

Full of excitement, Rosa went home, trying without success to remember the shoes Shraga had mentioned. In the evening she called all her children, and they hurried to her house for an emergency meeting. The girls were in favor of the marriage, and the boys were opposed to it. And when she saw that they were incapable of coming to an agreement, she asked them to leave her.

That night she informed her dead husband of her intended marriage. Joseph's eyes narrowed in alarm and his grimace of a smile froze on his lips in astonishment. Ignoring his knocks on the glass imprisoning him, Rosa switched off the bedside light, said good-night to him, curled up in bed, and dreamed of Shraga.

The next morning she avoided Joseph's betrayed, offended looks, and after sending Angel to her special day care, she put on her best dress and set off for the basement studio to reply in the affirmative to Shraga's marriage proposal. She found him sitting erect on a chair that had been upholstered in green velvet about twenty years before. When her eyes grew accustomed to the dim light they discovered gilded paper chains hanging from the ceiling and fluttering lightly and festively above her head.

"I was waiting for you," said Shraga. With regal stateliness he rose to his feet and put his arm around her waist.

There was no need for Rosa to put her answer into words. With a dancer's grace Shraga rose to the tips of his toes, bent her neck a little, and pressed an intrusive kiss on her lips, a kiss that was surprisingly similar to that first kiss in the school gymnasium, where the air was full of the smell of sweaty adolescent bodies and the faint, rubbery smell of new gym shoes. And as if Joseph had never existed, Rosa parted her lips, rolled her tongue round inside his mouth, sucked his lips as if they had always been hers, and smelled the sweet scent of oranges that she had dreamed of all her life, even though Joseph's smell of nicotine mingled with lavender had tried to banish it from her memory.

twelve

LOVE TO THE STEPS OF A DANCE

On the night before her wedding Rosa had an unexpected visit. Her mother came to her for the first time since she had departed for a better world. Rosa woke to the painfully familiar sounds of rubbing, sighs, and stifled cries rising from her pillow, and she sat up heavily in bed to find her mother next to her in a gleaming white nightgown. And as if she had not gone to her rest so many years ago, she opened her toothless mouth and unburdened her heart: "You must cancel this wedding. What do you need it for? Take an example from me. When your father died and I was left alone, it never occurred to me to look for someone else, even though I was far younger than you and I only had one child. And besides, it will upset Joseph. He's already told me that he intends to avenge himself and make your life a misery. You can still change your mind. What do you need trouble for? And think of Angel. Instead of concentrating on her and looking after her, you'll have to look after a strange man. And what if he doesn't love the child and makes you both unhappy?" Angela had her say, and when she realized that her words were falling on deaf ears, she vanished into thin air.

In the morning Rosa looked at her mother's white porcelain teeth, parted in a dazzling smile in the glass jar, and she wasn't sure if she had really seen her or if it had been a dream. In order to be on the safe side, she took the glass jar, and instead of brushing the dentures as she did religiously every morning, she threw out the water and hid the jar together with the teeth under the sink in the cupboard where she kept the cleaning agents. Her mother's warnings came back to echo in her ears when she removed the diamond-studded wedding ring she had received from Joseph in honor of their silver anniversary, hid it away in her bedside cupboard, and looked for a long time at her naked finger, where a band of white skin remained as a souvenir of her first husband. Then she tried on the ring Shraga had bought her and thought happily of the promise of the new life awaiting her, and when she took it off again and put it away in its box, the band of white skin looked at her accusingly, reminding her of forgotten things and rebuking her for the happiness she was demanding for herself.

Shraga, who was getting married for the first time, insisted on a big wedding with a lot of guests. And when Rosa hesitated as to what to wear, thinking it inappropriate for a woman in the prime of life marrying her second husband to wear white like a young bride, he overrode her objections and demanded that she wear a white wedding dress.

Reveling in the opportunity to deck herself out in a bridal gown for the second time in her life, Rosa got into Leslie-Shimon's car, squeezing in next to Ruthie, who was holding Angel on her lap. Rosa stroked the little girl's hair, straightened her tiny ruffled dress, made to match her mother's, and rubbed an invisible spot on her white doll's shoes. Excited by her new shoes Angel waved her little legs and kicked lightly at her mother's knees. Afraid of dirtying her dress, Rosa asked her to stop, and when she failed to obey her, she gripped her feet firmly in her hands. Shrieking and kicking, the little girl tried to free her legs, but Rosa refused to relax her grip. And thus she arrived exhausted and flustered at the wedding hall, her lacy knees covered with tiny gray footprints and Angel's screams echoing in her ears.

Large, solid, and determined, she stood next to Shraga under the wedding canopy, with Dror holding the train of her wedding dress, which was made of layers of gleaming ivory silk. With a sweet swooning sensation making her feel giddy and sending shivers of pleasure through her flesh, she imagined what was waiting for her at home in bed, in Shraga's eager arms.

From the heights of her tall body she looked down lovingly at her little bridegroom, encased in a suit whose size would have been more suitable for a bar mitzvah boy. Shraga stood on tiptoe and stretched up his arms in order to reach her veil and lift it from her face. Rosa lowered her eyes and looked at her husband leaping up in front of her. Then she opened her arms, embraced him tightly, and lifted him up until his eyes were on a level with hers. With difficulty he extricated his hands from her embrace, lifted the wedding veil from her face, and planted a quick, moist kiss on her lips, smeared with a thick layer of bright red lipstick. Blushing, she lowered her bridegroom gently to the floor, peeked down at his red lips, and recoiled as she suddenly found herself looking at Joseph, standing beside her in his wedding suit and pushing Shraga aside with his big hands and feet, his penis sticking up defiantly in front of him. With all her might she tried to banish the images of the past from her mind and to concentrate on the present and the words of the rabbi, which sounded like the nervous spluttering of a half-closed tap. But the images of her first wedding refused to go away, all but obliterating the little figure of her new husband.

Suddenly she saw the faces of her three young friends standing round her—Rachelle, Ruhama, and Ruthie—their bodies writhing, tears streaming from their eyes, and peals of stifled laughter breaking out of the hands covering their mouths. Shraga stole a look at his wife, standing smiling at his side, and stepped delicately on her foot, shod in the white silk shoe she had ordered specially from Grisha, the Russian shoemaker, in the commercial center of the city. As if waking from a distant dream she turned her attention to Rabbi Meir standing in front of them and mumbling unintelligibly, but to her dismay encountered instead the eyes of Rabbi Elbaz from her first wedding, staring at her with undisguised lust. Then his eyes had devoured her fleshy mouth, descended to her chest, weighed her heavy breasts swelling like rising dough in her pregnancy, and finally come to rest on her crotch. Rosa blushed in embarrassment and giggled when she saw Rabbi Elbaz's eyes moving from her to Joseph and focusing on the swelling in his trousers. Her giggles turned to peals of laughter when the rabbi let out a shriek, covered his eyes with the corner of his prayer shawl, and asked faintly for a glass of water.

The guests in the reception hall looked in astonishment at the giggling bride with her double chins quivering like jelly, and put it down to the fact that she was overcome with joy at her good fortune in having found this second husband. At a second nudge from Shraga's foot, Rosa recovered her gravity and made an effort to listen to Rabbi Meir, who was singing her praises as an excellent housekeeper and cook, while her ears rang with Rabbi Elbaz's stammering attempts to read the marriage contract with the forbidden sights piercing his eyes like spears.

"Mazel tov!" cried the guests surrounding Rosa and Shraga in a sticky, suffocating circle. Rosa didn't see them. She was absorbed in the past and the sight of Rabbi Elbaz fleeing the wedding canopy as if his pants were on fire. At the same moment Shraga took her hand in his and led her to the dance floor, where the Five Jokers band was playing a passionate Argentine tango. Shraga wound his arm round her waist, pressed her body to his, and found his head buried deep in the cleavage between her breasts, and his feet tangled in the long train of her dress. The guests sitting at the tables looked down in embarrassment at the plates of hummus, cauliflower salad in mayonnaise, and pickles, and stifled their laughter. As giddy as a drunk Rosa spun around with her husband in the stylish steps he had taught her in their private lessons in the shelter and the interminable rehearsals before the wedding, ignoring his feet stamping on the train of her dress and counting the steps silently to herself: One-two-three, One-two-three. When the guests joined them on the floor at the request of the emcee, Shraga led her to the family table, where her seven children were waiting for her with their spouses and their children, and with little Angel sitting on Ruthie's lap, admiring her new shoes.

All evening long Shraga kept refilling her glass and piling mountains of food on her plate, and Rosa ate until she felt the seams of her dress were about to burst. Gasping for breath as the wedding dress grew ever tighter around her waist, she pressed her offspring to eat and looked round the table with a satisfied air, congratulating herself at having produced all these happy, laughing people.

Laden with gifts and envelopes, tipsy and giggling, like a pair of youngsters intent on mischief, Rosa and her new husband arrived home. When she slid the key into the lock, she looked at her beloved and played with the idea of asking him to carry her over the bedroom threshold, in the gesture Joseph had copied from romantic Hollywood movies. But then she inspected his skinny body, his thin arms, and unsteady stance, and decided that their wedding night would be romantic enough even if the groom didn't carry the bride over the threshold.

With stylish little dancing steps, humming a Strauss waltz to himself, Shraga took Rosa by the hand and spun her into the bedroom. Then he began to warble a song by the Egyptian Umm Kaltoum, and took off his bar mitzvah suit, wiggling his hips in a belly dance as he did so. In the tiny tiger-striped bikinis he had bought for the occasion, he gyrated and twisted until the skin-tight shorts slid off his solid buttocks and down his skinny legs until they reached the floor.

A little pool of smooth, shiny black hair adorned his chest and flowed in a straight narrow line to his belly, where it separated into the many estuaries of a broad delta until it merged with the triangular black ocean below. A pointed pink member peeped out of the luxuriant hair, trembling in excitement.

Rosa gazed entranced at his mating dance, and, as shy as a virginal young bride who had never seen a naked man before, tried not to look at her husband's loins. Like an animal surveying its prey before devouring it, he advanced toward her, circling the bed to the left and the right, and keeping his eyes fixed on her as she watched him admiringly. With an agile, acrobatic leap he jumped onto the bed, slid under the quilt, and urged his wife in a coddled voice to hurry up and join him there. Blushing like a virgin Rosa slowly extricated herself from the confines of her wedding dress, clucking her tongue as she noted the black footprints of her groom all over the train. Then she pulled the tortoiseshell comb out of her elaborate hairdo, shook out her blond tresses, and let them fall softly down her back. Bashfully she turned her back to her bridegroom, who was watching her every movement with noisy pants and groans of lust, then twisted her arms around her back and undid the hooks of her giant-cupped bra, revealing deep red lines on the white flesh freed of its restraints. In her wide silk panties, with her cascading flesh trembling in desire, she joined the man waiting for her under the quilt. And when her body touched his, he kicked the quilt to the floor and gently cupped her left breast in his hands, groaning slightly beneath its weight, and began to stroke it, round and round in ever diminishing circles until he reached the pink nipple, which pricked up as soon as he touched it. Then he addressed himself to her second breast.

Rosa, who was becoming impatient, kicked off her panties and sent them flying over her head. The vast silk panties rose into the air, hit the ceiling, and floated lightly down again, swelling like a silver parachute, until they landed on the golden frame of Joseph's portrait. Watching the flight of her panties with riveted interest, Rosa found herself looking straight into the eyes of her first husband, peeping in astonishment at the sight revealed to them through the hole for her leg.

Rosa let out a shriek of laughter, looked at her new husband shrinking at her side, clasped him in her hands, and laid him tenderly on top of her body. Shraga was sucked into her flesh, his face sank into the deep cleavage between her breasts, and his modest erection vanished abruptly. With the terror of a drowning man he extricated himself from the depths of her body, floated to the surface, and then rolled down to her side.

"I can't concentrate with him looking at me like that through your panties," he mumbled apologetically.

"There's nothing to fear from the dead," she said, looking at the picture out of the corner of her eye. "Only from the living."

"Rosa, I can't. Please take the picture away," he begged.

"Tomorrow, my love," she replied, and rolled him on top of her again, burying his head between her breasts and rocking him on the folds of flesh that sucked him in like quivering quicksand.

With her breasts blocking his nose he gasped desperately for breath, raised his head with a mighty effort to her stalklike neck, took a deep breath, and freed himself from her embrace. Then he asked her to turn over on her stomach and tried his luck from behind. But his eager body was repulsed by her immense buttocks, and he asked her to turn over onto her back again, seated himself on her crotch and tried to thrust himself inside her, only to be prevented from doing so by a thick fold of shivering, jellylike fat covering her nether parts like an apron. When his attempts to shift this apron of fat aside failed, Rosa lost her patience and began energetically wriggling her hips underneath him, bouncing up and down and doing everything in her power to open up the way to him, but he remained inaccessible and remote.

For a long time they struggled together in a tangled melee of limbs, while Joseph, swathed in Rosa's panties, contemplated his rival's performance with a supercilious smile. Rosa could have sworn that she heard a nervous drumming on the glass, and she was afraid that her hotheaded dead husband was about to smash the glass, break out of the magnificent carved frame, and jump straight onto the bed to teach Shraga his job.

"I can't," Shraga said desperately, like a man begging for his life. "First get him out of the way." But Rosa was already busy energetically massaging his penis, which responded with a slight, promising tremor. When his erection met with her satisfaction and his penis throbbed in her hand, she parted her legs, hoisted Shraga onto her body, and guided him inside her. The member trembled weakly, knocked against her nether lips, and with a brief cough spewed out its contents and went limp.

"It doesn't matter," she said as if to console herself. "We'll try again in the morning, and now go to sleep." She turned him on his side and wrapped herself around him, swallowing him up in the mountains of her flesh. Protected, swaddled, and embraced in the warmth of her body Shraga fell asleep conciliated, and Rosa, with a tempest still raging in her nether parts, looked at Joseph's serious face peeping out of her panties, and when she looked away his eyes followed her. Then she looked down at her skinny bridegroom snoring in her bosom as if worn out by his efforts, and promised him that she would not allow Joseph to get in their way, to criticize their love-making, and to interfere in their lives.

Exhausted by the events of the day she switched off the light, fell into a heavy sleep, and woke with a start to see the first rays of the sun filtering through the shutters and covering the bed in golden stripes of light with glittering specks of dust dancing in them. She raised herself on her elbows and looked appalled at the strange man lying next to her. Full of guilt and fear, at that moment she wanted to shake him awake and send him packing before her husband came home and beat them both black and blue. Then she looked at the sleeping man again, and with Joseph's eyes contemplating her mockingly through her silk panties, she remembered the wedding. She curled up behind her new husband's back and showered his neck with wet kisses, ignoring Joseph's reproachful looks.

That same morning, before Shraga woke up, she climbed effortfully onto a chair, and in spite of Joseph's vociferous protests tore his picture off the wall, together with her panties hanging on the frame, ripping the nail from the plaster as she did so. The protests turned to insults, and then to threats, and when he saw that he was beaten, to a string of juicy curses. Quickly, so his threats and curses wouldn't make her change her mind, she wrapped the picture in the sheet on which he had found his death, and pushed it into the storage space between the bedroom ceiling and the roof. Later on she covered the rectangular mark on the wall with the new wedding picture in a shiny white plastic frame, showing the bride and groom standing side by side against a backdrop of red velvet. Only the sharp eyed noticed that the groom was standing on a little stool covered in black material while the bride was bending her knees in obedience to the instructions of the photographer, so that they would both be the same height.

After hiding Joseph in the storage space above, Rosa could have sworn that she heard him drumming on the glass with his fists and begging to be let out. To her daughter Ruthie, with whom she was particularly frank and from whom she hid nothing, she confided that at first he coaxed her sweetly, but when she failed to comply with his request he called her a whore, cursed her, and threatened that she would get her just deserts and feel the punishment of his strong right arm on her soft white flesh, even if he had to escape from the dungeons of hell to give her what she had coming to her.

Immediately after Shraga left the house with Angel in his arms to wait for the van transporting the handicapped children to day care, Rachelle burst in.

"So tell me, what was it like?" she demanded impatiently.

Rosa lowered her eyes and blushed.

"Why are you blushing like a virgin?" Rachelle mocked. "How was it?"

"It was," replied Rosa briefly, turning her broad back to her friend and putting the kettle on to boil.

"What do you mean, 'It was'? How was it?" insisted Rachelle. "You're so big and he's so small," she added spitefully.

"It was terrific," said Rosa. "Shraga's fantastic."

"But all your life you've been with Joseph, and now suddenly you're with someone else. Weren't you ashamed to get undressed in front of him?" Rachelle persisted with an innocent expression.

"No," Rosa replied briefly.

"Didn't it worry you that he would see you naked with all your fat? Didn't you try to hold your stomach in? Weren't you afraid that he would be put off when he saw the size of your butt? And those thighs of yours—didn't you try to hide them? Didn't it bother you that he would see you as you are?"

"No," said Rosa and tried to change the subject to the soaring price of tomatoes.

Only after Rachelle had left and she remained alone in the kitchen nibbling salty biscuits did she think of her friend's words in the context of what had happened the previous night. She didn't understand why she should be ashamed of her body. Shraga was her husband who loved her greatly, and why should a woman be ashamed in front of a loving husband? Perhaps it was thin women who should be ashamed of their bodies, women who had no bosom and no behind and who starved themselves to death. A hungry woman was an unhappy woman, and an unhappy woman didn't enjoy making love the way that she, Rosa, enjoyed it. And when she finished all the biscuits in the box and started on the leftovers of the wedding cake the caterers had packed up for her to take home, she came to the conclusion that if they conducted a survey and asked men if they preferred fat women or thin women, every last one of them would say that a plump woman in bed was a celebration of all the senses. And in general, Rosa convinced herself, men weren't dogs, men didn't like bones, men liked flesh, and a lot of it. Because going to bed with a fat woman was like going to bed with a lot of women at once. Whereas going to bed with a thin, hungry woman—whose pelvic bones stuck out and dug into you, whose arms were like twigs, whose breasts were shriveled as raisins, and whose face was sour—was no fun at all.

Proudly she remembered the pictures in the art books that Joseph used to show her, pictures of full-bodied women by Rubens, Rembrandt, and Renoir, and repeated to herself with relish the words that had been dinned into her all her life: "Men like big women." And she went on eating the wedding cake with its pink marzipan icing. When she had consumed it all, she sat and picked the crumbs from the plate with the tip of her finger, banishing all thoughts of Joseph from her mind, and persuading herself that tonight things would work out with Shraga.

thirteen

THE INVASION OF THE SHOES

Never in her life had Rosa seen so many pairs of men's shoes, outside a shoe store, as she saw the day Shraga brought his possessions to her house. Full of curiosity, Rosa pounced on the boxes as soon as the porters put them down, opened them, and peeked inside. In every box she opened she found herself staring at dozens of pairs of shoes, crammed together one on top of the other. Shoes of all kinds and colors: ballet shoes made of silk in pink, white, and black, with hard square toes; gym shoes, most of them shabby from use, in a variety of shapes, colors, and brands. Some of the boxes contained fancy patent leather pumps tied with broad ribbons. Before her astonished eyes there spilled onto the floor soft leather moccasins, tough-looking army boots, galoshes, cowboy boots, hobnailed work boots, sandals of every kind—plastic sandals, leather sandals, biblical sandals—wooden clogs, slippers, and a variety of health shoes.

In dismay she stared at the shoes lined up pair by pair in front of her like soldiers on parade, and wondered where she was going to put them. Once before, on television, she had seen something similar, the collection of footwear belonging to the wife of a fallen dictator, and she remembered how the camera had moved over the long shelves full of shoes, as in some vast supermarket of shoes.

Quickly, before she could regret it, she emptied out the closets and pushed her clothes aside to make room for Shraga's shoes. As she did so she noted that most of them were in a shameful state. The ballet shoes and gym shoes were stained and full of holes; the moccasins were shabby, and the laces were torn. Rosa sorted out the shoes, packing the shabbiest into big plastic bags and making several trips to the green Dumpster on the corner, which gobbled them up greedily in its gaping mouth. When Shraga came home in the evening and asked about his shoes, she led him proudly to the wall closets opened the doors, and showed him how she had arranged them neatly on the shelves according to type and color. Shraga turned pale. Like a man demented he fell on the closets, flung open the doors, and searched the shelves for the missing shoes.

"Where are the yellow running shoes with the blue laces?" he demanded in an ominous tone. "And where are the red moccasins and the pink ballet shoes?" Before he could go on she rubbed herself against him placatingly and said sweetly: "I threw them out. They were worn out. If you like," she added in a coaxing tone, "we'll go and buy you some new ones." Shraga sat down on the kitchen stool and buried his face in his hands, and Rosa saw that his shoulders were shaking.

"How could you do such a thing?" he said at last in a pitiful wail. "In those pink ballet shoes I won third prize in a ballroom-dancing competition in Ashdod; in the red moccasins I stepped for the first time on the soil of France; in the yellow running shoes I ran against the national champion when I was in the eighth grade, and there are a lot of other shoes missing too. How could you do this to me?" His lips trembled, and his eyes were red. Rosa, who couldn't bear to see him suffer, ran outside and retrieved the plastic bags from the Dumpster.

That night Shraga did not join her in bed. When she woke up to go to the lavatory at four in the morning she saw him sitting on the floor surrounded by mountains of shoes, sorting them patiently according to a classification system of his own. The next morning he explained to her that he had put all the shoes he had worn during his stay in France fourteen years before in one drawer. In another were the army boots and other shoes he had worn during his military service. After them, organized in a system only he understood, came all the dancing shoes thanks to which he had received prizes. Other shoes, lacking a distinctive history, were classified according to the year of their purchase, and thus Rosa's closets were filled with Shraga's shoes, while her own clothes were thrown into the middle of the room in a colorful heap of dresses, skirts, scarves, wide panties, and bras with gigantic cups.

The day after Shraga's all-night vigil Rosa got up early in the morning and left the room on tiptoe, in order not to wake her exhausted husband lying motionless on the bed. She hurried into Angel's room before she woke up with cries of hunger, and washed and fed her, keeping a watchful eye on Shraga through the bedroom door. And after she sent Angel to nursery school, while her husband slept, she sorted out the clothes she didn't need and put them away in the storage space under the roof. The clothes for use in the coming season she folded up and packed into the living room sideboard, pushing aside the photograph albums, two big fancy albums celebrating Israel's victory in the Six-Day War, tablecloths, half empty bottles of wine for *kiddush*, crystal glasses, and a large plate for the Passover seder.

On the first nights after their wedding, when Shraga tried repeatedly to penetrate her, ejaculating prematurely in his excitement and falling asleep immediately in her arms, her longings for Joseph would try their luck and knock hopefully on her heart, and she would banish them by dwelling resolutely on her new husband's kindness to her, on the way he never came home empty handed, but always brought delicacies and sweetmeats for her and a toy for Angel. She rejoiced especially in the good relationship between her husband and her daughter. Shraga insisted on getting up and going to her when she cried at night. He would carry her in his arms, take her for walks, and keep up with her progress in the special nursery school, as if he were her real father. Rosa would dwell on her new happiness and hope that her mother, who had objected so strenuously to her marriage, could see all these blessings from her vantage point in heaven. Then she would beg Joseph to leave her alone, not to trouble her with his complaints and demands, since her marriage to Shraga was an act of restitution for the injustice he had done her all those years ago by interfering with the natural course of her life. At last justice had been done, and she had been reunited with her childhood love in a meeting ordained by destiny.

One month after the wedding he came home and told her that he had been obliged to close down the ballroom-dancing studio. As soon as he got married, he said in a faintly accusing tone, as if she were to blame for his situation, the women had stopped coming to the shelter, especially after Charlie, a bachelor from Paris, opened a rival studio next door, with modern innovations and up-to-date new steps. And with no money coming in, he was reluctantly obliged to advertise in the local neighborhood paper that he was opening a new school for ballroom dancing and classical ballet for little girls.

And little girls with transparent skin and red cheeks, in pink and white tulle dresses made by their mothers, hopped round the shelter floor on the tips of their toes, fought for the right to dance with him, and battled their way through the Prelude to *Swan Lake*, Strauss waltzes, and sensuous tangos from Argentina. At the end of every lesson they would line up in front of him, push each other out of the way, stretch their tender necks, and receive a fatherly kiss of appreciation on their cheeks.

For six months he earned a decent living for his family in this way, until a rumor spread through the neighborhood that he had been seen secretly caressing the budding breasts of Yael Buzaglo, an outstanding student and the object of his special attention. Yael's father, known throughout the neighborhood for his violent temper, stormed into the shelter, and before the eyes of the little girls gliding about in their tutus, beat Shraga soundly and sent the dancers flying in all directions, like a flock of frightened chicks fleeing the dark shadow of a hawk. Afterward policemen came to the house, cuffed his wrists in steel handcuffs that sent cold shivers down his spine and brought his skin out in goose bumps, shamed him in front of the neighbors, and took him to the police station. Bruised and beaten, he went with them, shuffling his feet in their white silk ballet shoes, prevented by the handcuffs from waving good-bye to Rosa and Angel, who stood crying on the balcony and watched him being taken away.

Rosa, who was sure of his innocence, scraped up the money for his bail, and two days later he came home, his elegant clothes stained and torn and his wrists smelling repellently of steel and sweat. Shaking with sobs, he told Rosa that he had been ordered to shut down the dancing school. That same night he threw his jail shoes, as he called them, into the trash. "There are some things I'd rather not remember," he said.

Six months later the trial took place, and Yael Buzaglo reluctantly testified against him, together with three other girls who resented his coldness toward them. In an article about the trial entitled, "The Pedophile from Katamon G," the lawyer Yohanan Harel, who they had paid a lot of money to defend him, was quoted as saying: "The possibility exists that a dancing teacher, who in the nature of things touches his pupils in order to correct their posture, could give rise to suspicions of this nature. And perhaps such touches might be interpreted as crossing the fine line between contact necessary to the performance of the teacher's duties, and what could be perceived as the attempt to commit an obscene act."

After that the article quoted a number of Shraga's adult ex-students, headed by Rachelle, who gave him glowing testimonials as character witnesses. They testified under oath that the accused was a professional dancer, an excellent teacher, and a refined gentleman who had never touched any of them in an inappropriate way. Rachelle outdid them all, describing him as a saint, who despite the temptations surrounding him every hour of the day had never taken advantage of any of his students, until he remet the great love of his life, Rosa, and married her.

After hearing the evidence of the women who kept interrupting themselves to wipe their eyes and blow their noses, the court recessed. And when the proceedings resumed, Advocate Harel said: "The character witnesses we have just heard reinforce the impression that the accused is a warm and fatherly person, who enjoys good relations with students of all ages, and we must conclude that he is here as the result of a misunderstanding. It is not beyond the bounds of possibility that the young girls who pressed charges against him did so from psychological motives that should be examined by those professionally qualified for the task." The article concluded by quoting the judge, Zahara Yardeni: "I have my doubts as to whether the accused was actually intent on teaching his young pupils to dance. He may have been more interested in trying to teach these tender and innocent little girls a new language, one that they should by rights have learned only when they grew older, each in her own way." In the absence of hard evidence one way or the other, she gave him a sentence of two years' probation and forbade him to teach dancing to girls under the age of sixteen.

Surrounded by the women he used to teach, and with Rosa holding tightly to his arm, Shraga made his way down the courthouse corridors to the exit, where Leslie-Shimon was waiting for him with his car. As soon as they got home Rosa hurried to the kitchen to brew him chamomile tea to soothe his nerves, set a plate of sugar cookies before him, and watched him compassionately as he nibbled them, with sweet crumbs sticking to his lips and dropping onto his clothes.

"How could that judge have doubted you?" she said sadly. "They all run after you and try to start with you, and when you turn them down they make up stories to get you into trouble."

Shraga said nothing and stared at her blankly as if she weren't there.

"You didn't do it, did you?" she asked suddenly, doubt entering her heart.

"How could I?" he replied in a high, tearful voice. "You're my only love. I've never loved anyone else but you. Who are all these undeveloped little girls? How could they say such things about me?" he lamented.

And Rosa put her arms around him and whispered in his ear: "Shush, shush, shush," and rocked him in her arms just as she used to do with her children when they woke up at night after a bad dream.

Afterward he bathed and changed his clothes, and they sat together tired and frightened, with the article in the evening paper spread out in front of them, and discussed their economic future. After consulting the children and talking it over all night, they decided that Shraga would go to work at the big school for the dances of the sixties that had opened in Givatayim. Every morning he got up early and took the number 18 bus to the central bus station, where he got a direct bus to Givatayim. In the evening he came home, his body aching, his face fallen, the soles of his shoes worn out, and his toes covered with blisters. Rosa would wait for him with a steaming bath into which she poured almond oil to soothe his tired body. After his bath she would wrap him in a soft terry cloth robe, bandage his toes, give him his supper in front of the television news, and watch him with a gratified expression as he put the food in his mouth.

Every week he waited for Friday, his day off, when he went to the market for her. Ceremoniously he would put on his "market shoes"—leather boots with thick crepe soles—and slip on his khaki safari jacket with its many pockets. Like a hunter setting out at dawn to stalk his prey, he would take the bus to the Mahaneh Yehuda market with all the other husbands armed with pink and purple plastic baskets in patterns of fishermen's net or butterflies joined at the wings. He would elbow his way through the throngs of men taller than him by a head, stand on the tips of his toes, and cluster with them round the stalls in a fraternity of male shoppers. With relish he would feel the tomatoes, part the leaves of the artichokes, pat the bottoms of the watermelons, press the avocados, finger the nipples of the lemons, sniff the melons, weigh the grapefruit with his eyes, stroke the fuzz on the peaches, taste the grapes, and run his fingers down the cleavage of the nectarines. Together with his fellow shoppers he would inspect the size of the fresh carrots piled in golden heaps on the counters and measure the length of the asparagus stalks with his splayed fingers.

When he was through with the vegetables and fruit, he would proceed to the meat market, bend over the bloody counters, and poke around in the piles of chicken drumsticks and thighs, looking for the plumpest and juiciest, skipping over the scrawny necks and wings with their tips chopped off, and watching the butcher like a hawk as he cut the turkey breast into thick slices for him. With blood seeping from his basket he would then visit Tzedkiyahu's pickle stall, argue with him about politics, taste an olive, bite into a pickle, and decide on the fattest and creamiest cheese of all, the kind that left a sweet taste of butter on his tongue.

Then he would go to the fishmonger's, look into the churning pond full of flapping tails and gaping mouths, and choose an agitated, swollen-bellied carp. And when he pointed to it with his finger, the fishmonger, whose apron, hands, and hair were always full of gray scales, would grin at him and wink and ask: "How come you always manage to choose the fattest and most beautiful female fish in the pond?" He would quickly dip his net into the pond and fish out the "lady carp full of eggs." With one strong blow to the head of his victim, whose fleshy lips kept opening and closing alternately, he would silence the fish, throw it up in the air, and wait gleefully for it to fall onto the newspaper-covered counter. Then with the dexterity of a conjurer he would wrap its body firmly in the newspaper, leaving its orphaned tail to flap in blind anger on the wet counter.

Bowed down under the weight of his baskets, Shraga would go to the flower stalls to buy Rosa a big bunch of red and white gladiolus, with the request that the flower seller add a few ferns, to "give her a bit of green to look at." Then he would get on the bus, squeeze in among the baskets of his neighbors, compare their produce with his own, and conclude that this time too he had done well. On the way home he would rehearse the key sentences he would say to Rosa when she opened the door. Sometimes he would repeat to himself the stories of the stall owners bragging to each other about the politician or football player from Betar Jerusalem who had stopped at their stall to chat with them about the political situation. He would tell Rosa how he, Shraga, had entered into a loud argument with the politician in question about the need to hang on to the occupied territories and not to budge an inch. Sometimes he would repeat to himself the songs and slogans chanted by the stall owners, especially those celebrating the Betar Jerusalem victory over Hapoel Tel Aviv, trying to remember every word and not omit a single detail. And with sweetness seeping through his bones, he would imagine Rosa's beaming face and her soft hands nudging his ribs as she urged him to tell her more stories from the marketplace, to sing her the songs and describe the scents rising from the ripe summer fruits.

Rosa would wait for him with the Sabbath saucepans bubbling on the stove, with the dough for the *bourekas*, the phyllo pastry for the Moroccan "cigars," and the chicken livers fried with onions, wine, and garlic—whose smell made her giddy with pleasure—breaking off bits to taste. And since the livers were so delicious, she went on dipping her spoon into the pan until she realized that the level had sunk dangerously low. Then she would make haste to cram the deplenished contents of the pan into the grinder, and grind the livers into a fine paste. After that she would season the paste with salt and pepper, roll it up in strips of pastry dough, and fry the cigars in deep oil until they turned golden.

With a steaming cigar in her mouth she would open the door to Shraga, and when he unloaded the baskets she would gaze admiringly at the booty he had brought back from the market and say proudly to herself that her husband was the best shopper in the building. When she had finished cooking, she would sit in her armchair, and Shraga would sing the market songs to her, describe the summer fruits, convey their smells to her nose, and flavor it all with words of his love for her.

On Friday nights, after her daughters helped her to wash the dishes, all her children and grandchildren went home, and with Angel bathed and put to sleep, Rosa would wait for Shraga to join her in bed. And he would put it off as usual. First he would go into Angel's room to make sure that she was properly tucked in, and that not a single bloodsucking mosquito was circling her head. Then he would make the rounds of all the rooms, closing the blinds and locking the doors. Then he would go to the kitchen, to check that the faucets weren't dripping and the gas was securely shut off. When he was satisfied with his inspection, he would take the insect spray and attack all the danger spots, paying particular attention to the ants and searching out their hidden nesting places and those of their allies, the ticks. When he was finished with the insects, he turned his attention to himself. For a time that seemed to stretch into eternity Rosa would lie listening to the splashing of his urine in the lavatory bowl, to his gargling, and to the brushing of his teeth.

When the noises in the bathroom subsided, he would step into the bedroom and sit down lightly on the bed, which received his firm buttocks with a gentle sigh of its springs. Slowly he would take off his shoes and line them up neatly under the bed. He would roll his socks methodically down his calves and sniff them before rolling them up together in an inextricable knot "so they won't get lost in the wash." When he was done with his socks, he would raise his hands to his neck, loosen his tie, roll it into a tight coil, and put it away in a drawer. When he reached his shirt Rosa felt as if her heart would burst. He would undo the buttons slowly and deliberately, carefully feeling each one to make sure that it wasn't hanging by a thread and in urgent need of repair. When the inspection was over he would fold the shirt precisely along the lines left by the iron, even if it was dirty and destined for the laundry hamper. When he reached his trousers Rosa would hold her breath. Then he would unfasten his snakeskin belt with its gilt Dior buckle, roll it up neatly, and turn to his fly, holding the tongue of the zipper daintily between his index finger and thumb. In the silent house Rosa would hear the popping sound of the tiny iron teeth parting after a long day of symbiosis. After taking off his trousers he would align the seams, straighten them out, and hang them carefully in the closet.

And just as Rosa's patience was about to snap, he would slip into bed next to her. Then he would delicately feel her vast breasts, squeeze her nipples, stroke her belly overflowing in all directions, close her mouth with a kiss, and when she sighed, he would try to penetrate her. Groaning in an agony of passion Rosa would open herself up to him, and Shraga, panting as if he had been obliged to climb a mountain, would mount the hill of her stomach, cling to the cliffs of her breasts, and falter at the entrance to her body. No sooner did he succeed in penetrating her than he wet her with his seed, extricated himself from her embrace, and slid off her onto his pillow, after which he immediately curled up in the blanket and fell sound asleep like a satisfied baby. And Rosa would listen to his light snores and to the throbbing of the blood in her groin.

She soon learned to wet her finger and rub the flaming spot between her legs, ignoring as best she could the dull, stifled murmurs, the knocking on the glass, and the promises of assistance coming from the ceiling. The desperate sounds would grow louder when strong contractions wrung her body, bringing warmth, consolation, and calm in their wake. Then she would clasp the sleeping Shraga to her bosom and try to fall asleep despite the noise.

One night, as her husband lay snoring by her side while she rubbed the fount of her pleasure, the noises from above rose to an impudent crescendo, a shower of strangled curses and vituperation that succeeded in waking Shraga from his sleep. As soon as he sat up in bed, rubbing his eyes in confusion, the noises stopped abruptly.

"There are mice in the house," he cried in a shrill, squeaky voice. "As long as they don't gnaw holes in my shoes!" Then he recovered and announced in manly tones that on Friday he would buy mousetraps in the market.

By the next morning the incident had been forgotten, but as soon as he left the house with Angel, Rosa took the aluminum ladder and climbed up heavily to the storage space door. She lifted Joseph's picture out with difficulty and climbed down with it to the floor. Joseph's eyes gleamed at her expectantly through the glass. She avoided looking at him, loosened the screws attaching the picture to the gilt frame, and ripped it out. A sigh of relief escaped from Joseph's lips as he was freed from his prison. Indifferent to his imploring eyes, she flattened his face as if flattening a piece of dough with a rolling pin, and rolled the picture up. Then she pulled the rubber band out of her hair, uprooting a few curly fair hairs as she did so, fastened it tightly around the rolled-up photograph, and left the house with her dead husband in her hands. All the way to Ruhama's house Joseph begged for his life, promised not to bother her anymore, not to mock her new husband, not to sabotage her marriage, and even to try to like Shraga, the stink of whose shoes spread through the house and invaded his nose. With uncharacteristic sternness she ignored his promises and pressed her finger firmly on the bell of the door, which bore a bronze plaque inscribed in curly letters with the words: "Ruhama and Nissim Levy live here in prosperity and happiness."

Ruhama paled when she saw who was standing on the threshold

and smiling at her like an old friend. She recovered immediately and invited Rosa in with all the airs and graces of an aristocrat down on her luck. Rosa surveyed the miserable apartment, which had evidently seen better days, and her nostrils quivered as they were suddenly assailed by a storm of smells. It was an intolerable cacophony of roses and narcissi, jasmine and violets, all mixed up together and flavored with hints of strange and unfamiliar sweet scents. And the atoms of all these smells combined into a rare and inseparable chemical compound, producing a heavy scent that made it difficult for her to breathe and pressed on her chest. When she recovered, one smell rose in her nostrils, dominating all the others, sharp, tender, and mocking—the smell of Joseph's lavender soap.

At that moment she was sure that Joseph's head was about to pop out suddenly from the bathroom door, and she saw him in her imagination staring at the two of them in bewilderment, smiling the crooked smile that had been fixed on his face at the hour of his death. When she sat down heavily on the sofa, she noticed the walls of the room. What had looked at first like patches of color on a brightly patterned wallpaper turned out to be the heads of silk and plastic flowers attached to the wall by little steel nails. There were roses, narcissi, violets, gladiolus, carnations, and all kinds of exotic blooms she had never seen before. The flowers brazenly displayed their artificial reproductive organs to her as if they were desperately demanding to be pollinated.

Ruhama followed Rosa's curious glances and answered her unasked question: "Where there are flowers there must be butterflies." Her head spinning with the scents and sights, and with a shower of visionary butterflies descending before her eyes, Rosa accepted her old friend's offer of coffee. Ruhama opened the refrigerator door with a flourish to get the milk, but her hand returned empty. Except for a couple of eggs staring at her from blind white eyes, and a single carrot lying limp and shriveled on the tray, the refrigerator was empty. In the absence of milk, Rosa agreed to take tea, but since there was no sugar either, she found herself sipping lukewarm tap water from a dirty glass her hostess set before her as if it contained the nectar of the gods.

Apologizing for the lack of cake, Ruhama explained that there was nobody to eat it, and she didn't want to bake for herself because she didn't want to put on weight. Rosa examined Ruhama's slender figure with interest, and she couldn't understand what Joseph had seen in her, since he had always insisted that he liked his wife fat and juicy. But after looking deep into her rival's dark eyes, she realized how beautiful she was, and couldn't help congratulating her late husband on his excellent taste in women. And when she remembered Joseph, she recalled the purpose of her visit and pushed the rolled-up picture into Ruhama's hands.

"It's yours," she said. "I'm married now, and I don't need him anymore."

Ruhama unrolled the picture and turned pale as the face of her beloved was revealed.

"The first butterfly," she couldn't resist saying.

Ignoring this remark, Rosa watched Ruhama as she gazed down at the picture, hot tears falling from her eyes and spotting Joseph's face with round, wet stains.

"I miss him so much," she sobbed through clenched teeth. "I always loved him. I loved his serious face. When we were still living in the villa in Old Katamon I let him touch me, because he promised to marry me."

Rosa restrained herself. Encouraged by her rival's silence, Ruhama went on talking, trying to fill in the vacuum left by her lover's death. "You have no idea how I suffered when you married him. I was actually ill. I had no alternative, and I married Nissim, but I always went on loving Joseph."

"How did it begin?" asked Rosa grimly.

"When he opened Cinema Rosa. How I envied you when he named it for you. Every evening I sat there and cried my heart out over him. Until we began to sit together in the projection room, crying and embracing."

The two women sat in the kitchen, Rosa asking and Ruhama answering. They compared dates, days, and hours, and tried to work out which of them he had spent more time with. Unable to reach a common conclusion, they agreed that Joseph, as cunning as a devil, had calculated his every move and cleverly tricked them both.

"He told me that he wasn't going to bed with you anymore," said Ruhama, choking on a laughter that she didn't understand.

"And at the same time he couldn't keep his hands off me and he followed me around the house sticking to my backside like a leech," retorted Rosa.

"And when he told you that he was going to the movie theater to check up on a new movie, he was really with me," said Ruhama.

"He always came home and jumped on me as hungry as if he had been watching a blue movie instead of a Turkish tearjerker," reported Rosa, "and the next morning he was at it again, as if nothing had happened the night before."

Laughing wildly, they compared notes on positions, circumstances, and situations. Afterward Ruhama said that she didn't understand why Rosa was in such a hurry to get married. "All I wanted was for my husband to leave me and set me free so that I could begin to enjoy my life," she confessed. "In my heart of hearts I wanted him to die, among other things because black suits me. The moment he left I was free and I could do whatever I wanted. Including be with Joseph," she said, stealing a look at Rosa.

The two enemies parted like friends, and Ruhama promised Rosa that she would look after the picture and have it framed by Tzarfati. Since she was childless, Rosa offered her the services of Jackie-Ya'akov, her son with the golden hands, to drill a hole in the wall and hang the picture for her in the place of her choice.

But when she came home all the old angers against Joseph began to well up inside her, and she knew that from then on she would not allow him to trouble her anymore, and she would banish from her mind all the disturbing thoughts, feelings of guilt, and agonies of conscience that sometimes came to haunt her for having married Shraga. That night, with Joseph far away, rolled up tightly and fastened with a rubber band in Ruhama's house, she surrendered herself to Shraga's caring hands, and in the peace and quiet that had suddenly descended on her life she loved her new husband more than ever.

But the next day Ruhama showed up on her doorstep with the picture in her hands. "I couldn't sleep all night," she confessed. "All night long I dreamed that he was calling me a whore, cursing me, and demanding that I give him back to you." Silently Rosa took the rolled-up face of her dead husband, and as if nothing had happened invited her old friend and rival to coffee with milk and a slice of the fruitcake she had just taken out of the oven. And when Angel came home from her day care they both played with her until Shraga came back from work, and then Rosa invited her to supper, and watched her compassionately as she shoveled the food into her mouth as if she hadn't eaten a decent meal for years.

* * *

During this period Rosa put on so much weight that she had difficulty walking and was short of breath when she climbed the stairs. Shraga installed a little stool attached by a spring to the wall of the landing between the second and third floors for her, so that she could pull it out and sit down when she got tired. When her heart began to give her trouble, Dr. Sternschus, their family doctor at the HMO clinic, told her that if she didn't start exercising at once she wouldn't be responsible for the consequences. Accordingly Rosa went and registered at the health club run by the rabbi's wife, Leah-Tehiya, an establishment exclusively for women in the dank basement of the Helpmeets to the Righteous school for girls in the city center, next to the Geula Quarter. There Rosa found herself in the company of women with stomachs sagging from innumerable births, their heads bound in dark turbans that hid gleaming shaved scalps, and their bodies draped in shapeless, faded dressing gowns. They stood in rows, trying in vain to reach their toes with the tips of fingers scarred by the vigorous action of kitchen knives on wooden cutting boards. Together with worn-out wrinkled women older than she was, she took slow, tottering steps on the treadmills. Then she would wait her turn to lie down on the vibrating beds that twisted her body from side to side, threw her legs up in the air, forced her thighs apart, pushed her head in the direction of her neck, and mercilessly shook her rolls of fat.

She would go home hungry as an ox and gladly obey Shraga when he urged her discreetly to dig in. "You have to eat. Think of all the energy you used up today," he would say to her. On the days she visited the health club she would devour everything he set before her voraciously, until she grew so fat that she was tactfully asked to leave the club, since her prodigious weight was ruining the expensive equipment.

She began to find it difficult to cope with the housework, and Ruthie and Dror would show up every day to help her with Angel, who—just as the doctors had predicted—had stopped growing at the age of two. Ruthie would feed her, bathe her, and diaper her, and Dror would play with her and try to get her to walk on her thin legs. And since she was slow in talking, he would patiently teach her the names of the objects surrounding them in the house.

Freed from the burden of caring for the child, Rosa would drag herself to the plants on the balcony, pluck off dead leaves; water, fertilize, and prune the aromatic bushes; pack the herbs in rustling cellophane bags, and give them to Ruthie for distribution in the shops.

In her grateful love for her husband, Rosa made up her mind to cook delicious new dishes for him every day, and when she ran out of recipes she began to invent dishes of her own. For hours she would stand in the kitchen steaming the semolina in the special couscous pot; cleaning the mutton and roasting it; and boiling potatoes, beets, and zucchini on the side. Then she would roast squabs and chickens and stuff them with rice studded with raisins and almonds, and make sugared almonds and pecans for dessert.

She was particularly fond of making sesame sweets. First she would brown a few handfuls of the delicate seeds in a pan, shaking it with a practiced hand and breathing in the delicious smell of the oil they gave off. Then she would put two cups of sugar in a saucepan with a cup of water and bring the sweet solution to a boil, and when it began to seethe with transparent bubbles, she would add a little lemon juice and go on cooking the mixture until what Angela called "the right moment." This fragile and elusive moment was impossible to measure by the clock, but had to be sensed in the guts. It was the fraction of a second when a drop of the solution splashed onto the marble counter set into a tiny transparent column and stood upright by its own unaided efforts. Then she removed the sticky, honeyed solution from the flame, added the roasted sesame seeds, and stirred. Next she would prepare the marble for the syrupy task ahead of it: sprinkle it with water, flatten the mixture out on it, and press down with the rolling pin to join the sesame seeds tightly and irreversibly together: After the paste had cooled, she would cut it into triangles and rectangles with sure, rapid movements of a particularly sharp knife, crunching the leftover pieces between her strong teeth. She would store the rectangles and triangles piled up on the counter in a large tin bearing the modest legend, "Hadar Biscuits," hiding its true contents from visitors dropping in to "see if everything was all right" and looking around for something to munch. And when Shraga came home he would flare his nostrils at the delicious aromas wafting from the kitchen, nibble at the delicacies on his plate, and sit at the table with her for hours, urging her to eat in order to replenish her energy, pressing her to take another spoonful, another slice of meat, another sweetmeat, and watching her lovingly until her plate was clean.

And Rosa grew and swelled, with only her hands, feet, and head immune from the process. To Shraga's satisfaction she hardly ever left the house, and spent hours sitting and panting for breath in the vast armchair he had bought especially for her. Her flesh, which had not been exposed to the sun for months, turned an ivory white, and sometimes when she opened the shutters her eyes, accustomed to the gloom of the house would be blinded by the dazzling light. At night he would help her to get undressed, measuring the new tires of fat encompassing her body, and congratulating himself on his big, beautiful wife, and the fact that he alone could see and touch her, and no other man could contaminate her with his eyes or thoughts.

Since she hardly ever left the house, Ruthie and Dror would arrive every morning to dress and feed Angel. When the little girl was ready, Shraga would take her downstairs, Dror would go to school, and Ruthie would stay to help Rosa with the housework. Until the van arrived to take Angel to her day care, Shraga would hold her in one hand and wave the other vigorously to shoo away the crows assembling round them. In the evening he would wait for her downstairs, hoist her onto his shoulders, and climb lightly up the stairs to the third floor. At the door he would cry: "We're home," carry the little girl to Rosa's armchair, and offer her cheek to her mother's kiss. After supper he would carry her in his arms to the bathroom, put her in the bath, stroke her transparent skin with his soapy hands, tickle her under her armpits, and tell her funny stories, and she would reward him with her chiming laughter. When her body was shining with cleanliness he would dress her in her pajamas, and when she was safely tucked into bed he would turn his attention to Rosa.

On the night that Rosa's rolls of fat spread over the entire bed and pushed him so far to the edge that he was in danger of falling to the floor, he came to a decision and explained to her as tactfully as he could that tonight he would sleep in one of the children's beds. Every night from then on, before he retired to his bed, he would go into her bedroom, tuck her in, stroke her body, and kiss her goodnight. And, whispering words of love, he would promise her that if Angel cried in the night he would go to her himself, and there was no need for Rosa to get up. And Rosa would lie on her back, her arms and legs outspread, and fall asleep with a contented smile on her face.

One morning, when she rolled heavily out of bed and waddled to the bathroom, she discovered that she couldn't get through the door. With a mighty effort she drew in her stomach, flattened her breasts, and tried to squeeze in sideways, but to no avail. With her bladder bursting she dragged herself to the boys' bedroom where Shraga was sleeping in Leslie-Shimon's bed, and shook him awake. He woke up immediately and tried but failed to push her through the bathroom door. Weeping and wet with urine, she lowered herself into her armchair, while Shraga summoned Shlomo the Building Contractor, who arrived with Daoud the Builder from Beit Safafa. Armed with sledgehammers, they widened the door, and Rosa squeezed in and stayed there all day. A few days later, when she complained that she was having difficulty getting through the kitchen door and the doors to the rooms, Daoud was called in again and widened all the doors of the house, except for the front door, which Shraga said there was no need to alter, since in any case Rosa never left the house. And since she couldn't get into the bath, he knocked down the wall separating the bathroom from the back porch, enlarged the bathroom, and that same summer he installed a large oval Jacuzzi for her use.

Every evening, after Shraga had put Angel to bed, Rosa would get undressed in front of him and he would raise his eyes to heaven and utter the cries of excitement and admiration she loved to hear. And when she stood before him naked, he would lower his head and kiss the scar left by Angel's birth. With his lips and tongue he would glide over the long scar crossing her stomach as if intent on absorbing some of the pain of the operation into himself. Then Rosa would step carefully into the Jacuzzi, sink into the foaming water, and like a giant hippo in a fountain she would sit and delight in the currents of warm water lapping her body, tickling her breasts, and making her backside tingle. And Shraga would sit opposite her, staring at her admiringly, stroking bit by bit her smooth, rosy flesh, and tell her that nothing would happen if she peed in the water. And when he saw her eyes go glassy, the lines of her face relax, and the little yellow stain spreading until it disappeared in the warm water, he would kiss the nape of her neck and lovingly soap her back, which was free of cruel lines since she could no longer find a bra to fit her.

When the entire expanse of her back was covered by a layer of foam, he would lean back and marvel at the spectacle of her bathing: First she would take one magnificent breast in both her hands, hoist it over her shoulder, and scrub the skin beneath. Then she would take the other and repeat the performance. And as he would watch from behind, he would find himself gazing into the eyes of her pink nipples surrounded by dark haloes that had suddenly grown on her back.

And, with her breasts resting on her back, he would help her soap her armpits. Like a man making an important sacrifice, he would take his private, expensive French razor, blow off the superfluous stubble clinging to it, and carefully shave her armpits, first the left and then the right, tickling her and eliciting bursts of uncontrollable laughter as he did so. She would raise her hands alluringly and put them on her head, and Shraga would inspect his handiwork at close quarters, cluck his tongue approvingly, and go on to the next task.

Then he would take up his position in front of her feet and ask her to set one of them in his lap. Gently he would part her toes, trim her toenails one by one, and collect the hard clippings in his hand. After throwing them into the toilet bowl and flushing them away, he would take the pumice stone and get rid of the hard skin on her soles.

Only then would he turn his attention to her hair. With the expertise of a professional hairdresser he would carefully wet her long fair hair, not letting the water get into her eyes, pour a little fragrant shampoo into the palm of his hand, and rub it into her hair until her head was covered in a cap of lather. At the same time he would massage her scalp gently with his fingertips and listen gratefully to her gurgles of pleasure, which encouraged him to continue with the massage until his wrists swelled and the skin on his fingertips was as wrinkled as a plump prune. After rinsing her hair he would anoint it with a conditioner, and comb the soft tresses with a wide-toothed comb, lamenting the loss of every hair it uprooted.

And when she rose from her ablutions he would wrap her body in four towels and pat her dry. And when she stood before him dry and naked, he would inspect her pubic hair for any wayward curls, then bend down and clip the offender off with the nail scissors. And when his mission was accomplished, he would raise his head, and she would wait for him with pouting lips and cover his head, neck, and mouth with grateful kisses.

* * *

On their first wedding anniversary, Shraga came home early and handed her two parcels tied with red ribbons. As enthusiastically as a child receiving her first present, she undid the ribbons and tore the paper off the first parcel. With bated breath she lifted the lid and gazed at the two twin bracelets made of links of gold glittering on their velvet bed. The second box contained a collar to match.

"You shouldn't have, you shouldn't have," she murmured, and offered him the boxes with outstretched hands. Shraga took the first bracelet and fastened it around her right wrist, and quickly did the same with the second bracelet on her left wrist, as if loath to lose a second's time. Then he stepped slowly backwards to view the bracelets encircling Rosa's wrists like a pair of golden handcuffs, and turned to the second box. He lifted the thick gold collar reverentially from its velvet bed and fastened it around her neck. It fit perfectly, without enough room for even a finger to insert itself.

"I want you to wear them always," he announced, and Rosa, her head giddy and her face red from the pressure of the collar on her throat, nodded wordlessly.

A month later, on her birthday, he arrived with a large gift-wrapped box containing a pair of immense, flimsy-looking red leather shoes with spindly spike heels.

"How did you know my size?" she asked shyly as he knelt down before her with the ease of an experienced shoe seller, and slipped the shoes onto her feet with a regal flourish, like Prince Charming in the animated movie *Cinderella*. The shoes fit as if they had been made for her.

"I want you to wear these shoes when I come home from work," he whispered into her ear with his eyes glazed. "High heels improve the shape of the calves and the backside."

Giggling bashfully, she waved her feet in the air as if she were riding a bicycle.

"Stand up and let's see if they don't pinch," he whispered hoarsely.

Rosa stood up and towered above him.

"If Angel wasn't at home I would take you straight to bed," he whispered. "Walk to the bedroom with me, I'm dying to hear the tapping of the heels on the floor. It's such a sexy sound."

Rosa hobbled behind him, stumbling and twisting first her right ankle and then her left. Shraga took her in his arms, ready to waltz. Swaying heavily on her feet she tottered beside him. On the third turn the heels gave way and broke off neatly at the joint, leaving her flat-footed. Shraga stared at the slender heels, which had failed to bear her weight and were now lying on the floor, and announced that tomorrow he would buy her another, stronger pair. "Because the noise you made with the heels drove me crazy, and apart from that, you looked so unsteady that I thought you would fall into my arms at any moment, and I haven't been so aroused for ages," he told her after trying to penetrate her that night. The next day Rosa put the heelless shoes on her feet, and since they were so comfortable she decided to use them as slippers.

Since she was no longer capable of going out to visit her friends, Rachelle and Ruhama would come to visit her every afternoon to drink coffee and eat salty sesame biscuits. And Rosa, delighted at being reunited with both her childhood friends, would tell them about Shraga's kindness to her, about the presents he bought her, and about how he wouldn't let her do anything apart from the cooking. They would look at her gigantic body, which was growing bigger every day, and tell her tactfully that it wasn't healthy to be so fat and that she should start cutting down on her food. And she would look back at them pityingly and say: "But Shraga loves me like this."

"So what?!" Ruhama would explode. "You can't even go out of the house! You've turned into a prisoner in your own body!"

And Rachelle would nod in agreement.

And after they left Rosa would sit in her armchair and muse that even though they were her best friends, since there were no men in their lives they were probably jealous of her happy life with Shraga. Then Joseph would creep slyly into her thoughts, and she would think of her life with him and compare it to her present life with Shraga, racking her brains in the effort to decide which was better. When she thought of Joseph she remembered the even course of her life until Angel was born, the happy moments she had had with him, and the delights of their lovemaking, with their bodies entwined at night and in the morning in perfect union. Then she would banish her memories of Joseph and turn her thoughts to Shraga, her old and present love, who although he did not satisfy her as Joseph had, was a better husband than he had been, looking after her like a loving father, bathing and dressing her, buying her gifts, and taking care of all her needs and those of Angel. And when she thought of them both and compared them with each other, she thought how wonderful it would be if only she could combine the virtues of each of them and construct a new man who would be perfect.

fourteen

THE FATTEST WOMAN IN ISRAEL

*That year Rosa became the subject of a re-*newed wave of publicity, which turned her into one of the most famous women in Jerusalem. It all began when a reporter on a local paper heard about Rosa from his brother-in-law Elimelech, owner of the Fresh Fruit greengrocer's, was impressed by her dimensions, and wrote a two-page spread about her entitled "The Fattest Woman in Town." The article was accompanied by photographs of her and Shraga with Angel in his arms, and led to an interview on the local television channel. A team of four—a reporter, a photographer, and a light and a sound man—turned up at her house and behaved as if it belonged to them. They opened and closed the shutters, filled the bed with embroidered silk cushions, and instructed Rosa to lie down. Then they rummaged in the closets, examined Shraga's shoe collection, and snickered at the sight of Rosa's vast panties. In the end the reporter had the nerve to ask her to get into the Jacuzzi, "with your clothes on, but so that it looks as if you're naked." At this request Shraga lost his temper and told the reporter that she should be ashamed of herself, and this too appeared in the program that was broadcast on the local channel at half past seven in the evening.

Two days later she received a visit from Danny Barakat, the talk-show host who had interviewed her during her pregnancy. He burst into the living room with his crew and crowned her with a new title: "The Fattest Woman in Israel." Since he was the most popular TV host in the country, the house filled with the neighbors and their children, and many more gathered outside in the hope of getting a glimpse of him through the window. Rosa sat in her armchair, wearing her best silk dress, and wiped away a tear of excitement when

Danny stroked her dainty little hands, praised her pure, fresh complexion, extolled her beauty, and begged her not to lose a single gram.

"This is what a woman should look like," he roared, trying to make himself heard above the hubbub. "A lot of woman, fresh and beautiful as a picture by Rubens." Afterward he whispered in Shraga's ear that he envied him, "because the area of her skin is enough for five men, and her flesh is sufficient to accommodate ten. If I had a woman like her she would keep me satisfied for a year, and I wouldn't even look at another woman." But when he asked to see Angel, he took one look and recoiled. And the offended Rosa saw that he regretted his request that she get in touch with him when she grew up.

That night she was so excited she had difficulty breathing, and her loud wheezing woke Shraga, who was sleeping in the boys' room on Jackie-Ya'akov's bed. He found her blue in the face and struggling for breath, and rang for an ambulance in a panic. The ambulance men soon arrived, equipped with a stretcher and oxygen tanks to take Rosa to the hospital for tests. Since they were unable to fit her onto the stretcher, they were obliged to ask her to accompany them on foot. With harsh wheezes and whistles breaking out of her chest and frightening Angel, she hoisted herself out of bed and tottered toward the door, but she couldn't squeeze through it.

In the middle of the night they summoned Daoud, and in the faint light of the stairwell he enlarged the doorway with a few hefty blows of his hammer. But by the time he was finished Rosa's condition had deteriorated, and she lay on the kitchen floor with an oxygen mask attached to her nose, while her neighbors wiped her face with a wet cloth, her chest rising and falling as she struggled for every breath.

In the meantime the ambulance men had contacted the fire department and asked for a crane, and when it arrived they joined forces to dismantle the fence so that it could gain access to the apartment. Slowly the crane trundled up to the wall of the bedroom balcony, and with the press of a button the carrier rose into the air until it was level with the balcony floor. With a couple of blows Daoud knocked out the iron balustrade, and, supported by her neighbors, Rosa stumbled onto the carrier and lay flat on her back with her legs parted in front of her and her hands fearfully gripping the railings. In the light of the breaking day, to the cheers of the spectators gathered down below, the crane set off, groaning under its heavy burden, and trundled down the streets until it set her down at the entrance to the emergency room of the hospital.

With the joint efforts of the doctors and the bevy of nurses who gathered around the mountainous patient, Rosa's breath was restored, and she was warned of the dire consequences that would follow if she didn't lose weight immediately. The doctors also recommended that she sleep on her side, in order not to bury her heart and lungs under the intolerable weight of her fat. Armed with good advice, medication, and diet recipes, Rosa waited for the crane with Shraga at her side. Sailing through the air she waved weakly to the citizens of the town who lined the streets and applauded the gigantic woman they had all read about in the newspaper and seen on television, until the arm of the crane swung her through the balcony door and deposited her on her bed.

That night the worried Shraga decided to keep watch over his wife and listen to her breathing as she slept. He dragged Leslie-Shimon's youth bed into their bedroom, pulled it up to the double bed, and prepared to stay awake all night and save his wife from suffocating herself to death. Delighted to have her husband at her side and obedient to the instructions of the doctors, Rosa turned to face him, lying on her side in the recommended position, and breathing in the smell of oranges wafting from him as she stroked him tenderly until he fell asleep.

The next morning she found him blue and lifeless, crushed beneath the weight of her body.

And again the ambulance drove up to their house, waking the neighbors with its wailing sirens. Afterward they said that Rosa refused to let them take the body away. For a long time she lay next to Shraga, warming his cold body with her hands, putting her lips to his, and breathing into his gaping mouth until his crushed chest rose, only to sink again immediately. She stroked the body whose wide-open eyes looked at her in mute reproach and whose mouth gaped in a scream that would never be heard, whispered words of love in his ear, washed his face, and combed his hair.

And when they took the body away at last, she insisted on putting his favorite Sabbath shoes on his feet. But his swollen feet refused to slip into the shoes, and the weeping Rosa watched them putting him barefoot into the black plastic body bag. The metallic sound of the zipper closing went on echoing in her ears for days. Together with

Shraga, the smell of oranges, which she loved, disappeared from the house, and a smell of rotten fruit settled in the rooms.

HUSBAND SUFFOCATED BY WIFE'S BREASTS, the headlines screamed in the next day's paper. The report dwelled at length on the tragic story of Rosa, the fattest woman in Israel, who had killed her husband by mistake. It also said that the postmortem operation had revealed a number of broken ribs, one of which had pierced the right lung and contributed to the causes of death. The medical examiner reported dryly that the wife of the deceased had rolled onto her husband's bed while they were sleeping and crushed him to death.

The next day the fire department crane arrived at the house, hoisted the sorrow-stunned Rosa off the bedroom balcony, and drove at the head of the convoy of cars with their lights on that accompanied Shraga on his final journey. At the funeral parlor she asked them to take her to the purification chamber and leave her there. Exploiting her connections with the ritual purifiers, whom she knew from their devoted attentions to her previous husband, she pushed a handsome sum of money into their hands and asked them for one last favor.

"Before you wrap him in the winding sheet, put these shoes on him," she whispered, and removed from the plastic bag she was carrying an elegant box covered with shiny gold-lettered black paper. In the suspenseful silence that had descended on the little room she raised the lid and like a conjurer pulling a rabbit out of a hat removed Shraga's best shoes, gleaming in the light of the naked bulb. The purifiers held their breath at the sight of the alligator leather shoes the dead man had purchased for three months' wages at the fancy Italian boutique in Dizengoff Street in Tel Aviv, and worn only once, on the happiest day of his life.

"In these shoes he danced the tango with me at our wedding reception," she told them, wiping the tears streaming down her round cheeks. And when she remembered what those shoes had done to the train of her wedding gown, she smiled sadly.

"I'd like him to go on dancing up there in heaven," she wept, her body shaking. "Never to stop dancing and to make all the widows buried next to him happy," she added, with new tears of inappropriate mirth rolling down her face.

When she entrusted his most precious possession to the hands of the purifiers, Rosa had no idea that her dead husband would not be buried in his wedding shoes.

Hanna the Purifier, whose blind husband was unemployed and who had five hungry mouths to feed, coveted the shoes and betrayed her trust. She hid the shoes under her stained gown and smuggled them out of the purification room, and sold them for a few shekels to Menahem, the rag and bone seller from the marketplace, who displayed his wares on an old sheet in the alley opposite Rahmou's hummus shop on Wednesdays. Menahem, who insisted that there wasn't a man on earth with feet small enough to fit into the shoes, succeeded beating her down to a ridiculously low price. For a long time he debated with himself as to the best place to display his new acquisition, and in the end he placed them in a chipped enamel plate from the People's Republic of China, with cracked flowers decorating its rim. Opposite Shraga's shoes, for the sake of symmetry, he placed a pair of ladies' white kidskin pumps that boasted particularly high heels.

On the same day he succeeded in selling the shoes for twice what he paid for them to a worn-out cleaning woman who was looking for a secondhand bar mitzvah suit for her son. Stubbornly she rummaged in the piles of cast-off clothes smelling of the body odors of their previous owners, until she found what she was looking for. And when she held the suit out to him in her thin hands, Menahem waved the alligator shoes in front of her yearning eyes and told her that without a pair of splendid shoes like these her son would have nothing to celebrate. The woman bowed her head, and with fingers whose skin was flayed and peeling from detergents, she fingered the shoe size embossed on the shining leather soles, and informed Menahem with a sigh that her son, praise God, already took size thirty-seven.

"So let him curl up his toes," he barked. "You won't find shoes like this anywhere else. It's a bargain. Why should somebody else enjoy it?"

The woman sighed, plunged her hand into the depths of her bra, pulled out a tattered plastic bag, undid the knot, argued halfheartedly with Menahem, and paid him what he asked.

And thus it came about that the bar mitzvah boy stood in the synagogue in an old bridegroom's suit and new shoes made of fine alligator leather that pinched his toes, while Shraga, according to the cemetery director, Yochai, turned from side to side in his grave, barefoot, searching for his stolen wedding shoes and waking the dead with his complaints. In order to spare Rosa's feelings, the neighbors kept the story a secret from her. And Shraga too, who sometimes crept into her dreams, never complained to Rosa that in the end, despite all her efforts, he arrived in heaven barefoot.

Throughout the week of mourning, Rosa would beat her left breast and mutter to herself: "I murdered my husband. I murdered Shraga." And she told the condolence callers: "For forty years I waited for him, and when he came I killed him. I'm sorry I met him. We should never have met. We should never have married. I murdered my husband, I murdered my Shraga." So she sobbed, telling the tale of the crushing to anyone willing to listen, sniffing her fingertips and trying to bring back his vanished smell.

"I kill my husbands. Anyone who marries me will die," she cried to Peretz the Cabalist when he came to call.

"I should be locked up in jail," she cried to the reporter who came to report on the incident, and felt once more the old "Shraga pain" that had haunted her body ever since he had suddenly disappeared from her life so many years ago, only to reappear with the same suddenness and take her in his arms with an elegant dancer's step.

Every day she waited impatiently for the last mourner to leave, and until late at night, sobbing and beating her breast, she would occupy herself with his shoes. With the tears streaming down her cheeks and staining her dress, she would polish his leather shoes until she could see her face, swollen with crying, reflected on their gleaming surface; brush his ballet shoes and wash his sport shoes, trying to ignore Joseph's mocking laughter from the storage space under the roof. Then she would sit on the stool in the kitchen and arrange all the plates and trays with the food brought by the condolence callers on the Formica table. Only after everything was arranged to her satisfaction would she sigh and remember her bitter fate, and the tears would roll down her cheeks and wet the piquant fish, salt the vegetables in the couscous, and dilute the soup. Then she would begin greedily devouring the food, looking over her shoulder guiltily as she did so. But she soon discovered that the lump in her throat prevented the food from sliding down and that her stomach, contracted in pain, shrank from absorbing it.

In envious despair she watched the endless column of black-clad ants approaching to join in the funeral feast. No sooner had the news of Shraga's disappearance reached their anthills than they set out to take advantage of the fortuitous absence of their old enemy, the infamous insect hater who ground every creepy-crawly thing ruthlessly under his heel and sprayed them with lethal pesticides. Like an army of termites they advanced on Rosa's third-floor kitchen, and when they got there, famished and exhausted by the long, dangerous journey, they demolished every scrap of food left over from shiva. Sometimes Rosa found herself staring mesmerized at a perfect circle of gleaming black ants gathered around an invisible stain of sweetness. For what seemed to her like hours and to them like eternity, they stood on their jointed legs, their feelers quivering with the excitement of the discovery of food, and their stomachs filling with a delicacy invisible to the human eye.

After concluding her observations of the ants and sympathetically sensing their joy at the discovery of food, she vowed that she would never kill an ant again, even if they bothered her and demanded to share her food, for how could she kill something so small, so vulnerable, whose life was so short anyway? And she decided to take care not to tread on the tiny creatures by mistake either. And when she got into bed she went on thinking about them, and she came to the conclusion that God had created the ant in order to test the compassion of human beings. For the life of an ant was equal to the life of a human being. Death awaited them both at the end of the road, and who was she to cause the death of a fellow creature before God decided that its time had come? And with an aching stomach, a lump in her throat, and her head swarming with thoughts of ants, she covered herself with her thick quilt, summoned Shraga to join her, and told him apologetically about all the dishes she had been unable to get down that day, promising him that she would try to do better tomorrow.

Early in the morning, before the guests began to arrive, her body still aching with the "Shraga pain," she would wake Angel, open the window for her so that she could greet the crows, and with every spoon of food she fed her she repeated that her Daddy Shraga had gone and left them forever. Angel would open her blue eyes wide and look at her mother as if she understood, with a sad expression on her face. Rosa would stroke her golden hair and ask her to stay small, innocent, and loving forever.

Then Ruthie would arrive and take the little girl downstairs to wait for the transportation to day care, and when she returned she would find Rosa in the middle of the ritual she observed strictly throughout the week of mourning. Ruthie would help her to roll up the carpets, lift the chairs onto the tables, fill a pail with water, and begin to scrub the house. Again and again they washed the floors, cleaned the windows till they shone, and rearranged the closets. After the guests arrived she would wait impatiently for the last one to leave, so that she could sweep up the crumbs and wipe the greasy fingerprints from the gleaming furniture.

For seven days she sat in her armchair in the living room and received the condolence callers arriving with their offerings of patties, couscous, fish, cakes and candies, encountering their hard looks and overhearing their venomous whispers as they covered their mouths with their hands.

And after the week of mourning came the jokes, and the caricatures, and Rosa's house turned into a place of pilgrimage for curiosity seekers, until Ruhama, her old enemy, took it upon herself to stand guard in the entrance to the stairwell and chase away with her sharp tongue and the broomstick in her hands anyone who had no legitimate business in the building. And when she had banished the last of the nuisances, she would return to Rosa, sigh, and with a hint of envy in her voice she would say: "There are still two husbands waiting for you who probably have no idea that they're going to marry you." And Rosa would look at her through her tears and ask: "Don't you think I've done enough? Anyone who marries me is sure to die." But in her heart of hearts she prayed that Ruhama's butterfly prophecy would come true.

When the hubbub in the house died down and she was left alone, she finally realized the full significance of what had happened, and she fell exhausted onto her bed, turned her face to the wall, and refused to get up. She stopped eating altogether, and since she was incapable of taking care of Angel, Ruthie and Dror came to her rescue again. Rosa would look at the child when they brought her to her bed in the morning, kiss her on the forehead, and turn her face to the wall again. And she would only wake up in the evening when she heard Ruthie coming into her room with Angel in her arms.

A month later, with the unveiling of the tombstone, her daughters came to get her out of bed. They clucked their tongues approvingly when they saw how much weight she had lost. Like an infant taking its first steps, Rosa tottered to the grave, and there, in front of the large crowd that had come to pay their respects, she asked Shraga to forgive her. At the exit from the cemetery she sipped the glass of cold water offered her on a purple plastic tray by Yochai the Undertaker, who accompanied her to the car and with a theatrical flourish settled her skirts about her and closed the door behind her.

When she came home she asked them to bring Angel to her. With the silent child on her lap she paged through the photograph albums until she found what she was looking for. She removed her wedding photograph with Shraga and carefully cut it down the middle. Then she asked Ruhama to take the half with Shraga to the photography studio and have it enlarged. And when she came back with the poster-size picture rolled up in her hand, she asked her family to have the pictures of both her husbands, Joseph and Shraga, framed in identical frames and hung side by side opposite her bed. "Because that's the only way I can stop them from fighting at night," she said.

In the empty evenings after the visit to the cemetery for the unveiling of the tombstone, after her daily telephone conversations with her seven children, she would seat Angel on her lap and tell her about her fathers, first Joseph and then Shraga, and Angel would listen silently and shrink into her little body as if she blamed her mother for their deaths.

About two months after Shraga's death the miracle happened. When she went into Angel's room to get her ready for nursery school, she found her sitting up in bed and pointing at a crow flying outside the window and pecking at the glass with his hooked beak.

"Bird!" The little girl piped the first word she had ever pronounced in her life.

Rosa stood frozen in astonishment.

"Bird?" she asked.

"Bird!" she repeated firmly and smiled at her mother.

"Bird, crow," Rosa succeeded in saying, with the tears pouring down her cheeks.

An hour later, after sending Angel off to her day care, Rosa got busy on the telephone, calling all her children one after the other to tell them about the miracle.

"You'll see," she repeated seven times, "that child will still surprise us all, and the doctors and their theories can all go to hell."

After the child had uttered the first word of her life, Rosa began paying special attention to her. She watched television programs for children with her, read her stories, repeated words to her, supplied her with paper and crayons, and collected her drawings in books. It soon transpired that the only things Angel knew how to draw were birds and butterflies. And when Rosa tried to teach her to draw houses with red roofs and chimneys sending up smoke, the child would rebel, throw temper tantrums, and when she calmed down she would fill the pages with birds and butterflies again.

At this time Rosa was certain that Angel had stopped growing. Even though Angel was nearly four years old, she looked like a child of two.

"And that's how she'll stay," the doctors she ran to consult pronounced. "Your child won't grow anymore; she'll remain the same height, and there's nothing to be done about it."

And Rosa would go home, kiss her little girl, who would always stay small, and know that the requests she had made of all her seven previous children in turn had accumulated until they had come true in this last child.

In the first year after Shraga's death, when the old pangs of longing made her body ache, she would open the drawers of shoes, breathe in the familiar smell assailing her nostrils, stunning her heart with memories, and moving her body to feel old passions. Then she would commune with the shoes for hours at a time, arranging and rearranging them in their drawers and on their shelves. She kept this up until the day she opened the drawer of his ballet shoes and a sour, unfamiliar smell greeted her nose. In dismay she pulled the drawer out and discovered right at the back a pair of tattered shoes full of the clear marks of tiny teeth. The next day another pair of shoes was gnawed, and after a week, when the shoes were completely eaten up, she discovered at the back of the drawer containing the leather shoes, a nest padded with bits of silk, threads of gray woolen army socks, and scraps of Shraga's warm winter undershirts.

Alarmed, she asked Ruhama to bring her some mousetraps from the market, and every morning she examined them without discovering so much as the tip of a mouse's tail. The professional rat catcher she called in announced, as if he were giving her particularly good news, that she had a subtenant in the house, described to her the domestic mouse, also known as the common mouse, who had chosen her home above all others in the vicinity and decided to do her the honor of sharing his life with her. He told her that the mouse was especially active at night, that it ate everything, and that Rosa would have to resign herself to the fact that in order to build its nest and bring up its young, it would use any soft and available material it came across. And when Rosa asked him in horror about mouse offspring, he explained in a congratulatory tone that her mouse was apparently a pregnant female, since she had built a nest in which to give birth to her litter. The exterminator explained admiringly, as if he were speaking about his own children, that at the age of three months the babies turned into parents in their own right and built new nests for the next generation. Judging by the tone of his voice, she suspected that he was a mouse lover, and since it made no sense for a mouse lover to be a mouse exterminator, he had no doubt come to her house in order to rescue the creatures and not to destroy them.

Since she was a polite woman, Rosa thanked him for his informative lecture and decided that she would have to get along with them as best she could. After a few months of sharing the house with her unwanted lodgers, she went to check on Shraga's shoes and found nothing in the drawers but leather soles, plastic soles, and rubber soles. She gathered up the orphaned soles and put them away in a box that she relegated to the storage space under the roof, together with the magnificent gilt frame wrapped in the stained sheet, which had once held the portrait of Joseph. From the day that they finished chewing up Shraga's shoes, the rodents disappeared, never to visit her house again.

fifteen

JACOB'S DREAM

Ever since Shraga had departed this world and Rosa had hung his picture up next to Joseph's, it seemed to her that her first husband had calmed down. He no longer harassed her and hurled accusations at her, and at night as she lay alone in bed in the sideways position recommended by the doctors, lest her body with its internal organs collapse and suffocate her to death, she would think about both her husbands and try not to sell either of them short. In order to maintain strict equality between them, she would check her watch and allocate the same time to her reflections and memories of both Joseph and Shraga in turn. But try as she might, she failed in her endeavors, and Joseph always succeeded in stealing precious memory time at Shraga's expense. In the time allocated to Shraga, Joseph's face would invade her thoughts, and when she tried to remember Shraga's soft hands touching her, she would feel Joseph's big callused hands stroking her face. She would close her eyes and concentrate with all her might on Shraga and his tiny feet, and again Joseph's face would squeeze in through a split second of distraction, and again she would smell the nicotine on his breath and the lavender soap on his body rudely pushing aside Shraga's scent of oranges. Then she would surrender to her memories, ask Shraga to forgive her for sending him to his untimely death, and to take into account the fact that she had spent some fifty years more with Joseph than she had with him.

In the days when she was sunk in grief she found herself unthinkingly skipping meals, and suddenly she became aware that her dresses were loose on her body. After a few months of losing weight, "at a satisfactory rate," as her doctor told her, she succeeded too in ridding herself of the permanent pressure on her chest, which she did not always know whether to ascribe to her excess weight or to the pangs of conscience she had felt since Shraga's tragic death.

Every morning she would weigh herself and find that she had lost a little more weight. Then she would stand naked in front of the mirror and look for the pink stretch marks left on the bodies of fat women when they lose weight. First she would examine her thighs. Then her eyes would climb to her stomach, and finally she would swing her breasts from side to side and peek underneath them. Satisfied with the results of her examination so far, she would turn around, look over her shoulder, and check on her backside. To her gratification, she discovered that her skin was taut and shiny, her breasts were full, and her buttocks as firm as ever.

After examining herself in the mirror Rosa would turn her attention to Angel. With every spoonful she fed her she would repeat new words and recite old nursery rhymes to her. When the child imitated her and answered her questions correctly she would hug her and admire her rapid progress.

Every day after school her grandson Dror would come and teach Angel everything he had learned that day. With a protective canopy of black crows accompanying them to the sound of excited caws, he would take her out into the fields that surrounded the neighborhood and reached the houses of the Arab village of Beit Safafa. Round and round the crows would circle over the children's heads, chasing away rival birds, sparrows and wild pigeons, which were obliged to worship Angel from afar. When she sat down with Dror in the field, the crows would fly down, cluster around them, and chatter loudly and excitedly in their throaty language. Angel would throw them crumbs of the bread Rosa had spread with chocolate for their expedition, and the birds would hop up and receive the gracious gifts of their adored queen with bowed heads and drooping wings.

Then Dror would show her the flowers and teach her their names. And he would tell her about the butterflies and the bees, and tell her to stand still next to a flower and watch to see how the butterfly sucked up its nectar. With spots of color from flowers and butterflies dancing before their eyes, he would tell her about the world below the ground, too, Hades, that black place that nobody knew and where all the bad souls were destined to go. In order to illustrate his words he would walk round the fields with her until he found what he was looking for, a little rock sunk in the ground. Laboriously he would dig it up, and together they would stare at the wound revealed in the earth, exposing to every eye what the rock had been trying to conceal. Dozens of tiny creatures, silvery and albino white, which had never seen the light of the sun, groping their way blindly in the sudden glare, searching for a crack through which they could be swallowed up in the darkness again. Gray insects with scaly chain-mailed backs curled up in panic, turning themselves in a second into tiny armored balls against harm from any quarter. Transparent snails sent out their feelers, trying at their slow pace to escape the sun that melted soft unprotected tissues, leaving shiny trails of slime behind them. Among the commotion of fleeing insects were the tangled white roots of invisible plants, some delicate and feathery and others thick, rough, and woody.

And when the sun went down, turning Angel's head to gold and painting the fields red, and all around the air echoed with the din of chirping crickets and cicadas desperately searching for their mates, he would tell her in a whisper the story of Jacob's dream, a story he took care not to repeat in the presence of his grandmother. Because when she once heard him tell the tale to Angel, she asked him to stop and not to fill the little girl's head with nonsense, since it wasn't too strong to begin with. There in the abandoned fields surrounding the neighborhood like a hangman's noose, far from Rosa's vigilant ears, in an unchanging ritual, he would put his head next to Angel's, and with his curly hair touching her golden tresses, he would whisper the story into her ear.

He told her about the ancient patriarch Jacob, who, weary with the long journey, lay down and fell asleep on a stone. In his dream he saw a tall ladder with its top in the heavens and angels going up and down it. All the angels wore long robes of silk, their hair was long and shining, and their little feet went up and down the ladder made of solid gold. "And in that band of angels there was one special angel," Dror would say and bring his head closer to hers. "It was the smallest and most beautiful angel of all. Its eyes were azure blue, just like yours, and its hair was long and gold and wavy and reached all the way to the ground. Because this angel was so small, it was afraid of heights. All the time it was climbing, on the advice of its friends, the little angel tried not to look down at the ground. But since it was very curious and wanted to know exactly what the people down there in the fields looked like, it looked down, got giddy, and *boom*!—it fell off the ladder. Because of the noise it made Jacob woke up, and as soon as he woke up the dream vanished and the golden ladder with all its angels disappeared into the sky. And the fallen angel couldn't go back to heaven, because it didn't have a ladder to climb up on. For years it wandered the world looking for a way back to its fellow angels. Every night it would visit people in their dreams, but none of them ever dreamed Jacob's dream. Some people dreamed of ladders and some people dreamed of angels, but nobody dreamed of a golden ladder with its top in heaven and angels going up and down it. And since it never found the ladder, it looked for a new body to live in until it could return to heaven. For years it searched among the children of the world, but it never found the right one. With every new child born the angel hurried to its side to see if it suited its needs, and so it examined all the children in the world, but all the children grew too fast to fit the little angel. Until you were born. The day you were born it saw you even before your mother saw you, and it rejoiced and decided to enter into your body, because it knew that you wouldn't grow and that with your help it would succeed in getting back to heaven. And in order to return to heaven it made you a pair of wings."

Dror would conclude his story, stroking the little humps on her back, and repeating the last sentence like a soothing mantra in her ears: "And one day, you'll spread your wings and fly straight up into the clouds, and you'll go back to heaven and play with all the other angels there." Then he would look deep into Angel's eyes and she would repeat after him: "Angel will fly up to heaven and play with the angels." And Dror would hug her little body, kiss her forehead, and say: "Yes, Angel will fly up to heaven and play with the angels."

And when the song of the insects subsided in the fields, black shadows crept into Angel's hair and darkened its color, and a cold wind penetrated their clothes and chilled their flesh, they would go home and the crows would return to their nests.

And when Dror brought Angel home, Rosa would see that her cheeks were red with the sun, her hair was full of bits of grass and crumbling dry leaves, and her eyes were shining as if she had discovered new worlds in the fields that she couldn't tell her mother about.

She would press her to her bosom and feel the warmth of the sun seeping into her and penetrating her bones. And when she undressed her and combed her hair the fresh scent of the fields would rise in her nostrils, and her eyes would cloud over with memories as a thick shower of bright butterflies rained down before them.

sixteen

CHEERFUL HANDS

The morning after a particularly hard night, most of which she had spent in painful memories, bitter regrets, and repeated pleas for forgiveness for having killed Shraga by mistake, Rosa woke with difficulty to the sound of knocking on the door.

She dragged herself heavily to the door and looked through the peephole. A tall thin man in the prime of his life, holding a large cardboard folder in his hands, stood there, shifting his weight nervously from foot to foot. Since he appeared harmless enough, she opened the door.

The strange man drew back slightly and looked at her with an admiration he did nothing to hide. Rosa examined the brown beret flattening black hair streaked with white, and the shabby white shirt on which reposed a limp pink bow tie. Then her eyes traveled down to the trousers, faded in the wash, and the cracked shoes under innumerable layers of shoe polish. To her surprise she saw that his hands were large, strong, and cheerful.

Later on, when she tried to understand what she could have meant by thinking his hands were cheerful, she remembered that they were dotted with bright spots in all the colors of the rainbow, and seemed to her when she first set sight on them like the giant wings of an exotic butterfly of incomparable beauty.

The stranger's gray eyes, which were surrounded by a fan of fine wrinkles, twinkled at her warmly, and his narrow lips parted in a tentative smile, revealing a row of gleaming white teeth. Rosa gazed into his eyes, examined his strong teeth, appraised his lean body, and decided that he was rather a handsome man.

"You're Rosa!" he cried joyfully in a deep baritone voice, as if he had discovered a long-lost relative. "You're as beautiful as I imagined you," he went on, gasping for breath, either from excitement or the tiring climb up three flights of stairs. When he saw her questioning look, he held out his right hand. Hesitantly Rosa put her hand in his, and as he grasped it eagerly she felt his palm rubbing against hers and the lines of their fate merging in perfect harmony. The stranger hurried to introduce himself.

"Shmuel. Shmuel Evron. You might have heard of me." And when he realized that his name wasn't making the desired impression, he added, on a note of disappointment: "I'm a painter."

With her hand in his she looked at him in silence and discovered the little tic that made his upper lip twitch and tremble in a way that aroused her compassion and melted her heart.

"May I come in?" asked the painter, his self-confidence eroding and the tremor in his lip growing more severe.

"Yes, of course, forgive me," she said and moved aside to let him in.

His eyes opened wide, as if reluctant to lose even a fraction of the crown of creation preceding him, gazed admiringly at the vast backside swaying in front of him with the rise and fall of great ocean breakers. The magnificent posterior, attached to the broadest back he had ever seen, led him into the depths of the living room. From one of the doors in the passage a curly little head peeked out. A minute fair-haired child, built with perfect symmetry, resembling in every respect a cupid in a classical painting, stood in the doorway and looked at him curiously. In spite of her charming appearance, Shmuel felt a cold shiver running down his spine and contracting his heart with an inexplicable pain. Ignoring the ominous foreboding, he turned to look at Rosa again, his eyes dazzled by the whiteness of her skin, drowning in her eyes, and riveted by the vast bosom bouncing freely before him in perfect coordination with the movements of her body. Rosa asked him to excuse her, bent down to the child, picked her up in her arms, and murmured soothingly in her ear. The child closed her eyes and nestled against her mother's bosom. Shmuel contemplated this maternal scene, and to his horror saw the two little humps sticking out of the miniature creature's back and spoiling the harmonious lines of her body.

"Who's he?" the child asked in a whisper.

"A friend," replied Rosa, with her eyes fixed on his.

"I'm a painter," he repeated, as he sat down on the armchair after

Rosa had cleared away the pile of linen waiting to be ironed, staring at the gigantic mother and her tiny child. He immediately remembered that he had already introduced himself to her, and he blushed hotly, feeling like a fool.

Rosa looked at him pityingly, well aware of the effect of her appearance, which was capable of paralyzing stronger men. Experience had taught her that her dimensions always gave rise, even in large-bodied and well-built men, to a passing feeling of weakness, puniness, and physical inferiority. Their faces turned red, their speech faltered, they talked nonsense and made themselves look ridiculous to her.

"I'd like to paint you." Shmuel overcame the obstruction in his throat at last, and succeeded in saying the sentence he had been rehearsing with every step as he climbed the three flights of stairs to Rosa's apartment. With the twitch wreaking havoc on his lip, he examined the effect of his words on her. It seemed to him that Rosa had not taken in his request, and so he repeated it, this time more loudly, as if he were speaking to a woman who was hard of hearing or feebleminded.

"I want to paint you."

"What does the man want?" asked Angel in a piping voice.

"The man wants to paint me," she said, and as she took in the meaning of what she had just said her chin began to tremble. The tremor spread to her double chins and made them quiver, crept to the unconfined breasts bouncing up and down in front of her like a couple of giant balls, took hold of her belly that shook like a vast mound of jelly, slid down her thighs, and eventually reached her feet, which kicked gaily in the air. A couple of seconds later the laughter broke out in a roar that sounded to the furiously blushing Shmuel like the bellowing of a calf about to be slaughtered. Angel's little body shook in her mother's heaving arms as she joined in with tinkling chimes of mirth.

"Paint me?!" she roared. And when she recovered she apologized for her outburst and asked him: "Why?"

"You're a beautiful woman." He repeated the speech he had rehearsed during the long bus journey. "You're a big, beautiful woman and I've wanted to paint you for years," he confessed, and pulled out of the shabby cardboard portfolio a collection of newspaper cuttings all about Rosa.

"I've been following your career from an early age," he announced with lowered eyes like a youngster declaring his love for the first time in his life. "To my regret, I was obliged to paint you from the photographs that appeared in the newspapers. I've been dreaming of painting you for years, ever since I arrived in the country," he said shyly. And when she looked at him questioningly, he added that now that he had improved as a painter and gained a reputation and held exhibitions in Israel and abroad, he had finally plucked up the courage to knock on her door and request what he had dreamed of requesting for nearly forty years.

Then he removed several large sheets of paper from a separate compartment in the portfolio and showed Rosa his paintings. She gazed in embarrassment at the large woman smeared in pastels spread out before her in poses that brought a blush to her cheeks. The woman looked back at her curiously. Rosa could not ignore the fact that the woman in the pictures bore an astonishing resemblance to her. Shmuel watched her as she looked at his work, gathered up the drawings, and apologized for portraying her in this manner.

"Please understand," he tried to explain. "Since I couldn't paint the original, I painted you as you appeared in the pictures in the newspapers, and added a lot of imagination."

"She really does look like me," she admitted in the end, after a long, embarrassed silence.

"Would you like to see more of my work?" he asked shyly.

"Gladly," she replied, and watched him as he removed more paintings from the portfolio with trembling hands. Slowly and carefully he laid the drawings on the living room table, and when there was no more room, he spread them on the floor, on the sofa next to Rosa and on the chair standing by its side. From all the drawings fat women looked out at her, most of them naked and some of them seminaked.

"This is Eve," he explained as he picked up a picture of an enormous woman. Her crotch and heavy breasts were symbolically adorned with tiny fig leaves, and a thick, brightly colored snake with a vicious expression was slithering revoltingly round her rolls of fat.

"And this is the matriarch Sarah." He pointed to a picture of a giantess whose face bore a strong resemblance to Rosa's. "And this is Bathsheba bathing on the roof, and this is the Queen of Sheba and this is Jezebel." He jerked his chin in the direction of the immense figures filling the pages. It seemed to Rosa at that moment as if Shmuel were introducing her to his closest kin and the women nearest and dearest to him in the world.

After presenting all his women to her, he quickly put all the pictures back in the portfolio, as if he regretted having exposed his loves in their nakedness, and had decided from now on to guard their privacy from the eyes of the world. When he took his leave of her at the door, he avoided looking at the defective child who spoiled the beauty of his vision, and asked Rosa again if she would agree to pose for him. With a blush spreading over her cheeks and creeping down her chest, she replied in a confidential whisper that she would have to think about it and that he should come back the next day.

That night she consulted her seven children on the telephone. The girls were excited and told her that it was an opportunity not to be missed, and it was only the queens and princesses of Europe that had their portraits painted by famous painters. The boys sounded suspicious. Leslie-Shimon, Jackie-Ya'akov, and James-Gad demanded in one voice, as if they had agreed beforehand, that if she agreed to pose for him, it had to be on condition that she was fully dressed. On no account, they added threateningly, was she to take off her clothes. And Rosa, to whom such a thing had never even occurred, was insulted and hung up on all three of them angrily.

The next day, when Shmuel arrived, she answered in the affirmative.

"Then come to my studio tomorrow morning," he said quickly, before she could change her mind.

"I hardly go out of the house to do the shopping. If you want to paint me, it will have to be here," she announced, hoping that he would agree.

Shmuel opened the shutters, drew the curtains, examined the light, and agreed. But before he left he told her that she would have to be very patient, because the work could take a long time.

When Ruthie came to take Angel to her day care she stared shamelessly at Shmuel, who was making himself at home and setting up his easel in the living room with a lot of noise. She looked at his colorful hands, examined him from top to bottom, winked encouragingly at Rosa, and left the house with Angel in her arms. Rosa settled down heavily on the sofa wearing a silk dress patterned with big red poppies. He looked at her with his eyes shining, grinning from ear to ear, went up to her, and showed her how he wanted her to sit, casually touching her hand as he did so.

Afterward she would tell Rachelle and Ruhama, who wanted to hear all the details, that when his hand brushed against hers, she felt as if her hand were on fire. For hours she sat opposite him like a stone, and after the pounding of her heart was stilled, her limbs went to sleep one by one, until she fell asleep herself. She woke to the sound of the easel being folded up and the tubes of paint being returned to their box.

"Show me how I came out," she asked drowsily.

Shmuel refused. "Strictly forbidden," he said with a mischievous smile. "I can't show it to you until it's finished, otherwise you'll refuse to sit for me."

The next day he came at eight on the dot, and he went on coming during the following weeks, and Rosa's taste for life returned. Every morning she would wake up two hours before he was due and prepare herself in his honor. First she would bathe in the Jacuzzi, and after the hot water had turned her skin red and sent the blood coursing through her veins, and she felt her flesh tingling enjoyably in the bubbles, she would rub the hard skin off her soles with a pumice stone, separate her toes, and wash carefully between them. When she was through with her feet she turned her attention to her armpits, scrubbed and shaved them ruthlessly, and went on from there to her breasts, lathering and massaging them in ever-diminishing circles until she reached the pink circles round the erect nipples. With her flesh prickling deliciously she would descend to her nether parts and lather her tangled bush of curls. Finally she would soap a finger, crook her hand behind her, fondle her buttocks, and absentmindedly insert her soapy finger deep inside her rectum, cleaning it thoroughly.

When her body was clean inside and out she would turn her attention to her hair, washing it with imported shampoo, anointing it with a conditioner that made it feel like silk, and combing it in the elaborate curls she favored. As she sat in front of the mirror and made up her face and eyes, she would feel the sensations of cleanliness, freshness, and anticipation that used to make her body tingle when Shraga washed her. But she would quickly push aside these memories of her old love in order to make room for the new one that was beginning to ferment inside her. After eating her breakfast she would paint her lips with shiny red lipstick, repair her eye makeup, put on her silk dress with the poppy pattern, and wait excitedly for him to appear. And when he set up his easel with the painting and looked at her with adoring eyes, her body would be racked with the sweet pain of a vacuum longing to be filled. With her eyes glazed, she would settle into her position on the sofa and wait for the first strokes of the brush on the canvas, which made her flesh prickle with a pleasure such as she had never felt before, as if the brush were sweeping over her actual flesh and tickling it in the most sensitive places.

After three weeks, when he told her that the painting was finished, she asked him to show it to her. Shyly and hesitantly, as if it was himself he was about to bare before her, he carefully removed the white cloth covering the canvas. Rosa stared speechlessly at her portrait.

"Is that me?" she asked weakly when she recovered her voice.

Shmuel laughed in relief. He knew that Rosa liked what she saw. "Yes, it's you," he whispered, as if revealing a secret to her.

"Is that what I look like? Are you sure?" she asked again, and her heart beat as if it wanted to burst through the barrier of her gigantic bosom.

"Yes, exactly."

The big woman looking at her was more beautiful than anything that Rosa could have imagined. She lay languidly on her side on a red silk sofa like a princess in a harem, her slanting blue eyes half shut and smiling. Her head was crowned with thick, shining curls, and her face was free of wrinkles and signs of age.

The next day he arrived with a new canvas, and this time he demanded to examine her wardrobe. After rummaging briefly among her dresses he chose one with lace and ruffles, a shorter hem, and a lower neckline. When she sat in front of him in the dress he had chosen and the pose he had requested, with a big bowl of gleaming summer fruit next to her, he asked her to raise the hem a little, so that he could paint her legs from the ankles to the thighs. Rosa did as he asked. A month later she found herself gazing at the picture of a beautiful, fleshy gypsy—half sitting, half lying—with a darkly seductive look in her eyes.

During the many hours of her sittings, she would look at his paint-spotted hands, and imagine them undressing her, stroking her body, and massaging her breasts. Full of anticipation she examined his mouth, sensing his lips pressing on hers and his tongue touching hers. When he bent over her to correct her pose she would examine the swelling in his trousers, look into his gray eyes, which softened under her gaze, and smell the turpentine and oil paint that seemed to be on his breath.

Without understanding how it happened, she began exposing more and more of herself to his brushes, until she found herself one day lying on her side on the sofa, one hand on the backrest, the other supporting her right breast, her legs drawn slightly back, as naked as the day she was born.

Her nudity seemed to make things difficult for him, and he would sit staring at her for a long time with his brush in his hand and a hesitant expression on his face, as if he couldn't decide where to begin and how to proceed. For hours at a time she would lie still in the pose he requested and wait for him to begin, but he seemed dissatisfied. Every now and then he would shake off his paralysis, go up to her, push a stray curl off her forehead, alter the position of the hand supporting her breast, and measure her with admiring eyes.

On the fifth day of the nude pose she had already lost hope, and she resigned herself to another day passing without a single brushstroke making its appearance on the bare canvas. She lay on the sofa, and Shmuel, as usual, got up to correct her pose. As if by mistake, his hand brushed against the soft, white flesh of her shoulder, and he withdrew it in alarm, as if from a burning coal. Resolutely Rosa seized hold of his hand and passed it over her shoulders. As if lacking a will of its own, the hand slid down her arm and hovered over her right breast. Her nipple pricked up in response, and without a thought for the pose they had labored over for days she held up both her arms, clasped them firmly around his neck, and pressed his lips to hers. Thrusting her tongue into his mouth she felt the smooth surface of his white teeth and tasted the flavor of his peppermint gum.

After a moment that felt to her like eternity, Shmuel freed himself abruptly from her embrace, took a deep gulp of air, and dived for her lips again, nuzzling and nibbling hungrily at their smooth, slippery fleshiness. Rosa opened her mouth wide into the kiss, her tongue plunged into the depths of his mouth, examining the roughness of his palate, probing between his teeth, and flicking against the inside of his cheeks. He began wrestling with her inside the cavern of his mouth with his tongue coiling and tightening around hers, alternately crushing and caressing as it twisted and vibrated.

Rosa knew that she would not be satisfied with his tongue. She wanted all his mouth, all his head, all his body, all of him. Generously she opened her mouth until her jaws hurt, and allowed him to win the battle. Like a victor his tongue lay heavily on hers, throbbing and salivating sweetly.

A moment later they were writhing together on the floor. Tugging and tearing, Rosa ripped from his body the clothing that separated her from her pleasure. As she struggled with him she felt the pain of the void yawning in her body and crying out to be filled. And when he buried himself inside her, filling her with his love, with his flesh and his warmth, she sucked him into her, thrilling to the electric currents running through her body from top to toe. Once she was the penetrater and once the penetrated, once the hollow and once the protuberance, until she could no longer distinguish between what was his and what was hers and what she gave him and what he gave her and what she received from him and what he received from her. Together with him she climbed the steps of pleasure, step after step, higher and higher, until she reached the top and could no longer stop herself and plunged joyfully into the abyss yawning below.

Lightly and airily she threw herself off the cliff together with her lover into the black hole sucking them deliciously in, and she heard herself pleading and shouting in a voice she didn't recognize: "More, more, more!" A long time later she lay in her pose on the sofa with her body satiated, her nipples stiff with pleasure, her cheeks pink, and her chin grazed and scratched with the stubble of his beard. With sparks of light in her eyes she looked at Shmuel hastily pulling on his shorts and trousers, composing his features into their previous expression, and trying with trembling hands to paint her.

After this she would wait for him in the mornings with her flesh melting in anticipation. As soon as he came in she would lead him to the sofa, take a few steps backwards, and with her eyes fixed on his she would slither out of her clothes, wriggling her butt around in imitation of the striptease she had seen the one time she went to Cinema Rosa. Completely naked she would stand before him, waiting in suspense for the touch of his bright hands on her body. And when his hands began to roam over her, she wanted to feel his body joined to hers, uniting with her and pulsing inside her. Then Shmuel would rapidly remove his trousers and shorts, always leaving his long-sleeved shirt on, and penetrate her with urgent force.

When their bodies were satiated, she would lie down on the sofa in the familiar pose, her eyes smiling serenely, and wait for the first brushstrokes on the canvas to send thrills through her body. And when the painting was finished, and he unveiled it with a flourish, Rosa gazed at herself in growing astonishment. The body she knew so intimately was reflected with the accuracy of a mirror, every dimple in its place, every fine blue vein in the lacy network covering her great breasts captured on the canvas. Shmuel had reproduced the expression on her face, the light in her eyes, the smile on her lips, and the relaxed position of her hand. The precision of the details was so great that she could have sworn he had counted every hair on her head and groin.

She confided in Rachelle that as soon as she saw the picture she became aware that Shmuel knew her intimately, both inside and out. He knew what her internal organs looked like, he had made friends with the heart beating under her gigantic bosom, breathed in the air exhaled by her lungs, was familiar with the road through her intestines traveled by the food she chewed, with the electric currents passing through her brain, and with the size and depth of her womb. And from that moment Rosa knew that she wanted to share her life with this man.

"But you don't know anything about him," said Rachelle, who was suspicious by nature. "All you know about him is that he's a painter. You don't know who he is, where he was born, who his parents were, if he's married or not, if he has any children, how old he is, where he lives, how much he earns. I'm surprised at you! He's been painting you for so many months, and you've never asked him any of these questions. There's something fishy here. He must be married. I simply can't understand how a woman your age loses her head again and behaves like a silly young girl falling in love for the first time."

"So what should I do?" asked Rosa helplessly after hearing her friend list all these questions.

"If you're serious about him, ask him," said Rachelle firmly.

The next day Shmuel arrived with his huge shabby portfolio and, as if he had read her thoughts and overheard her conversation with Rachelle, announced that since they had become so close it was time for her to know everything about him. With an angry movement he overturned the portfolio and shook out its contents. Rosa looked in horror at the pictures spread out before her, painted on all kinds of rags and tatters and on notices printed in curly Gothic script. As soon as she took the pictures in, she knew for certain that not only had she seen them before, but even worse, that she herself was one of the figures in the terrible scenes etched in charcoal with harsh, cruel lines.

Suddenly she felt a terrible, gnawing hunger, and the emaciated skull-like face of Mischa, who had occupied the kitchen in the villa in Old Katamon, pushed Shmuel's face out of her field of vision. Mischa's stories came back and echoed in her ears, stunning her and pulverizing her from within, consuming her flesh, and leaving her skin and bones, a walking skeleton. She was the woman in the picture, whose sacks of breasts hung on her body like a pair of pockets emptied of their contents, herded into the showers of death and then shoveled into the gaping mouth of the fiery furnace. She was the shriveled body from whose mouth a haggard man in striped pajamas was extracting gold teeth while her eyes stared through him with the baffled look of the dead. She saw the skeleton of her body walking naked, its feet leaving bloody prints on the thick blanket of snow while a tall, stout man in a black uniform whipped the exposed flesh hanging on her bones.

"During the war, when I was a young boy, I worked in a *Sonderkommando* in Auschwitz," he said in a soft voice that sounded in her ears like a sharp, jarring scream. "I was responsible for removing the bodies from the gas chambers and transferring them to crematorium number five. I was a child of twelve, but since I looked much older than my age, I said I was seventeen and got the job that saved my life. At the same time I started drawing like a lunatic. I drew on every scrap of paper or material that I could find. I drew the women I saw in the gas chambers and the crematoria, naked and emaciated; I drew sexless bodies and women's skeletons. Since I had no paints, I made them from chicory coffee and a mixture of earth, leaves, and bark," he said harshly. And when he felt her body shivering in his hands, he added with a grim smile: "Perhaps that's why I like painting fat women now—beautiful, healthy women, just like you."

Afterward he sat with her for a long time and told her that at the beginning of the war his father was taken away to a forced-labor camp and never heard of again. He and his mother and his two little brothers were taken to Auschwitz, where they were separated from one another. At first he had dug mass graves and watched the Germans throwing in the bodies of murdered men, women, and children. Then he had been ordered to remove the dead bodies from the gas chambers and burn them in the crematoria. He also told her how the Germans had discovered his talents as an artist and calligrapher and set him to writing illustrated letters to the mistresses of the camp commanders, drawing birds, flowers and angels on their love letters. Worst of all was when the commandant of the women's camp saw his pictures of angels and forced him to decorate lampshades made of human skin with them.

"When I drew the angels, I always wondered who the skin belonged to, and I was afraid that it might be the skin of my mother or one of my brothers, whom I hadn't seen since the selection on the railway platform."

Rosa hugged him tightly and rolled up the sleeve of his shirt, which he never took off, not even when they made love, and exposed the blue number tattooed on his arm. Again Mischa's face rose before her, obliterating Shmuel. However hard she tried to banish it, it kept on surfacing, bringing with it the touch of his hands on her body. With her mouth full of the taste of the stale cookies he used to feed her, she gazed at the number tattooed on her lover's arm, repeated the digits to herself, and compared them with the ones on Mischa's arm. When she was sure that she remembered them by heart, she kissed them one by one, licking, sucking, and nibbling, trying with her tongue and lips to obliterate them and bandage the pain.

With his head clasped in her arms, he told her that he couldn't look at the number tattooed on his arm and etched into his soul. And in his attempts to forget the accursed numbers branded on his body for the rest of his life, he was unable to deal with any numbers at all. He needed help in making the simplest calculation; the easiest sums confused him. And because of the tattoo branded onto his flesh he never wore short-sleeved shirts on even the hottest summer days, and never exposed his torso in bathing trunks. It always seemed to him that people's eyes were drawn to the number on his arm, which betrayed him, telling everyone where he came from and what he had suffered there.

And when she asked him to tell her more about his life in the camp, he said that even if she had heard all the stories from the lips of the six million, read all the testimonies, visited all the camps and lived day and night in Yad Vahem, she would still be incapable of imagining the horror. And when she pressed him, he told her in a whisper that the ghastly work he had been forced to do had made him feel disgust for himself. "After the war, when we were liberated by the Russians, and I looked in the mirror, I saw a man with no feelings, sick and repulsive."

Rosa felt as if a barbed-wire fence had been erected between them. He was standing on one side and she was standing on the other, and they reached out for each other with their hands but could not touch. Then she banished all such thoughts from her mind and listened in pain and pity to his stories. And when the lump in her throat melted, she made up her mind to compensate him for everything he had been through and make him the happiest man alive. She asked him hesitantly about his marital status, and when he told her that he was divorced and childless, she breathed a sigh of relief. She asked him curiously about his ex-wife. Shmuel closed his eyes in pain and told her about the refugee girl, the survivor of the hell of the camps that he had met on the ship to Israel. Since they both felt alone in the world they fell in love and married on board ship, with the captain performing the ceremony. When they arrived in the country and began their lives together they found themselves suffocating in memories of death, unable to break out of the circle of horror, and after a few years they decided to part and try to find happiness with partners who had not been through what they had. "She remarried immediately and had a family," he told Rosa. "And I painted you and waited for us to meet."

And when he asked her before he left if she would allow him to hold an exhibition of his paintings of her, she couldn't refuse him. When she told her children in seven separate phone calls, she closed her ears to the warnings of her daughters and the yells of her sons and decided that she would stand by Shmuel to the end.

The exhibition *Rosa* opened in the Artists' House in Jerusalem and caused a sensation in the town. The evening of the gala opening was charged with tension due to the many anonymous phone calls threatening to burn down the gallery, throw acid on the offending pictures, and cut the abominations to ribbons. The more the threatening calls—which were widely quoted on the radio, in the press, and on the local

TV channel—multiplied, the surer Shmuel was that this exhibition would succeed above and beyond anything that had preceded it. And indeed, from the day the Artists' House had been founded, nobody could remember anything like the crowds who lined up to see it day after day. They came from all over the country. Young people dressed in the latest fashions arrived from Tel Aviv; residents of Haifa and the north, the Negev and the south, farmers with callused hands, waited patiently next to Jerusalemites with loaded plastic shopping baskets who came straight from the market to see "our Rosa." They all waited for hours in the blazing sun to see the exhibition, and afterward, over bowls of sunflower seeds on Friday night, they told their friends about the splendors of Rosa's naked flesh.

For the first time in his artistic career there was no question as to the quality of Shmuel Evron's work. In a long, illustrated article entitled "Mother Earth," Debbie Jiavon wrote in the local paper:

> The exhibition by Shmuel Evron shows only one figure in a number of variations: a woman stripping herself bare. The stripping here is of layers of pretense, of concealment. What distinguishes Rosa from other strippers is the unpolished nature of her nudity, which is far from any conventional definition of beauty. This nakedness is fully revealed in the last, most moving painting. Lying on the sofa, Rosa is painted in great detail in a naturalistic style that hides nothing. She presents herself as she is—a very fat woman, a sagging stomach falling in endless cascades of flesh, two mountains of fat challenging the viewer on her chest, things which have lost their original shape, and at the top—a sad, delicate, haunting face. Uncharacteristically, the eyes in this face are not open in an explicit invitation, promising an earthly paradise to the viewer. On the contrary. All her attention is turned inwards, to the understanding of her body. Beneath the closed lids is an inner attention to her body, her suffering, her past. This is a face that offers itself to us, frankly conveying the life lived by Rosa. It makes no attempt to please or to seduce. It reveals its owner, and makes us feel close to her.

> Evron gives us at last an intimate experience of closeness. He touches the flesh of this woman, and allows us to place our hands in his so that through him we too can touch the abundant flesh of Rosa. For us, both men and women, since her femininity is maternal, its invitation inspires trust, for Rosa is the great, the ultimate mother figure.
>
> It is obvious that Evron desires Rosa. The patient treatment he devotes to every inch of her flesh is that of someone who delights in the touch of her skin and is eager to share his pleasure with us. But he also sees who she really is. He penetrates her soul and accepts her as she is, a long-suffering woman who has borne many children and who bears the weight of her body as she bears the weight of her life. For where acceptance exists—there love grows.

Despite the explicit prohibition imposed by her sons, her daughters took no notice and stole into the gala opening of the exhibition. They stared in embarrassment at the huge canvases groaning beneath their mother's weight. The painted Rosa looked back at them defiantly. From painting to painting they followed the gradual stripping until they reached the end of the hall and the crowd of people clustered round *the* painting. They elbowed their way through the crowd with their sharp elbows, treading viciously on the feet of the people who stood gazing at the big naked woman like worshipers at a shrine. In astonishment they looked at the many men standing there in silence, stretching their necks like turkeys with swollen crops, their eyes fixed unembarrassed on the intimate parts of their love-saturated mother.

Her forehead creased with worry, Ruthie made her way through the crowds surrounding Rosa, who was dressed for the occasion in an elegant new purple silk dress, and whose eyes were sparkling. Furiously she hissed into her ear: "Just don't dare get married again. We're sick and tired of your nonsense."

Rosa, who looked as if she was in the middle of a sweet dream, woke up and looked at her eldest daughter, who at this moment seemed to her to be dreary, gray, and skinny, and surprisingly similar to her grandmother Angela. "How did you know?" she asked in astonishment.

"I know those looks of yours by now," Ruthie replied. "You'll make the whole family look ridiculous if you get married for a third time. Apart from that, you've already killed two husbands. Do you want to endanger the life of the new one too?"

"I was told that I'd marry four times, and I've only managed twice," said Rosa with ostentatious composure, and looked round for Shmuel, who was circulating among the crowds in a borrowed tuxedo, a black velvet tie choking his neck. She took Ruthie's hand in hers and went up to him.

"Are you going to marry my mother?" demanded Ruthie, looking disbelievingly at the colors covering the back of his hand.

Shmuel blushed. "I haven't really thought about it yet, but since you ask—," he added, and then and there he went down on his knees, took Rosa's hand in his brightly colored one, and in front of everyone, under Ruthie's melting eyes, he asked: "Will you marry me, Rosa?"

In reply Rosa pulled him to his feet, planted a kiss on his lips, and said, "Yes," in a resounding cry loud enough to be heard outside in the street.

All that night Rosa spent in long conversations with her two previous husbands, telling them about her new love and excusing her decision to get married again. Joseph, who refused to accept the news, gave her his hardest look, the look he saved for those rare occasions when he argued with Rosa and disagreed with her. In days gone by, this look was enough to make her submit, but this time, since she knew that he was buried in the earth, she stood her ground and heroically ignored him when he cursed her as a whore. Shraga received the news with a sour face, and it seemed to her that he accepted it, however reluctantly, since unlike Joseph he had only spent the briefest of times with her, even though he had waited for her all his life.

And before she fell asleep she cast one last glance at the thick wedding ring Shraga had bought her. She turned the ring, made of heavy links of gold, around her finger with a dainty, ladylike gesture, and then whipped it off, leaving her finger bare and free. Without giving it a second glance she dropped it into the drawer of her bedside table, added the gold bracelets and gold collar he had given her for their first anniversary, and as she firmly slammed the drawer shut, she heard the clink of Shraga's and Joseph's wedding rings hitting each other.

The night before the wedding both her late husbands appeared to her, and this time they brought Angela with them. Like a couple of bodyguards Joseph and Shraga stationed themselves on either side of her mother, exchanging amused looks and giggling like a pair of naughty children perpetrating a particularly mischievous prank. They didn't dare look her in the eye and left it to Angela to persuade her. With the ominous expression she saved for her most devastating prophecies of doom, Angela looked at her daughter, theatrically rustling her black silk dress, which was full of holes, dust, and cobwebs.

"Tell me, have you gone mad?" She spat the words at her from her toothless mouth. "Weren't two husbands enough for you? You need a third? Where will you get the strength to bury another one? Do you want the rabbis to pronounce you a lethal woman? And what about Angel? I can see that he can't stand the sight of her. You want another catastrophe? Haven't you had enough? What will the neighbors say?"

Rosa shut her ears and told herself that she was having a very bad dream.

But Angela kept on at her. "Don't come crying to me afterward and say that you didn't know," she warned her. "I see a catastrophe. Beware. Cancel the wedding." And when she realized that her words were falling on deaf ears, she asked her two escorts to try to dissuade Rosa from her reckless course. Joseph and Shraga shrugged their shoulders helplessly, looked at each other, and snickered like a pair of youngsters telling dirty jokes.

"That's enough! If you can't help me at least don't hinder me!" Angela shouted, waved a crooked finger in Rosa's face, and repeated her warning a number of times, until her words sounded like a muffled echo rising from the depths of the earth. "Stop and reconsider before catastrophe strikes!"

Rosa woke up in a panic, saw a shining ball of orange light fading before her eyes, and smelled the bittersweet scent of her mother's ruinous flowers. On trembling legs she went to the bathroom and examined the glass in which she kept her mother's false teeth. They were there, dry and full of dust, and this morning they didn't part to greet her in a cheerful grin.

This time Rosa decided on a modest wedding at the rabbinate. Wearing a simple dress, surrounded by her daughters, her grandchildren, and Rachelle and Ruhama, she looked lovingly at Shmuel standing next to her with an aged relative in a shabby suit at his side. At that moment she felt at peace with her decision, she knew that she had done the right thing, and even if her sons were ostracizing her and her new husband, her happiness was more important than their approval.

And when Shmuel slipped the wedding ring on her finger, she promised herself that she would make up to him for the terrible years in the camp, that she would love him to her dying day, and that she would end her life with him at her side, in spite of Ruhama and her butterfly prophecies.

seventeen

ANGELS ON THE CEILING

*The night after the wedding the couple se*cluded themselves in the King David Hotel, which presented them with a day and a night in its royal suite as a wedding gift to the famous painter and his model. There, on the bed whose softness had cradled the high and mighty of the world, presidents and kings, movie stars and billionaires, Rosa sank into the wide mattress and flattened its springs. Groaning heroically under their load, the steel springs divided her weight equally among them and trembled in response as she received her bridegroom with happy sighs and tears of gratitude.

"Would you ever have believed that we would make love on a bed that was warmed by the bodies of princes and princesses, kings and queens?" she asked Shmuel, opening her fingers and pressing the sheet, trying to feel their royal imprints on the mattress with her fingertips. Then she buried her nose deep in the plump pillow, sniffed it, and tried to breathe in the smells of sweat, soap, and shaving lotion left behind them by her aristocratic predecessors.

"You're my queen," murmured Shmuel and kissed her on the mouth. And when she pursed her lips and opened her mouth to trap his lips with hers, he pulled away and slid his tongue down her neck. And when she arched her neck in delight, he slid down to her breasts and from there to her belly, went on a foray into her private parts with his nose, and quickly brought in reinforcements in the shape of his lips and tongue. Rosa giggled shyly and then groaned with deep, throaty growls that surprised him with their volume. Encouraged by the warmth of her response he kept at it until the shock waves stiffened her body and shook her limbs in a series of involuntary spasms. And when the wave subsided, she lay on her back exhausted, her limbs outspread, and whispered weakly: "More."

"You're my queen," he told her again, and whispered a string of royal titles into her ear: "My czarina, my duchess, my empress, my countess, my princess." And thus, with her husband snuggled in her arms and two new wedding rings glittering on their interlaced fingers, Rosa fell asleep. Early in the morning she woke up to a sense of impending catastrophe. A feeling so tangible, threatening, and malevolent that she could actually touch it, hear it approaching with rude steps, smell its stinking breath, and hear its mocking laughter. Desperately she tried to turn her thoughts to the pleasures of the wedding night and looked lovingly at the face of her new husband lying at her side with his hands folded behind his head, his skin pink and healthy, and his breathing quiet and regular.

Suddenly she saw the faces of Joseph and Shraga under his features, and with terror striking at her heart she remembered her mother's prophecies and the fourth butterfly, and she knew that Shmuel would not be the last. As if comforting a hurt child, she gently stroked his face, kissed his lips, and smoothed his hair. Shmuel turned toward her in his sleep, put his arms around her, and pressed her to his chest as if she were about to slip away from him.

The numbers tattooed on his arm leaped out at her. She read them from left to right and right to left, seeking the hidden number with the new significance in her life. Against her will she found herself comparing Shmuel's numbers to Mischa's, trying to crack the message encoded in the living flesh. Unable to decipher the unintelligible code, she stroked the blue numbers gently with her fingertip, as if trying to atone for all the pain he had endured in his life and all the pain he was still to endure in the future. And when he murmured his words of love straight into her mouth, she felt a heavy depression spreading through her body and rudely pushing aside the pleasures of the night before.

With a terrible sobriety she sensed the catastrophe on its way to destroy her love for her new husband. Precisely at this joyful moment, with her husband cradled warmly in her arms, she was unable to escape from the painful memories of the past and their message of the evil in store. Painfully she remembered Rina and Mischa, the childhood she never had, the birth of the flawed Angel, the deterioration of Joseph, and the cold body of Shraga underneath her in bed. And when she remembered her friend Ruthie, who had died so young, the dam of tears burst, and she wept without restraint and woke Shmuel with her sobs. Blind to what was happening before his eyes, Shmuel rocked her gently in his arms, his mouth murmuring soothing words and his heart brimming over with the sweetness of his love for his new wife, who was weeping tears of joy.

"I love you," he whispered into her ears, where the tears had collected like miniature salt lakes. "I love you," he repeated, as if accustoming himself to the sound of the sentence. "For me you're all the women in the world, a whole harem of women concentrated in one woman, my queen," he whispered, and lapped up the pools of tears collected in her ears as greedily as if tasting some rare delicacy.

Afterward, when she told Rachelle about the terrifying premonition she had experienced precisely at the moments of her greatest happiness, her friend would tell her that love was always accompanied by a sense of doom, since nothing ever stayed as it was. Everything passed in life, and even the greatest love would vanish and give way to another. And it didn't surprise her that Rosa should have felt this way precisely on her wedding night, for great happiness was always accompanied by the fear of its loss. She would also explain to her that happiness and pain were the Siamese twins of fate. They always came together in an inseparable pair, a reminder of the fears of abandonment experienced in infancy.

The morning after the great weeping, Rosa put ice cubes on her eyes to bring down the swelling, and with the help of the sunbeams filtering through the blinds she succeeded in banishing black thoughts and conjuring up a bright future full of happiness, flowers, and birdsong. After eating the breakfast rolled into their room by the waiter, they went back to bed, and remained cradled there until noon, whispering words of love in each other's ears. And at noon they filled the vast bathtub with hot water and poured in all the little jars of foaming bath salts and oils they found there. With the upper halves of their bodies emerging from the airy bubbles cascading merrily over the sides of the tub, they splashed about in the water, scooped up handfuls of foam and threw them at each other, and soaped each other's bodies. And when they emerged from the bathroom they devoured the bowl of exotic fruits, wrapped the champagne in the hotel bathrobes, and crammed them into their suitcase together with the little bottles of shampoo, body lotion, shower caps, and unused sewing kit, and went home, exhausted with happiness.

Ruthie, Dror, and Angel were waiting for them in the apartment, which was full of flowers. And when Angel limped up to them in the fancy party dress she had worn only once, when Rosa married Shraga, her mother hugged her tightly and asked her to welcome Shmuel. Obediently the little girl extricated herself from her mother's embrace, stood shyly in front of Shmuel, and silently raised her arms in the air in a mute request for him to pick her up. Flushing with embarrassment, Shmuel averted his face from the tiny hunchback standing in front of him with her hands held up in a gesture of surrender and the lace-trimmed edges of her new panties peeking out below the hem of her dress. Rosa watched his evasive look and a pang of foreboding and anxiety tore away a piece of the happiness he had bestowed on her. A tense, heavy silence descended on the room like a smothering gray blanket, and unsaid words hovered in the air, threatening to crash down on their heads. Rosa hurried up to Angel, took hold of the little hands she was still holding up in the air, picked her up, and kissed her hair.

"Isn't Angel the prettiest little girl in the whole world?" she asked Shmuel, with a note of uncertainty in her voice.

"Yes, of course," he replied unwillingly, without looking at the child, and another piece of happiness fell silently to the floor, where it dissolved into a murky pool of disappointment.

The next day Shmuel's boxes arrived, a lot of cardboard boxes, containing all the worldly possessions he had collected in his leaking studio apartment in Nahalat Shiva, which Rosa had visited once and sworn she would never set foot in again. Then she had been appalled at the sight of the stacks of cardboard boxes filling the single room, the bare mattress lying on the floor, and the jars full of paintbrushes, empty tubes of dried-up paints, and rags smeared with congealed paint strewn all over in a hellish mess that made her shudder with horror.

"It's dank, stinking, dark, full of spiderwebs, and scary," she told Rachelle and Ruhama when they asked her to describe it to them. After she left, they discussed the subject and came to the conclusion that as a famous painter he must earn well, and the only reason that he lived in such conditions was that he didn't like spending money.

They wondered whether they should warn Rosa about his miserliness, but decided in the end that it wasn't up to them to do so.

And now all those boxes were in Rosa's house. The first box she opened with him contained his clothes—a few long-sleeved shirts gray with washing, frayed at the collars and cuffs; a pair of scuffed shoes with worn soles; and two pairs of trousers shiny at the seat and unraveling at the cuffs. "I wouldn't insult a beggar by giving them to him," she told Rachelle later. Shmuel hung these precious possessions in Rosa's closet, and began happily unpacking the rest of the boxes.

Dozens of paintbrushes stiff with use fell out of the first box he opened. Some of them were fine, thin brushes with only a few surviving hairs, and others were completely bald, only the paint stains on their handles hinting at their creative past. There were flat, medium-size brushes and thick, stiff ones that looked like the tail of an old horse. The next box contained similar ware, and so did all the rest. The house soon filled up with all kinds of strange receptacles—glass jars, mugs, plastic bottles with the tops cut off, pails, vases, little laundry hampers, and old tin cans, all of them holding what looked like unusual floral arrangements of curious flowers with wooden stems and stiff, hairy heads.

"Why do you need so many paintbrushes?" asked Rosa in despair as her house filled up with bouquets of stiff, dry brushes.

"I keep all the brushes I ever used," replied Shmuel, holding a pail full of paintbrushes in his arms and looking around for a place to put it.

"But why don't you throw the stiff, bald ones away? In any case you don't use them," she said, and found herself sobbing fearlessly at the end of the sentence. And another tiny piece of happiness fell away from her.

"How can I throw out brushes that served me faithfully for so many years and even brought me a living?" he replied. "We don't throw out elderly relatives just because they aren't any use to us anymore. And that's the way I feel about my brushes. I know them all, I remember when I painted with them, and what I painted, and if you throw out a single paintbrush I'll know immediately that it's missing," he added with a warning note in his voice.

But the worst of all was still to come, when the paintbrushes declared war on her plants. On busy days Shmuel would splash his brushes about in turpentine until all the paint came off the hairs, then wash them in water, and afterward he would throw the dirty water collected in the jars and tins straight onto her fragrant herbs. The results were soon apparent. Strange diseases began to attack her precious plants. First the delicate leaves began to shrivel at the edges. And when they turned brown they began to fall off the bushes, spotting the balcony floor with the dry, crumbly, autumnal remains of their premature deaths. And when the stems dried up too and the roots lost their hold, Shmuel would pull them up and empty the flowerpots with a vigorous shake over the balustrade, showering the passersby as he did so in a rain of soil dyed all the colors of the rainbow by oil paints, watercolors, and gouache. Then he would take the windfall of flowerpots, wash them well, and cram them full of paintbrushes. Soon the rosemary disappeared, the mint shriveled, the lemon balm was uprooted, and the wild thyme in the pickle barrel was usurped by giant paintbrushes resembling brightly colored brooms. And when Rosa gave him dirty looks, careful not to scold him in front of Angel, he would lecture her again on the importance of the paintbrushes in his life.

On the day the last plant died he promised to make it up to her, and told her that some of his paintbrushes could be used to paint on all kinds of surfaces, not only canvas. And with bated breath, as if afraid of being refused, he asked her permission to paint on the walls.

"Up to now I've lived in rented rooms, and I've never had a chance to paint on the walls. Please let me have the opportunity to do it now," he pleaded. Rosa, whose happiness was marred by his attitude to Angel, agreed on condition that he start with the child's room. Perhaps in this way, she thought, she would influence him to come closer to her daughter. When she saw the results, she promised him, she would decide about the rest of the apartment.

Shmuel asked her to leave him alone in the room, put his meals on a tray outside the door, and let him work undisturbed. For three days and three nights he worked without a break. Angel would fall asleep happily next to her mother in her big bed, and Rosa would lie awake counting her breaths. When she was sure the little girl was sound asleep she would pick her up and move her to one of the beds in the boys' room, and then she would go back to bed and wonder what Shmuel was up to in Angel's room before she fell asleep.

On the fourth day he emerged from the room with a pale face and his paint-stained clothes hanging on him as if he had lost kilos of weight. With a huge, happy smile he invited them to come in and see the results of his labors.

"Birds, crows!" Angel squealed in delight when she saw her new room.

"Angels," breathed Rosa in astonishment as she looked wide-eyed at the beauty before her. On the ceiling of the little room whose walls had been painted pink shone a bright blue sky dotted with fleecy white clouds, which looked so real that for a moment she thought he had torn the roof off to let in the sky. Between the clouds friendly, smiling gray crows glided on the blue sky. Rosa looked at the crows and it seemed to her that their sharp eyes were following her closely, accompanying her wherever she went just like their real brothers did when she walked through the neighborhood streets with Angel.

All around the ceiling Shmuel had painted a ring of dozens of plump angels. Their bodies were clothed in white robes, their golden hair shone, their faces beamed, and in their plump hands they held musical instruments. Rosa could have sworn that she heard them playing. She turned to Shmuel and looked at him as if she was seeing him for the first time in her life, too moved to speak.

"Well?" asked Shmuel, doubt gnawing at his heart.

Rosa couldn't say a single word.

"Do you like what I painted?" he asked, and this time he sounded desperate.

Speechless, Rosa put her arms around him and hugged him.

At that moment she remembered the stories he had told her about the camp and how they had forced him to paint angels on lampshades made of human skin, and her joy was dulled at the thought of these very same pictures now decorating the ceiling of her daughter's room. But she banished the disturbing thoughts from her mind, and that evening she told him it was the most beautiful painting he had ever done.

"Would you like me to paint the other walls too?" he asked, and his confidence returned.

Rosa considered his offer carefully, and asked him to paint the kitchen cabinets, which were covered in white Formica. "I spend all day in the kitchen," she explained. "At least let me have something cheerful to look at."

Shmuel didn't wait for another invitation. For a week the kitchen was out of bounds, and Rosa went down to eat at Rachelle's with Angel, until he announced that the paint was dry and she could come in and see the paintings.

He had painted the cabinets a glorious sunset red, and covered them with a field of wildflowers and herbs. The field spread over all the cabinets, and continued to the fridge, the stove, the door, the white porcelain tiles, and the sink. Rosa widened her nostrils, and she could have sworn that they were assailed from all directions by a medley of overpowering evening scents, more intoxicating than anything she had ever smelled in her life. At that moment she knew that her herb garden had not been sacrificed in vain and that she had been richly rewarded for its loss.

So beautiful were the flowers, and so real, that it was rumored in the neighborhood that Rosa's kitchen had been invaded by bees, butterflies, and various kinds of nectar-imbibing insects, who had discovered the flowery field and come to feed on its sweetness. With empty stomachs the winged insects flew giddily round the kitchen, trying to force their way into the field and exploding with little popping sounds against the cabinets and tiles, until Rosa took pity on them and set out saucers of sugar water for them on the windowsill, which Shmuel had covered with beds of violets.

"If they've flown all the way to my kitchen, at least let them get something for their trouble," she said to her astonished neighbors.

The kitchen became Rosa's favorite place, and dishes never seen there before began to appear on her table. With her eyes gazing at the field of flowers she cooked more gladly and willingly than ever before. And when she served her dishes to the guests who came flocking to see the blooming kitchen, they would swear that the food gave off a heavy scent of flowers, a potpourri of scents blended into one rare and exquisite new smell.

Rosa talked about her new kitchen to everyone she met, and even allowed a team of photographers from the magazine *Homes and Gardens* to photograph it for a special issue about kitchens. She welcomed anyone who asked to see it close up and share in the beauty of her husband's creation. But only to Rachelle and Ruhama did she confide the secret of the sink. When she was washing the dishes, she told them in the strictest secrecy, and looking deep into the sink, she could see four bright butterflies circling around the petals of a particularly beautiful bloom set right in the middle of the plug.

"How could he possibly have known?" she would conclude, a question that had no answer.

eighteen

POOR MADAME BUTTERFLY

*In the early days of her marriage, Rosa no-*ticed that her children were beginning to avoid the traditional family dinners on Friday nights, and when she urged them to come and taste something, they would turn up unwillingly, sit down at the table reluctantly, eat in silence, and get up, make their excuses, and leave as soon as the meal was over. After a few weeks of this they told her they were busy and they weren't sure if they would be able to make it, and when they failed to show up they would find new excuses to explain their absence, until she decided to leave them alone.

Only Ruthie remained faithful, and she would drop in to visit from time to time, snooping on Shmuel and his doings, peering at his pictures, fingering the paintbrushes in their various receptacles, examining the shriveled plants, and looking at her mother in concern. At these moments Rosa would feel that the natural order had been turned upside down. Ruthie, her daughter, had become her mother, and she had become the daughter. And when Ruthie tried to tell her that all her children were very worried, and that they were especially disturbed about Shmuel's attitude to Angel, Rosa would interrupt her angrily, insist that she was happy, and ask her and her brothers and sisters not to interfere in her life.

Dror, who always accompanied Ruthie on her visits, would listen miserably to the quarrels between the mother and daughter and take Angel out of the house, go for walks with her in the fields, and tell her the story of Jacob's dream. And when he brought her back in the evening, Rosa would smell the scent of the fields on Angel's skin and stroke her sunburned cheeks. Then they would eat supper alone in the painted kitchen, because Shmuel, who avoided any contact with Angel, would pretend to be busy with his painting. And when she put the child to bed in her angel-festooned room, she would tuck her in, kiss her forehead, and try to endow her with a double quantity of love to make up for the love she was missing from her stepfather.

Angel would lie on her back and stare at the ceiling, and the crows and angels surrounding her would laugh and smile at her. And the moment Rosa left the room and switched off the light, a glittering golden ladder would descend from among the painted clouds on the ceiling and invite her to climb up and reach the sky and play there with the angels.

When Shmuel received an invitation to exhibit the *Rosa* show at a prestigious gallery in Rome, their excitement knew no bounds. Rosa, who had never been out of the country, began to prepare for the trip a month in advance. Ruthie agreed to look after Angel as a matter of course, and Dror promised to take good care of her and told her not to worry. Before they set out for the airport, Rosa checked again to make sure that all the blinds were drawn, that the gas was turned off, that the boiler was switched off and the fridge empty, and only then made her way laboriously down the stairs.

Leslie-Shimon's car was waiting for them downstairs, and this time Rosa was too excited by the prospect of the journey ahead of her to take any notice of the oppressive silence in the car. Shmuel and Leslie-Shimon didn't exchange a single word throughout the drive to the airport, but nothing could spoil Rosa's happiness.

In time to come, when she tried to recall the flight, on which she occupied two seats to enable her to sit comfortably, she could only remember the terrible pressure in her stomach that lasted throughout the four and a half hours, which seemed to her like eternity.

Her bladder was so full that it threatened to leak, and then to burst, because despite all the combined efforts of the flight attendants she was unable to squeeze into the toilet. Throughout the flight she sat cramped with pain, refusing all the drinks offered her and looking enviously at the other passengers lining up outside the toilets to relieve themselves. And when the plane finally landed Shmuel pushed his way through the crowds, dragging her behind him, and shut himself up in the men's toilets with her, after ordering all the men standing in front of the urinals to vacate the place immediately. Then she squatted in front of the urinals that assailed her nose with an overpowering smell of ammonia and brought tears to her eyes, and as soon as she had emptied her bladder she emerged from the toilets, free at last to look around her and marvel at the sights.

The city welcomed them with blue skies and human warmth. The *Rosa* exhibition received glowing reviews. For a week they toured the city, from the Fountain of Trevi to the Coliseum to the Baths of Caracalla, where they saw the opera *Madama Butterfly* under the open sky. And when they came back to the hotel and Shmuel took a big handkerchief out of his pocket and wiped away Rosa's tears, which flowed without stopping, she told him that she was so happy that she would rather kill herself like poor Madame Butterfly than live for a single minute without him. And when Shmuel whispered that he would do the same thing if God forbid she died before him, she felt that her happiness was complete, even though Joseph caught up with her even in distant Rome, and when she said what she said to her new husband, he bared his nicotine-corroded teeth in a mocking smile as if to say: *Let's see you do it.*

On the second day of the exhibition the Genius, as the famous director was known in Cinecittà, turned up to see it. For five minutes he looked at Rosa, his bald head flushed, the tuft of his surviving hair dyed blond and sticking up like the crest of a parrot, and his eyes popping out of his head. Then he told her with a help of an interpreter that she was "the most woman he had ever seen in his life," called her affectionately, "My fertility goddess," caressed her breasts with his eyes, invaded her dress with his looks, swallowed his saliva, and whispered to his assistant: "She's worth five women to me." After the excitement had died down a little, his eyes, armed with lenses as thick as the bottoms of wine bottles, penetrated hers, and with a heartrending groan, as if stricken by a wave of pain, he told her that he was in the middle of making a new movie, and that he would like her to take part in one day's filming, which for her sake he was even prepared to move up. All she had to do was hover in the air, held up by an invisible harness, dressed in a white toga, and shower the heads of the people looking up at her adoringly from below with rose petals.

Rosa looked at Shmuel, who asked the interpreter how much she would be paid, and on hearing the reply agreed immediately without asking his wife's permission.

When they returned to the hotel an argument broke out between them.

"How dared you agree without asking me first?" she screamed, her waterfalls of flesh quivering with anger. "Since when am I some kind of object for you to shift from place to place? What do you think, that I'm a circus elephant to be put on show? It was only to spare you embarrassment that I didn't bawl you out on the spot, and now you'll pick up the phone immediately and tell that genius that I don't agree. There's a limit to everything. To float in the air dressed in a toga, indeed! This time you've gone too far."

Shmuel turned pale with fright, cleared his throat, and said weakly: "Rosaleh, we could live for a year on the money he offered you without my having to sell a single painting. Think about it."

Rosa turned a deaf ear to his pleas based on pecuniary considerations, and was only appeased after he told her that if she appeared in the movie she would be known to many millions of people all over the world. In the end she said that she would agree to float over the heads of her worshipers dressed in a toga, but only on condition that they showed her the toga first.

After lengthy negotiations the Genius unwillingly agreed to her conditions. The contract was signed, and Rosa received a check with an advance of an immense sum ending in tens of zeros. "Don't forget that they're lire, not dollars," Shmuel said, and tried to dampen her enthusiasm when she embarked on a shopping spree in the most glamorous department store in Rome, buying everything she could lay her hands on: white cashmere sweaters, leather bags and shoes for her daughters, and mountains of toys for Angel and her grandchildren. When she tried to replenish Shmuel's wardrobe, he refused and said that he was quite content with the clothes he had.

On their last day in Rome a long limousine drew up outside the hotel, and Rosa squeezed into it, giggling with delight. She vividly remembered the day she spent in Cinecittà. They dressed her in a wide, pleated white toga and combed her hair in elaborate ringlets, and when she looked at herself in the mirror she remembered with an ache the ringlets her mother used to make her when she was a child. Afterward they put her into a strong leather harness hidden under the folds of the toga, and hoisted her into the air on a crane. At first she screamed in terror, her ears went deaf, and she couldn't hear the Genius's directions, translated into Hebrew by a young Israeli who was studying medicine in Italy and supporting himself in bizarre ways. The instructions relayed to her by a microphone set in her left ear made no sense to her at all. Only after three hours, when everyone was about to give up in despair, did she adjust to her airborne position, and at the Genius's request she scattered yellow rose petals on the crowd of extras wearing Roman army uniforms and gleaming helmets adorned by silly-looking red plumes. The crowds gathered below gaped in astonishment at the spectacle of the flying matron as she dipped her hands into her golden pouch and showered them with handfuls of sweet-smelling, velvety rose petals.

Rosa giggled at the sight of the Roman soldiers with their heads, shoulders, and open mouths full of yellow petals. And when the technicians wanted to bring her down she pleaded to stay in the air a little longer, and demonstrated impressive rowing movements that made the flesh under her arms shiver and shake. When her feet touched the earth at last, she thought of her late husband Joseph and how she would have loved to see him now, looking up at her as she realized his most secret dream, a dream he never dared put into words, to act in a movie, any movie at all, never mind one directed by the Italian Genius. If he were still alive, she thought, how proud he would have been to show her movie in Cinema Rosa, even if it wasn't a sad one.

When she returned to the hotel and tried to explain to herself why she had so enjoyed being in the air, she felt once more the sensation of weightlessness and freedom she had felt in the sky and remembered with longing the days when she had been lighter. When she shared her feelings with Shmuel and asked him if he didn't think she should start cutting down on what she ate, he scowled and said angrily: "Don't you dare. All your beauty is in your size." And Rosa submitted and bowed her will to his.

And when the movie came to Israel and was shown in the theaters, people lined up to see "our Rosa" acting in an Italian movie, and greeted her flight through the air with cries of admiration and rhythmic clapping, while the film critics sang her praises and those of the brilliant Italian director.

In the days following their return to Israel, Rosa's attitude toward Shmuel underwent a radical change, and she became impatient and hostile. She soon found herself raising her voice to him for no reason, scolding him, finding fault with everything he did, feeling ashamed of his paint-stained hands and clothes, and arguing with him almost daily. Rosa couldn't understand what caused the bad blood between them. Even when she racked her brains and tried to reconstruct the story of their relationship from the beginning, she couldn't understand what had brought about the rift in their marriage, spoiled things between them, and caused her to hate her husband and regret that she had married a man she hardly knew. Sometimes, when she contemplated the ruins of her herb garden, she was convinced that it all began with the killing of her plants by the water he rinsed his brushes in. When she bumped into the paintbrushes standing in their tins and jars and pails all over the house, she was sure that they were to blame, and on Friday nights, when she sat down to eat alone with Angel, she blamed her husband for estranging her children from her.

But above all she felt that her love for him had turned to hate because of his rejection of Angel. With terrible pain she had witnessed the pitiful attempts of the child who never grew to please Shmuel and come close to him. With tears welling despairingly in her throat she would watch every day as Angel said good-bye to him at the door, called him "Daddy," and tried to cling to his leg with her little arms. With an involuntary movement he would push her away, as if she were suffering from a contagious disease. He never hugged her or picked her up in his arms, never took her out for a walk, never asked her how she was, never praised her or bought her a present, not even on her birthday. In the heavy silences that descended on the house then, Rosa would see Angel shrinking and trying to efface herself, and a bitter lump would block her throat.

And when at long last she poured out her heart to Rachelle, her friend told her that one day she had seen Shmuel striding down the street with Angel tottering behind him on her little legs, trying to catch up with him and begging him to slow down. "Shmulik, wait for me, Shmulik, wait for me!" Rachelle imitated Angel's piping voice. And he ignored her, as if he saw and heard nothing, even when she fell down and grazed her knee. Even when she cried he didn't turn his head or pause; he went on walking as if nothing had happened, leaving it to strangers to pick the little girl up and bandage her wound. Rachelle told her that she had kept the incident from her because she didn't want to grieve her, or to come between a husband and wife, but once Rosa herself had brought the subject up, she felt it was her duty to tell her the story. Before she went home she added that a lot of people in the neighborhood had seen what happened, and they had asked her afterward how Rosa could stay married to such a heartless man.

That evening she tried to talk to him about his attitude to Angel and about the incident Rachelle had told her about. Shmuel answered her rudely and impatiently, saying that that he was the way he was, that he couldn't change his behavior, and that the child would have to get used to it. Rosa was unable to reply, because everything she wanted to say was choking her.

And the last, precious scrap of happiness fell away from her and dropped to the floor, where it melted into a reeking, murky puddle of disappointment.

That night she sat for hours next to Angel's bed and tried to calm herself with the help of the peaceful breathing of the sleeping child. Only when she heard Shmuel snoring did she get into bed and turn her back to him. From then on she stopped talking to him, except for the few words necessary to the running of the household.

Shmuel tried to placate her. He stopped eating garlic before going to bed and painted her in the most flattering way without making her pose. When she refused to be appeased, he brought her her favorite delicacies to eat, and when this too failed, he used Angel as a last resort.

One day Rosa returned from visiting Rachelle and to her horror she saw Angel sitting naked in front of him, her long fair hair covering her body, holding a bow and arrow in her hands, while Shmuel gave her orders such as "Don't move," "Smile nicely," and "Show your teeth." Thrilled by the sudden attention he was paying her, Angel did her best to obey his commands and tried with all her might to please him. Rosa looked in horror at the canvas and saw Angel on it in the shape of a plump, pink, dimpled cupid. Her humps were hidden under downy little wings, her fair hair illuminated the painting with a glowing light, and the face revealed through the curtain of her hair was the most beautiful face Rosa had ever seen in her life, perhaps the most beautiful face that Shmuel had ever painted. When she looked harder at the painting, however, she noticed a tiny male organ, erect and uncircumcised, added with a few brushstrokes to the bottom of her daughter's body.

Shrieking like a banshee, she set about him, beating him and stabbing him with the paintbrush she snatched from his hand, until her shrieks and the terrified Angel's screams brought the neighbors running, and they dragged her off him, leaving red finger marks on the white flesh of her arms. With his body riddled by holes, his legs covered with blue bruises from her kicks, and his face with red scratches, as if all the cats of the neighborhood had gone to war against him, he said to her humbly that night in bed, after she had refused to talk to him all day: "All we wanted to do was give you a nice surprise for your birthday, Angel and I. I wanted to paint you a pretty cupid to strengthen our love." Exhausted by rage Rosa looked at him pityingly and said: "Never mind that you painted her in the nude, you pervert; never mind the wings, but a *penis*? You gave her a penis, you maniac!"

"Have you ever seen a cupid without a penis?" he asked in all innocence.

This was too much for Rosa to bear, and with one hefty kick to his behind she turfed him out of the bed and onto the carpet.

From that night she no longer wanted him, and she exiled him from her bed. Lonely and pathetic, Shmuel would wander round the house looking for a bed on which to lay his head. But Rosa remained stubbornly blind to his suffering, ignored the fawning, hangdog looks he sent her from his moist gray eyes, and devoted herself to cleaning the house and scouring the windows and floors until they shone.

"Of course you'd rather kill yourself like poor Madame Butterfly than live one minute without your husband," Joseph said to her with a wicked smile. "Well, let's see you! You've been sleeping without him for two weeks now, and you don't seem to be suffering too much. In one blow you got rid of him."

"Between the two of us it would be better if he killed himself," she replied with clenched teeth, and with strong movements full of hate she went on scrubbing the floor until she could see her sweating face reflected in the tiles and Joseph's satisfied grin gleaming at her from the little puddle of water.

nineteen

BUTTERFLIES OF ASH

*If Rosa had been able to predict the conse-*quences of her decision regarding the paintbrushes that had taken over her house and filled every unoccupied space with their thorny decorations, she might have acted differently. It all began with Rachelle's daily visit, and the ritual of sympathy and complaint in which they indulged when Rosa's sorrow and despair overwhelmed her, and Rachelle listened patiently to her troubles and responded with warmth and good advice.

On this particular afternoon, while she drank her coffee and nibbled the salty sesame biscuits fresh from the oven, Rachelle watched Shmuel as he trailed drearily around the rooms. His body was hunched, as if he had spent the night lying on a bed of nails on the floor; his feet shuffled aimlessly in shabby slippers; his eyes were downcast as if searching for a lost coin, his mouth gave off a faint smell of garlic, and his paint-stained hands wandered nervously and suspiciously among the paintbrushes scattered throughout the house in their vases, tins, jars, and buckets as if he were counting them.

Curling her lips in a spiteful expression Rachelle said to Rosa: "Chuck them out."

"Chuck what out?" Rosa stared at her friend.

"His paintbrushes. Aren't you fed up with those demented flower arrangements in their crystal vases and mop pails taking over your house? Enough already! Chuck them out, and finish with the business."

"It would kill him," said Rosa, lowering her voice in case he was eavesdropping on their conversation.

"All the better." Rachelle snickered nastily.

Rosa looked at her in horror, and then burst into hysterical laughter, spilling her coffee as she did so. With cookie crumbs soaked in lukewarm coffee spraying from her mouth, she kicked her legs in the air and laughed: "Why not? After all, I've still got another one to go." And Rachelle, infected by her laughter, took up the refrain: "Another one, another one, one more butterfly to go! Fly down pretty butterfly . . ."

"Don't be afraid. Come sit on my hand," Angel chimed in happily, hearing the children's rhyme.

"And fly away into the sky!" shrieked Rosa and Rachelle, and fell into each other's arms, sobbing and weeping with wild laughter that left them gasping for breath.

"What were you laughing at like that?" asked Shmuel, coming into the kitchen in the evening and looking at Rosa and Angel eating their solitary supper, wondering what his wife, whose bed he had not shared for over a month, had to be so cheerful about.

"Girl talk," Rosa said briefly, and urged Angel to finish the food on her plate.

"That's not true, Mommy." Angel corrected her with the honesty characteristic of children. "You and Auntie Rachelle were talking about butterflies."

Glad to volunteer information, dispel the fog, and perhaps even please Shmuel, the little girl recited with her mouth full of bread, making the appropriate movements with her hands:

Fly down pretty butterfly,
Don't be afraid.
Come sit on my hand,
And fly away into the sky.

"Butterflies?" Shmuel looked at her incredulously.

"Hurry up, swallow your food!" Rosa broke in, with the words of the rhyme in her daughter's chiming voice echoing threateningly in her ears.

"We have to talk," Shmuel said to her after she put Angel to bed and began to wash the dishes with a noisy, angry clatter.

"What's there to talk about?" she retorted, her eyes on the sink full of dirty dishes.

"You avoid me, you don't sleep with me, you won't talk to me, and in the end you'll throw out all my paintbrushes," he said, as if he could read her thoughts and predict the future.

"If I do you'll deserve it. I'm sick of those damned paintbrushes all over the house. Yesterday one of them nearly poked Angel's eye out when she bent down, and I almost tripped and fell over a pailful of them. Apart from which, you killed all my plants with that filthy water of yours. And that smell of garlic again. I'm ashamed to invite my friends to the house with you stinking the place up. Look at your clothes, your hands. Aren't you tired of walking around with all those paint stains? It's high time you removed them with turpentine."

Shmuel tried to efface himself and said in a meek voice: "Once you called my hands cheerful and you loved them. Tell me, what's the matter with you?"

Rosa didn't reply, because she didn't know the answer. For the last month she had been racking her brains in the attempt to understand what was making her hate and detest everything she had once loved about her husband. When she thought about the great love between them, which had disappeared overnight and given way to hatred, misery, helplessness and despair, she couldn't understand what had happened to ruin their marriage.

People in the neighborhood said that Rosa had been given the evil eye. Her undisguised happiness with her third husband must have brought the troubles on her head. Those who favored this theory argued that unhappy people couldn't stand the sight of other people's happiness, and they must have given her the evil eye, even if they didn't mean to. If Angela had been alive, she would no doubt have told her that it was all because of her former husbands, who were expressing their dissatisfaction with her marriage from the grave. Angela had always drummed it into her that a widow should never remarry, or she would feel the punishment of her dead husband's jealousy. And Rosa knew that if she were alive to see her present plight her mother would undoubtedly repeat the sentence she hated so much: "You see, I told you so."

Rachelle and Ruhama both said that her marriage had been doomed to fail, and summed up their diagnosis with the words: "You're not suited, and we never understood in the first place what you saw in him or what he saw in you."

During the long days of their estrangement Rosa refused to sit for him, and Shmuel painted her body from his memories, which were still vivid and loving. When he went out for a breath of air Rosa slipped into the boys' room, which was now his, examined the new paintings, and felt a new and terrible rage when she saw that he had not spared her. Shmuel had emphasized her double chin, sprinkled her hair with gray, etched in the delicate lines that had begun to appear around her eyes, made her breasts sag, and traced the veins that netted the translucent skin of her legs. And when he came home she received him with a sour face and refrained from asking why he had chosen to paint her thus. In the evening, when she examined her naked body in the mirror on the closet door and compared it to the paintings, she knew that Shmuel was right. He had scrupulously recorded the changes wrought by time in her face and body, without concealing anything.

On the day she found herself staring at a new painting draped in a sheet like a corpse wrapped in a winding sheet, she knew that the end prophesied on their wedding night had come. Like an unseen monument waiting to be unveiled, the painting confronted her ominously. With one swift movement she whipped away the white sheet and stood there staring at the mouth torn open in a scream that went on echoing soundlessly in her ears for days to come.

The painted eyes bulged out of their sockets, staring in terror, as if at a spectacle of nightmarish horror. Paralyzed with fear, Rosa looked at the sunken cheeks covered with hard, white bristles. At that moment it seemed to her that the toothless mouth was eating away at the inside of the cheeks and sucking the marrow out of the bones. With a sense of terrible foreboding, she suddenly saw Mischa's face rising before her eyes and covering Shmuel's face painted on the canvas. Panic-stricken, she stared at the painting, and before her astonished eyes she saw the faces of the two men struggling with each other on the canvas, first Mischa and then Shmuel gaining the upper hand.

When the vision faded, she looked at the painting again and she couldn't tell if the face was that of a man or a woman. At that moment, as time froze and began to go backwards, she knew that she had seen this face before, many years ago, in the extermination camp she had never been in, only imagined from Shmuel's descriptions. And when she closed her eyes in an attempt to banish the image from her mind, it flickered in front of her like a pale square on a black background impressed on the optic nerve to remind the closed eyes of what they had witnessed when they were open.

Suddenly Rosa knew that Shmuel had been trying in this painting to memorialize the faces of all the victims, all the murdered millions. And she saw them all superimposed, one on top of another, six million times. As she sat there and looked at the picture, as if she were performing a forbidden act, she saw Shmuel's death mask in front of her, and she was sure that he had painted the moment of his own death. And when she heard his footsteps on the stairs, she quickly covered the painting with the sheet, and all that evening she avoided looking her husband in the eye.

And the next day, when words returned to her, she broke her silence and asked him to keep the painting covered all the time, since it was liable to frighten Angel. Afterward she thought that perhaps she should have taken advantage of the opportunity to ask him what the subject of the painting was. But she immediately dismissed the thought, on the grounds that a question of this nature would have been sure to lead to a serious discussion, and Rosa felt unable to talk to her husband about anything on earth, and certainly not about the six million dead.

On the day she felt that she had come to the end of her rope, that she could no longer bear Shmuel's presence—his smell, his appearance, and his paintbrushes filling the rooms and leaving her no room in her own house—she escaped to Rachelle's apartment, where her friend told her again to throw them out.

"What can happen, already?" She brushed Rosa's objections aside. "I've never heard of anyone who killed himself because of paintbrushes."

The next morning, when Shmuel went out to do his chores, the perfect opportunity to act presented itself. Rosa looked out of the window and saw groups of children collecting firewood in the neglected yards for Lag b'Omer bonfires. "Come upstairs, I've got lots of wood for you," she called down to them quickly, before she could regret it. Like a swarm of famished locusts the urchins descended on the house and emptied all the receptacles of their brushes. A few hours later all the paintbrushes, large and small, were piled up in the core of the huge bonfire erected on an empty lot on the outskirts of the neighborhood. The biggest paintbrush of all, whose hairy head was stuck on top of a broomstick like a red, bristly, punk coxcomb, they dressed in old clothes, stuffed with newspapers and rags, and added a scary mask. After the effigy was complete, they settled down to argue over whether to call it Haman the Wicked, Hitler, or Saddam Hussein.

About what happened when Shmuel came home, many stories were told in the neighborhood. The moment he opened the door and encountered the emptiness, he uttered a shriek that brought all the neighbors running to see who was being slaughtered there. Like a balloon with all the air expelled from it, his body collapsed, leaving his clothes hanging loose as if they were three sizes too big for him. Rosa was afraid that if he went on shrinking, all that would be left was a pile of shabby clothes and a pair of orphaned shoes standing in the middle of the floor. When he was finished shrinking he flopped down on his meager behind and sat on the floor, buried his face in his hands, and wailed like a banshee.

Rosa couldn't bear the sight of his suffering. Bitterly regretting what she had done and furious with Rachelle for egging her on, she burst outside and hurried as fast as her fat would allow her to make the rounds of the bonfires about to go up in flames all over the neighborhood, searching for her husband's paintbrushes. At last the familiar red coxcomb rising high above all the rest caught her eye and led her to the bonfire of the paintbrushes.

With the help of an exceptionally long paintbrush, she penetrated to the depths of the bonfire and raked out the brushes waiting for the last rites of their cremation. And when she grabbed hold of the broomstick paintbrush and began to undress it, its stiff red crest bristled wickedly and brought the children running to rescue their effigy. They stood around her and, with the bows in their hands, began to shoot the paintbrushes at her like arrows that pierced her soft flesh.

While Shmuel's paintbrushes were revenging themselves on Rosa for taking them away from him, he opened all the windows of the house and like a man demented began flinging all his paintings to the ground. First he threw out all the Rosas. Rosa in her clothes, Rosa as a gypsy, Rosa naked, and Rosa in red all crashed noisily down on the brambles of the yard below. The wooden frames splintered on the stones, the stretched canvases slackened, and the thorns and nettles joined in the work of destruction, scratching and slashing and tearing Rosa's painted flesh to tatters. After the Rosas, the new biblical women came crashing down, from Eve to the seductive Bathsheba, until Shmuel's whole harem was empty. After he had finished with his fat women, he took his tattered cardboard portfolios and shook all the shriveled, skeletal women he had painted in the camp out of the window. Torn notices, scraps of paper, pieces of striped pajamas covered with charcoal drawings, rags, and strips of bark spotted the paintings of the fat women with black and brown. In conclusion he threw out the painting of Angel as cupid, and after it the painting of the six million.

A pile of torn, crushed, slashed, and bruised paintings covered the nettles and brambles in a patchwork quilt of color. Then the children of the neighborhood descended in a horde and fell on the loot, grabbing everything they could lay their hands on and breaking up the frames as the vicious thorns scratched their little fingers till they bled. On limping, stolen supermarket carts they pushed their booty to the bonfires, and threw the skeletons of the frames, the pieces of paper, the rags and tatters, and the torn canvases bearing the vestiges of Shmuel's paintings, onto the flames.

And when Rosa returned home there wasn't a single painting left. Stabbed and hurting, her arms laden with paintbrushes, she found Shmuel sitting on the floor. Full of remorse, she threw the brushes into Shmuel's lap, but he only looked at her blankly with unseeing eyes.

In order to gain his attention she picked up one of the brushes and tickled him with its thick, thorny hairs. Starting with the soles of his bare feet she climbed up his thighs, roamed over his arms, invaded his armpits, tickled his chest, and concluded by lightly brushing his face, taking care to insert the hairs into his nostrils and ears. And when he failed to respond to the tickling, she turned the paintbrush around and stabbed him angrily in the backside with its pointed end. But Shmuel didn't even blink. In despair she began to shake his shoulders, and with the force of her shaking his head swayed to and fro like the head of her old doll, Belle. His expressionless eyes looked right through her to an invisible point on the wall.

When he failed to react to her cries and refused to eat the soup she prepared for him, she decided to resort to a measure "guaranteed to wake the dead from their graves," as she described the steps she took later to Rachelle, who said that she had always suspected her friend was crazy, but now she was absolutely sure.

Heavily she seated herself on a chair in front of him, trying to take up his whole field of vision with her body and examining him like a hunter surveying her prey. She began with her slippers, which were made of velvet and decorated with red parrot feathers. She shook her feet lightly in the air, and the slippers dropped off, revealing long, narrow white feet and manicured toenails painted dark brown. She dragged her chair up closer to him, waved her feet in front of his dead eyes, and offered her toes to his mouth. But Shmuel didn't part his lips to seize her toes in his mouth and suck them one by one as was his wont in days gone by. Disappointed, she turned her back to him and slowly unbuttoned her dress, let it fall to the floor, and kicked it in his direction. Dressed only in her panties she began dancing round the room in the steps of the waltz taught her by Shraga, her breasts bouncing up and down like pale balloons. Shmuel's eyes, which were still fixed on the invisible point on the wall, now stared unseeingly at the dancing nipples that had once aroused his passionate desire, and a shining trickle of saliva drooled from his half-open mouth. In a final act of despair she slowly slithered out of her panties, wriggling her thighs and rear as she did so. Naked as the day she was born, she bent over her comatose husband to check the effects of her performance on his groin. His member was limp and droopy, slipped out of her grasp, and failed to respond to her ministrations.

Put to shame, she got dressed again and waited for Angel to come home from her day care. And when she went to bed Shmuel went on sitting on the floor, deaf to her pleas to come and join her.

All that night the bonfires blazed, consuming the effigies looming over them like scarecrows in their flames, and snapping and crackling merrily as they devoured Shmuel's contribution to the conflagration. Scraps of half-burned paper and material and smoldering cinders and particles of sooty black dust floated through the open windows of the house and circled through the rooms like sad, ashen butterflies, soiling the hands of all who touched them. More and more gray butterflies fluttered around the rooms, and when they grew tired they fell to the floor, covering the tiles with their dark wings and scattering black butterfly dust on all who crossed their path.

With no one to stop it, the ash covered Shmuel's bright hands, spotted his clothes, and settled into the many wrinkles on his tired face, filling them with a dark, aging greasepaint and emphasizing the lines of suffering etched on his cheeks and brow.

The next day Rosa swept up the layer of ash that had accumulated everywhere, scolding herself for not having remembered to close the windows, as she did every Lag b'Omer. When she wanted to wash the living room floor and was unable to make Shmuel move from his place, she summoned her sons to help her. They raised his frozen body from the floor, removed his filthy, sooty clothes, and forced him into the shower. The clear water covered his body, wet his hair, penetrated his wrinkles, washed the black color from his pores, and ran down his legs in dark, dirty streams that disappeared down the drain. When he was clean and dry they dressed him in striped pajamas and carried him to bed. Shmuel turned his face to the wall, and the tears streaming from his eyes soaked through the pillowcase and wet the feathers inside the pillow.

When the situation continued unchanged for three days, and Shmuel stayed in bed, refused to eat, and didn't answer when she spoke to him, she called the doctor.

"How did it happen?" he asked her.

"I have no idea. I hid his paintbrushes, and he went mad and threw out all his paintings. But now he's quiet. I wish he would yell. His silence is driving the whole house crazy."

The doctor passed his hand before Shmuel's eyes and called his name. Shmuel did not react.

"He's in a catatonic state," he said at last, after testing Shmuel's reflexes and measuring his blood pressure. "He doesn't react," he added in explanation, as if Rosa didn't know this for herself. "He has to be hospitalized."

Rosa, who was sick of the inanimate object surrounded by paintbrushes, consented, on condition that they didn't hurt him too much. "He's a good man, taken all in all," she said to Rachelle later when she told her what had happened.

That same evening, when the sky was painted purple and the smell of frying eggs and fresh vegetable salads dressed with lemon juice and olive oil rose from all the houses, men dressed in white suits arrived at the house, strapped Shmuel onto a stretcher with strong canvas straps, and carried him down to the ambulance waiting outside.

"Well, and what have you got to say for yourself now?" Joseph bared his teeth in a spiteful grin as soon as she walked back into the house after laboriously climbing upstairs. "I'd rather kill myself like poor Madame Butterfly than live a single minute without you." He mimicked her voice. "I'd rather kill myself like poor Madame Butterfly than live a single minute without you," he repeated mockingly. Rosa stopped her ears to the voices echoing inside her head. But all that night and all the next day the sentence went on ringing in her ears. She tried to ignore the voices and do the housework, endeavoring not to think about her husband tied up like a calf, and what they were doing to him there in the hospital.

When she was overcome with longings for Shmuel, she gathered up the paintbrushes she had managed to save from destruction, fastened them together with a strong rubber band, and put them in her best crystal vase. If Shmuel came back from the hospital, he would be greeted by a bouquet of paintbrushes. The thickest, tallest paintbrush, which the children had dressed up as Haman or Hitler or perhaps Saddam Hussein, she decided to exploit for her own private use, and she set its stiff red crest to work on clearing the cobwebs from the dustiest corners of the ceiling. The paintbrush performed its menial task meekly and faithfully. And the more worn and gray its splendid quiff coxcomb became, the more Rosa succeeded in overcoming the pain and insult it had caused her when it betrayed her into the hands of the children who shot at her with their paintbrush-arrows.

Once a week she went to visit Shmuel. In a thunderous silence and with an expression that said plainer than words "We told you and you wouldn't listen" Leslie-Shimon would drive her to the entrance to the hospital, which looked like a detention camp because of all its prefabricated huts. There they stored the tortured souls of the survivors of hell, imprisoned in their inner worlds and detached from reality. Laden with food she would walk down the path in the glade of ancient, rustling pine trees, which welcomed her with an excited waving of their arms that shook the soft hairy caterpillars cradled in its boughs. The pines that accompanied her to the door of hut number three sprinkled her with yellow pollen and pelted her with ripe cones.

Gasping for breath, Rosa would reach the hut and bump into a patient named Feiga, who would bawl her out at the top of her voice for treading on the wet floor and try to hit her with the mop. Feiga never parted from her sole possessions on earth—the pail and mop that were welded to her hands like extensions of her arms, and which by some accounts she even took to bed with her at night. In the camps, the nurses said, after they bayoneted her baby before her and her husband's eyes, raped her in front of her husband, and then shot him while she watched, they had forced her to clean the blood turning the gravel in the yard red. And after she had performed the task with distinction they put her in charge of cleaning the officers' quarters, with special emphasis on the lavatories. For which they rewarded her by putting out their cigarettes on her flesh. Ever since then she cleaned. She scrubbed when the Russians arrived and liberated the camp. When she refused to evacuate the camp with the other survivors before making everything shine, they dragged her away with the cleaning agents in her hands. She went on cleaning on the ship, she disinfected the detention camp in Cyprus, and if they hadn't stopped her she would have cleaned the huts of the guards and the quarters of the British officers too. As soon as she arrived on the kibbutz she set to work energetically scouring and scrubbing, and she was still cleaning to this day. Even lying in bed at night, the nurses told Rosa, her hands went on compulsively performing their task. Her hands were crooked and swollen with rheumatism, their skin was red, rough, and chapped and full of burns from the disinfectants. But Feiga felt nothing. Her pain-saturated body blocked the distress signals sent to her brain.

After hopping over the obstacle of the wet floor, Rosa entered Shmuel's room. She always found him sitting on a chair with his back to her, facing the window, his hands, which had grown white in the meantime, sketching her portrait in the air with the help of a paintbrush only he could see. When she stood in front of him he would blink admiringly, open his mouth, and fail to utter a single world.

And when she left him and walked down the path to her son's waiting car, her long hair sprinkled with yellow pollen and her feet treading on the hairy caterpillars that had come down from the trees to greet her, she thought of his bright hands that had turned white, felt their touch pleasuring her body, and dozed off on the backseat of the car until Leslie-Shimon woke her and announced that they were home. Heavily she mounted the stairs and fell fully clothed into bed, where she spent a sleepless night, full of memories.

Once, when she succeeded at last in falling asleep in the wee hours, she found herself dressed in a black uniform and high black boots. With a vigorous kick of her boot she broke down the door of hut number three. Scores of prisoners in ragged striped pajamas, with Shmuel among them, lay crowded on wooden bunks and looked at her in terror. With a terrible anger Rosa cracked the long whip in her hand, which resembled the whip of the animal trainer she had once seen in the circus. The prisoners climbed down from their bunks obediently and gathered around her in a circle, waiting expectantly. But Shmuel remained sitting on his bunk, his eyes looking right through her and his hands stubbornly drawing an invisible picture in the air. She felt her anger rising and cracked the whip again. The pointed tip of the whip, armed with a heavy pellet of lead, hit Shmuel in the face, and he fell onto the floor. There he lay, bent over in pain, with his hands etching the endless lines of his paintings in the air.

Rosa woke in tears with a bitter taste in her mouth. She sat up in bed in alarm, trying in vain to calm her racing heart and escape the sights of the dream. But the sights surrounded her and attacked her from every side, poking obscenely pointing fingers into her eyes, pinching her flesh, sawing her bones, tearing out her heart, and stopping her breath. At that moment she understood that she had failed and knew that she was to blame for everything that had happened. Shmuel had been entrusted to her in order for her to atone by her love for all the suffering he had experienced in his life, and she had failed to keep this trust. And even worse, she was responsible for his deterioration and his present condition; she was to blame for causing him new suffering, which may have been even worse than everything he had endured before, because this suffering had finished him off.

Appalled, she went into the kitchen, drank water from the tap, and tried to get rid of the terrible taste in her mouth. But the taste only grew stronger, entrenching itself in her taste buds and refusing to go away. To her horror she suddenly smelled a stench coming from an undefined source, which accompanied the taste like an inseparable twin. She brushed her teeth, gargled with Shmuel's mint-flavored mouthwash, and drank strong coffee. But the ghastly taste and smell remained, settling inside her, becoming a part of her and refusing to go away.

With a terrible feeling of failure she went into Angel's room and looked indifferently at the old crow tapping its beak on the windowpane as if asking to be let in. When she averted her eyes from the crow, she felt the stab of the beady black eyes of the painted crows looking at her with hatred from every corner of the room, and she woke Angel up to a new day.

twenty

THE MIRACLE WORKER

"One day Shmuel will open his mouth and talk to me." Rosa repeated this sentence firmly to herself, convinced that if she only repeated it enough it would come true. She would sometimes confide her belief in Ruhama and Rachelle and the nurses at the hospital. "In my opinion," she told them, "Shmuel is still angry, and that's why he doesn't want to talk to me. But since our love was strong, it will overcome everything. I'm sure that one day when I look deep into his eyes and whisper into his ear that I love him and ask him to forgive me, he'll wake up from this strange sleep that he's imposed on himself, open his mouth, and talk to me."

They would look at her pityingly, and wonder behind her back how she could fail to read the writing on the wall. Everyone knew that after each of her visits his condition deteriorated, and the hospital director was even thinking of forbidding her visits.

In spite of the optimism she radiated, she realized that the disease that had wrought havoc with his mind had ravaged his body too. His back began to curve, his hands grew swollen and puffy and his face bloated, black circles were smudged as if by crude brushstrokes under his eyes, and a deathlike stench rose from his body.

Muhammad, the male nurse who looked after him every day, was prepared to tell her, in exchange for a few shekels slipped into his hand, what the doctors and nurses refrained from telling her.

"Shmuel," he whispered into her ear for fear of being overheard by the head nurse, "goes to bed every night in his clothes and shoes. When I try to undress him, he yells at me and hits me." He told her too how her husband took with him to bed the plastic bag containing all his possessions, the bag with which he wandered round like a zombie all day and into which he threw whatever he could lay his hands on. And here Muhammad listed the contents of the bag, as if taking an inventory: stinking wet floor rags he stole from Feiga, pine cones he collected from the yard, used toilet paper, empty toothpaste tubes, shampoo bottles, black pawns from the chessboard, moldy slices of bread, a porridge bowl, a half-eaten apple, and a crooked soup-spoon. Muhammad admitted that the bag undoubtedly contained a lot of other things that Shmuel added daily to his hoard, and that he, Muhammad, had not yet succeeded in examining, since Shmuel clung to his bag and it was impossible to pry it from his fingers. "And he takes it all to bed with him every night and goes to sleep in his shoes and clothes. So what's the wonder if he gets up crooked and stinking?"

"Have you tried to get rid of the bag?" asked Rosa in a conspiratorial whisper.

"Of course we've tried. I took it away from him in his sleep, and he woke up and screamed and woke all the lunatics, and there was a terrible racket, and in the end I got it in the neck. So now there's nothing we can do, and he takes that bag with him everywhere and keeps putting more things into it."

And when Rosa consulted the doctors and asked them to tell her when her husband would be coming home, they lowered their eyes and told her that in their opinion Shmuel was a lost case. He would never return to himself. He would never talk and respond. He had taken flight from reality and sunk into the madness that was his refuge.

Hope came from Tzila, the head nurse of hut number three.

"Shmuel's talking," she announced one day on the telephone in a voice choked with excitement.

"I'm coming," said Rosa, and the lump that had been blocking her throat for so long dissolved in tears. Immediately she called Leslie-Shimon and told him to come and pick her up, never mind how many customers were waiting. "Shmuel's started to talk, and I'm going to him right now," she informed him in a tone that brooked no arguments.

Breathlessly she made her way down the path under a persistent drizzle to hut number three. She submitted to the blows of Feiga's mop and her screams that she was ruining her nice clean floor and messing everything up with her mud, and breathed in the reek of fermenting garbage mingled with a faint smell of garlic that greeted her when she entered Shmuel's room. She found him in his usual frozen position—his back to her, his face reflected in the windowpane bringing low gray rainclouds into the room, and his hand sketching her portrait endlessly in the air.

"Shmuel!" she cried as she hurried into the room. He hesitated for a moment and his hand trembled as it sketched the contours of her breasts in a movement painfully familiar to her, leaving a broken, crooked line in the air. Then he recovered and went on drawing briskly, as if to make up for lost time.

"Shmuel, it's me, Rosa. I've come to visit you!" she cried.

Shmuel went on drawing the endless line of her breasts.

"Shmuel, talk to me!" she shouted in his ear as if he were deaf.

Despairingly, his white hand dotted in the halo around her nipples. "Shmuel, I'm sorry, forgive me, I shouldn't have thrown out your paintbrushes. I've bought you a lot of new ones," she said in a sweet, coaxing voice.

Shmuel didn't blink an eye, as if she were speaking a language he didn't understand, and his hand slid down to draw her stomach.

Rosa burst out of the room in tears. "He isn't talking," she complained to Tzila, who was waiting for her at the nurses' station, and shook her shoulders violently as if she were to blame for Shmuel's silence.

"Now he isn't, but before he talked," the nurse replied, and told her about the strange fellow who had showed up at the hospital in order to cheer up the inmates.

"You should have seen him," she said. "A tall, thin man with beautiful eyes carrying an ancient accordion. No sooner had he arrived than the miracles began to happen in our ward."

"You see Zalman?" She pointed to the skeletal old man huddled up in a wheelchair. "What he went through and witnessed in the camps is impossible to describe. Ever since he arrived in the country forty years ago he hasn't walked or talked. Every year he folds up further in his wheelchair, and in another few years, if he isn't dead by then, I'm sure we'll find him as flat and folded as an old sheet, and we won't be able to straighten him out again. He's so old and ancient that we've almost despaired of him. But then this odd fellow with the accordion and the heart of gold arrived, looked compassionately at Zalman, and asked me where he was from. I looked at his file, which is the oldest file we have here, and it turned out that he was born in the Austro-Hungarian Empire and actually fought in the First World War. And what does this fellow do? He opens his dilapidated old accordion and plays an Austro-Hungarian march, something jolly and springy. And guess what happened? Zalman's head began to rise, little by little, like a movie in slow motion; his back straightened, he got carefully off his chair on those skinny, shriveled legs that forgot how to walk decades ago, and began marching around the room, left-right, left-right, left-right. After he had marched for an hour and driven everyone crazy, he collapsed on the floor like a clockwork doll that had run out of steam. If I hadn't seen it with my own eyes I would never have believed it."

"And Itzik." Tzila pointed at a young man sitting in the corner, his watery eyes fixed on an invisible point on the wall and his swollen penis sprouting through the open zipper of his pants. With a stiff, distorted hand Itzik gently stroked its fleshy pink head as if it were a rare, exquisite flower. "Itzik wasn't there himself, but his parents were, they named him after their baby son who starved to death in the ghetto and told him horror stories until he went mad. Ever since then all he does is fondle himself, day and night. And then along comes this guy with his accordion, plays him a few tunes, and he forgets about the thing burning in his pants, and for the first time since he arrived here I saw him taking his hand away to clap.

"And after he was finished with Itzik he played for the whole ward, and you should have seen them dance. Even Feiga forgot her cleaning and danced. Everyone danced. In slippers, in clogs, barefoot, with clumsy movements and with bodies full of joy."

"But Shmuel, what did he do to Shmuel?" asked Rosa impatiently.

"With Shmuel it was a lot harder. He sat down next to him and played him songs, and Shmuel didn't react. Until this man, this angel, saw that Shmuel was drawing in the air. Then he stood in front of him, as if he were holding the painting in his hands, and told him it was the most beautiful painting he had ever seen, and asked him who the beautiful woman in the painting was."

"And Shmuel talked?" demanded Rosa.

"You bet he talked. The first word he said was 'Rosa.' "

"I don't believe it," said Rosa breathlessly.

"Wait till you hear the rest. And then the man asked him: 'Who's Rosa?' "

"And what did he say?" interrupted Rosa.

"He talked about you. He described you with a lot of love and warmth. He said that you were the biggest and most beautiful woman in the world. How he had waited for you all his life. How he had followed your career and cut out every newspaper article published about you until he got up the courage to knock on your door. And how when he saw you in real life for the first time he was so excited that he couldn't breathe or talk and he felt as if he were paralyzed."

The tears began to stream down Rosa's cheeks, and she buried her head in her hands and asked Tzila in a whisper to go on.

"And then he began to cry," Tzila continued. "He said that he couldn't see you. And when the man asked him why, he said that you'd been burned in the crematorium. And when the man asked him how it had happened, he told him that it was his fault because he had burned you; with his own hands he had thrust your body into the crematorium and seen the fire burning your hair and melting your flesh, until all that was left was a little heap of ash. Then Shmuel called himself a murderer, and started crying so loudly that everyone came to see what had happened. When he calmed down he told the man that ever since he had burned you he was painting you from memory. And you should have heard how he cried over you. Poor man. He mourned you as if you were really dead and kept saying that he was to blame."

"And why is he silent now?" asked Rosa, her body heaving with sobs. "Why won't he talk to me?"

"Because the man's gone. The minute he left Shmuel shut his mouth and resumed his position in front of the window. If he comes back I'll call you," the nurse promised.

The day after her visit to the hospital, early in the morning, there was a soft knock at the door. Rosa peeped through the peephole and saw Rachelle standing there. She opened the door in alarm. This time Rachelle didn't burst noisily into the apartment and wake Angel, as usual. She stood silently on the threshold with an embarrassed, pitying look in her eyes. And when Rosa saw them standing behind her in their white coats, she knew that even though Rachelle was her best friend, she enjoyed being the bringer of bad news. Tzila, the head nurse of hut number three, and Dr. Cohen, the medical director of the hospital, looked at her nervously. They asked her to sit down on the kitchen chair, which Shmuel had covered with painted anemones, and as Rachelle gave her a glass of water, the doctor told her that the night before, a gray, rainy night, Shmuel had disappeared from the ward. "We searched for him everywhere, and we couldn't find a trace," they told her, in a confidential whisper. In the morning, when the rain stopped, they found him lying under an ancient pine tree, buried beneath a pile of dry cones. His hands were still gripping the plastic bag, which by some miracle hadn't been torn in the fall. "It seems," they told her, "that he tried to climb to the top of the pine tree, but the tree was old and dry and hollow and couldn't bear his weight, and it fell to the ground together with him. It was almost like a suicide pact between the tree and the man."

When they left, with their heads hanging and their eyes on the ground, Rachelle remained by her side. Rosa looked at her curiously, suddenly discovering the hard black bristles growing on her upper lip; the scanty, orange-hennaed hair exposing bald spots on her scalp; the brown blotches that had appeared on her cheeks between the pock-marks; the fingers crooked with rheumatism ending in hooked nails like a vulture's claws. She shook her head angrily, trying to get rid of the ugly sight, and then she remembered the terrible news, and lifted her voice in a howl that woke Angel, who crawled out of bed and curled up in her mother's lap, trembling with fear.

"It's all your fault!" she shrieked at Rachelle. "You made him die, you and your advice. 'Nobody commits suicide over paintbrushes.' " She mimicked her voice mockingly. "I should never have listened to you. I always knew that you were jealous of me, and here's the proof. You wanted me to be alone, as lonely as you are. Well, you got what you wanted." And boiling tears of pain streamed down her fleshy cheeks, collected in the deep cleavage between her breasts, and wet Angel's fair head pressing fearfully against her.

When Rachelle left and she remained alone in the painted kitchen with Angel, she told her that Daddy Shmuel had gone and he was never coming back.

"Like Daddy Joseph and Daddy Shraga?" the little girl asked sadly.

"Yes, just like Daddy Joseph and Daddy Shraga." She found herself echoing the child's words.

That evening she asked her children and neighbors not to come, because she wanted to be alone. And when she lay on her bed, with Angel holding her hands in her tiny ones as if trying to comfort her, she felt the anger welling up and seething inside her. This time she was angry at herself for listening to Rachelle and throwing out Shmuel's paintbrushes. When she had exhausted her anger at herself she began to direct her rage at Shraga for leaving her a widow and free to marry Shmuel. And as she continued to examine her life she came up at last with the main culprit—Joseph, for if he hadn't died none of these terrible troubles would have descended on her.

Late at night, when an oppressive silence lay over the house and black shadows lurked with malevolent expressions, she looked at the peaceful face of the child lying next to her, and came to the conclusion that all her troubles had begun with the birth of her daughter. She pushed these cruel thoughts away in alarm, and with her whole body aching and her eyes blinded by tears, she lay and waited for morning, afraid to fall asleep lest she smother the child who had ruined her life. And when morning came, sending hesitant rays through the slats of the blinds, painting the dust motes gold as they danced before her eyes and lay in stripes and squares on the floor, she woke Angel to a new day.

That same day she returned to the hospital to inquire about what had happened to Shmuel and to collect his few possessions. With her back and buttocks bruised by Feiga's mop, whose blows were harder than usual, she reached Shmuel's room, panting for breath. The bed was made, and a strange old man was sitting beside it in a wheelchair with his back to her, staring at the cloudy sky. She looked at the nape of his neck and felt a new pain pinching her chest. Hesitantly she took hold of the handles of the wheelchair and turned it toward her. Eyes full of ashes looked at her curiously and a toothless, narrow-lipped mouth gaped at her. Rosa looked at the old man, and slowly, as if trying to gain time, she rolled up his pajama sleeve. Five blue numbers leaped up at her. Rosa read the numbers aloud, and they immediately began to play before her eyes as if in a game of chance on television, adding and multiplying, subtracting and dividing themselves.

When all the sums were done, and she arrived at the final result, the final figure, she collapsed onto the bed, looked at the old man, and called him by his name. Mischa blinked his eyes and began to mumble all the horrors about human beings turned into soap, babies whose skulls were smashed, crematoria that emitted red dust, into her ears. But Rosa didn't want to hear. With shaking hands she crammed the last months of her dead husband's life into two black plastic garbage bags, and left the room knowing that she could help no more, that however much she tried to atone for everything that had been done to them in the camps, even if she tried to help only one individual survivor, she would never succeed. Because the horror that had happened there was too great and too heavy, and even if she mobilized all the resources of her body and her soul, it would not help.

Defeated, she went to look for Muhammad. And when she found him and asked him what had happened, he told her that Shmuel had climbed the tree because he wanted to achieve greatness, and a man who wants to achieve greatness and climbs high sometimes succeeds and sometimes falls. Rosa didn't agree with this theory; she thought that Shmuel had climbed up a tall tree because he wanted to find a good vantage point to search for his wife who had vanished in the chimney smoke among the scraps of cloud. Whatever the truth may have been, many different explanations of Shmuel's final act were put forward by the patients and the staff, and the next day the newspapers reported dryly that Shmuel Evron, the painter who loved fat women, had died a solitary death in a hospital for the mentally ill.

On trembling legs, her face wet with tears, and her eyes dazzled by the glare of the sun that had emerged from the clouds, Rosa made her way heavily to the gate, where her son's car stood waiting. Two frayed shirts, a pair of shabby shoes, a pair of new pajamas she had bought for him, which he had never worn, long johns, warm undershirts, and a watch with a cracked face—weighed accusingly on her arms in a vengeful burden. Wet pine trunks, sawed off by the gardener for fear they might uproot themselves like Shmuel's tree, barred her path. She zigzagged among the amputated trunks with the pungent smell of the oozing resin pinching her nostrils, and the sticky amber tears gluing the pine needles to the soles of her shoes. She looked at every trunk blocking her way with hatred and hostility, in case it was the one that had killed Shmuel. At the end of the path she tripped over a trunk oozing congealed teardrops. She lay on top of it, her belly crushing dry pine cones and her face sticky with resin. When she opened her eyes she found her head buried in a hole gaping like a wound, padded by thick, torn roots like a warm eagle's nest dug in the ground.

"This is Shmuel's tree," whispered a tall, very thin man with beautiful light eyes who had been following her without her noticing him. Gently he bent over her, took hold of her wrists with his strong hands, and lifted her up as easily as if she were a weightless rag doll. Rosa stood on her feet, shook the dirt off her clothes, picked the pine needles from her hair, and tried to scrape the resin off her nose with her nails. When she had completed her preparations and felt better about herself she looked curiously at her savior, knitting her brow in the attempt to remember if she had ever seen him before. When she failed in the attempt, she suddenly noticed that he was carrying an accordion on his back. The man bent down gracefully, put the accordion on the ground, and carefully gathered up the imaginary canvases and paintbrushes that had existed in Shmuel's madness and had scattered around him when he fell.

"You forgot to take his paintings and brushes," he said in a kindly tone of voice. He led her gently to the car, as if she were a fragile object, and when she sat down heavily in the backseat he laid the pile of airy brushes and canvases on her lap. Rosa refused to cooperate and tried to evade the burden of Shmuel's imagination, but when she felt the stab of a nonexistent paintbrush she took fright and held out her arms to take the bundle.

"If you don't mind," said the stranger delicately, holding a roll of air. "I'll keep this one for myself." With a flourish he unrolled the painting before her. "This is the last portrait of you he painted from memory." He went on to describe the empty, resinous air he was holding spread out in his long hands. "It's his finest painting," he said as he rolled up the nonexistent canvas. "I hope you don't think it's cheek on my part to ask for it. I think Shmuel would have agreed to let me have it."

Rosa looked in embarrassment into the stranger's beautiful eyes and said that every painting Shmuel had ever painted was his finest painting, and with her lap full of imaginary paintbrushes and nonexistent paintings she asked Leslie-Shimon to drive her home. All the way there she looked at the back of her silent son's neck and suddenly she saw that it bore an astonishing resemblance to the nape of Joseph's neck, and she remembered her sons' solemn warnings, and thought that parents should sometimes listen to what their children told them.

When she came home she pushed the imaginary paintbrushes into the red pottery vase standing in the corner and put the crystal vase with the real paintbrushes next to it. After that the pottery vase always stood empty, and when visitors suggested that she fill it with dry branches bearing fluffy cotton blossoms, purple nettles, or even flowers, she would smile and say that she kept this vase for Shmuel's paintbrushes. And when they asked her where the paintbrushes were, she would explain: "We may not be able to see them, but Shmuel can see them from where he is, in heaven."

The imaginary canvases, which the man whose name she didn't know had placed in her lap, she rolled up tightly and stored away carefully in the closet. To keep the moths away from her dead husband's last paintings she strewed mothballs among them. Perhaps these paintings were not the kind that could be seen or felt, but Rosa knew that if they existed for two people, they must be real.

twenty-one

ONE CHILD AND THREE FATHERS

Rosa sat paralyzed among the dozens of people who came to comfort her during the week of mourning, her face empty and expressionless. Most of their visits were prompted by sincere sympathy, but some came out of curiosity to see the woman who had buried three husbands, and a few came to gloat. Bombarded with dozens of roast chickens, kilos of boiled potatoes, hard-boiled eggs, fresh salads, and baked goods, Rosa sat motionless next to the laden table, her eyes dull, her hair greasy, her face fallen, holding the crystal vase with Shmuel's paintbrushes on her lap, waiting for him to come and paint with them to his heart's content.

Since she had broken off relations with Rachelle because of the poor advice she had given her, she told no one but Ruhama that as she sat with the crystal vase between her thighs and listened to the paintbrushes whispering inside it, she felt as if Shmuel were choosing a paintbrush to paint a new picture. Every evening during the week of mourning she would put the vase down next to her bed, count the paintbrushes, learn their colors, and the order in which they were arranged, and pray that he would smell them from afar and be tempted by the bait to visit her bed in the night.

In the morning, before she washed her face, she would count them again and check the order in which they were arranged, and she was prepared to swear that he had used them during the night. On the seventh morning, feeling the dampness on one of the brushes with her fingertips and seeing the dark color on another, she knew that Shmuel hadn't gone, that he was there with her just like Joseph and Shraga.

This time she felt uneasy about framing his picture, and she discussed her doubts with Ruhama, who told her that she had no right to discriminate against any of her husbands, and that Shmuel deserved a memorial too. Again she found herself sorting through the photographs of her dead husbands until she finally chose the best one, a studio portrait taken on their wedding night showing the beaming bridegroom with his arm around his bride. She cut herself carefully out of the photograph and left Shmuel with one broad, brightly colored hand dangling uncomfortably in the air. She set off for the photographer's studio and came home with a poster-size enlargement rolled up in a cardboard cylinder. Then she went to the framer's, and a week later she took delivery of her last husband's beaming face and half his body in a frame identical to those imprisoning the portraits of Joseph and Shraga.

Impatient as a little girl she summoned Leslie-Shimon to come over the same evening and hang the picture. Muttering to himself in protest, her son reluctantly drilled a hole in the wall and hung the new picture in a straight line with the portraits of Joseph and Shraga. Through their glass the old husbands looked disdainfully at the newcomer swelling their ranks, and even though they had never been on the best of terms, it seemed to Rosa that they were joining forces to conspire against the latest addition. Shmuel, who was shy and aware of the hostile atmosphere surrounding him, did his best to be as unobtrusive as possible.

The next day Angel woke up and joined her in bed, in the new regime she had instituted since Shmuel had left, and peeked over the blanket at the three male heads hanging on the wall like the trophies of a scalp hunter. Pointing at them with her slender finger she announced: "That's Daddy Joseph, and that's Daddy Shraga, and that's Daddy Shmuel." She repeated this announcement several times, as if to make sure that she remembered all their names and didn't deprive one of them of his rights.

And when Rosa helped her to get dressed, the little girl chanted a chilling refrain: "First Daddy Joseph went away, and then Daddy Shraga went away, and then Daddy Shmuel went away, and now they're all in the sky." And when she came to "all in the sky" she raised her hands above her head, and Rosa slid her sweater on. Angel went on singing her song as she hopped downstairs and got into the minibus coming to collect her, and with the horrifying refrain ringing in her ears, Rosa climbed laboriously back up to her apartment.

All that day she was unable to concentrate on her housework, and she wandered around restlessly, humming the song that refused to go away, angry at herself for not being able to banish it from her mind and deal with more important things. In the end she switched on the radio and listened to the cheerful tunes, hoping that they would drown out the infectious song and make it go away. But the terrible song rose mockingly above the music from the radio, repeating itself over and over again, until she couldn't stand the sound of it. Suddenly she felt worried about Angel, and she called Dvora, the kindergarten teacher, to ask her if she was all right.

"With her everything's weird," said Dvora, as if she had finally received permission to say what was in her heart. "Never mind those crows that wait for her every day outside, and the way she talks to them; never mind that story about Jacob's ladder she tells us all the time and how she claims that she's a fallen angel. But now, for a change, she's made up some song about her dead fathers, and she won't stop singing it. During the games, during the quiet time, at lunch, and even now, after I've put them all down to sleep, she's still singing it and disturbing the other children. And worst of all, that song's stuck to us all like glue, and now we're all singing it, the teachers, the assistants, and the children who're capable of talking. It just won't leave us alone."

And that evening, when Rosa hummed the song in bed, Joseph disappeared from her life in a silent protest, taking the easygoing and weak-charactered Shraga with him. Rosa, who was so used to his jibes and curses that she couldn't do without them, lay awake in bed, concentrating on Joseph's picture and trying to summon him. When he refused to come, she humiliated herself and begged him to return, promising him all kinds of things if he would only come back to her. And when he persisted in his refusal, she threatened to stay away from his grave, to burn his portrait, and to wipe his memory from her heart. But Joseph took no notice of her threats and stubbornly refused to appear.

When she despaired of Joseph, she began to negotiate with Shraga, concentrating on his picture and coaxing him sweetly to come to her. And when he too failed to respond, she called Shmuel, rattling the paintbrushes with her hand. When this had no effect, she peeled a few plump cloves of garlic, slashed them with her long fingernails, and squeezed their juice over the paintbrushes. But Shmuel refused to come to her, to eat the garlic, or to pick up the paintbrushes.

She felt utterly abandoned. And when she looked at the pictures of her three husbands she knew that they had joined forces against her. They ignored her existence, surveyed her with cold, glassy, distant looks, and ostracized her in the most hurtful way. But in spite of all these ominous signs, Rosa knew that they would come back one day. After all, they needed her no less than she needed them.

In anticipation of the unveiling of the tombstone thirty days after Shmuel's death, she went into town and bought a bunch of new paintbrushes at an art supply shop. She crammed the slender paintbrushes with their soft, shining tufts of hair into a bag and drove to the cemetery. After the ceremony she waited impatiently for everyone to leave. When she was alone, with only the dark looks of Yochai the Undertaker following her from afar, she took the new paintbrushes out of her bag. Then she stood doubtfully in front of the grave, at a loss as to what to do with them. In the end she bunched them all together into one, thick brush and used it to sweep the dust and the little stones that had accumulated on the new marble tombstone. Finding no further use for the paintbrushes, she planted them in the loose soil around the grave with their wooden stems buried in the ground and their tufts sticking up.

Surrounded by a little forest of soft, rustling coxcombs, she turned to Shmuel and told him that now that she had provided him with a fresh supply of paintbrushes she expected him to paint a lot of angels and beautiful women in his new heavenly home. Then she asked him to keep the paintings for her, so that she could see them when she joined him in the fullness of time.

After concluding her conversation with Shmuel, she turned to Shraga. She sat down heavily on his tombstone, and although she was certain that he already knew, she told him about the death of her new husband, and in order to gladden his heart she danced his favorite waltz for him, with the very same steps as on their wedding night. She skipped and capered in the space between the tombstones, feeling his tender feet treading on her toes and getting entangled in her train. When she ran out of breath she sat down on the stone to rest, and after taking her leave of Shraga she set out to find Joseph.

Joseph's grave was covered with lavender bushes, their long stems crowned with purple blooms. Rosa plucked the scented flowers and crushed them between her fingers. The sharp, piercing smell, strong enough to wake the dead, spread through the cemetery. When the scent invaded her nostrils and reminded her of the touch of Joseph's hands, she pulled up her skirts and sat down on the chilly tombstone. Her smell, merging with the heavy scent of the lavender, was sucked in greedily by the rich clods of earth and penetrated to the depths of the underworld.

In a whisper she implored the eldest of her husbands to collect the other two and come home. Joseph, who was busy breathing in the incomparable scents that had momentarily vanquished the rot of death, did not reply, but Rosa knew that her offering had been accepted.

Wearing a grave, solemn expression, like the mask of an actor in a Greek tragedy, Yochai the Undertaker was waiting for her at the gate with a glass of cold water to restore her. Ceremoniously he opened the door of the taxi for her, took her hand, and with a theatrical gesture helped her in, thrust her trailing skirt in after her, tucked it around her lap, and closed the door with a soft slam. Then he watched with lifeless eyes as the taxi drove away, and after it disappeared from view he returned to the cemetery at a light run, unbecoming to his somber calling.

First he visited Joseph's grave, where he filled his lungs with the smell she had left behind her, and stroked with his lean fingers the smooth stone storing the warmth of her body. Then he turned to Shraga's grave and gently swept his outspread hands over the footprints she had left in the ground as a souvenir of her dance. After stepping in all her footsteps, he turned to Shmuel's fresh grave with its shiny new tombstone, wrinkled his thin nose, and stroked the heads of the delicate paintbrushes waving at him in the light breeze.

The next day, when she went to wake Angel from her sleep, the little girl woke up with a beaming smile. Her eyes blinded by tears, Rosa immediately noticed the change that had taken place in her. The long fair hair curling down to her knees parted like a curtain, and her face shone through. It was the most beautiful face that Rosa had ever seen in her life. And when she looked again, as if she couldn't believe her eyes, she saw that it bore an astonishing resemblance to the face Shmuel had given her when he painted her as a cupid. Her light eyes were open wide with a dreamy expression, her ripe rosy lips were parted in an angelic smile, and it seemed to Rosa that her nose had straightened overnight and taken on the classical shape beloved of painters. Alarmed, she examined the child's back to see if her little humps had turned into the downy wings that Shmuel had given her in his painting. To her relief she saw that the humps were unchanged.

Angel looked up at her mother and, in her chirping voice, asked for breakfast. Rosa's happiness was almost complete. Angel wasn't growing like a normal child, but in defiance of the doctors' gloomy predictions she was changing in front of her eyes. She talked, she laughed, she walked, and she was the most beautiful creature Rosa had ever seen, exactly like an angel in a painting.

That night Rosa couldn't contain herself, and after the seven phone calls to her seven children, she told her three dead husbands in excitement about the miracle. As if by common consent, all three had decided to come back to her, and the silence of her bedroom was broken by three male voices. Again Joseph began to shower her with the cursing and teasing, the complaints and obscenities, she had so sorely missed; again she heard Shraga's kindly chirping and the drumming of his bare feet as he danced. This time they were joined by Shmuel, and she could hear the two senior husbands harassing the newcomer, tormenting and insulting him. Joseph mocked his nudes, called them cheap pornography, and spoke slightingly of his paintbrushes. And Shraga, noticing Shmuel's shabby shoes, pounced on them and kept at him all evening, saying that they were a disgrace and demanding to know why he couldn't buy himself a new pair of shoes. After that, as if by common consent, they both began to make fun of his paint-spattered hands and shabby clothes. Then Joseph turned his attention to Shraga, reminding him of his poor performance in bed and the embarrassing circumstances of his death, and Shraga retaliated with the story of Joseph's last days on earth, and the grotesque position in which he had been buried, which they were still talking about in heaven, and which made even the angels laugh. And so it went until Rosa's patience snapped; she scolded them as if they were naughty children, and warned them that if they went on quarreling none of them would be allowed into her bed.

During the nights when she conversed with her husbands, separately and together, all three of them tried to get into her bed. With a heavy heart she would decide which of them to spend the night with and kick the other two out. Since it was hard for her to choose, she would flip a coin until it transpired that Joseph, the strongest of the three, would shoulder the other two aside and turn the coin to suit himself when he picked it off the floor. When she discovered this piece of trickery, she decided to make a roster and allow each of them in turn into her bed. Sundays and Wednesdays were devoted to Joseph. Monday and Thursday it was Shraga's turn, and Tuesdays and Fridays were set aside for Shmuel. In order to avoid superfluous arguments she decided to spend the Sabbath alone in self-examination, until Joseph demanded it for himself, since he was the senior husband and had lived with her the longest.

"That's it; I've had enough. I'll never get married again," she announced to Ruhama after paying another visit to Shmuel's grave and taking the opportunity to visit the other two as well.

"It doesn't depend on you," Ruhama replied dryly, in an ominous tone of voice.

"I haven't got the strength left to marry and bury, marry and bury, marry and bury," Rosa pleaded, as if Ruhama, who had invented the butterfly game and sealed her fate, had the power to change her destiny. "And it's lucky for me that the three of them are buried in the same place," she added. "Imagine if I had to run to three cemeteries all over the country! This way it's easy. Whenever I visit one grave I visit the others too, and none of them can complain of being left out. But a fourth grave—the very thought of it gives me the shivers. Who's got the strength for it at our age?"

"But who says you'll have to bury the fourth one too? Maybe he'll bury you—don't forget he'll be the last," Ruhama said spitefully.

Rosa, who felt the words burning her flesh, laughed apologetically. "Look at me, fat, old, a mother of eight with a disabled child to look after. Who would want me?"

Ruhama didn't answer and looked enviously at her friend's perfect face, sucking up her beauty as if to absorb it into the darkness of her body. And before they parted she told her that she should consider herself lucky, since she had already had three husbands and it wasn't over yet, whereas the only man she, Ruhama, had been close to in recent years, after Joseph's death, was the faceless man burdened with shopping baskets who sat next to her on the number eighteen bus on the way home from the market, and who was so tired that he fell asleep and let his head fall onto her shoulder. And she was so happy to have a man sleeping at her side at last that she didn't shake him off, not even in order to get off the bus at her stop. And when he woke up and got off the bus in Katamon H, she got off with him. "And he didn't even turn his head to see who had been acting as his pillow," she said bitterly. "He got off the bus and walked away as if I didn't exist, as if he hadn't been sleeping on my shoulder. As if he was something to write home about! A tired middle-aged man in stinking old clothes, with unshaved cheeks and red eyes. And to think that I got off the bus and followed him just because he did me the favor of sleeping on my shoulder," she said painfully, and as if she regretted her confession, she quickly left the house.

During this time Rosa ignored the living and concentrated on the dead. Angel's beautiful face smiling at her in the morning no longer thrilled her, nor did her grandchildren succeed in bringing a smile to her face when they came to visit. The warm weight and good smell of the babies in her lap, which usually filled her with intense feelings of love, did not warm her heart. Rosa's life centered round the anniversaries of her husbands' deaths. She visited their graves, cherished their mementos, and kept three memorial candles burning in the living room.

Before she could recover from the anniversary of Shmuel's death, it was followed by Shraga's, which was followed by Joseph's, and then came Shmuel's turn again. She began to wonder if her mother had been right never to remarry, and if satisfying the demands of one dead husband was difficult, taking care of three was almost impossible.

"It's impossible to share your attention among three dead husbands without depriving any of them," Rosa would complain to Rachelle, with whom she had made friends again in the meantime, and to Ruhama, who always liked hearing about her troubles. And at night too they gave her no peace, keeping her awake with their incessant quarreling, their whims, and their complaints.

The days passed so quickly that she complained to Rachelle that her years were growing shorter, that before she could turn around she had already observed three anniversaries and the year was already over, and with the years getting so short she would die before her time. Rachelle pondered what she had said and then remarked that she felt the same way, that her years too were getting shorter, and every year was shorter than the one before, and the year to come would probably be shorter still, and the one after that would be over before it began.

And Rosa, who felt time racing and her days disappearing, began to mark the passing days in little lines on the wall behind her bed. At the end of the year, when she counted the lines she had drawn, she saw that she had not missed a single day, but nevertheless the year had passed more quickly than the one before it.

"I'm afraid," she said to Rachelle, "that I'll go to sleep one night and when I wake up in the morning I'll discover that another year has passed." And when they invited Ruhama for a joint consultation, they revived memories of bygone days, when a year was a year, and with longing filming their eyes they recalled how slowly time had passed then, and how they had counted the days before summer vacation, and how they had almost died of anticipation until it arrived, and how the time between one birthday and the next when they were children had seemed like an eternity.

And again they spoke gravely and at length about how their days were getting shorter, until Rosa put an end to the barren discussion and announced that she was going to see Peretz the Cabalist. "He's the wisest man I know," she said, "and I'm sure he'll come up with an answer. And besides, I haven't seen him for ages and he's probably got a lot to tell me," she added apologetically.

This time Rosa did not have to wait her turn with the dozens of women assembled outside his door. As soon as he heard that she was there he sent his assistant to bring her to him. He looked into her eyes, peeked down the neck of her dress, weighed her breasts in his imagination, and listened to the problem of the shortening days. Although she asked him, he refused point-blank to tell her when she would be reunited with her husbands, but he was prepared to explain why her days were growing shorter, and reassured her by saying that many people of her age felt the same.

"The reason is simple," he said. "When we're children the years pass slowly, that's a fact. Because your year and a child's year are the same from the point of view of the number of days they contain, but his is very long and yours is very short. Don't forget, for a four-year-old a year is a quarter of his life, and for a five-year-old a year is a fifth of his life. Whereas we, who would love to make time go slower, one year at the age of fifty is a fiftieth of our lives, and one year at the age of sixty is a sixtieth of our lives—so you see, everything is relative, and time really does fly. And besides"—he suddenly changed his tone and began to speak like a university professor, and Rosa felt that he really was the cleverest man she knew—"if we look at the scientific study of the time mechanism in humans, we're talking about a physiological process taking place in the brain. The longer we live, the more this process wears down, and so the sense of time in an old man is different from that in a young man."

Before she left he asked her how Angel was doing and when she told him about her he nodded his head in satisfaction and asked her to look out for anything unusual in her behavior, because he saw something for which he had no explanation at the moment. And when she asked him what he meant, he said that he couldn't say for sure, and asked her again to watch the child carefully.

Rosa went home, called her friends, and told them what the cabalist had said.

After this Rosa began to watch Angel like a hawk, trying to make up for all those years when she had been too busy getting married, taking care of her new husbands, burying them, mourning them, and appeasing their spirits to pay her the proper attention. Now she began to look after her like a mother again, rejecting the attempts of her daughter Ruthie, who had grown accustomed to her role of surrogate mother, to take the child under her wing. And in the evenings, when she put her to bed, she would gaze intently at this different child to whom she had given birth, who had smashed to smithereens the ordinary, uneventful life to which she had once aspired.

Sometimes, when she thought about Angel and worried about what would happen to her when she, Rosa, departed this world, she would suffer agonies of conscience that kept her awake at night, and she would blame herself for arresting the child's growth, since an old wish of hers had come true in Angel. Painfully she remembered Angela's strictures: "When you wish for something, you don't always know what the results will be if your wish comes true. The realization of a wish can cost a heavy price." Once Angela had caught her in the middle of performing her secret nightly ritual over baby Ruthie, and when she heard Rosa asking her daughter not to grow up, she was furious. "Did you ever think about what would happen if your wish came true and Ruthie really didn't grow?" she scolded her. Rosa didn't bother to reply, and she didn't think of the consequences, and at night, behind her mother's back, she continued to ask her children not to grow up.

And in her last child the wish had come true, as if all the previous wishes had come together and materialized in her. And even after the doctors told her that Angel wouldn't grow, she couldn't stop herself from repeating the words she had repeated every night over all her other children: "Don't grow." Rosa hoped that thanks to the arrested growth of her last child time would stop for her and she wouldn't grow old, as if Angel's refusal to grow would stop the years from encroaching and keep the end at bay. And when she listened to the neighborhood women talking about the "goslings that had grown wings and flown away" and even read in the women's magazines about "empty nest syndrome," she knew that she would always have Angel at her side; her nest would never be empty, and she would not grow old.

When she looked at the results of her wish that had come true—at Angel's tiny feet, like those of the Chinese girls whose mothers had bound their feet to arrest their growth, sticking out of her baby dresses—she would almost swoon with joy.

The neighborhood women would exclaim loudly over Angel's beauty and tell Rosa that her baby was a doll. And Rosa knew that this was not far from the truth. When she looked at Angel playing with the doll, Belle, she could see the resemblance between them. Both had golden curls, small straight noses, pink cheeks as perfect as if painted by a master painter's hand, and blue eyes fringed with long dark lashes. Belle's eyes were glassy and expressionless and never closed, and Angel's eyes were always smiling.

When she went out for walks with Angel now, she would dress her in wide blouses to hide the little humps on her back. With maternal pride she would see how the passersby stopped to look at the child. Enchanted, they would bend over the tiny little girl, cooing and gurgling in the usual way that adults consider suitable for talking to babies. This was the moment both of them were waiting for. After her admirers had run out of baby talk, Angel would open her mouth and talk sense, leaving her audience speechless. A look of astonishment would cross their faces as they stared at the exquisite baby who could talk like a big girl. Sometimes Rosa would take fright at her own great pride in her daughter, and suspect the people looking at her curiously of wanting to give her the evil eye, and she would spread her five fingers wide and raise her right hand to her forehead, as if to wipe away invisible beads of sweat, and whisper five times to herself the magic charm against the evil eye: "*Hamsa, hamsa, hamsa, hamsa, hamsa.*"

At night, after bathing Angel in the baby tub, shampooing her hair, kissing every dimple and soft fold of flesh, nuzzling her toes, and breathing on her pink cheeks, she would put her to sleep and stand by her bed, counting her rhythmic breaths. For a long time she would stand there and listen attentively, trying to discern the familiar sound of children growing in the night. Then she would bend over her bed and whisper in her ear: "Don't grow, don't grow, don't grow."

And the child did not fail her. Obediently she would wake up after a long night during which all the children grew, and her height would be exactly the same as the day before.

"It's not that she's a dwarf, God forbid," Rosa would say to her friends. "All her proportions are right; it's just that she hasn't grown, and at least one of the doctors' predictions has come true."

Behind Rosa's back Rachelle would say to anyone who asked her: "Rosa is to blame for everything. It's because she asked all her other seven children not to grow up. And now her wish has come true in her eighth child to punish her. The child doesn't grow, and if you ask me it's not normal for a child of her age to look like a child of two." And then she would add: "In my opinion Rosa neglects that child. Instead of behaving like a responsible mother and running to doctors with her, she's proud of her abnormality and does nothing to stop it." And, lowering her voice to a confidential whisper, she would continue: "How come she lets her play with those crows? Crows bring bad luck. How come she doesn't understand that anyone who plays with bad luck is putting his life at stake?" And Rosa would hear from her neighbors the things that were never said to her face, and push another clove of garlic against the evil eye under Angel's pillow.

In time to come, after Angel was gone, when the elders of the neighborhood would debate the matter and try to pinpoint the moment of her disappearance, violent disagreements would break out. One would say that she had reached the age of five, another would argue heatedly that she was seven, while a third would claim that she was no more or less than ten years old—but since her body refused to grow with the years, she looked like a baby.

twenty-two

THE BELOVED OF THE CROWS

As Rosa grew closer to Angel she became more sharply aware of the "phenomenon," as the neighbors referred to the unique relationship between her daughter and the birds in general, and the crows in particular. After Angel was born, when a great flock of crows began to circle the house, Rosa at first refused to see it as a "phenomenon," and claimed that it was simply coincidence. But when the "phenomenon" repeated itself, and the whole neighborhood started to talk about it, she began to look for explanations, hints, and signs.

Rosa thought that it all began when she first brought Angel home, because of the vociferous welcome accorded her by Joseph's cuckoo clocks. She liked to tell the story of how she came home from the hospital with the baby in her arms, and the minute she walked in the door all the wooden birds chorused, "Cuckoo! Cuckoo!" ten times to mark the hour of ten o'clock in the morning. And the cuckoo cries continued to resound in the baby's ears every hour on the hour until her father, Joseph, died.

The neighbors told a different story. They described a motley crew of gray crows massing on the wires of the telephone poles opposite the house and cawing curiously, ignored by Rosa who was too excited to notice them. The fourth-floor neighbors, looking down from their balconies, liked to describe how the crows screwed their necks around at an angle that made their feathers bristle and enabled them to fix their beady eyes on the tiny flawed baby in its mother's arms. And when their curiosity was satisfied, they began to fly around and around the house and utter their agitated cries. The cacophony went on for hours, the neighbors said, and ever since the crows had flown past the baby's window in formation every morning, taking turns tapping on the windowpane with their strong beaks and showing a keen interest in her development. And the child, who the doctors predicted would never grow and would spend her life lying on her hunchback, would turn her head in the direction of the tapping, stretch out her tiny arms, and coo with delight.

At first Rosa dismissed the idea of there being any kind of connection between the child and the neighborhood crows, but as time went by she grew accustomed to the strange spectacle. When she emerged from the house with Angel, she would raise her eyes to the sky and look for the dark legions casting their terror on the birds above and the people below.

Angel soon learned to follow the black birds that had become an integral part of her life with her eyes, and before she could say "Mama" she learned to say "birds." When she grew older, Rosa would open the window of her room and stand her on a chair, and the little girl would thrust her golden head outside and call in her weak voice, "Cuckoo crow!" at the black birds streaking the sky as they soared and swooped over the house, cleverly exploiting the whirling currents of air, and they would answer her with calls of their own.

Angel knew them all, from the leaders to the youngest and most insignificant among them, and she gave them all names. And when she was asked how she distinguished between them, since they all looked the same, she would laugh her chiming laugh and claim that this one had a thick beak, and that one a drooping tail feather, and the other was faded as if it had been too long in the sun; another had gleaming round spots on its down, another was vain and spent all day grooming its feathers, another was the smallest, another was the biggest, and yet another had a red glint in its eyes. And when Dror and Rosa tried to see the signs she gave them, they soon gave up in despair, because all the crows looked identical to them.

Rosa would look at Angel in astonishment as she called the birds by their names. Even when they were otherwise occupied and far away, they would immediately drop whatever they had in their beaks, spread their black wings, and come flying to see what she wanted. And when she went around the neighborhood, one of them would always accompany her and keep watch over her. Wagging its tail to keep its balance, the crow would hover over her head, and when she lagged behind, it would turn its head and observe her every movement with its beady eyes.

The story of the "little Jerusalem cripple and the neighborhood birds" first appeared in a small item on the back page of the local paper. Soon the neighborhood was swarming with reporters, photographers, nature lovers, bird-watchers armed with binoculars and tape recorders, and scores of curiosity seekers beating a path to Angel's door like stubborn suitors, raising their eyes to the sky to watch the gray birds flying past in formation and waiting for Angel to come out of the house so that they could witness the spectacle reported in the newspaper. Even the skeptics and those of little faith streamed into the neighborhood in order to scoff at the credulous who arrived there in droves. The former argued that any kind of bond between humans and crows was impossible, and to prove that they were wrong the neighbors would show them the indelible traces of the bird droppings lining the pavements in stripes.

The enterprising boys who set up stalls to sell lemonade and almond water did good business. The long hours of watching and waiting for Angel and the crows, and the endless arguments that raged on the pavements between the believers and the skeptics, dried people's throats and they drank eagerly.

A learned article appeared in the journal *Nature and Landscape* about the little girl in Jerusalem and the crows. Dr. Jonathan Tzafrir, the well-known ornithologist, wrote that it was not unusual to find such friendships between people and birds, and that the phenomenon was especially common among crows, who were considered intelligent birds with a particularly well developed social and couple-oriented life. In the introduction to the article, which was entitled *Friendly Birds in Jerusalem*, it said:

> The state of Israel can claim the title of being the country with the densest population of crows in the world. For every square meter of the country today there are seventeen crows, and every day an average of eight distress calls are received from people all over the country who have been harmed by a crow. The confrontation with the crow sometimes concludes with the wound-

> ing of the bird, but there are other cases in which the crows nurse a grievance and persist in treating the person who harmed them as an enemy. The opposite case too occurs, and Angel's case is not unique. Here the flock has adopted this child, and taken responsibility for her welfare.

And when the author went around the country with his slides, lecturing on the subject of crows at high schools and community centers, he would include the story of Angel and the crows in his lectures, but he was unable to answer the question that troubled Rosa and kept coming up among his audiences: "Why Angel, of all people? Why didn't they pick somebody else?"

And Rosa, brooding about the unsolved mystery whenever she heard the cawing of the crows over the house, would remember Angela drying the black watermelon seeds on white cotton sheets in the yard of the "House of Notes" in Old Katamon. Sheets and blankets in all the colors of the rainbow would be spread out in the summer months and covered with the wet black seeds of recently eaten watermelons. Around the sheets the women in their bright kerchiefs would crouch on low stools with wicker seats, their heavy breasts sagging to their waists and their vast behinds spreading in all directions. As they gossiped and chatted merrily, they would bend forward and reach automatically for the mountain of seeds, taste them, and mix them so that each and every one would receive its daily dose of sun. And when greedy sparrows and impudent crows approached, their placid chatter would turn into an uproar, and their voices would turn into shrill agitated shrieks. Then they would rise heavily from their stools, take up their posts by their sheets, and wave their arms vigorously to frighten the hungry birds and chase them away.

Only Angela would stand at a distance and watch the birds pecking greedily at her watermelon seeds. And one bird brought another until her sheet was covered with birds of every type and kind, and they would hop about among the seeds and feast on them to their hearts' content. In spite of these aviary attacks, Angela never found any bird droppings or feathers on her seeds, and there was never any lack of watermelon seeds to grace her table after the Sabbath meal was over.

And Rosa remembered too, as if it were yesterday, how Angela would take her out into the broad fields surrounding Old Katamon in the twilight hours, always carrying dry pita wrapped in a bandanna. And when they sat down to rest in the shade of the carob tree, she would crumble the bread and scatter it around for the birds.

When she shared her memories with Rachelle, the latter told her that it was a classic case of the reincarnation of the grandmother's soul in the granddaughter, since Rosa's mother had died only two months before the birth of the baby who had received her name, and there was no need for Rosa to be surprised, for the soul of Angela, God have mercy on her, was simply continuing to work through her granddaughter, and who but the crows were the first to recognize her? And since they were the first to make the discovery, they had succeeded in claiming the child for their own. Rosa pondered her friend's words, which sounded logical enough, hugged Angel, and looked deep into her daughter's eyes, seeking traces of her mother's lost soul.

twenty-three

"MY LITTLE ANGEL HAS FALLEN!"

All that night, the last of her nights, Angel couldn't sleep. In addition to her fear of the thunder and the storm banging at the windows and threatening to break in, she was concerned for her friends the crows, huddling, exposed and frozen in their nests, their feathers bristling with cold. As she struggled with the troubling thoughts about the storm and the crows, her anxiety was diluted by expectation. The reason for the expectation seeping sweetly though her body was lying on her bed: a magnificent bridal gown, a long veil, and a pair of new patent leather shoes, waiting like her for the next morning. This ensemble was to be her costume for the Purim holiday, when all boys and girls dressed up.

Before she went to bed she had tried on the dress. And Rosa, with her mouth full of the pins she was sticking in the hem of the dress to shorten it and adapt it to Angel's short stature, muttered, as if to herself, that tomorrow Angel would be the fairest of all the girls, the most beautiful bride in town. When she had finished putting up the hem, she examined the results of her work with satisfaction, hung the dress over the back of the chair, added a long veil decorated with flowers, and put the new patent leather shoes under the chair.

After Rosa, with heavy sighs, got into bed, Angel couldn't control herself. She jumped out of bed, took the dress, tried it on again in front of the mirror, put on the new shoes, and inspected her little body all clad in white. Then she took the dress off, and since she was unwilling to part with it, she laid it on her bed, careful not to crease it, and thought happily of how she would surprise Dror the next day with her bride's costume.

In the morning she woke up from a brief sleep earlier than usual.

In days to come, when Rosa told Rachelle and Ruhama about

the sequence of events, she would choke with tears and blame herself, and say that she was still sure that Angel had woken up because of the strange silence that had fallen on the town.

The thick, fluffy, white blanket that had frozen on the ground smothered the sounds before they broke out into the cold air, and dimmed the usual noises of the morning. The blanket deceived the innocent, tricked the ignorant, and lied to those who were seeing it for the first time in their lives. They say that it starts its long journey high up in the sky, close to God, in the form of isolated feathery flakes that whirl and dance in all directions until they multiply in a mysterious process of reproduction hidden from the human eye. Overnight they accumulate on the ground and merge into a cold, deceptive, short-lived blanket covering the earth.

At the sound of the magical silence Angel woke from her sleep in her room where crows and angels sailed through the clouds. She waited expectantly in bed for the morning crows to greet her, and when they tarried she called them in her thoughts. They made haste to obey her summons, leaving their warm nests and the sheltering wings of their mates, flew with ominous caws over the treetops adorned in their honor with caps of white that only God and the birds can see, and swooped down to her window. As they did every morning, they tapped on the windowpane, which that morning was decorated with perfect flowers of frost in shapes never seen before.

Angel did not want to wake her mother, who opened the window for her every morning to receive the blessing of the crows. Slowly she dragged the wooden chair to the wall, climbed up on it, and opened the window. A blast of freezing cold burst into the room, which had been warmed all night by the heat of her body and breath. The crows beat their wings in delight, gave her their blessing, cawed their farewells, and disappeared into the gray sky, flying between the snowflakes whirling around without aim or direction in their fleeting lives.

At that moment the white radiance of the earth dazzled her eyes. Angel was beside herself. First she raised her head to the gray sky as if seeking an answer, following the flight of the crows between the white feathers. Then she followed the dance of the snowflakes whirling opposite her, until her eyes grew tired and her head spun. With black spots dancing before her eyes, she looked down at the earth covered with a tempting blanket of soft, woolly clouds. In the excitement of seeing snow for the first time in her life, she forgot all about the Purim party and the bridal gown waiting for her on her bed, and hurried from her room to Rosa's giant bed in order to share the scene with her mother, and shook her gently awake.

"There are clouds on the ground," she cried joyfully, "lots and lots of clouds on the ground. Clouds like the ones on my ceiling. I want to go down and play with the clouds."

Rosa turned over on her side, trying to preserve the warmth of her body under the thick blanket.

"Go back to bed," she said firmly. "It's too early to get up."

Chastised, Angel went back to her room, picked up the doll, Belle, and climbed onto the chair with her so that she too could enjoy the spectacle. When she leaned out of the window, the snow covering the yard winked at her with a thousand starry white eyes and promised her angelic games and soft pamperings.

"I have wings," she murmured to herself, hugging Belle to her chest. "I can fly, I have wings, I can fly." With great difficulty she climbed onto the windowsill holding the doll in her arms. Her feet sank into the frozen droppings of the crows, and before the horrified eyes of Mazel, the first-floor neighbor from the building opposite, who had opened her shutters to check out the suspicious silence, Angel's bare feet slipped on the frozen slime. Her wings did not spread as her body cut through the air.

To the accompaniment of shrieks of grief from the crows who rushed to the place and looked on in terror at her last flight, she fell to the ground, cleaving through the snowflakes fluttering around her. In an instant she sank into the deceptive blanket of white, which sucked her little body into its softness and flung it furiously against the hard, stony, frozen ground. Mazel's horrified screams were swallowed up in the cries of fear and pain uttered by the crows, which came flying from all directions.

Rosa was woken by the cold invading the house through the open window in Angel's room. Deaf to the screeching of the crows and Mazel's screams, she went into Angel's room and slammed the window shut, fully intending to scold the child for leaving the window open on such a cold day. After looking for her all over the house she heard a loud knocking on the door, opened it, and ran into the yard behind the bearers of the evil tidings. She found her there lying in a bed of scarlet clouds, with her flannel nightgown, whose pattern of fleecy sheep had been dyed red, hiding her broken body. Angel's smiling face was as pale as the snow, her golden hair was spread out around her like a halo of light, mingled with the hair of the doll, Belle, who was lying beside her with her china head smashed.

"My little angel has fallen!" screamed Rosa as she gathered up the broken body that dangled in her frozen hands like a rag doll. Gently the neighbors tried to part her from the dead child, but Rosa held on, digging her nails into her body and leaving ten bleeding crescents in her cold flesh.

"My little angel has fallen." She repeated the sentence as if she were afraid of forgetting it as they hoisted her step by step up the stairs to her house, her nightgown sour with blood, the little girl clasped tightly to her bosom, her bare feet swaying lifelessly in the air with every step her mother took.

"My little angel has fallen," she mumbled when they succeeded in prying the child from her arms, removed her bloody nightgown, dressed her in heavy winter clothes, and supported her step by step downstairs to the ambulance waiting to take her and the little body to the hospital.

"My little angel has fallen, my little angel has fallen," she repeated all the way to the cemetery, as if to convince herself that the tragedy had truly happened.

"My little angel has fallen," she screamed into the little pit dug with difficulty in the frozen ground of the plot Rosa was saving for herself, next to Joseph. And Dror stood next to her and screamed and screamed until he fainted.

To the sound of the despairing screeches of the crows, which merged with the weeping of the people and Rosa's grief-stricken screams, they buried the little bundle wrapped in its shroud in the muddy ground. When it was all over, they revived Dror with light slaps, and when he came back to life he refused to leave and asked to be buried with her, whispering to himself that now that Angel had turned into one of the angels in the sky he would join her there, and they would celebrate their wedding in heaven.

Like a sad, ragged flock of wet black crows they left the fresh grave. At the exit of the cemetery they were met by the frozen face of Yochai, by the purple plastic tray and glass of water that had turned to ice. "My little angel has fallen," Rosa flung at him accusingly, as if he were to blame for her death, and ignoring the glass of icy water she walked heavily away, dragging her feet and supported by her sons. Shamefaced, Yochai stood rooted to the spot, watching the column of mourners filing past him in their heavy coats, with black umbrellas that afforded scant protection from the lashing rain mixed with sleet and hail.

Soaking wet, they returned from the cemetery and huddled silently around Rosa's kerosene stoves until vapors rose from their heavy winter clothes and the air filled with the reek of the kerosene, mingled with the smell of the mothballs that had seeped into their clothes during the long summer months. And when Rosa for the umpteenth time repeated the sentence, "My little angel has fallen," in a howl that sounded like a jackal lamenting its lost cubs, she pressed the doll, Belle, to her breast. Suddenly the doll, who hadn't uttered a sound for years, joined in and cried in a soft, squeaky voice: "Mama, mama, mama."

Horrified, Leslie-Shimon ran out of the room and returned with the heaviest hammer he could find in Joseph's toolbox. With his mouth full of nails clenched between his lips, and his cheeks sucked in, he burst into Angel's room, climbed onto the chair with the tiny pair of patent leather shoes waiting in vain underneath it, and furiously nailed the window to the wooden frame. The furious hammering brought the neighbors running to the scene of the fall, where they trampled the muddy, bloodstained snow, wringing their hands and sadly nodding their heads. They all agreed that Leslie-Shimon was right to nail the window up, so that nobody could jump out of Angel's window again. For suicide, so they said there in the muddy yard, was contagious, and people who wanted to commit suicide were like criminals returning to the scene of the crime. And people who chose to end their lives by jumping from a high place were liable to follow in the footsteps of their predecessors who had succeeded.

And when the snow melted two days later, the bit of ground where the little girl and her doll had been smashed was revealed. The bed of death that had crushed the little bodies was lined with sharp stones, broken bottles, dirty diapers, torn newspapers, and dog excrement.

Many months later, so the neighbors said, the crows were still searching for the little girl standing in the window, until they lost hope, folded their wings, abandoned their nests, and left, never to return.

* * *

In time to come, on the dreamy summer nights that covered the town in a steamy blanket of heat that made everybody forget the harsh winter, the neighbors would hear Rosa's lament again.

The lament, which was repeated as if in her sleep, always ended with the scream of dismay: "My little angel has fallen!" which she repeated in the middle of the night with her nightgown soaked in sweat and clinging to her body. And when the children of the neighborhood woke up at the sound of the terrible scream breaking into their sweet childish dreams, they would go like sleepwalkers to their parents' rooms, cuddle up with them in their big beds, and ask their mothers fearfully why Angel had fallen. Sleepy eyed, their mothers would wrap the children in their arms and explain to them that Angel had fallen because she had played with her life and not taken care, and when people played with their lives the wind blew them away or they were run over by a car, and that was what happened to children when they weren't careful.

And a year after Angel's death, Rachelle could say to Rosa what she had thought and not dared to say before: "Angel fell because she had no grip on reality, and anyone who has no grip on reality ends up by disappearing and turning into a legend."

twenty-four

THE PUNISHMENT OF TIME

At the end of the week of mourning, when the condolence callers went away and Rosa remained alone at home for the first time in her life, she summoned her three dead husbands for a hard talk.

"Why didn't you tell me?" she demanded.

The three men exchanged embarrassed looks and said nothing.

"At least you could have warned me against the fall. Where are your hearts?" she reproached them and listened to their silence.

When the silence dragged on she stood in front of them and shouted at the top of her voice, mobilizing all her sorrow and all her anger and all the resonance of her mighty chest: "Answer me!"

Shraga and Shmuel looked desperately at Joseph, the senior husband and Angel's father. Joseph avoided their eyes, smiled the same fatuous smile that had appeared on his face at the moment of his death, shrugged his shoulders, and said: "We couldn't have known. And even if we had warned you and Leslie-Shimon had nailed down all the windows, our destiny is written in advance and nobody can change it. She would have fallen anyway." And he added hesitantly: "And if you want to know my opinion, it was all because of Dror. If he hadn't kept on telling her that she had wings, and telling her that silly story about Jacob's dream, I doubt if she would have tried to fly."

Shraga nodded in agreement, picked absentmindedly at his bare toes, and since he had always detested animals of every shape and form, added: "It's true that it's all Dror's fault, but the crows are to blame too. They enticed her to fly with them."

Then they looked at each other and with the silent complicity of old friends they both turned on the last husband, Shmuel, who sat between them like a schoolboy in disgrace, with his eyes fixed on the tips of his shabby shoes, spattered with paint in all the colors of the rainbow.

"It's Shmuel's fault too. He painted her with wings and filled her room with angels. Is it any wonder that she thought she was one of them?" they chorused. Then all three of them looked at one another, nodded their heads in agreement, and turned on Rosa, raising their voices and rebuking her with words that went on ringing in her ears long after they had left.

"And it's all your fault too," they said. "If you hadn't called her Angel to begin with, she might never have tried the wings she didn't possess and the story might have ended differently."

Rosa raged against them as she had never raged against anyone before. Yelling furiously she chased them out of her room, declaring that this time she really never wanted to see them again, and for many nights afterward she refused to allow any of them into her bed. Even when they sent her their sweetest smiles from behind the glass of their pictures and coaxed her with tender words, reminding her of the happy days they had spent together and holding out the promise of future delights, she hardened her heart against them.

As a last resort they recruited Angela to their cause, calling her up from the depths of the underworld. One evening she appeared among them, her shriveled body draped in a black lace mourning dress full of tears that exposed her sickly white skin. The roses blooming on her faded cheeks and the unfamiliar glitter in her eyes led Rosa to the happy conclusion that her parents had finally been reunited, and that her father was apparently showering her mother with love again. And when she tried to ask her how her father was, Angela wagged her finger at her and admonished her as in days gone by, speaking in a hoarse, dull whisper from her toothless mouth. "I told you that it was forbidden to name the living after the dead. Who asked you to give her my name?" she demanded in a voice that sounded as if it had been conjured up from the bowels of the earth. Then she gave the three men one of her withering looks and continued in a rebuking voice: "I told you that it was forbidden for a widow to marry. You set the dead against you, and you didn't ask their permission, and here's the result. You are a lethal woman."

Rosa forgot that her mother had long been dead and gone, and old, unresolved resentments that always began with the words "I told you so" began rising in her throat. She stopped her ears with her fingers and told them all to get out of her room or she wouldn't be responsible for the consequences. All four vanished in an instant, and she felt cold shivers running down her spine, from the back of her neck to the tips of her toes. With her whole body shaken by sobs and the word "lethal" ringing in her ears, she got into bed, where she spent a sleepless night, knowing that she never wanted to see her dead husbands again and that she would never miss them as long as she lived.

Try as she might, Rosa was unable to conjure up the figure of her dead daughter in her memory. Even when she pressed the new patent leather shoes to her bosom, sniffed her clothes, gathered up the golden hairs that had become entangled in her hairbrush, and looked again and again at her drawings, she could not sense Angel's presence. Nor did the huge portrait she had made and hung on her bedroom wall help, a picture in which Angel looked out at her with her a bright, clear, pensive gaze, so different from the looks of her three husbands with the wrinkles round their eyes. And when she tried to conjure up her memory with the aid of the doll, Belle, who looked so much like Angel, she would scold herself afterward, for how could you compare a little girl full of life to an inanimate doll with a smashed skull and beady blue glass eyes? Belle's white dress, which reminded her of the bride's costume Angel had not lived to wear, was blood-stained, and whenever she touched it she felt the pain in her heart and the wounds gaping open again, and for the umpteenth time she wondered why she didn't throw the doll away.

But Belle reminded her of her first friend, Rina, too, in whose bed she had slept in the villa in Old Katamon, and she was afraid that if she threw the doll away all her memories would be wiped out. And Rosa would hug the doll and think about her secret bedfellow, about her life in the House of Notes, about her mother, Angela, and about her little daughter who had smashed against the frozen ground with the doll clasped in her arms and its golden hair tangled with hers. For hours she would sit in the dark on the flowery chair in the cheerful kitchen, pressing the doll to her bosom, shaking it up and down and listening in wonder to the word it had begun to repeat again after the fall: "Mama, mama, mama." And Rosa would interrupt the doll and repeat in time to its cry: "My little angel has fallen, my little angel had fallen, my little angel has fallen," until the first rays of the morning sun filtered through the slats of the shutters in long narrow stripes of faint light and crept stealthily toward her. First they licked at her feet, cold from the night chill, then they climbed to her calves and thighs, lingered between the tops of her legs to warm and tickle her there before climbing to her belly, invading her breasts, and penetrating her tear-blinded eyes with their merciless glare.

Then Rosa would rise from her chair, go to Angel's bedroom, and lay the doll with its broken head on her rumpled bed, which was still just as she had left it, with the bridal gown and veil waiting for her in vain. Gently, so as not to hurt it, she would shake the doll a little, listen with a gratified expression to its cry of "Mama," tuck it into Angel's blanket so it wouldn't catch cold, and go exhausted to her room, lie down in the deep dent in her mattress, close her eyes, and try without success to recall the last time she saw her daughter lying on her icy bed.

On the thirtieth day after Angel's death she came home from the cemetery, and this time she did not call on her three husbands, not even to say good-bye to them. And when she mounted the stairs on her feet swollen from standing next to the grave, she knew that her life had frozen at a single point in time. When her consolers told her that "Time heals everything," Rosa already knew the truth. She knew that her time, the time that had gone past so swiftly in her life and that she had often complained of to her friends, had decided to punish her. The time that was supposed to pass quickly and heal her, according to her comforters, had begun to deceive her, mock her, and play tricks on her in dark corners and in secret. Just now, when she wanted it to pass quickly, it stretched out endlessly as if its feet were grounded in the earth. When she tried to describe the phenomenon to her friends, she explained to them that her time had changed. Now she had a different time, not at all like theirs, because on the day that Angel had died a little stone had entered the hourglass of her life, got stuck in the transition between one period and the next, and stopped the grains of sand allotted to her from flowing.

Every night she would wait for the morning light to come and make her forget her troubles, rid her of the painful memories and disturbing thoughts floating about in the darkness of her head like hairy, malevolent bats uttering their hateful squeaks before swooping down on their prey. And in the morning she would drink her coffee anxiously, afraid that the day would never end, evening would never come, and night would not fall on the town. She would spend her hallucinatory days and nights prowling endlessly around the rooms and stealing glances at the clock. At those moments, which stretched into hours, she could have sworn that time was tormenting her, the time that didn't want to pass had maliciously stuck the hands to the face of the clock to prevent them from moving. Exhausted, she would find herself imploring it to pass quickly, for the seconds, the minutes, the hours, the days, the weeks, the months, and the years to pass until her allotted span was over, her sufferings would come to an end, and calm and happy she could at long last be reunited with her loved ones.

One particularly hard night, when bad thoughts pierced her body like raptors tearing at her flesh with iron beaks and hooked claws, she stole a look at her watch and saw that time had stopped. At that moment, which lasted an eternity, she decided not to give in to the tyrannical dictates of time. She got out of bed and filled the sink with a strong cleaning acid, ran around the house collecting all the clocks, and plunged them into the sink. She didn't forget the kitchen clock, the alarm clock next to her bed, the elegant gold wristwatch Joseph had bought her as a present, and the wristwatches that had belonged to Joseph, Shraga, and Shmuel. In order not to leave a single breach for time to slip through, she threw in all the metal insides of the cuckoo clocks too, even though they had stopped working long ago and the little wooden houses had been eaten by woodworms. Tired out, she sat in the kitchen, looking with satisfaction at the clocks dissolving in the acid and listening to the fermenting of the water, which was like music to her ears. In the morning she removed the remains of the clocks and watches from the sink, crammed them into a black plastic bag, went downstairs, and threw the allies of time into the garbage bin. Then she went back home as triumphantly as if she had won a great battle.

But after a few minutes, which seemed like an eternity in the clockless house, she felt time breathing down her neck again. She looked around in alarm and her eyes fell on the flickering green digits winking at her maliciously from the timer on the oven and confidently announcing the hour, the minutes, and the seconds. Furiously she pulled the plug out of the wall and sank defeated into her armchair in the living room.

And again she heard it mocking her from the darkness of the

house. She looked around and to her horror she saw the flickering, phosphorescent figures changing on the VCR. In a rage she disconnected the instrument and decided to give it to Dror as a gift, since she had never liked watching movies and never used it anyway.

Even when all the allies of time had been destroyed, she did not feel the joy of victory, and she knew that in this battle too her opponent had gained the upper hand. A new time, not measured by clocks, had dug itself into its battle stations and refused to be budged. At the moment of recognition, which lasted forever, she was overcome by weakness and by a terrible fear. She broke out in a cold sweat, her body ached, and a feeling of suffocation gripped her throat. Rosa knew with frightening certainty that her body, her loyal ally throughout her life, was beginning to betray her. In an unexpected move that took her completely by surprise, it had rebelled against her, broken through her fortifications, entered into an alliance with her enemies, and invited them in.

Taking advantage of the opportunity time rushed into the breach, penetrated the depths of her body, settled down inside her, and proceeded to dictate the measurements of a new meter to her, that of the beating of her heart. Defeated, she went to bed and all night long she lay awake counting her heartbeats, and every time she reached sixty she knew that another minute had passed. Beaten down by the cruel games of time, she knew with certainty that from now on it would dictate the rhythm of her life to her, and only it would decide when to run out and when the last grain of sand would drop through the waist of the hourglass of her life.

After making this discovery she lay in bed with her eyes open and saw the pictures of her life flashing past her. Like the Technicolor images of a riveting movie they unrolled before her, husbands, children, friends, landscapes, smells, and tastes. And by the time she had counted sixty heartbeats the movie was over, and she went on counting the time planted inside her body that ached with a pain she had never known before. The grief, the sadness—the pangs of conscience and remorse that she tried in vain to banish—settled heavily on her heart measuring out its beats, and refused to go away.

And when she found herself at the dawn of a new morning, she knew that she had lost the taste for life. "Not only because she had lost three husbands and daughter and her time had stopped," the neighbors would say, "but because of a new punishment that she couldn't bear."

The punishment delivered a fatal blow to the center of her pleasures. In the privacy of their homes, in stairwells and shops, people whispered that Rosa had lost her sense of smell, and in the wake of her sense of smell her sense of taste too had disappeared, never to return.

The first warning came when she went into the kitchen and failed to smell the flowers. When it happened she thought that since she had grown accustomed to her painted kitchen, and since she was sunk deep in her sorrow, it was only natural that she should fail to smell flowers that weren't real in the first place. But later on Rachelle dropped in for her daily visit, and when she flared her nostrils and expanded her lungs as usual to breathe in the medley of colorful, flowery scents filling the kitchen, Rosa pretended that nothing had changed in her life.

After Rachelle left Rosa hurried to her vanity, took out the heavy perfume that Shraga had once bought her, and with trembling fingers removed the cap and breathed in the bubble of air sealed inside the elegant glass bottle. Not a single particle of scent invaded her nostrils and engraved the word "perfume" on the smell center in her brain. Frantically she tore the cellophane off a new bottle of perfume, and when her shaking hands had finally succeeded in removing the stopper, she fell on the bottle, thrust the slender neck into her nostril, and took a deep breath. When she failed to smell the scent in the new bottle too, she let it drop from her hand with a loud crash. Sharp splinters of glass, dotting the oily yellow liquid, spotted the floor. Too tired to sweep up the broken glass, she collapsed onto her bed, insensible to the heavy smell aggressively invading the room.

That night her sleep was restless and disturbed by frightening dreams. She saw herself moving about her herb garden, which had died long ago due to the murderous treatment it had received from Shmuel, from which it had never recovered. A magnificent basil bush fixed her with a challenging green stare. Laboriously she bent down and plucked a few leaves and green blooms from the bush, crushing the delicate leaves in eager anticipation of their pungent aroma. But the leaves refused to delight her with their smell. In alarm she raised them to her mouth and ground them between her teeth. Something dull and lifeless filled her mouth. Rosa spat out the chewed leaves and discovered to her horror that they were made of plastic. As if bitten by a snake, she let them fall from her hand and they floated slowly and silently, like real leaves, to the ground. Panic-stricken, she stumbled to the pickle barrel with the medicinal sage, pulled up an entire bush in her alarm, crushed a few stalks and raised them to her nose. This plant too was made of plastic, and so were all the other herbs on her balcony garden.

She forced herself to wake up and stumbled into the kitchen, put the kettle on to boil, and made her morning coffee. The aromatic steam that usually greeted her nostrils was absent. The worst of all awaited her when she carefully sipped the boiling coffee. There was no taste, as if all the taste buds on her tongue had joined forces with her nose to deny themselves any pleasure. The coffee was as tasteless and muddy as the ersatz coffee she remembered from the days of austerity of her childhood. Rosa poured the coffee into the sink, put her mouth to the nozzle of the tap, and in order to get rid of the tasteless coffee grounds clinging aimlessly and meaninglessly to her tongue and palate, drank until her stomach hurt.

At that moment she knew for certain that she had been deprived of her sense of smell. Overcome with a feeling of grief, she sat on the little kitchen stool, rocking her body as hot tears poured down her cheeks. She wept for the smell of the first rain, for the smell of the new-mown grass, for the delicious aromas of the dishes she cooked, for the fragrant smell of her freshly bathed grandchildren, and for the smell of a newborn baby, which she would never smell again. And then she remembered that together with the sense of smell she had been deprived of the sense of taste, and she wept for her double loss.

In a final act of despair she emptied the kitchen cabinets and sniffed and tasted everything she found there: fresh crackers, sesame seeds, finely ground black pepper, olive oil, sharp vinegar, vanilla pudding powder, sugar, bicarbonate of soda, and a big bar of cooking chocolate. When she failed to discern any smell, she tried to discern their taste, cramming everything she could lay her hands on into her mouth. Urgently she stuffed herself with big grains and small grains, crumbly textures and hard textures, dense liquids and thin liquids, and all of them rolled around in her mouth, penetrated her throat, slid down her gullet, and churned around in her stomach, but left no impression at all on the area in her brain responsible for discerning taste.

In her despair she hung the chain of garlic round her neck and raised the bulbs one after another to her nose. But the pungent smell, which had once reminded her of the reek of Shmuel's breath, did not greet her nostrils. At this moment, with the braid of garlic adorning her like a necklace, she felt the hand of fate tormenting her with a vengeance. Seized by intense longings for Shmuel and his smell of garlic, she tore the white bulbs from her neck and crushed them savagely in her hands, trying to force them to give up the smell that had disgusted her in the days of her happiness. The dull, odorless liquid slid down her fingers, burning old scratches and invisible wounds with its touch.

When Rachelle arrived she found Rosa sitting in the middle of her flowery kitchen, half-open packages of groceries scattered on the floor, and tears rolling down her cheeks.

Rachelle stared at her in alarm, thrust a bunch of tissues into her hand, and tidied her wet, crumpled clothes.

"What's wrong with you now? Why does the house smell like a brothel where a pot of garlic soup has exploded? And what are all these groceries lying around for, and what's the meaning of all this mess?" she scolded, and with a finger crooked with rheumatism tidied Rosa's rumpled hair.

"My sense of smell has gone," sobbed Rosa.

"To hell with your sense of smell! You can live without it for another hundred years. The worst thing that can happen is that you'll lose a bit of weight because your food will be tasteless now. If you can't smell you can't taste either," lectured Rachelle, who always knew how to take the right view of life.

And since she was a practical woman, she added: "Never mind the smell of the flowers and the smell of food. Something else worries me more. What will happen if, God forbid, you leave the gas on? If you don't smell it, you'll suffocate to death. And what about food that spoils, something burning on the stove, the smell of smoke? These are the things that worry me."

That same day Rosa rushed round to the neighborhood HMO clinic and explained her problem to a blond woman doctor who answered her with demonstrative impatience in a foreign accent. With her breasts sticking out in front of her as if they were independent of the rest of her body, she scribbled something on a slip of paper and instructed Rosa to swallow the drops twice a day.

And when the drops failed to have any effect, she went to consult a specialist, who tested her sense of smell. He gave her about twenty pieces of paper, each of them saturated with a different smell, and instructed her to tear them one by one and breathe in the odor. Obediently she did as he told her, and when he asked her to describe the smells, she burst into despairing tears and said that she couldn't smell a thing. "They all smell the same, of nothing." The doctor clapped his hands, told her that he had no cure for her affliction, and asked her to pay him a few hundred shekels.

Rosa walked all the way home, trying desperately, until her lungs hurt, to smell the honeysuckle and the jasmine twining around the fences of the houses in Old Katamon, thinking angrily about the doctor who had taken her money without finding a cure for what ailed her. When she got home she put a pot of lentil soup on the stove to heat. In a moment of forgetfulness she raised a steaming spoonful of the hot, rich brown liquid to her mouth. The soup was tasteless. Rosa could not taste the coriander, she could not smell the heavy aroma of the soft lentils, and even the generous handful of chopped onion and garlic she had thrown into the soup the night before turned into bits of tasteless plastic in her mouth. Resolutely Rosa picked up the heavy pot, threw its contents into the lavatory, and flushed. A few solitary lentils that had escaped the drain floated on the surface of the water as a gloomy reminder.

Rosa went to bed hungry, and she couldn't sleep all night. Loud noises and terrible sounds whose like she had never heard before joined the beating of her heart as it counted out her time, disturbing her rest and preventing her from sleeping. She heard the water gurgling in the copper pipes set deep in the walls. She listened to the idle conversations of her neighbors, which she could hear as clearly as if they were conducting their lives right there in her bedroom. She heard people breathing in their sleep, she heard their snores and their bodies moving in their beds, she heard the sighing of the mattresses. The moans of pleasure of a couple making love in a distant apartment jolted her body as if they were coupling beside her in bed. When she heard the snapping of the woodworms' teeth, the whisper of the feelers of the cockroaches burying into the food, the fermenting of the garbage rotting in the bin, and the sound of the blood streaming in her veins—she knew she had received a compensation that had turned into a curse. Now that she had been deprived of her sense of smell and taste, her sense of hearing had been sharpened in return for what she had lost.

As she lay paralyzed with fear, listening to the sounds of the night with her eyes wide open in the darkness, she was horrified to hear the dull sound that took her back to her earliest memories. With tears streaming down her sagging cheeks, Rosa remembered the sounds of dragging she had once heard as a child, the dragging of bodies, a great many bodies, which she was later told were actually carpets. At that moment she felt Rina's gloved hand wiping away her tears. She was not surprised to find her old friend here in her house, lying in her bed and covered by her blanket. Rina had not grown; she had remained a child. After overcoming her emotion she raised the blanket and looked at her closely. Her beautiful lace dress was tattered and full of dark stains, the soles of her shoes were worn out, her ringlets were dusty and covered with spiderwebs, her blue eyes were sadder now, and there was an ugly scar on her head. When Rosa told her about Angel and her fall, Rina put her arms around her and whispered in her ear that now Angel was sleeping in another little girl's bed, for the whole world was full of little girls sleeping in the beds of other little girls, who were sleeping in the beds of other little girls, and there was no end to it.

At the end of the week, when her children came for dinner with their husbands and wives and all the grandchildren, she saw them exchange embarrassed looks, and she couldn't avoid noticing the frequent use of the salt and pepper passing from one end of the table to the other. And when they went home and she was left with pots full of food, she knew that together with the loss of her sense of taste and smell, she had also lost her magic touch as a cook. The next week some of them stayed away. And after the meal, which was eaten in oppressive silence, Ruthie asked her: "Tell me, Mother, what's happened to your cooking? Why is the food so tasteless?"

At the end of a month Rosa noticed that her dress was no longer as tight as it used to be, and she knew that she was losing weight. And after two months of the diet that had been imposed on her against her will, when she walked down the street she noticed that the men passing her no longer stared or turned their heads to look at her, as if she had suddenly become invisible. Defeated, she looked at her reflection in the window of the florist shop, and found herself staring at a faded old woman with her dress hanging loosely on her heavy body. Her dry hair showed its white roots and stuck up wildly around her head, her sunken eyes had an expression of obscure hunger, and her mouth was turned down at the corners, like the mouths of women whom life had treated badly. Rosa tried to smooth her unruly hair, but it resisted her efforts and sprang back rebelliously, as if to spite her. She tried to turn the corners of her mouth up in a forced smile, but they immediately drooped again, deepening the expression of bitterness on her face.

She hurried home in alarm, panting for breath, slowly climbed the three flights of steps, and collapsed onto her bed. And with the doll, Belle, crying, "Mama, mama, mama," in her arms, she made up her mind that she had to do something to change what was left of her life.

twenty-five

A GOLDEN LADDER

One day, when Rachelle knocked on Rosa's door as she did every morning, the door failed to open. Nor did it open when she tried her luck in the afternoon, or the next morning. Two days later she pressed her ear to the door, and when she didn't hear anything she remembered the spare key Rosa had given her, which she had never used, and she fetched it and opened the door. She was greeted by a smell of flowers mixed with heavy perfume and rotting food. Hesitantly she went into the bedroom. The room was empty, the bed made, and Rosa's three husbands, with Angel in their midst, looked at her sadly from the wall. Apprehensively she inspected the other rooms. Rosa was not at home. Her shopping basket was in its place in the kitchen, and her purse lay on the dressing table in the bedroom. In growing alarm she opened the bedroom closet and found that all Rosa's dresses were hanging there and nothing was missing. And when she went into Angel's room she found that the bed was empty. The doll, Belle, which had been lying on the dead girl's bed ever since the accident, had disappeared.

Beside herself with worry, she called Ruthie, who informed her calmly that Rosa had gone away. Where she had gone, who she had gone with, and when she was coming back, Ruthie refused to say. When Rachelle brooded about it all night, angry with Rosa for not telling her about her plans and causing her unnecessary worry, Rachelle knew that Rosa had left her house and locked the door behind her with no intention of returning.

When the neighbors discovered that she had left without saying good-bye to anybody, they began to ask questions accompanied by speculations, rumors, and arguments, and the atmosphere in Katamon G grew heated.

First they asked where Rosa had disappeared to, and for many days the question stalked the neighborhood like an independent entity with a form and substance of its own. Like the car of a newly married couple with pots and pans tied to its bumper and clattering loudly behind it, the question dragged in its train a host of speculations, guesses, prejudices, suspicions, and fears. After that the question of who Rosa's fourth husband was came up, and everybody knew that the answers to both questions were connected, and the solution to the first riddle would inevitably lead to the solution of the second.

At first they thought that the answer lay with her good friend Rachelle, but from the day of Rosa's disappearance Rachelle sealed her lips and refused to speak about her friend for good or for ill. On a very warm spring evening, when her rheumatic pains let up a little and her usually tense expression relaxed, the women sitting downstairs with her in the yard dared to ask her for her opinion on the matter. Sucking the scorching air into their lungs with little sighing noises, the women sat on the low wicker stools they had placed in a circle on the concrete path leading to the entrance of the building, their backsides spreading in all directions, fanning themselves with their swollen hands, and waiting for the right moment—the split second of grace when it would be possible to ask their question.

"Why a fourth husband?" replied Rachelle with a question.

"People said she would have four husbands. You said so yourself. Don't you remember? Four butterflies, four husbands."

Rachelle said nothing. Again she felt the burning insult and the gnawing longings for Rosa, her best friend, who had excluded her from her plans and vanished without even saying good-bye.

"Come on," they urged her as if trying to refresh her memory. "Fly down pretty butterfly, don't be afraid, come sit on my hand, and fly away into the sky."

Rachelle was silent.

"Come on," they repeated impatiently. "There's one more butterfly to go. There were three, and now there's one missing. Who's Rosa's fourth husband?"

"I'll tell you the truth," she said frankly, "I have no answer."

"So what happened to Rosa after Angel died?" they persevered.

"I don't know."

"Where is she?"

"God knows," said Rachelle in resignation, pointing at the sky with her finger, distorted by rheumatism. Those who watched closely saw that she was actually pointing at the graffiti sprayed in huge black letters on the wall: LIFE IS LIKE THE HAIRS ON MY ASS—, SHORT, HARD, BLACK, AND STINKING.

"A woman disappears and nobody knows where she is?" they demanded angrily. "Especially such a big, well-known woman?"

"I'm sure they know where she is, but they're not telling," said Rachelle reluctantly, apparently in a hurry to change the subject.

"Who's they?"

"Her children, of course."

"Is there any point in asking them?"

"They didn't tell me, so you think they'll tell you?"

The women stretched out their swollen legs, inspected the peeling polish on their toenails, and studied the vegetation growing all around them as if seeing it for the first time in their lives. The brambles, the nettles, the thistles, and the thornbushes running riot in the yard were still green and tender, before putting on the yellow-brown of summer and growing hard, spiky, dry thorns.

A great wave of guesses and speculations engulfed the neighborhood. Tzadok the Grocer argued that he was the one who knew her best, after Rachelle, of course, since she had been coming to his store every day at nine, regular as clockwork, when she was able, to do her daily shopping. And he was ready to take a solemn oath in public and swear that she was living in a log cabin on an abandoned outpost in the Upper Galilee and growing organic vegetables with her fourth husband, whose identity was unknown, since she had married him in secret, in a quiet, private ceremony, and no doubt she had also opened a vegetarian restaurant there on the hilltop, overlooking the most beautiful scenery in the world. And when they asked him how he knew, he answered simply that he had been told that this was what she wanted to do with her life. And if she had disappeared, she must have gone to make her wish come true.

Others in the neighborhood claimed that Rosa had married Yochai the Undertaker in secret. All those years when she had been visiting the graves of her dead husbands, he had been following her in secret with his dark looks, they explained. His black garments full of shadows from the world of shades held no terrors for her, and his gaze, which met death face-to-face on a daily basis, was understanding and sympathetic, and held a healing balm for her broken heart. His always-melancholy face; his eyes, which turned down sharply at the corners; and his lips, which drooped toward the ground and never parted in a smile—reminded her of her first husband, Joseph, to whom she was attached by the ties of habit. In proof they pointed to the fact that Yochai had left his house at the cemetery gate, next to the stonemasons' yard, and disappeared without a trace.

And when they were on the subject of cemeteries and undertakers, the more pessimistic of the neighbors claimed that Rosa had simply gone to a better world. At last she was united with her nearest and dearest—with her father, whom she had never seen, her mother, her three husbands, her friend Ruthie, and above all with Angel, who had vanished from her life. And if anyone asked why nobody had heard of her death, why no death notices had been posted, where was the funeral, the eulogies, the shiva, they replied that her children might well have buried her in secret, at her request, which they had honored, and with the help of Yochai the Undertaker, who had always loved her from a distance. And since burying the woman he loved had broken his heart, he had abandoned the profession, closed his house, and gone to seek a livelier occupation.

But the men who used to hang out at Mousa Zilka's hut argued that Rosa had eloped with Mousa. Now that his wife had died, the two of them were finally able to consummate the love that had been denied for so many years. And for proof they offered the fact that Mousa had locked up his hut at exactly the same time as Rosa had disappeared, gone off without saying good-bye, and had no doubt vanished into the blue together with Rosa.

Some people were convinced that the answer lay with Ruhama. Rosa's disappearance had hurt Ruhama just as much as it had hurt Rachelle, since it was inconceivable that she should have gone off without consulting them.

In the days following the disappearance, Ruhama walked round the neighborhood looking angry and insulted. After hearing the news from Rachelle, she tossed and turned all night, grinding her teeth furiously and disturbing the sleep of her new husband, until the idea came to her. Drawing on the grimmest stories she had heard during the course of her life, she succeeded in putting together an intractable family problem, and after making sure she had the details straight, she went to consult Peretz the cabalist. As they spoke, she thought, she would be able to slip in her question about Rosa, to which there was no doubt he had the answer, since he knew all there was to know about her, and she never did anything without consulting him. Skipping over the overturned garbage bins and shooing away the frightened cats, she reached the dirt path leading to his house, where she was surprised to find that the usual queue of women seeking his succor was absent. The door was locked, and the yellowing note pinned to it announced to all who sought him that the old cabalist had gone away for an unspecified period of time.

"Are you looking for Peretz?" asked a woman leaning on the gate of the house next door. "He isn't here. He's gone away."

"When is he coming back?" asked Ruhama.

"Nobody knows. He locked up and left."

"Did he go alone?"

"I don't know," came the indifferent answer from behind the fence.

"Do you know Rosa?' the interrogation continued.

"Fat Rosa from Katamon G?"

"Yes, fat Rosa. Perhaps he went away with her?"

"Search me."

"Did Rosa come to him before he left?"

"So they say. They say that after her third one died and then her daughter too, she came to Peretz and asked him to perform a widows' *Tikkun* for her."

"What's a widows' *Tikkun*?"

"Peretz told me that when a woman's husband dies, and she wants to marry again, the spirit of the first husband is jealous and makes trouble for her, and therefore it has to be placated so that it won't pester her and give her grief. And so Peretz, so they say, performed a widows' *Tikkun* for Rosa, and all her husbands are quiet now and they won't trouble her anymore, and she can get married again."

"Where is Rosa now?"

"Peretz told her that she had to move to a new apartment, leave everything behind her, even her clothes, because all her husbands are waiting for her in the old apartment, and if she wants to start a new life, she has to leave her old apartment and her old life behind her."

"Where did she move to?"

"Nobody knows."

"Maybe she and Peretz went away together?" Ruhama tried to put words in the woman's mouth.

"I don't know." The woman's voice suddenly sounded sullen and impatient, as if she would be severely punished if she went on talking, and without another word she turned her back, went inside, and slammed the door behind her.

When she went home Ruhama decided not to share her sensational discovery with anyone, including her new husband. A mysterious smile appeared on her lips, announcing that she knew the answer but was not about to share it with anyone else. Some said that she didn't even tell Rachelle. And when the latter begged to be let into the secret, for the sake of their long friendship, she pursed her lips meanly and locked the secret up inside her as if it were a treasure not to be shared with others. Now, more than ever, she knew that she had been right when she said that Rosa would marry four husbands, because of the four butterflies that had alighted on her head. And even though, when Ruhama had taken one more husband than she'd had butterflies, and told herself it was a childish game, clearly it wasn't. It was the game of life.

In the evening, when she reflected on the story of her life, which had diverged from the destiny prophesied by the butterflies, she excused the outcome by telling herself that the rules could be changed at any stage of the game, even after it was over. Because the rules of the game were capable of changing reality. You only had to know how to act and how it was possible to change reality. And anyone who wanted to play with their life and make changes in it had to want it very much. Ruthie, Rachelle, and Rosa didn't know the rules. They didn't know how to play, and they weren't strong enough to change the rules. Only she had passed all the tests and succeeded in winning the game. And with a triumphant smile on her lips, she went to the kitchen to make her new husband a cup of strong coffee.

But many of the residents of Katamon G dismiss all these speculations and believe that the right answer, the one and only answer, lies with Rosa's grandson Dror, who loved his grandmother and Angel more than he loved himself, and was therefore the only one who knew for certain where Rosa had disappeared to. If they had pressed him, perhaps he would have told them about that clear, starry night when a golden ladder came down from the sky in his grandmother's dream. Rosa gazed at it in wonder, cradled the doll, Belle, in her arms and asked Dror to join her in her dream. And Dror, who had always wanted to dream his grandmother's dreams, watched it with her. Like a pair of spectators sitting alone in an auditorium and watching a movie on a giant screen spreading over the entire star-studded sky, with the doll, Belle, lying on their laps, they raised their heads and looked at the angels robed in white silk, their fair hair falling in curls to their shoulders, climbing up and down the ladder, ascending and descending and ascending again, until their eyes tired of the sight.

And when they wanted to wake up they suddenly saw him. The little fallen angel scurrying and scrambling between the feet of the big angels. Rosa and Dror rose to their feet, called out loud, held out their arms to him, and begged him to come down to them. But the little angel was afraid of heights, and he was too frightened to lower his eyes to the ground. And when they went on calling him in loud, demanding voices, he sat down on one of the rungs of the ladder and looked in bewilderment from Dror to Rosa and back again, and when he couldn't decide what to do he flapped his wings at them and beckoned them to climb up after him. Dror made haste to put his foot on the first rung of the ladder but his grandmother pushed him aside. Tucking the doll, Belle, firmly under her armpit she gripped the ladder with her other hand, then raised her foot and set it resolutely on the first rung of the ladder. When the little angel saw her taking the first step he smiled down at her with a familiar smile and encouraged her to keep on climbing. And when she gripped the ladder with her other hand, and Belle slipped from her grasp and fell to the ground, Rosa did not look back. With her eyes fixed on the little angel, she set her second foot on the ladder and started to climb up behind him, while he hopped lightly from rung to rung, going on ahead and showing her the way, until they both turned into little dots in the sky.

As soon as they disappeared from view Dror tried to follow them. But when he put his foot on the first rung the ladder rose into the air and was swallowed up by the clouds, leaving a blinding flash of golden light behind it. Dror was left alone in the world, holding the doll, Belle, in his hands. Doubled up in a terrible pain that hit him like a fist in his stomach, he knew that Rosa had reached the sky and would never return to the earth, not even for a brief visit. For her eyes were now feasting on the sight of the angels, her ears were full of the glorious music of the harps playing in her honor, and her hands were delighting in the touch of the soft, downy wings spread out to welcome her.

When he woke up crying with his stomach aching, he found Belle next to him, her wide-open eyes looking at him sadly. And when he hugged her, squeezing her soft body in his hands, she consoled him with her high, squeaky voice: "Mama, mama, mama." Dror promised that he would take good care of her, better care than he had taken of Angel. And when he calmed down he told her that now that Angel had reached heaven at last, nobody in the world would ever dream again of a golden ladder with its head in the sky and angels going up and down it. But he was sure, so he told her, that one day Angel would miss him and want him by her side. Then she would send a new ladder for him, and it made no difference to him at all if the ladder was made of gold, or silver, or metal, or even of wood. As long as she sent him a ladder and he could climb up it and meet the little girl who was an angel, and whom he loved more than anything else in his life.